Third Voice

Published by Hesperus Nova
Hesperus Press Limited
28 Mortimer Street, London W1W 7RD
www.hesperuspress.com

This edition first published by Hesperus Press Limited, 2015

Cilla and Rolf Börjlind assert their moral right to be identified as the authors
of this work under the Copyright, Designs and Patents Act 1988

First published by Norstedts, Sweden

Copyright © Cilla and Rolf Börjlind 2013 by Agreement with Grand Agency

English language translation © Hilary Parnfors, 2015

Typeset by Sarah Newitt
Printed and bound by CPI Group (UK) Ltd, Croydon, CR0 4YY

ISBN: 978-1-84391-555-3

Third Voice

Cilla and Rolf Börjlind

Translated by Hilary Parnfors

Chapter 1

Barefoot, I stand looking down from the roof. Nine floors below, I see the grey road. It's empty and the city sleeps without a breath of wind in the air. I take a few steps along the edge and stretch out my arms for balance. A bird swoops down and perches a little way away. I think it might be a jackdaw. The bird looks out over the silent houses. We both have wings. Mine are white, its are black.

It'll get light soon.

I take a few steps towards the jackdaw, carefully, so as not to scare it. I want it to understand why I'm here, at this time.

I want to explain.

I left my body last night, I whisper to the jackdaw, even before I was dead. I was already hovering over my body when he started beating me. I watched it all from above. I saw the straps cutting into my throat. He'd pulled them too tight. I knew that I'd suffocate. That's why I screamed so horribly. It hurt so much. I'd never screamed like that before. That's probably why he started hitting me, over and over again, and the heavy ashtray shattered my temple.

Now I feel the breeze.

It's the first balmy breeze to come in from the sea in ages. The jackdaw looks at me with one eye, and far away I see the mighty golden Madonna. She stands on the highest hill, her face turned towards me. Did she see what happened last night as well? Was she in the room too? Couldn't she have helped me?

I look at the jackdaw again.

Before I died I was blind, I whisper. That's why it was all so terrible. We weren't alone in the room, he and I. I could hear other voices. I was frightened of what I couldn't see, of those men's voices I heard, foreign words. I didn't want to be part of this any more. It all felt wrong. Then I died, and it was just him and me left in there. He had to clean up all the blood himself. It took such a long time.

5

The jackdaw is still in the same place, motionless. Is it an angel bird? Did it get caught in a net and break its neck? Or was it hit by a lorry? Now I hear noises from the road down below, someone has woken, and I can sense the smell of burning rubbish all the way up here. Soon there'll be people milling between the houses.

I have to hurry.

He carried me out in the dark, I whisper to the jackdaw. No one saw us. I was floating above it all. He lifted me into the boot of a car and folded up my thin legs. He was in a rush. We went to the cliffs. He laid my naked body on the ground next to the car, in the gravel. I wanted to reach down and brush my hand over my cheek. I looked so violated. He dragged me by my arms, far off in amongst the trees and rocks. And there he dismembered me. First he cut off my head. I wonder how he felt when he did it. He did it so fast, with a large knife. He buried me in six different places, far apart. He didn't want anyone to find me. When he left I flew here. To this rooftop.

Now I'm ready.

Far away, in the mountains of the north, the first rays of sunshine are bursting over the ridge, the dew sparkling on the rooftops. A lone fishing boat is heading back into port.

It's going to be a beautiful day.

The jackdaw next to me is falling out into the breeze with its wings outstretched. I lean out and follow it.

Someone will find me.

I know it.

Chapter 2

'Cut out of my murdered mother's womb.'

Olivia tormented herself day and night. Dark, vile thoughts occupied her mind at night. During the day she hid herself away.

It went on for a long time, until she was more or less apathetic.

Until it couldn't continue any more.

Then one morning, her survival instinct kicked in and pummelled her out into the world again.

There, she made a decision.

She'd complete her final term at the Police Academy and be a police officer.

Then she'd go abroad. She wasn't going to look for a job. She was going to disappear, go far away, and try to reconnect with the person she was before she became the daughter of two murdered parents.

If that was even possible.

She followed her plan, borrowed money from a relative and set off in July.

Alone.

First to Mexico, the homeland of her murdered mother, to unknown places with unknown people and foreign tongues. She travelled light with only a brown backpack and a map. She had no plan and no particular direction. All places were new and she was nobody. She had to spend time with her inner self, moving at her own pace. Nobody saw her cry. Nobody knew why she sometimes just sank down by a stream, letting her long black hair flow through the water for a while.

She was in her own universe.

Before the trip, she'd had some vague thoughts about tracing her mother's roots, and maybe finding some relatives, but she'd realised that she knew far too little about them for it to lead anywhere.

So she just got on a bus in a small town and got off in an even smaller one.

Three months later, she ended up in Cuatro Ciénegas.

She checked into Xipe Totec, the hotel of the flayed god, on the outskirts of town. At dusk, she walked barefoot to the beautiful square in the centre. It was her twenty-fifth birthday and she wanted to see people. There were coloured lanterns hanging in the plane trees with small groups of young people huddled beneath them, young girls in garish skirts and young boys with handkerchiefs stuffed into their trousers. They were laughing. The music from the bars drifted out into the square, the donkeys stood still by the fountain and many strange smells swirled through the air.

She sat on a bench like an outsider and felt very safe.

An hour later she headed back to her hotel.

The evening air was still warm when she sat down on a wooden veranda, looking out over the vast Chihuahua Desert, as the cicadas' sharp song mixed with the clatter of horses' hooves. She'd just treated herself to a cold beer and was considering having another. Then it happened. For the first time she felt some solid ground beneath her.

I'm going to change my surname, she thought.

I'm actually half Mexican. I'm going to take my mother's name. Her name was Adelita Rivera. I'm going to change my surname from Rönning to Rivera.

Olivia Rivera.

She looked out over the desert in front of her. Of course, she thought, that's how I'll start over. Simple. She turned around and gestured with the empty beer bottle towards the bar inside.

She was going to drink the next beer as Olivia Rivera.

She looked out over the desert again, and saw the light breeze blowing a couple of dry bushes over the hot quivering ground. She saw a green and black lizard scamper up a three-branched prickly saguaro, she saw a couple of silent birds of prey glide off into the burning horizon and suddenly she smiled at nothing at all, unhindered. For the first time since late summer last year she felt almost happy.

Simple as that.

That night she went to bed with Ramón, the young bartender who'd lisped a little as he politely asked her whether she wanted to make love.

She was done with Mexico. The trip had taken her to the place she'd needed to reach. Her next destination was Costa Rica and the village of Mal Pais, the place where her biological father had had a house. He'd called himself Dan Nilsson there, even though his real name was Nils Wendt.

He had lived a double life.

On the way, she made a number of decisions, all spawned by Olivia Rivera, from the strange power she had gained with her new surname.

One was that she was going to put her police career on hold and study history of art. Adelita had been an artist, weaving beautiful fabrics. Maybe they could connect in some abstract kind of way, she thought.

One rather more crucial decision concerned her outlook on life. As soon as she got back to Sweden, she would follow her own path. She'd been hurt by people she had trusted. She'd been naive and open, and had had her heart smashed to pieces. She was determined not to take that risk again. From now on she would trust one person alone.

Olivia Rivera.

It was late afternoon by the time she got out of the sea at a beach on the Nicoya Peninsula. Her long black hair fell down over her tanned body – she'd spent four months in the tropical sun. She climbed up on the deserted beach and threw a towel over her shoulders. A green coconut rolled back and forth at the water's edge. She turned towards the sea and knew that she had to go over it again.

Right here, right now.

'Cut out of my murdered mother's womb.'

The image departed from her consciousness again. The beach, the woman, the moon. The murder. Her mother had been drowned in a spring tide, buried on the island of Nordkoster. Before I was born, she thought, she died before I was *born*.

She never got to see me.

Now she was standing on a very different beach trying to accept – much harder than trying to understand – the thought that their eyes had never met.

Being born unseen.

She looked out to sea. The ocean stretched all the way to the blazing amber horizon. It was about to get dark. Calm swells were moving in towards the land, soft warm waves rolling up towards her feet. In the distance she saw a group of dark heads bobbing around on the surface.

She pulled on her thin white dress and started walking.

Small grey-white crabs scuttled into their holes in the sand as she passed by, the water filling her footsteps behind her. She had walked along the beach for almost an hour, slowly, from Santa Teresa all the way out here, to the cliffs at Mal Pais. She knew it would be like this, that the images and thoughts would come flooding back.

That was the point of the walk.

She wanted to submerge herself in the pain again, one last time, she wanted to be prepared. In a few minutes she would meet a man who would take her back even closer to her mysterious past.

The man was sitting on a long tree trunk by the shore. He was seventy-four years old and had lived in the area his whole life. He had once owned a bar in Santa Teresa. Now he mostly sat on the veranda of his peculiar house drinking rum. He'd come to terms with most things. When his beloved boyfriend died a few years ago, the last thing keeping his flame of life alight had disappeared with him. Breathe in, breathe out. Sooner or later it all comes to an end. But he didn't complain. He had his booze. And his past. Many people had come and gone during his lifetime, some had stuck in his memory. Two of them were Adelita Rivera and Dan Nilsson.

And now he was about to meet their daughter.

The daughter neither of them had had the chance to meet themselves.

He regretted not bringing a swig of rum to the beach.

Olivia saw him from afar. She sort of knew what he was going to look like. Abbas el Fassi had told her. But she couldn't be completely sure. So she stopped some distance away from the tree trunk and waited for the man to look up.

He didn't.

'Rodriguez Bosques?'

'Bosques Rodriguez. Bosques is my first name. And you're Olivia?'

'Yes.'

Then Bosques looked up. When his old narrow eyes caught sight of Olivia's face he shuddered. Not very noticeably, but enough for Olivia to get a clear flashback. That's exactly how Nils Wendt had reacted when he'd seen her in a doorway on the island of Nordkoster last year, not having a clue who she was. Especially not that she was his and Adelita Rivera's daughter. And Olivia had had no idea who the man in the doorway was either. That's how they'd parted ways, and it was the first and last time she'd seen her father alive.

'You're a spitting image of Adelita,' Bosques said in his croaky voice.

'I'm her daughter.'

'Sit down.'

Olivia sat down on the tree trunk, well away from Bosques, which he noted.

'You're very beautiful,' he said. 'Like her.'

'You knew my mother.'

'And your father. The big Swede.'

'Was that what he was called?'

'By me, yes. And now they're both dead.'

'Yes. You wrote that you had a photo of my mother?'

'A photo and a few other things.'

Olivia had been given Bosques' email address by Abbas el Fassi. Somewhere in Mexico she'd gone into an Internet café, emailed Bosques, explaining who she was, and saying that she was planning to come to Costa Rica and wanted to meet him. Bosques had responded very quickly. He only received personal emails once in a blue moon, and he told her that he had quite a few of her parents' personal belongings.

He lifted up a small oblong metal box, red and yellow in colour, which had originally housed some very exclusive Cuban cigars, opened it and picked up a photograph. His hands were trembling slightly.

'That's your mother. Adelita Rivera.'

Olivia leant over towards Bosques and took the photograph. She smelled a slight waft of cigar. It was a colour photograph. She had seen a picture of her mother once before, on a photograph that Abbas had taken home with him from Santa Teresa last year, but this one was much sharper and more beautiful. She looked at her mother and saw that she had a slight squint in one eye.

Just like Olivia.

'Adelita got her name from a Mexican heroine,' said Bosques. 'Her name was Adelita Velarde and she was a soldier during the Mexican Revolution. Her name became a symbol for women with strength and courage. There's a song about her too. *La Adelita*.'

Bosques suddenly started singing, softly, in gentle melodic Spanish, the song about the strong and brave woman with whom all the rebels had fallen in love. Olivia looked at him, at the photograph of her mother, the old man's trembling song touching her innermost soul. She glanced up and looked out over the ocean. The whole situation was absurd, magical, far removed from her daily life in Stockholm.

Bosques fell silent and his gaze sank down into the sand. Olivia looked at him and realised that Bosques was also grieving. He had been a close friend of her mother and father. She moved nearer, almost right next to him. Carefully he put her hand in his. She let him do so. Bosques cleared his throat a little.

'Your mother was a very talented artist.'

'Abbas told me. He sends his regards.'

'He's very good with knives.'

'Yes.'

'Shall we go up to your father's house?'

'Soon.'

Olivia turned towards the water again and saw a massive wave pulsating through the sea. All the dark heads she'd seen earlier were hoisting themselves up onto surfboards. They caught the wave with their bodies hunched over and were carried away from the burning horizon at furious speed.

She got up.

Chapter 3

Sandra Sahlmann was happy. She whizzed through the November darkness, in the pouring rain, on her new white scooter, feeling happy. Elated thoughts filled her mind – there were so many great things happening at the moment. Her volleyball coach had told her she'd be playing in the first team next season and she'd got an 'A' in her religious studies exam, rather unexpectedly as she hadn't thought it had gone very well. She quickly rode along the edge of the golf course, up towards the residential area and sped up a bit more.

Then the engine died.

She turned the ignition a few times, but soon realised that she'd run out of petrol. She stopped at the side of the road and got off. She wasn't far from home, only a few hundred metres, but pushing a scooter in this weather wasn't much fun, so she took out her mobile and called her dad. He could come and meet her and bring an umbrella.

No answer.

He tended to put his mobile on silent when he watched TV, it helped him concentrate, he claimed. Or maybe he was out doing some shopping and couldn't hear the phone ring. He had promised to buy tacos, her favourite food, as a reward for her 'A'. She'd just have to handle the situation herself. I'll put the scooter here and we can collect it later, she thought. She pulled the scooter under a tree and locked it up. She kept her helmet on. Then she tried calling her dad again. Maybe he'd turned his phone off silent? Or got home?

No.

She started to walk.

Luckily the light in the underpass was on, she could see that from afar. Sometimes it was broken. It wasn't that she was afraid of the dark, but if there was someone else down there, you couldn't really see who it was and she didn't like that.

As she reached the underpass, she saw a man coming in the other direction. She knew most of the people living in the area, but she didn't recognise him. She started walking a bit faster as they passed each other, half-ran the last stretch and turned around.

The man was gone.

Had he run too?

Sod it.

Now all she needed to do was get across the narrow path and through the woodland, and she'd almost be home.

The harsh wind flung wet leaves at her and the mist seemed to envelop the trees. But she felt safe in the woodland, even though it was quite dark tonight. She'd almost reached it when she remembered the bag. With her house keys. It was in the scooter's storage box. If her dad was out shopping she wouldn't be able to get in. She turned around and scurried back the way she'd come. Her mood had deteriorated significantly. On top of that the light in the underpass had gone out. She was so pissed off that she just hurried through it and over to the scooter, pulled open the storage box, got the bag and started walking back in the rain. When she saw the dark tunnel in front of her she thought about the man who'd disappeared.

Where had he gone?

She stopped before she went in and tried to look through to the other side. It wasn't that far and it looked empty. She took a deep breath and ran straight through it. Ridiculous, she thought, once she'd reached the other side.

What am I afraid of?

In the distance she could see that the lights were on in a neighbouring house. For some reason that suddenly made her feel safe. At least there were people around. She crossed the wet grassy slope and approached the woodland again, and tried to cheer up. It wasn't much further and then they'd collect her scooter together and eat tacos.

She was in the woodland now.

The wet leaves squelched beneath her shoes.

She walked along the poorly trodden path, a path that she'd walked a hundred times, it stopped just outside their garden hedge. Then she heard the noise. As though a branch was being broken off. Right behind her. She turned around, her helmet was restricting her view.

What was that noise?

She looked at the trees, the dark trunks and the branches weighed down by the rain.

A deer?

Here?

She turned back and started walking faster. She knew where the path went, but still walked straight into a tree trunk. She staggered and pulled off her helmet. Then she heard another noise. Much closer.

There's someone here!

She threw her helmet on the ground and rushed between the trees. It wasn't that far to the garden hedge and she'd be safe there. Though not until she'd reached the gate. It was quite a high hornbeam hedge that surrounded her house and she had to run around it before she reached the gate. She ran as fast as she could until she suddenly fell to the ground. A mound of compost had tripped her up. Right next to the hedge. She lay still for a few seconds, her face pressed into the wet clay, not daring to look behind her, and felt the tears welling up in her eyes.

'Dad! *Dad!*'

She screamed out loud. If her father was home, he might hear her! She was just on the other side of the hedge! She straightened her arms and pushed herself up from the ground and started running again. Towards the gate. It was open. She ran through, towards the door, took hold of her bag and tried to open it. The zip was stuck. Finally she managed to open it, found the key and put it in the door, turned the lock, pulled the door open, rushed inside and slammed it shut, locked it twice, breathed out and turned around – five metres in front of her she saw her father hanging from the ceiling by a blue tow rope, his tongue hanging out and his wide-open eyes staring straight at her.

* * *

Dinner was great, everything from the madeira-flavoured chanterelle soup to the veal and the delicious panna cotta.

'Did you make the panna cotta as well?'

'It's not that hard.'

Olivia smiled. Not much in the way of cooking was hard for Maria Rönning, her adoptive mother, a lawyer of Spanish origin with long black hair. They sat at Maria's kitchen table in the terraced house in Rotebro. Maria had collected Olivia from the airport and insisted on cooking her dinner. It didn't take much to persuade Olivia. Many long hours spent flying across the Atlantic with tasteless food and dry biscuits with watery coffee had made her mother's offer hard to refuse. What she had really wanted to do was to head back to her two-room flat on Söder to sleep and recharge her batteries before delivering some difficult news to Maria.

It had to be done at the right time.

Having dinner with her in her kitchen, jetlagged, plied with wine, would create an intimacy between them that Olivia would have preferred to avoid.

But now it couldn't be helped.

So she'd decided to disclose most of it in the car on the way back from Arlanda airport.

'Change your name?' Maria said at the wheel.

'Yes. To Rivera.'

'When did you decide that?'

'In Mexico.'

'Olivia Rivera?'

'Yes.'

'It's a beautiful name.'

Maria kept her eyes on the road. Olivia observed her from the side. Did she mean what she'd said? Did she mean that it was a beautiful name in general or what?

'It suits you,' Maria said.

Olivia was stumped. She had expected a very different reaction and had put together a barrage of arguments for wanting to take her deceased mother's name. 'It suits you.' What was she supposed to say to that?

'Thanks. And I've also decided to take a break from the police force. For the time being at least.'

'Good.'

'Good?'

'What would you want to be a police officer for? It's not for you, I've said that all along.'

Which was true. Maria had never been keen on Olivia's decision to join the police. She had supported it, but without any great enthusiasm. But Olivia still felt slightly irritated. Why shouldn't she be a police officer?! Even though she didn't want to be one any more? She suddenly felt unsettled. Maria had responded to her two most important decisions as though they were trivialities. Or at least not as important as they were to Olivia. During the rest of the car journey Olivia described the various places she'd visited, and they aired their mutual relief at Obama's victory in the presidential election.

'So what are you going to do instead, then?'

Maria poured some more wine while looking at Olivia.

'Instead of what?'

'Becoming a police officer?'

'I'm thinking of studying history of art.'

Just don't say 'good' now, Olivia thought.

'Smart. A bit of a link to Adelita.'

'Yes.'

Maria smiled and looked at Olivia.

'What is it?'

'You're very tanned.'

'I'm half Mexican.'

'Calm down, darling, that was a compliment.'

'Thanks.'

Olivia felt she needed some air. She'd steeled herself for this first meeting with Maria and had felt a kind of obstinate need to provoke her with the name change and things, and it had ended up in a strange kind of nothingness.

'Shall we go for a walk?' Maria suggested.

It had stopped raining. But Olivia was still quite shocked when she stepped outside. She'd spent quite some time in a tropical climate – here it was about zero degrees and a harsh November wind was blowing. Maria had dressed her up in an old down jacket and a hideous woollen hat.

And Olivia was soon very glad that she had.

Side by side they walked up the row of houses where Olivia had spent most of her childhood. Maria pointed at the houses as they passed by, telling her who still lived there, who had died, who had got remarried to a neighbour and so on, and Olivia nodded every now and again to appear interested. Her thoughts were elsewhere, with Arne, her adoptive father, Maria's husband, who had died of cancer when Olivia was nineteen. Olivia had idolised Arne. He'd been her rock during those tough teenage years, always by her side when she needed his support, felt lost, wanted to die or run away or just curl up next to someone who consoled her without making comments.

Maria always made comments.

Olivia hated that.

Then Arne died, leaving her with deep sorrow and a white Ford Mustang. She still had the Mustang, but the sorrow had morphed into something else entirely.

From the moment she found out that Arne wasn't her real father.

Both he and Maria had hidden it from her. But more than that, he'd hidden Olivia's terrible story from both her and

Maria, in a way that she couldn't understand and probably never would. She wouldn't get any answers. He was dead. But it was a betrayal that dragged her much-loved adoptive father down into a snake pit of chaotic emotions. Eventually she came to accept things as they were. Why waste your energy being angry with a man who's dead and buried? She had ultimately reconciled herself with what had happened.

She'd had to.

She had loved Arne and he had loved her. Deeply and sincerely, as long as he lived. There was no reason to spoil that.

'What are you thinking about?' Maria asked.

They'd just turned into Holmbodavägen.

'How Dad would have reacted to my new name.'

'He would have reacted like me.'

'How do you know?'

'Because he was… what's going on?!'

Maria stopped and pointed. There was an ambulance outside one of the houses at the end of the road. A couple of uniformed police officers were just coming out through the gate. Mary took hold of Olivia's arm.

'That's the Sahlmanns' house, isn't it?'

'Yes.'

Olivia knew who the Sahlmanns were. She'd babysat their youngest daughter Sandra quite a few times when she lived at home. After Sandra's mother Therese died in the tsunami eight years ago, Maria had been one of those in the neighbourhood who'd supported her father Bengt and helped him with various legal formalities.

'What's happened?' Maria said.

They walked over to the ambulance. Olivia saw that there were a few neighbours standing half-hidden behind their curtains, peering at the Sahlmanns' house. When they were almost there, she was surprised to see that one of the officers at the gate looked very familiar. It was Ulf Molin, one of her classmates at the Police Academy. He was the most persistent of all the guys who'd hit on her during those couple of years. Olivia quickly pulled off the ugly woollen hat.

'Hi Ulf.'

Ulf Molin turned around.

'Olivia? Hi! What are you doing here?'

'Visiting my mum, she lives nearby.'

'So, how are you doing, then? You're so tanned! I heard that you'd...'

'I've taken some time out. What's happened? This is Maria, by the way, my mum.'

Ulf greeted Maria. A bit too smarmily, Olivia thought. Hasn't he given up yet?

'We know Bengt Sahlmann and his daughter Sandra,' Maria said and repeated Olivia's question. 'What's happened?'

Ulf took a few steps to the side and Olivia and Maria followed him. Consciously or unconsciously, he lowered his voice slightly.

'Sahlmann has killed himself. Hanged himself. His daughter came home a while ago and found him.'

Maria and Olivia looked at each other. Hanged himself?

'Oh, the poor girl!' Maria exclaimed.

'Where is she now?' Olivia asked.

'In the ambulance. They've given her a sedative. We've asked her where her mother is, but she won't answer.'

'Her mother is dead,' Maria said.

'Oh, I see.'

'Have you contacted any relatives?'

'We've tried to get hold of her aunt, but she seems to be at some conference in Copenhagen, so we haven't reached her yet.'

'No one else?'

'She hasn't mentioned anyone else.'

'Can I talk to her?' Olivia asked.

Ulf nodded and went over to the ambulance and opened the back door. Olivia stepped forward and looked inside. A female paramedic was sitting on one side. On a narrow bench opposite sat a thin teenage girl, slumped over, in muddy clothes and with a red blanket around her shoulders. Her blonde hair hung down over her eyes, her hands clasping her mouth. It took a little while before Olivia recognised her, but no time at all before she felt a lump in her throat.

She swallowed hard.

'Hi Sandra. Do you remember me?' Olivia said.

Sandra turned her tear-stained face towards Olivia.

'I used to babysit you when you were little. Do you remember?'

Sandra looked at Olivia for a few seconds and nodded almost imperceptibly. Olivia leant in a little more.

'I've just heard what happened and…'

'I don't want to go into the house.'

Sandra's voice was thin and virtually inaudible. She pulled the blanket over her eyes and hung her head down towards her chest.

'You don't have to,' said Olivia.

'I don't want to stay here.'

'I understand… you're more than welcome to come to our house, if you want.'

'I want to go to Charlotte's.'

The voice came from deep within her chest.

'Who's that?'

'My aunt.'

'She's in Copenhagen apparently. As soon as the police get hold of her I'm sure she'll come home, but it might not be until tomorrow. Don't you want to come over to our place?'

Sandra rocked back and forth. Olivia turned around. Ulf and Maria were standing behind her. Olivia looked at Ulf and whispered as quietly as she could.

'Where will you take her if she doesn't want to…'

Suddenly Sandra got up from the bench. Olivia quickly reached out her hand and helped her climb down onto the road. Maria took a step towards her.

'Hi Sandra.'

Maria put an arm around Sandra's shoulders and started walking away from the ambulance. Olivia turned to Ulf.

'Is it all right if we take her with us?'

'Absolutely, no problem, if that's what she wants. Are you still using your old mobile number?'

What's he after now, Olivia thought. Here?

'Why?'

'If we get hold of her aunt, it's probably good if I can let you know as soon as possible.'

'Sure. Of course. Yes, it's the same number.'

'Good. We'll be in touch. Nice hat, by the way.'

Ulf nodded down at the woollen hat in Olivia's hand.

Ulf called half an hour later. He'd got hold of Sandra's aunt in Copenhagen, told her what had happened and said that Sandra was at Maria Rönning's house. Charlotte had been given Olivia's mobile number and called immediately. The conversation with Sandra was short and pretty monosyllabic. Both of them were crying down the phone. Finally Sandra passed the phone back to Olivia and Charlotte explained that she would take the first plane back in the morning.

'Can Sandra stay with you until I get back?'

'Of course,' said Olivia.

'Thank you.'

Olivia ended the call.

The three of them sat in Maria's kitchen. Maria had lit a few candles on the table and made some tea with her special blend, a kind of universal panacea that had already healed a great many wounds. More than anything, it was soothing. Maybe mostly for Maria and Olivia, Sandra was already noticeably affected by whatever she'd been given by the paramedics and was pretty zoned out. Shocked, tired and drugged. She didn't say anything. Maria and Olivia sipped their tea and were a little unsure about how to handle the situation when the thin voice found its way out.

'I ran out of petrol... '

Sandra stared into her cup as she said this, so quietly that Olivia and Maria had to lean towards her.

'…I called my dad, but he didn't answer, I thought he might have gone out to do some shopping, he was going to buy tacos, my favourite, we were going to celebrate…'

Sandra fell silent. Heavy tears ran down her cheeks and dripped into her cup.

'What were you going to celebrate?'

'I don't want to go back home.'

'I can understand that,' said Olivia. 'Can you stay with Charlotte?'

'When is she coming?'

'Tomorrow morning. She'll come straight here.'

'Am I going to sleep here?'

'Don't you want to?'

Sandra didn't answer. Maria put her hand on her arm.

'You can sleep in Olivia's old room.'

Sandra nodded slightly. She pushed her teacup away and looked up at Olivia. Her gaze was absent, her eyes bleary.

'I want my computer.'

'And where is it?'

'In Dad's office. We shared it. I have loads of school projects on it. It's in a cork computer bag, a checked one.'

'I'll go and get it, then.'

Olivia stood up. Maria looked at her and Olivia shrugged her shoulders a little. If Sandra wanted her computer, she would get it. It was, after all, a source of continuity for her.

'Have you got a house key on you?'

Sandra put her hand in her pocket and pulled out a key. Olivia took it from her.

'I'll be right back.'

Olivia hurried out through Maria's gate. Ulf was probably no longer at the house. Maybe I should check with him, she thought. She got out her mobile and called the last dialled number.

'Molin.'

'Hi, it's Olivia.'

'Hi! How's it going? How is she feeling?'

'Crap. Ulf, she's asked me to collect her computer from the house, is that all right? She's given me the door key.'

'No problem, we're done there. But you should tread carefully, you know.'

'I know. We did the same training.'

'Did we?'

'Stop it.'

Olivia ended the call. 'Tread carefully.' Where did they pick up these idiotic expressions? In the sauna? But she understood what he meant and realised that she should have been wearing gloves. She checked the pockets of her jacket and pulled out some tattered mittens. Mittens? She put them back in her pocket and turned in towards the Sahlmanns' house. It had started raining again and the wind was whipping between the houses. She squinted and hesitated a little. There was a dark figure standing by the gate. Or was it the shadow of a tree? She carried on walking up towards the house. The ambulance and the police car were gone, but the neighbours were still hiding behind the curtains. She felt their peering eyes following her down the poorly lit street.

She reached the gate.

There was no one there. Probably a shadow, she thought, and walked up to the front door. She opened it with Sandra's key and stepped into the house. Suddenly the door slammed shut behind her with a loud bang.

It was pitch dark in the hallway.

In the whole house.

And totally silent.

A dead man had been hanging here not so long ago. Right in front of her. Hanging by a rope from the ceiling. Olivia suppressed these thoughts and started feeling for the light switch. Then her police training kicked in. She quickly pulled out the mittens and put them on. A few seconds later, she realised what a sensitive instrument the human hand really is. Feeling around for a switch in the pitch dark wearing thick mittens is no easy feat. Finally she found it. The hallway light showed her the way into the living room, where she found another light switch. The room lit up. Olivia looked around. An ordinary living room with a sofa, a television, bookshelves, a floor lamp, an armchair, some paintings on the wall. She went to have a look at some photographs on a bookshelf. In quite a large photo she saw a younger Sandra and a younger Bengt Sahlmann with a dark-blonde woman of Bengt's age. Therese, Sandra's mother. Olivia vaguely recognised her.

A family.

And now there was only Sandra. Olivia felt her stomach tighten. She carried on into the adjoining room and turned on the ceiling light. Along one wall was a large square desk with various electrical devices, a modem, a printer, a router and a tangle of wires.

But no laptop.

And no checked laptop bag made of cork.

She had a good look around. On the shelves, chairs, and again on the desk. It wasn't there. Perhaps it was in another room? Although Sandra had been very clear: 'It's in the office.' But she could have been wrong. Her father could have moved it.

Olivia turned off the light and went back into the living room. A shiver ran down her spine. She looked back up at the ceiling, at the lamp hook that Sahlmann had probably used to hang himself, since Sandra had seen him immediately as she came into the hallway. She realised that she was breathing quietly. Why was she doing that? There hadn't been a murder in here. Just an unhappy man who'd ended his life with a rope. The only unsettling thing that might be found here was his soul. But Olivia was the last person in the world to engage with such hocus-pocus, so she headed towards the kitchen.

The ceiling lamp was casting a dim light across the room. Olivia had another look around. No laptop. Just a kitchen like any other. White cabinets, magnets on the dishwasher, a fruit bowl, a worktop with various little bottles, a table in the middle with a green plastic tablecloth, a half-drunk glass of water next to the cooker. Just a mundane, everyday place until only a few hours ago.

Now it was something else entirely.

Olivia felt that stinging sensation in her stomach again, how life could suddenly be thrown into disarray, from the safety of daily life to shock and sorrow. She looked at the kitchen worktop. A packet of taco shells, a jar of taco sauce, a can of sweetcorn and a bag of corn chips lay on the side. She remembered Sandra talking about her favourite food, and saying that her father was going to buy it to celebrate whatever it was they were going to celebrate. She opened the fridge. There was an unopened packet of mince on the top shelf.

All the ingredients for her favourite meal.

And then he'd gone and taken his own life.

Olivia turned the light off in the kitchen and went back out into the living room. Something was bothering her. She didn't really know what, but something wasn't right. She sat down on the sofa and looked down at her mittens. The silence in the room enveloped her. What had happened in here? Slowly she turned her head and looked towards the hallway where Sandra had come in, up at the ceiling where her father had been hanging, down at the floor where the remains of a stain showed where the police had cleared up, and then at the dark corridor that led into the bedrooms.

Should I go and have a look there as well?

She rubbed her mittens together and made a decision. It wasn't far from the sofa to the corridor. A couple of metres in, she stopped. She had heard a noise. A scraping noise.

Was it the branches brushing against the bedroom windows?

She took another step forward and stood still outside the half-open door. The scraping noise had stopped. It was deadly silent. She reached for the door. Just when she was about to push it open, a sharp sound cut through the house. A phone. A shrill signal that made her rush back out into the corridor. With a few quick steps she was back in the living room. The phone was on the shelf opposite the sofa. It rang again. She approached the shelf. When it rang a third time, she picked up the handset and almost dropped it on the floor because of her mittens.

But she answered.

'Yes?'

'Hi, it's Alex Popovic. I'd like to speak to Bengt. Is that Sandra?'

'No.'

'Is Bengt there?'

'No. Are you a friend of the family?'

'…who am I speaking to?'

'Olivia Rivera. Bengt Sahlmann has committed suicide. If you'd like more information, you should contact the police.'

Olivia put the phone down and went towards the front door.

She'd done what Sandra had asked her to do.

Almost.

There was no sign of any computer.

* * *

The ash at the end of his cigarillo was just a centimetre from his yellowed fingertips. Soon it would fall down in front of his bare feet. Nevertheless he'd hardly smoked it: he'd lit the cigarillo, taken one big puff and then been swallowed up by the music, and *Scheherazade*. And that's where he remained. He'd positioned the speakers so that the sound intertwined just where he was sitting, naked, eyes closed, in the middle of the large room. The light from a couple of alabaster lamps shone onto the beautiful floorboards, the shadow of his lean body crept up as a silent figure on the wall. The large, bare north-facing wall that he loved so. The opposite wall was covered from floor to ceiling with books with dark spines, thick, quiet books that he'd never read and never planned to read. They'd been there when he moved in. He turned his naked body slightly, as though there was a bar of music he couldn't reach. There wasn't. All the tones and sounds had gathered in there, in his head. In the same place as that woman. The woman who bled and screamed and died, over and over again, right in front of his helpless eyes, until his closed eyes lost sight of her and just the music remained. The loud, beautiful music had done it again. Purified him. Cleansed him. Eliminated all the horror from his brain.

This time.

He lowered his head slightly and opened his eyes. A new sound had forced its way in, a sound he didn't want to hear. He stepped to the side and turned off the music. His mobile was on the amplifier. He saw who was calling and answered, the familiar voice reaching into his consciousness.

'Bengt Sahlmann has hanged himself.'

The ash fell onto the floor.

* * *

Sandra's eyes closed straight away. Maria tucked her in and saw that she was already asleep before the blanket was pulled over her. She looked at the young girl for a few minutes before switching off the bedside lamp. She subconsciously avoided drawing parallels between Sandra and Olivia – she didn't want to face those thoughts tonight.

'There was no laptop there.'

Olivia threw the jacket over a chair in the kitchen and slumped down at the table. Maria filled up her teacup.

'Sandra has fallen asleep.'

'Good. I basically looked all over the house and it wasn't there.'

'Well, you can't do any more.'

'I can check if it's at Bengt's work.'

'Yes. But her aunt can do that too.'

'She asked me to do it.'

Maria nodded. She realised that the parallels she had wanted to avoid had taken root in Olivia. She had already made room for Sandra.

'What did Bengt do?' Olivia asked.

'He worked for Customs and Excise. Are you staying the night?'

'Yes.'

What did she think? That she was going to go back to Söder in the middle of the night and let Sandra wake up here on her own? Not that she mistrusted Maria's kindness or her ability to serve Sandra an excellent and nutritious breakfast. But it was Olivia who'd made a connection with Sandra.

At least from her perspective.

'You can sleep in the spare room, the sheets are clean. I think I'm going to go to bed now,' Maria said.

'You do that. I'll clear this up.'

Maria got up and hesitated for a second, wondering whether she should bend down and give Olivia a kiss on the cheek. Olivia Rivera. She decided to stroke her daughter's cheek instead.

'*Te amo.*'

'Sleep well.'

Maria headed towards the kitchen door. Halfway there she turned around and looked at Olivia.

'You can empathise with her situation, can't you?'

Olivia didn't answer.

'Goodnight.'

Maria disappeared. Olivia watched her go. She was right. Olivia had empathised with Sandra's situation ever since she'd seen the thin girl sitting in the ambulance in shock, having just lost her father. And having lost her mother in the tsunami just a few years earlier. Both her parents had died in dramatic circumstances. Like Olivia's own. She had no difficulty at all imagining being in Sandra's shoes.

On the contrary.

Even though her own shocks had come one after the other, in a completely different way. But the girl asleep upstairs in her old room would wake up to an orphaned existence and be forced to shape her life alone.

Now you're being unfair to Arne and Maria, Olivia thought. You did actually grow up with two parents, one of whom is still alive. You were not left empty handed when the shocking news was delivered. Your real parents were not ripped out of your life. You didn't even know they existed.

Olivia could feel herself flagging, both physically and mentally. The long flight was catching up with her – the tiredness, the tension, and then the tragedy she'd been caught up in. Just when she thought she would sleep a thousand hours and then step back out into the world.

Strong. Ready.

Things were seemingly not going to be that simple.

She pulled her rucksack towards her and opened it. She had wrapped Bosques' beautiful cigar box in a couple of unwashed T-shirts. She gently picked it up and put it on the kitchen table. She stared at the door and listened.

Silence.

She didn't want to show it to Maria. Especially not what was inside. It was a very private heirloom that she didn't intend to share with anyone. She opened the lid and smelled that familiar scent of old cigars again. Carefully she picked up the photograph of Adelita. Under it lay a black lock of hair, tied together with a thin transparent piece of string. Who had kept it? Nils Wendt? When had he got it? When Adelita had travelled to Sweden just before she was murdered there? She placed the lock of hair next to the photograph. At the bottom of the box were a few handwritten letters. She had already looked at them on the plane and realised that her Spanish wasn't good enough to understand what was written in them. One day she'd get someone to translate them. Not Maria, but Abbas perhaps? He was good at Spanish. Abbas had crossed her mind a couple of times during her long trip. She liked him, a lot, without really knowing him.

Bosques had liked Abbas too. 'He's a man,' Bosques had said. And Olivia hadn't thought that sounded silly. She understood exactly what Bosques meant. I'll call Abbas tomorrow, Olivia thought and looked inside the box again. There was only one thing left in it. A gold brooch. Olivia picked it up and realised it could be opened. She hadn't seen that on the plane. Carefully she snapped open the top to reveal a small photo graph inside. Of a dark-skinned man. Who was it? His appearance was neither reminiscent of Adelita's nor her own. He looked a bit like Bosques but she didn't think any more about that.

She snapped the brooch shut and put it back in the box.

And thought about Sandra again.

The orphaned teenager sleeping in her old room.

Chapter 4

The light grey jumper elegantly fitted Abbas's slim, supple body. He was freshly showered and dressed in brown chinos. His feet moved slowly down the stairs. Frozen in time, he thought. Some of the gently curved stone steps were adorned with beautiful fossils of million-year-old squid. Orthoceratidae. They fascinated him. He carried on going down, a little faster. He was on his way to check the letterbox in the hall. There was an expectant spring in his step: with any luck there would be a thin book with Sufi poetry in there. Ronny Redlös, who ran a shop selling old books, had posted it yesterday, so it should be here today.

Should.

But given the poor reliability of the postal service, it might well take another day. That would be annoying. He had been desperately longing for some spiritual catharsis before his nightshift at the casino. So he hurried on down the stairs.

'Abbas!'

Abbas stopped. He knew who that voice belonged to. When he turned around, he saw Agnes Ekholm standing at her half-open front door. Her silvery grey wig wasn't on properly and her tattered dressing gown was wrongly buttoned.

'Are you going to get the post?'

'Yes. Should I get yours too?'

'If you don't mind.'

Abbas went back up to take the little key from Agnes.

'I'll wait here,' she said.

Abbas nodded and carried on down. He reflected that older people with frail bones and a shaky sense of balance were now forced to go up and down the hard stone staircase to get their post. Often several times a day, because no one knew when the post actually came. All so that postmen no longer needed to put it through their individual doors. It was one of the reasons he disliked the letterboxes being down by the entrance. Another was that certain people, if so inclined, probably had all the time in the world to steal various bits of personal information and bank details.

The postal service had laid it all out for them.

Abbas opened Agnes's box first: a thin letter from the Church of Sweden and a postcard that should have gone to her neighbour. His own was rather more well filled. A few letters, an ugly pamphlet from an insurance company and a thick newspaper. His subscription.

But no book.

At least the newspaper had come, he thought, and quickly climbed up the stairs to Agnes' floor. She looked at him expectantly.

'There wasn't much today unfortunately,' he said.

Agnes took the letter from the Church of Sweden and tried to hide her disappointment.

'Maybe there'll be more tomorrow?' she said.

'Yes.'

'Here!'

Agnes passed him a small piece of carrot cake wrapped in a white paper napkin.

'I didn't make it today, but…'

Abbas took the piece of cake. It was a ritual. Every time he went to get the post for Agnes, she gave him a piece of her carrot cake. The second time he'd tasted it he realised that it was probably the same cake as last time, a week later. The third time he'd left it in a dog bowl in the stairway one floor up.

'Thank you,' he said.

'I do hope you'll enjoy it.'

Abbas nodded again and carried on up the stairs. The cake ended up in the same bowl as the others had. He reached his own front door and opened it while glancing at his letters. Two bills and a pay slip from Casino Cosmopol. He pulled the door closed, put the post on the small table in the hallway and opened up the newspaper he'd collected.

The one he subscribed to.

Before the front page was completely unfolded, he had already taken a few steps into the living room. He stood still. For the first few seconds he read the headlines and scanned the large black and white photograph. He then spent the next few minutes reading the article. For fifteen minutes, he held the newspaper in the same position in front of him, standing on the same spot on the floor, the only difference being that his hands were now trembling and his eyes had stopped reading. He was just holding an object made from paper.

Totally detached.

Suddenly he managed to free himself. He carefully folded up the newspaper and put it on the sleek glass table in front of the sofa, making sure it was in line with the edge of the table. Then he took two steps towards the window and pulled out the thin black pole that he used to adjust his wooden blinds. His gaze wandered through the window and towards the Matteus Church on the other side of the road, staring at it without actually seeing it. Then he closed the blinds and stood still, just staring out in front of him.

The hoover?

Where have I put it?

He walked away from the window and went to get the hoover. It was where it always was. He plugged it into the socket and started hoovering. First methodically, all over the living room floor, under the sofa and the glass table, and then back over the floor again. Eventually he got stuck in one spot. He hoovered the same bit over and over again, back and forth, until cramp set in.

First in his chest, then in his stomach.

He put the hoover down and went into the kitchen. He just about managed to think, 'Maybe I should paint the walls?' before he threw up into the sink, repeatedly, until it was just green bile that came up. By the end he was just retching. He hung his head down over the sink, his hands let go of the worktop, he slowly slid down onto the floor and onto the kitchen rug. He curled up into a foetal position. His eyelids slid shut.

The last thing he saw was the strange, whirring machine in the middle of the living room.

Chapter 5

Stilton had gained weight. It was largely muscle. Most of his body had withered away during the years he'd lived on streets, his collarbones serving as a bony hanger for a sack of skin. He'd put a stop to that. Slowly but surely, he had restored his worn body, exercising, taking care of himself, and all the saggy skin had filled out again. Now he was almost back to his former self.

Physically.

He ran a hand over his head. His long straggly hair had been cropped and replaced with a blond crew cut with streaks of grey running through it. A white scar in the corner of his mouth shone through the thin stubble, reminding him of the young lad he once was, just before he turned twenty. A young Swede of few words on a Norwegian oilrig, an oilrig that had suddenly exploded and unleashed full-scale panic in all but him, the Swede, who'd dragged a couple of colleagues from the distorted steel inferno with a muted contempt for death and saved their lives. A year later he had submitted his application to the Police Academy in Stockholm.

He carried a blue Adidas bag in his hand and headed down from Hornsgatan towards Långholmen. He walked quickly to keep warm. It was that inspiring time of year when the colour scheme delighted with different shades of grey. He buttoned his brown leather jacket right up under his chin. It was still a bit too big, but did the job in the icy cold winds. He'd inherited it from his grandfather, a tough old seal hunter on the island of Rödlöga whose shoulders were as wide as a doorframe.

He'd never match that.

But his grandfather was dead and the jacket was his and he wore it as well as he could.

He reached into the inside pocket, took out his mobile and tapped in a number. It didn't ring for long.

'Luna.'

'Hi again, it's Tom Stilton.'

'Yes?'

'I was just wondering if I could come over.'

'Now?'

'Yes.'

'OK.'

'I'll be there in ten minutes.'

Stilton ended the call and pulled out the piece of paper that he'd found stapled to an old oak tree on the edge of the Långholmen Park. He read the text again.

'*Sara la Kali.*'

Why not, he thought.

Luna pulled a wire brush over one of the iron ribs on the front deck. The rust came and went. It came when she didn't notice it and went again when she paid attention. What a Sisyphean task, she thought. The barge had been built in 1932, and although it was in good condition, it required constant maintenance. She stood up and glanced over at the Pålsund Bridge. A lone figure carrying a blue bag was making his way over the bridge, the wind forcing him to lean forwards slightly as he walked. It's probably him, she thought. He'd called twice in quick succession and now he was on his way here. What an efficient man. Luna liked that. She put down the brush and flicked her thick mane of blonde hair with her somewhat grubby hand just as the man looked over at the barge. Luna waved at him. She didn't really know how to begin – probably best just to be upfront about it. It was the first time she was doing this and she wasn't entirely comfortable with the situation.

The man was soon at the gangway, a rather primitive construction made from wood and tar. He crossed over it in four steps and stood still on the deck.

Luna stepped forward.

'Hi. Luna Johansson.'

'Tom Stilton.'

He's tall, she thought. She was six foot and this man was clearly taller, this man with a deep voice, worn face and a nice brown leather jacket. She was dressed in a pair of dirty green dungarees. Did he look a little dangerous? Maybe that was a good thing. There had been an attempted break-in a week ago and it could happen again.

'Is this your boat?' Stilton asked.

'Yes.'

'Do you live here alone?'

Luna had thought that she would be the one asking questions, but OK.

'Yes.'

'Can we take a look inside the cabin?'

'In a sec. Do you have any references?'

'I was homeless for five years, getting by selling *Situation Stockholm*, and this past year I've been living on Rödlöga.'

'Are those your references?'

'Are you worried about the rent?'

'No. I'll take an advance on that. Do you have a job?'

'Not yet.'

'What did you do before you were homeless?'

'I was a police officer. At the National Crime Squad.'

This man was either a compulsive liar or very strange. Luna hadn't quite made up her mind when Stilton said: 'I come from a family of seal hunters.'

He was strange.

'The cabin is this way,' said Luna.

She gestured behind her and expected the man to go first. He thought otherwise, so there were a few seconds of nervous silence before Luna turned around and headed towards the stern.

Stilton followed her.

He studied the woman in front of him. She was tall, quite broad shouldered and although her overalls didn't reveal much about her frame, he got the feeling that she was in good shape.

When she tossed her head her blonde hair fell over onto one of her shoulders, partially revealing her neck. Not much, but enough for Stilton to see a tattoo snaking its way up to her ear.

'So here it is.'

Luna moved away so that Stilton could take a step forward. He looked in and saw a wall-mounted bunk, a square table under a small round porthole, wooden bulkheads, nothing more.

'It's the largest cabin on here,' she said. 'Seven square metres.'

The cells at Kumla Prison are ten, Stilton thought.

'Looks good,' he said. 'Can I lock this?'

Stilton nodded towards the cabin door.

'No, but I can put a bolt on the door if you want.'

'Yes, please. Where do you sleep?'

'At the other end. My cabin has a lock.'

Stilton didn't really know how to react to that and then Luna said: 'You have access to the shower, lounge and kitchen. There's only one fridge. You can use the two bottom shelves. We share the loo.'

'OK. Three thousand a month?'

'Well, yes, in principle.'

Stilton peered at Luna.

'I'd consider reducing the rent in lieu of some renovation work on the boat.'

Stilton nodded. He was no handyman: he was busy enough fixing himself. But the offer was OK.

'Will there be a contract?' he asked.

'Do we need one?'

'You're taking a month's payment in advance. How do I know that the boat will still be here in a week?'

'You don't.'

'No. So…?'

'What difference would a contract make?'

'Bugger all.'

'Yep, so you may as well trust that I'm not going to screw you over.'

'Apparently so.'

Stilton felt himself getting defensive and he didn't enjoy being in this position. One of his major assets as an interrogator had been his ability to steer the dialogue in the direction he wanted until interviewees were pushed into a verbal corner that they could not escape.

Luna had certainly not ended up in that corner.

'When do you want to move in?' she asked.

'Now, if that's all right.'

Luna looked at his blue bag.

'I have another bag at a friend's house.'

'What about the rent?'

Stilton pulled out a black wallet from his inside pocket, opened it and took out three thousand-kronor notes. There were a few more in there. Four months ago he'd sold a piece of land out on Rödlöga to an eager stockbroker from Gothenburg. His grandparents were probably turning in their graves when the sale went through, but Stilton needed money and it was his inheritance. He now had a pretty decent amount of money sitting in a savings account at Swedbank.

'Thanks.'

Luna took the notes from him.

Stilton went into the cabin and pulled the door closed.

* * *

There was a lot that was different about this day. The sun, for example, was shining. And it hadn't been for the past week. Now it had crept over the rooftops just to show it was still there. Soon it would soon be descending again.

But nevertheless.

The beams of sunlight shone into Maria's kitchen, casting a warm yellowy glow over the room. Things were different there too. Maria had been called to the Svea Court of Appeal to assist a colleague and neither of the people sitting at the kitchen table lived in the house. One of them was a daughter who'd flown the nest and was thinking about changing her surname, and the other was Sandra, the girl who had found her father hanging from the ceiling by a tow rope less than eighteen hours ago. She had woken late. Her face bore clear traces of shock and nightmares, but above all she seemed to have woken up to the realisation that she no longer had parents.

Olivia saw this realisation in her face as soon as she stepped into the kitchen. She gave Sandra a long, long hug. Silently. A few minutes later, she felt her thin jumper was soaked with Sandra's tears. After a while Sandra freed herself from Olivia's hug and asked to use the toilet. Olivia showed her where it was. Meanwhile she laid out whatever she could find in Maria's fridge and before long they were each sitting with a bowl of cereal in front of them. Not many words had been exchanged across the table. Olivia waited. Sandra moved her spoon around the bowl.

'Has Charlotte been in touch?' she asked.

'Yes, she's on her way. She's landing in half an hour and she's coming straight here.'

'Did you get the computer?'

'It wasn't there.'

Sandra looked up from the bowl.

'In the office?'

'No, I looked everywhere. Could he have taken it to work?'

'I don't know. He tends to keep it at home.'

'OK. I can have a look at his work. What kind of computer is it?'

'A MacBook Pro. It's quite new. I put a little sticker on the inside, a pink heart… Why did he do it?'

'Who?'

'My dad!'

'Commit suicide?'

'Yes!?'

Sandra was suddenly staring straight into Olivia's eyes. As if she thought that Olivia would have an answer.

'I have no idea.'

'But why do people commit suicide?'

Olivia saw that Sandra was steeling herself to talk, to put the horror into words, to try to comprehend the incomprehensible. A father taking his own life. Without any kind of warning, leaving his only child an orphan.

'I don't know, Sandra. I never knew your father. Was he sad about something?'

Olivia heard how foolish that sounded: 'sad about something'. She wasn't speaking to a child. Sandra was a teenager, about to enter adulthood in a way that no one should have to.

She deserved more respect.

Olivia pulled her chair towards Sandra.

'Sandra... there are a thousand reasons why people commit suicide, but there is one thing that you can exclude. He did not take his life because of you. I don't know why he did it, maybe the police investigation will tell us: there might be financial reasons or it might be something to do with your mother. I mean, she died...'

'He'd got over my mum's death. We both had. Once, about six months after she died, he came into my room and talked about his grief, how he was sometimes so sad that he didn't know whether he could carry on living if it wasn't for me. We held each other and got through it.'

This corroborated what Olivia's intuition had told her. Sandra wasn't a child.

'Having said that, he was very sad about what happened with my grandfather,' Sandra said.

'What happened to him?'

'He died a while ago. He was living in an old people's home and died there. Dad said that they hadn't taken proper care of him and that made him very sad. He didn't really show it, but I saw it in his eyes.'

'Was your grandfather old?'

'He was eighty-three, and he was quite ill. We knew that he was going to die soon, so it wasn't that…'

Sandra ate a spoonful of cereal. Olivia saw her hand shaking. I hope that Charlotte is a good person, she thought, who knows how to deal with Sandra. She should be, her sister died in the tsunami, so she's faced crises of her own.

But you never know.

'Where's your father?'

Sandra spoke as she pushed her bowl away. Olivia was completely unprepared.

'He died a few years ago. From cancer.'

'Well, at least you still have your mum.'

'Yes.'

Olivia could have ended the conversation there, with a half-truth. But she didn't want that. She didn't know how close she would get to Sandra in the future and she didn't want her to stumble upon the real truth at a later date. She didn't want to do what others had done to her.

So she started telling her what had happened.

It took quite a while. It was not a straightforward story. But when she'd finally recounted all the tragic things that had happened to her and her various parents, and answered several of Sandra's questions, Sandra looked at her and said.

'Poor you.'

As though it was Olivia who needed comforting.

The young women went out through the gate of the terraced house in Rotebro, off to collect Sandra's scooter. The feeble November sunshine barely managed to dry up the small puddles on the road. It was pretty cold, but the wind was not nearly as severe as the night before. They walked quite slowly. From a distance they could have been mistaken for best friends, or sisters, one a little older than the other. They were neither, but the hours in Maria's kitchen had created a connection between them, as though they shared the same fate.

Which they did to some extent.

Sandra's mind was still filled with Olivia's account of brutal murders and painful betrayals, allowing her to repress her own anguish.

For the moment anyway.

Very different thoughts were running through Olivia's head. When they reached the underpass, she remembered what she'd wanted to ask.

'Do you know someone called Alex Popovic?'

'Not very well. I know who he is, one of Dad's friends, a journalist. Why do you ask?'

'He called your house when I was there looking for the computer.'

'What did he want?'

'I don't know, I ended the call pretty quickly.'

'Did you tell him about my dad?'

'Yes.'

They walked through the underpass. Olivia peered at the girl next to her. The night before she had walked this way on her way home, happy, looking forward to celebrating her exam result. Now her entire existence was crushed.

They emerged on the other side.

'Where did you put your scooter?'

'Over there, by the tree.'

Sandra walked ahead towards some trees where she'd left her scooter. But there was no scooter to be found.

'It's gone!'

Olivia caught up with her.

'And this is where you left it?'

'Yes.'

Olivia looked around and saw the severed lock on the ground, half-hidden by wet leaves.

'It looks like it's been stolen.'

'Yes.'

Olivia thought that Sandra might break down again. But she didn't. It was as if the missing scooter was just a part of the greater tragedy, that everything was connected.

'It must have been that bloody man,' Sandra said.

'What man?'

'The one I walked past.'

'Where?'

'In the underpass, on my way home. He was walking the other way and then he disappeared. I ran back to the scooter to get my bag with the key and he was gone. Imagine if he was hiding and saw me when I got to the scooter and then went back? He would have seen that it was just standing there. And then stolen it.'

'Yes, maybe. You didn't recognise him? From the area?'

'No.'

'But when he walked past you, was he coming from the direction of where your house is?'

'Yes, what do you mean?'

'Nothing.'

Olivia got out her mobile.

'I'm going to report the scooter missing.'

* * *

Mette Olsäter pulled out a small paper napkin and wiped under her nose – she could feel there were beads of sweat on her upper lip. She'd asked for a window to be opened in the cramped boardroom to keep the temperature down, as the thermostat wasn't working properly. Her bulk and the inescapable tension would make her sweat, she knew that, and sweat undermines authority. She couldn't be doing with that – she needed some authority for what she wanted to say. She looked at her watch, a thin black Rado watch that she'd been given by her husband when she turned fifty, and realised there was less than one minute to go. She took a last glance around her sparsely decorated office, one of the oldest at the National Crime Squad headquarters. Before, she'd had private photos on her desk and various pieces of pottery that she'd made in the windows. Now everything was gone. She'd reached a phase when she wanted to keep her work and her private life completely separate. She was approaching retirement.

She picked up her blue file and headed towards the open door. She knew there'd be questions over there, some more intelligent than others. She was able to foresee and prepare for most of them. The less intelligent ones. But the others, the intelligent questions, the ones that would come when she least expected them, and from where she could not predict, they worried her. They could stump her, or at least demand answers she couldn't give. She could ill afford them. She knew that the people gathered in the room would meet for an evaluation afterwards, and that the outcome of this would determine the ongoing investigation. And maybe even her role in it. Sweden had been tasked with putting together a strategy for a coordinated international response to the explosive growth in online drug sales. Mette Olsäter had been put in charge of the project. Now she was about to present the strategy advocated by the Swedish police to sixteen foreign police representatives.

She pulled the door closed behind her and headed towards the boardroom. Just before she was about to go in she felt her mobile vibrating in her pocket. She pulled it out. Olivia had texted: 'What time?' Mette answered: '7.00 p.m.'

She had invited Olivia for dinner.

* * *

Stilton arranged his things in the cabin. It didn't take long. A few clothes in the tiny wardrobe and a tattered portrait of One-eyed Vera on the narrow shelf by the bedside lamp. It was as close to home as he could get in his situation. He didn't care. Just over a year ago he was living in a borrowed caravan that burned

47

down – some kind of arson attack. Now he lived in a cabin on an old barge. A bit more cramped, but untainted by broken memories.

It suited him perfectly.

He left the barge without bumping into Luna. He thought he'd go and see Abbas. He knew that Abbas seldom started work at the casino before eight o'clock. Stilton wanted to begin some private investigations into the shit that had happened before he became homeless, and he might need Abbas's help.

They had a pretty special relationship, based on mutual respect. Stilton had once taken care of Abbas when the young Frenchman had been arrested for counterfeit sales of this and that, and was close to attacking a fellow inmate with a knife when his back was against the wall. Stilton made a connection with him, found a way into his closed world and saw something that no one else saw back then.

A good person.

Damaged and closed, with baggage that Stilton could only guess at, but still. He organised a special programme for Abbas with two supervisors he trusted. Mette and Mårten Olsäter.

Over time, it turned out that Stilton's evaluation of Abbas had been right. He was a good person. So good in fact that he was eventually considered family by the Olsäters, decided to train as a croupier and began studying Sufism. He never forgot what Stilton had done for him.

During the years that Stilton was homeless, Abbas was given the chance to repay some of his debt of gratitude.

And now Stilton was ringing at his door on Dalagatan.

No answer.

He's probably with Ronny Redlös, thought Stilton, with his phone turned off. Or maybe he's in the bath with his earphones on listening to music. Abbas often had baths. Stilton did not. He rang the doorbell again. As the sound faded away he leant against the door. What was that? A dull whirring noise could be heard inside the flat. Was he hoovering? Stilton knocked on the door a couple of times, hard. The whirring noise continued. Stilton concluded that Abbas el Fassi, who was rather anal about tidiness, was hoovering with his earphones on. And he might well be doing that for quite some time.

Stilton stepped out onto Dalagatan and started walking towards Odengatan. It was that time of year again when people didn't look at each other. That cold and harsh time when it was dark almost all day, before the snow came to brighten things up a bit. Everyone he passed was looking down, channelling their bodies to somewhere warm.

Stilton didn't care about the weather, not in that way.

People who've grown up on the flat islands in Stockholm's archipelago have a different relationship to the weather than people in the city. Out there, the weather is a matter of life and death. When storms lash in at thirty metres a second from the open sea, you can't just glide into a posh restaurant like Sturehof to complain about how bloody cold it is!

So Stilton walked towards Odenplan not paying any attention to what was blowing around him. He'd stood outside underground stations selling *Situation Stockholm* in far worse conditions than this. With one major difference. Back then he was totally drained, absent, without a single relevant feeling in his body.

Now it was quite the opposite.

He was extremely fired up. Focused. He had a task. He was going to deal with Rune Forss, the detective chief inspector who had manipulated him out of the police.

A very unpleasant man.

The pressure rising inside Stilton forced him to clench his teeth until his cheeks were straining. He stopped outside the Hellmans toyshop on Odengatan and watched his reflection in the window. He'd never done that when he was homeless. Never. The first time he saw himself in a mirror, after five years on the streets, at home with the Olsäters, he'd had quite a shock. Not now though. He saw himself as the person he had restored.

On Rödlöga.

For the past year he'd lived alone out there in the house he'd inherited from his mother – her parents' old fisherman's cottage. Before that he hadn't been there since he went off the rails in 2005. Abbas had come out to visit him a couple of times and he'd gone into the city to meet Mette and Mårten a couple of times too. Mette was one of his oldest colleagues from the squad, the only one there for whom he had total respect, which had over time resulted in a close personal relationship as well. And subsequently also with her husband Mårten, a slightly eccentric child psychologist.

But the visits to the city were short lived, as he longed to get back out to the island again. Back to isolation. In the beginning he spent time getting the house in order. It was a simple house, wooden panelling on the walls and a stone floor, a tiled roof that had withstood the worst of the weather. It had been standing there for more than a hundred years and Stilton intended to ensure that it would remain there throughout his lifetime.

Once he'd got the house in order he started to clear the land.

Several years had passed since anyone had tended to the plot and many trees had fallen down during storms. It suited him perfectly. He got to work with his grandfather's old bow saw, cut, stacked and then started chopping. Every morning he went out to his chopping block, grabbed a new piece of wood and took up his axe. Hour after hour, until his arms were like putty. Afterwards he went to lie down on the bed just next to the kitchen and checked his arms and legs for ticks.

Then he read.

The Manhattan series. Whodunnits from the fifties. The only books there'd ever been at his grandparents' house. His grandfather had loved them. Peter Cheney, James Hadley Chase, Mickey Spillane. He'd read them over and over again when he was young, when he lived out there with the old folks, smuggling the well-thumbed paperbacks to the outhouse to lose himself in the hard-boiled stories. He still recalled many of the heroes' names. Lemmy Caution. Slim Callaghan. Mike Hammer. Sometimes he'd wondered how much his juvenile fascination with these crime stories and coppers had influenced his choice of profession.

He read the books again, until he fell asleep.

When he woke, he ate whatever he'd been able to get hold of – either from the small island shop or from the Vaxholm boat deliveries, depending on the time of year.

Always food that was easy to prepare.

Then he'd sit down and look out through the hand-blown windowpanes. At the sea, the stars and the lights on far-off ships. He had no dreams about the sea, or a life at sea – he wanted firm ground under his feet. But he enjoyed sitting by the window.

He was biding his time.

As his physical strength returned, through wood chopping and fishing and long walks over the island, his brain also started working again.

For better or for worse.

He did some serious soul-searching. It was quite painful. He forced himself to recall the names of all those he had betrayed during his years in the force. People he'd abandoned, cut ties with, treated like shit. People who had loved him, tried to support him, been there for him. People who had eventually given up hope.

It took its toll.

But it led him onwards.

First into shame. That took a couple of months to process. But when he finally realised that the first step forward was to respect himself more, for the person he now was, the pressure eased a little. He was who he was and he dealt with it as best he could. And he would try to draw new self-respect from that.

That's when he started feeling a sense of rage.

Not immediately. He still wasn't up to it, but he began mulling over certain things. 'Lost years.' He'd lost a number of years in his life. Why? He knew what had sparked it, he knew there weren't any medical explanations, but was that the whole truth?

That's when he came closer to rage.

He got closer to Rune Forss.

Stilton peered at himself in the toyshop window again. An older man in a stiff coat came and stood next to him.

'You don't have a poo bag, do you?'

'Poo bag?'

'Little Wiffin has pooed on the pavement and I forgot to bring a bag.'

Stilton looked down and saw an odd-looking ball of fur circling around the man's legs.

'Sorry, I haven't got a poo bag.'

'All right, sorry to bother you.'

The man pulled Wiffin away. Stilton turned back to face the shop window. He had no trouble connecting to what was taking place inside him. It had been going on for quite some time now and had recently escalated. A kind of frenzied need to get back. And assume a place in the world again.

Make up for lost time.

Yet he didn't quite know how. He'd dedicated a great deal of deep thought to the matter. Where should he go? What was he going to do with his life? He had given it up once and now he'd got it back again.

Or reclaimed it.

What was he going to do with it?

He'd spent the majority of his adult life working in the police, successfully. He had a good moral compass, a sense of right and wrong, perhaps even more clearly now than before his years on the streets. But he couldn't possibly imagine returning to that police environment.

He needed to go in another direction.

But he first had to deal with Rune Forss.

It was the first step towards the closure he was looking for.

He looked past his reflection into the toyshop. He saw electric train sets and puzzles and large boxes of Lego and caught himself missing children.

Children playing.

With him.

Children who were his.

He'd never have any, he was sure of that. That time was over. When the time had been right, during his marriage to Marianne Boglund, he'd been consumed by murder investigations and made it quite clear that he wasn't ready to have children. That was probably one of the reasons for the divorce.

But there were others.

He pulled himself away from the toyshop and walked towards Odenplan. He glanced over at the Tennstopet restaurant on the other side of the road. It was crowded in there, away from the cold and desolation. That sense of community had never appealed to him. He got out his mobile and called Mette Olsäter. She answered after a couple of rings.

'Hi, it's Tom.'

'Hi! Are you in the city?'

'Yes. I want to deal with Rune Forss.'

'Really? Oh!'

'Are you surprised?'

'No. But I can't speak at the moment. I've just been asked to join the steering committee for an international drug operation and I need to email out a million things. Can we meet up tomorrow?'

'I could come and see you at home this evening?'

'That's not very convenient.'

'Why?'

'I've invited Olivia for dinner.'

'So?'

There was silence at the other end of the line and Stilton knew exactly what it was about. Olivia had blamed Stilton for a load of shit that happened in connection with the Nordkoster case. Her mother's murder. With some justification, he knew that. He'd buried his head in the sand and hadn't dared to tell her the truth about some things. When he eventually did she was furious, and she probably still was.

Again with some justification.

So he understood what Mette meant.

'So when can we see each other tomorrow then?' he said.

'Eleven.'

'Where?'

'Here.'

'At the office?'

'Yes, I don't have time to traipse all over the city. Have you heard from Abbas, by the way?'

'No, why?'

'I've tried ringing him so many times, but he's not answering.'

'He's hoovering.'

'Hoovering?'

'Or he might be in the other world, the world yonder.'

Abbas had once tried to explain to Stilton what Sufism was about. Stilton had listened. When Abbas began talking about a world yonder, Stilton suggested that they should play a game of backgammon.

And that was that.

'But I can give him a ring,' he said.

'Thanks. Bye.'

Stilton ended the call.

He folded up the collar on his leather jacket and walked towards Odenplan. He fancied a sausage and thought that there was a sausage stall there.

There wasn't.

* * *

Olivia sat in the beautifully aged kitchen relishing Mårten's latest stew experiment. She'd really longed to come here, to the semi-chaotic, green and white, dilapidated old mansion out in Kummelnäs on the island of Värmdö, with children and grandchildren milling around. It was a long time since she'd been here last. The wounds had not yet healed then, and she'd still had that long journey ahead of her. Yet it all came flooding back as soon ,as she stepped through the gate. It was here in this house that everything had been revealed, just over a year ago. Both Mette and Mårten had been there, but it wasn't them who had shocked her. It was Tom Stilton. He wasn't here now – if he had been she would have left.

She put a warm, delicious-smelling spoonful into her mouth.

'Tom seems to be back on his feet again,' Mette suddenly remarked while topping up Olivia's glass with red wine.

'Oh, really. What a delicious stew, Mårten! What spices did you use? Lots of garlic?'

'Yes,' Mårten said. 'And some cayenne and garam masala.'

'He's been living out on Rödlöga for almost a year now,' Mette continued.

'Are we going to talk about Tom Stilton?'

Olivia sounded a bit blunter than she'd intended and regretted it. She knew that Mette only meant well, but she didn't want to talk about him. And Mårten could see that right away.

'Tell us about your trip,' he said.

She was happy to. A couple of glasses of wine later, Mette and Mårten had been updated about most things that had happened during her trip.

The exception being Ramón.

When she'd finished Mårten looked at her.

'So are you going to change your surname?'

'Yes, but I haven't dealt with the formalities yet.'

'And where are you going to apply for a job then?'

It was Mette who asked and Olivia had been dreading that question. She knew it was coming, of course, she also knew that Mette wasn't Maria, who'd just said 'good'. Mette was a detective chief inspector at the National Crime Squad.

'Nowhere,' Olivia replied.

'What do you mean?'

'I don't know if I want to join the police. Not the way I feel now anyway.'

'But you've just completed your training!'

'Yes.'

'But why don't you want to join?'

Mårten saw how upset Mette was and Olivia felt the mood around the table change. But she'd made a decision and she was standing by it.

'I want to do other things.'

'Like what?'

'Study history of art.'

'Are you just going waste all that training?'

'Mette.' Mårten put his hand on Mette's arm. 'That's up to her,' he said.

'Sure.' Mette spoke directly to Mårten without looking at Olivia. 'But I thought she was passionate about this. That she wanted to do something. Make a difference. Accomplish something. Apparently I was wrong.'

'That's not very nice,' Olivia said. Mette was about to answer, but Olivia went on: 'You have no reason whatsoever to sit there and judge me. You have no idea what I want and what I can achieve. There are plenty of people who make a difference and who aren't in the police. I thought you were a bit more broadminded.'

Mårten looked at Mette. It was quite a while since anyone had dared to speak to her like that to her face. Particularly a young person. His respect for Olivia grew immensely, but he made sure not to let his wife know that. Mette watched Olivia for a few seconds, her hand moving up and down her wine glass while Olivia's words sank in.

'I'm sorry,' she said. 'You're right. It's just that I got so disappointed. I know how skilled you are, and what kind of person you are. We need people like you. It feels like a waste. You could have become an amazing murder investigator.'

'I haven't said that I'll never join the police. I might change my mind.'

'I'll keep my fingers crossed.'

Mette raised her glass to Olivia and both of them had a sip of wine. Mårten felt that a ceasefire had been reached.

A ceasefire of sorts.

Mette wasn't going to let this go.

'One of our neighbours hanged himself yesterday,' Olivia said, mostly to change the subject. 'Out in Rotebro.'

'Bengt Sahlmann,' Mette said.

'Yes. Did you know him?'

'Not personally, but I know who he was. He worked at Customs and Excise. We were in touch when they did a major drug crackdown a while ago. I just heard the news this morning. He was a good person.'

'Yes.'

'Did you know him?'

'Maria did. I used to babysit his daughter Sandra ages ago. She was the one who found him.'

'Awful.'

Mårten got up and started clearing the table. He wanted to give the ladies a chance to reach some neutral ground. And Olivia wanted that too. Mette meant a lot to her, both professionally and as a friend. She didn't want there to be tension between them, so she said something that she thought would catch Mette's attention.

'But I do think there's something weird about his suicide,' she said.

'What?'

'Many things.'

Olivia saw Mette topping up her glass and pulling her chair up a bit closer.

'Tell me.'

It caught her attention straight away.

'The first thing that struck me was that he knew that Sandra was on her way home. He knew that she was going to find him. Hanging from the ceiling. His only child. Isn't that a bit odd?'

'Yes.'

'He'd also promised Sandra to buy her favourite food for dinner, which he did. Everything was in the kitchen.'

'Did you go into the house?'

'Yes. After the suicide. We were taking care of Sandra, she slept at Maria's. She asked me to go and get her laptop, so I went.'

'And that's when you saw that he'd bought all the food?'

'Yes. And then he takes his own life?'

Mette took a sip of wine.

'Do you have more?' she asked.

'Yes, there was no suicide note, for one thing.'

'People don't always leave one. In Sahlmann's case, knowing that his daughter was on her way, there should have been. But you never know. Anything else?'

Mette was clearly paying attention now. Out of general curiosity, but also for reasons unbeknown to Olivia.

'The laptop,' said Olivia. 'Sandra said that they shared a computer, and that she had some school projects saved on there that she needed. It was supposedly in the office.'

'And it wasn't?'

'No. I looked, but it I couldn't find it anywhere.'

'What was Sandra's reaction?'

'She thought it was weird. Apparently he always kept it in the office.'

'Maybe he'd taken it to work?'

'Yes, maybe.'

'But you don't think so?'

'I have no idea.'

'Do you think it was stolen?'

'If it was stolen then maybe it wasn't suicide.'

'No. But we don't know that.'

'Not yet,' said Olivia.

'Now you sound like the murder investigator you don't want to be.'

58

But Mette smiled a little as she said it and Olivia smiled back and Mårten felt that the situation was sufficiently defused that he could tempt them with a cheese board.

Olivia gave both Mette and Mårten a warm hug in the hall as she left. There was enough of a bond between Mette and her to withstand a bit of confrontation.

As soon as Olivia had disappeared through the door, Mette got her mobile out. She had intentionally kept information from Olivia. Police information. Things that were no longer any of Olivia's business – she was going to study history of art. Otherwise Mette would have told her that a large stash of drugs had recently disappeared at Customs and Excise. Part of the major drug haul earlier that autumn. No one knew where the drugs had gone. There was an internal inquiry underway that until yesterday at least was being run by Bengt Sahlmann.

Who'd just hanged himself.

In circumstances that had roused Olivia's suspicions.

And now also Mette Olsäter's.

The conversation was brief. Mette requested that Bengt Sahlmann's autopsy be speeded up. When she rang off, Mårten was staring at her with that look on his face. A look that seemed innocuous to all but his partner of thirty-nine years.

She knew exactly what that look meant.

'Yes, I pushed her, I know, but I apologised.'

'Only because you had to.'

'Yeah, maybe. But I think that she's a fool. One of the most promising and talented future detectives I have ever met "doesn't feel like joining the police". It's just typical.'

'What do you mean "typical"?'

'Kids! They want to travel, think about stuff, jump from one thing to the next, everything is possible without any obligations, everything is just focused on themselves. It annoys me.'

'Now you're doing her an injustice. She's had exceptional issues to deal with and you know it. She, more than anyone, needs to find her own path. If she can.'

Mette nodded slightly. Mårten was absolutely right.

'In any case, I think it's definitely the wrong way to get her to come back to the force,' he said.

'What do you mean?'

'By provoking her. She's like Tom. She goes on the offensive. She hates to be questioned. You'll have to think of something more cunning if you want to get anywhere.'

'Cunning is your department.'

'Thanks.'

Mårten pulled Mette towards him and was just about to give her a slightly tipsy kiss, when the door burst open and one of their sons came in with a laughing Jolene in tow.

'I scored!'

Jolene was twenty and their straggler. She had Down's syndrome. A week ago she'd started playing basketball with the Skuru Specials and tonight she'd managed to get the ball in the basket.

It was a big moment for her.

Olivia sat on the bus back home. She felt the effects of the red wine. It was the second night in a row and she wasn't used to that. She felt slightly queasy as the bus lurched up the motorway to Slussen. That faint aroma of urine wasn't making things easier. She'd decided to sit right at the back, she always did if it was free, and it seemed that someone had taken a piss back there. She got up and moved forward a few rows. There were only three passengers other than her. She sank down into the window seat and tried to focus her gaze.

'You could have become an amazing murder investigator.'

Mette's words resonated in her head. They were big words from one of Sweden's most experienced murder detectives, hardly known for dishing out compliments willy-nilly. Am I making a mistake? Maybe I should go down the police route after all? I've wanted that the whole time. Suddenly she felt tired, sad and drunk.

Then her mobile rang.

'Hi, it's your BFF!'

Lenni's voice could be heard almost as far as the bus driver. Olivia was forced to hold the phone away from her ear.

'And I really want to see you while you're still nice and tanned!'

'Of course,' Olivia smiled. 'We're going to see each other tomorrow.'

'But I want to see you now! Where are you?'

'On my way home?'

'Good. Because I'm sitting on your doorstep.'

Lenni's sudden urge to see Olivia turned out to have its reasons. She'd locked herself out and was in no mood to go to her mum's in Sollentuna to get the spare key.

Olivia just about managed to step out of the lift on Skånegatan before her face disappeared in a blonde, freshly washed ball of frizz and she was enveloped by Lenni's giant hug.

'You're never allowed to leave me for this long again! Promise!'

'I promise,' Olivia giggled.

'But my God you stink of booze!'

'Wine, not booze.'

Olivia extracted herself from the hug and looked at Lenni.

'And you've cut your hair since we last skyped.'

'Yes, I decided that I should have a fringe.'

Lenni quickly tried to pat down her messy fringe with her fingers.

'It suits you! You look great,' said Olivia.

'And what about you! You're so bloody tanned! There's no way you're walking next to me for the next few weeks.'

Olivia laughed again and felt the sadness fade away. God, she'd missed Lenni! Their friendship was so straightforward and natural. And despite their differences, both outward and inward,

Lenni was one of the few people whom Olivia still trusted. She fished her keys out of her bag and opened the door. When she stepped into the hallway and switched the light on, she saw that half of Lenni's lipstick was now on her cheek. She smiled and rubbed it off with her hand. Lenni appeared behind her in the mirror.

'Well, that's as close as you get to putting make-up on,' she said. 'But I do my best. I'll make some tea to sober you up.'

And that's what Olivia did – sober up – while Lenni gave her an update about all their friends. Olivia was pretty clued up, at least about the things they'd chosen to put on Facebook, but of course Lenni was able to tell her a load of details and embarrassing stuff that they hadn't wanted to boast about online.

Then Olivia told her about the trip, down to the very last detail.

'And what about Ramón? What happened?'

'Stuff happened. But then I left.'

Lenni laughed.

'There's something different about you, you know that?'

Olivia looked at her.

'Well, I mean, I know that loads has happened,' Lenni said. 'But it's not just that. Before, you would never just have had random sex with some guy in a little Mexican shithole.'

'No, but then again I'd never been to Mexico before.'

Olivia smiled.

'And what are your thoughts about Ove?' Lenni wondered.

'What do you mean "my thoughts"? What's he got to do with anything?'

'What's he got to do with anything?' Lenni mimicked. 'You know exactly what I mean.'

But Olivia didn't. Ove Gardman was the boy who'd seen her mother being drowned and he'd actually saved her life. Literally. If he hadn't been there that night, twenty-five years ago, then she would not be here today. Now he was no longer a boy, but a man of thirty-five who'd spent his life traipsing around the globe saving coral reefs, dolphins and whales. He was a marine biologist. Their paths had crossed last year, when she returned to Nordkoster to see the beach where her mother had died and she was born. When she broke down, he was the one who took care of her. She'd stayed with him for a week. He'd listened, supported her and made sure that she got some food inside her. He'd been her rock. And since then they'd been almost like brother and sister, two only children who understood one another.

But nothing more.

As far as Olivia was concerned.

'Ove is in Guatemala or somewhere like that,' she said. 'We skyped the other day.'

'And he was missing you desperately? Am I right?'

Lenni dramatically laid one hand on her heart and pressed the back of the other against her forehead.

'Stop it, we're just friends, as you very well know.'

'Yes, but I don't know why. Such a waste! He's seriously hot, nice and...'

'And?'

'Perfect for you. It's only his name that's a bit dull – Ove Gardman – but you'll just have to live with that. He can always change his name, like you.'

Olivia laughed. Lenni always had opinions about everyone. And guys with the wrong haircut, wrong clothes and wrong name for that matter were a serious no-no in her world.

But then again, she could pick and choose as she pleased.

'I'm not in love with Ove and he's not in love with me. And that's that.'

Lenni fixed her carefully made-up blue eyes on Olivia.

'Have you asked him?'

'Of course I haven't.'

'Have you asked yourself?'

Olivia hadn't. She'd never even thought about Ove in that way. When he came into her life, there was no room for such feelings, there were simply too many others she had to deal with first. And now that she'd dealt with those feelings she… well, what feelings did she have for Ove?

Olivia lay awake for a while after Lenni had fallen asleep next to her in the bed, in the middle of a sentence. She listened to Lenni's deep breaths, and after a while these became gentle snores. Was Lenni right? Was there something more between them? She'd missed him, she knew that, and he'd always been happy to see her when they skyped. But… No, they were like brother and sister and that's how it would remain. A love affair would just destroy what they had, Olivia concluded before disappearing into her dreams, to the tune of Lenni's snoring.

* * *

Stilton had headed on down to the city. He called Abbas twice, but there was no reply. Was he hoovering the whole neighbourhood? Then he switched his mobile off to save some battery. He didn't have that many other people to call. The Olsäters were having dinner with Olivia. And that's where his friend list ended. He could have rung Benseman or Arvo Pärt, or one of the other homeless guys who'd sort of become friends during his years on the streets, but he felt that he'd moved on.

Instead he just roamed around the city.

He preferred the dark, narrow streets a few blocks away from the hustle and bustle. Fewer cars, fewer shops, less noise. He wanted to avoid people, he still felt that they were staring sometimes, as they had done not so long ago. He still avoided the gaze of unfamiliar people.

So he walked along with his head hanging low, looking at the pavement.

For a long time.

He felt that he had to make time pass. There was too much going on in his head for him to remain cooped up in that cell he'd just rented on Luna's barge, he had to walk off some of that restlessness. When he was in his cabin, he just wanted to detach. Tomorrow he'd be meeting Mette to talk about Rune Forss. He had to kill time until then.

So he walked through the city centre a few times before heading back to Söder. He saw former colleagues sail past him in police patrol vans and turned away slightly. Not that they'd recognise him, he'd never been on patrol duty, and the people inside the vans were too young to know who he was.

But they were police officers.

That was enough.

They reminded him of the wrong things.

Eventually he reached the barge, late at night, in a state in which he finally thought he'd be able to creep into bed and disappear. He climbed up the ladder. It was dark on deck. That Luna sure doesn't waste electricity, he thought, and went over to the steps down to the cabin.

'Hi.'

The voice came from the darkness over by the railings and it made him jump. He recognised the voice, but he couldn't see anyone.

'Hi,' he said. 'I was heading to bed.'

'You don't want to have a whiskey?'

Luna stepped out of the darkness and into a beam of light from the quayside lamp. Her dungarees had been replaced with a pair of worn jeans and a grey woolly jumper. She held a thick blanket around her shoulders.

'I'm quite shattered,' Stilton said.

'Have you been working?'

'No.'

Stilton hesitated a little. Luna was standing a couple of metres away. Her thick hair was hanging over her shoulder, tied in a ponytail.

'Are you going to get up early?'

'I get up when I wake up.'

Luna nodded a little and kept Stilton's gaze.

'But I'd like to have a whiskey,' he lied.

Luna turned around and headed down towards the lounge, in front of Stilton. She'd put on a few lamps, there was gentle country music coming from somewhere out in the darkness, coupled with a light whiff of tar in the air. Two small olive trees and two larger lemon trees were placed along the bulkheads. Luna gestured towards a long wall-mounted bench. There were a couple of framed pictures hanging above it, small abstract oil paintings in bold colours. Stilton sat down. It was the first time he'd been down here. He immediately liked it. All the dark worn wood, brass fittings here and there, the rounded oblong table in front of him, full of scratches. He thought about Rödlöga, about the old wherries out there, the old fisherman's cottages. He felt a strange longing for home. Luna walked towards the wooden cupboard on the wall and took out a bottle of Bulleit Bourbon and two small glasses.

'Surely it's all right to celebrate my first lodger,' she said.

'I think so.'

She poured the whiskey and held out a glass to Stilton.

'Cheers.'

Stilton raised his glass and sipped the dry whiskey.

'So this is the first time you've rented out a cabin?' he said.

'Yes. I need to boost my income.'

'What do you do?'

'I'm a caretaker at the Norra cemetery and the pay is pretty bad. How did you end up on the streets?'

The question came out of nowhere and Stilton didn't have a chance to duck. He looked down into his glass. He'd been asked that question enough times to be able to present a number of different responses, depending on who was asking. Right now he didn't feel like answering at all.

'It's hard to answer that,' he said.

'Why?'

'Because I don't know who you are and what response I should choose.'

Luna smiled without saying anything. Stilton felt uncomfortable.

'What's that music?' he said, trying to change the subject.

'"Lover's Eyes." Mumford & Sons. What music do you like?'

'None in particular.'

Luna looked at him and took a small sip from her glass.

'Luna,' said Stilton.

'Yes?'

'Quite an unusual name.'

'Mum christened me Abluna, some family name.'

'Sounds foreign.'

'Abluna is an old Swedish girl's name. But then Mum disappeared and Dad didn't like the name so he called me Luna instead. Moon in Italian. I like it.'

'It's beautiful.'

'Thanks.'

'When did your mum disappear?'

'When I was twelve. She was a "wind walker".'

'What's that?'

'It's an old Sami term, he who walks with the wind. Who goes his own way.'

'Was she Sami?'

'No.'

'Oh right.'

That's where Stilton's conversational stocks began to run dry, but he went for something within easy reach.

'How long have you had the barge?'

'I came across it two years ago, in Toulouse, I fell for the name.'

'*Sara la Kali.*'

'Yes. It's the name of a Roman saint. I took it up the canals.'

'On your own?'

'No, my dad's a sea captain. He came too.'

Stilton nodded and drank up the whiskey. He felt how the accumulated fatigue hit him with full force. Yet he still wanted to remain seated. On one level. And on another he had Rune Forss to deal with.

'I'm going to hit the sack now,' he said.

'Thanks for the company.'

'There'll be other times.'

Stilton looked away as he said it. Luna smiled again and followed him with her gaze. She slowly poured herself another splash. When she put the glass to her lips Stilton had disappeared.

'I come from a family of seal hunters.'

Luna gulped the whiskey and put the glass down. As she let go she saw her hand was trembling slightly. It was a sinewy hand, divided by furrows, some from hard work and others were secrets. She turned it over and looked at her nails, broad, evenly cut, unpainted. She wasn't one for nail polish. She was vain in a different way.

But the trembling?

She clenched her fist to calm it. The trembling was troubling her. She'd had it that morning too, and at the cemetery the day before. A light tremble in both hands that she couldn't explain. She was forty-one years old and had been fit as a fiddle her entire life, apart from the odd allergy. She looked at the corridor into which Stilton had disappeared. Shame that he wasn't been a doctor, she thought. Former coppers probably didn't have much to say about trembling hands. She leant back and put the lights out in the lounge. The lamps on the quay were casting a dull raking light through the portholes, and her silhouette was visible against the dark wood-panelled wall behind her. She lowered her body onto the wooden bench and stretched out a little. She'd had trouble falling asleep recently. Sometimes she went up to lie down in the lounge, just to get a change of environment, and every now and again she fell asleep there. She shut her eyes and felt that she was drifting off, the booze rocking her in the darkness. Just a second before she was about to surrender to sleep, she heard the scream.

It came from Stilton's cabin.

She sat up, her heart pounding. She was just about to lie back down when she heard another scream. Luna got up and went over towards the corridor. She stopped some distance away from Stilton's cabin. There was no light seeping under the door. She stood there in silence. Then there was another scream, lower now, shorter, followed by a long protracted whimper.

He's dreaming, she thought. Nightmares.

When Stilton asked whether he could lock the cabin door, she'd already felt that there was something mysterious about this man. As though the rent he was paying was just a necessary evil, a quick and easy way of getting an abode, a place to sleep and nothing more.

She went back into the lounge.

* * *

The little round beam of light slowly slid across a bare white bedroom wall. Carefully it brushed against the edge of a framed poster, paused, hesitated, and then slid back across the bare wall again.

Abbas sat on the floor with a small torch in his hand. He'd wrapped himself in a grey bedspread. His eyes were just about visible in the light, sore and red from all the rubbing and crying, and lack of sleep. He tried to look at the wall opposite, tried to reach the part that was shadowed in darkness, but he didn't dare. He closed his eyes to win some time. He knew he had to look at the poster.

Now.

He'd been sitting here for hours, waiting for the darkness to fall, trying to gather his strength. To no avail. His entire body was drained, the arm holding the torch was limp and weak, the signals from his brain hardly reached his hand.

'I have to look at it now.'

He heard himself utter those words. He repeated them again. Slowly he opened his eyes and began steering the shaft of light across the wall and towards the poster again, held back, the light trembling up and down, and then he allowed it to spill over the edge, carefully.

It was a large, beautiful poster, a circus poster from France, Cirque Gruss, from the mid-nineties, in red and blue. The light explored the energetically charged image, the jugglers, the trapeze, the elephants; it took a while before he dared to move all the way to the bottom, towards the texts with the performers' names.

There it remained.

Suddenly, the light went out and it became pitch dark. The only sound to be heard was a heavy inhalation.

The hoover had fallen silent.

Chapter 6

Just before reaching the top of the stairs, Agnes Ekholm had to stop and take a breather. She had trouble with stairs, especially going up, and she was now on her way to the fourth floor. She'd pulled a coat over her pink dressing gown and put her feet in a pair of soft fluffy slippers. When she reached the landing she hesitated a little.

Which door was it?

Her vision now required different glasses for different distances, and she had of course taken the wrong pair with her. She stuffed them back into her coat pocket and leant very close against the door. Yes, it had to be this one. With a slight tremble, she rang the doorbell. The noise on the other side was clear even to Agnes with her massacred hearing. After a couple of minutes she rang again. Maybe he wasn't at home? She rang once more, waited and pushed down on the door handle. The door was locked. Agnes sighed and turned to leave. All that mountaineering for nothing. Just as she shuffled towards the first step, the door behind her opened. She turned around. There was a man standing in the doorway, she could see that, wrapped in a bedspread. He had thick stubble, his hair was all over the place and his eyes were nestled into a couple of dark cavities. Agnes recoiled a little.

'Sorry. I was looking for Abbas.'

'Yes?'

Agnes stared at the man and was forced to realise that it was indeed Abbas standing in the doorway. In a state in which she'd never seen him. She'd never even seen him unshaven.

'I'm so sorry, I didn't see that it was you.'

'What did you want?'

'I just ran into the postman and he said that your box was full, there was no room for today's post, it looked like it hadn't been emptied for a while.'

'I've been unwell.'

'Well, I can see that, poor boy. What's...'

'I'll empty the box.'

'Good. Well, I do hope that you feel better soon. You don't want some carrot cake?'

'No, thanks.'

Agnes nodded slightly and made her way back down. Abbas quickly pulled the door closed.

A full letterbox?

He took a few steps into the hallway and looked at himself in the narrow mirror. He immediately understood Agnes's reaction. He looked terrible. How long had this been going on? He let go of the bedspread and saw a couple of large stains on his jumper. Did I throw up in the kitchen sink? He vaguely recollected that. He stepped into the living room and saw the hoover on the floor. Have I been hoovering? Why? He was rooted in the middle of the room. There was something in here that this was all about. What? Slowly his eyes wandered down onto the glass table. Towards the newspaper. His subscription. It was exactly where he'd left it, one side perfectly in line with the edge of the glass. He looked at it. Was it that?

It was.

What had to return slowly returned.

Little by little.

When everything was restored in his memory, he headed straight for the shower.

First hot, for a long time, to emerge from his descent, then gradually colder. When it was freezing cold he'd caught up with himself and made a decision.

The first thing he got out was the knives.

Five Black Circus knives.

Double edged.

* * *

Mette walked through the corridor very quickly, without nodding through the glass at any of her colleagues sitting in their offices. She was in a hurry. She turned the corner with a thick file under her arm and opened the door into the meeting room she'd chosen. Bosse Thyrén and Lisa Hedqvist, two of her favourite young investigators, were already in the room. For now she wanted to keep the group as tight as possible. She dumped the file on the table at the front and sat down in the chair behind it. She'd had the reply from forensics less than an hour ago: Bengt Sahlmann had been killed. There was no doubt about that.

'He was dead before he was hung up. The murder was probably preceded by a scuffle, he had fragments of skin under his nails.'

'DNA?'

'It's being dealt with.'

Mette had also got door knocking underway in Rotebro and sent technicians to his house.

'We've lost valuable time,' she said. 'Sahlmann was found hanged the night before last by his daughter Sandra and there was nothing at the scene to indicate that it was anything other than suicide. The preliminary report is impeccable. Which means that the murderer or murderers are more than thirty-six hours ahead of us. I've asked Lagerman to check Sahlmann's finances. Elin is mapping out his social circle. His wife died in the tsunami. He has a sister-in-law who lives at Johan Enbergs Väg 8 in Huvudsta. Her name is Charlotte Pram. His daughter Sandra is with her now. She has not been informed that this is a murder inquiry. You take care of that, Lisa, but be careful. Bosse and I will go to Customs and Excise.'

'So why are we dealing with this investigation?' Bosse wondered.

'I wanted it.'

'Why?'

'Because there are links to an international drug trade. A large stash of 5-IT drugs recently disappeared at Customs and Excise. It was part of that massive drug raid earlier in the autumn, you know the one?'

'Yes,' said Lisa. 'But what's Sahlmann's got to do with it?'

'He was in charge of the internal inquiry at Customs and Excise that was trying to find out where those drugs had disappeared to. He eventually uncovered some information that put him in danger.'

'Is that speculation?' Lisa asked.

'Yes. What's less speculative is that Sahlmann's laptop was stolen from his home the same night that he was murdered.'

'How do you know that?'

'From a source.'

For some reason, Mette didn't want to name her source, Olivia Rönning. Or Rivera. Both Bosse and Lisa knew Olivia since the Nordkoster case, she knew that. At that very moment she realised that they needed to speak to Olivia of course. She was at the murder scene just an hour or so after it had happened.

So Mette took a step back.

'Olivia Rönning was the source.'

'And how did she know about it?' Bosse asked.

'She'll have to tell you that herself. Why don't you speak to her before we head over to Customs and Excise?'

'OK.'

Bosse and Lisa got up. Mette got out her mobile. Lisa took a couple of steps towards her.

'So Olivia is back?'

'Yes.'

'And how is she?'

'She's going to change her surname. To Rivera.'

'Really?'

'And she's decided not stay in the force.'

'Why?'

'Let's work now, OK?'

Lisa got the message and headed towards the door. Mette picked up her mobile and prepared to call Olivia. When Bosse and Lisa had closed the door she pressed the call button. Olivia answered immediately.

'Hi, Mette! Thanks for last night!'

'Well, thank you for coming. Did you get home all right?'

'Yes, thanks. A little more tipsy than I'd thought, but it was fun that –'

'You were right.'

'About?'

'Bengt Sahlmann was murdered. I got the report a short while ago.'

Olivia remained silent. Mixed feelings. Positive because it confirmed her suspicions, negative because of Sandra. Or perhaps not. Maybe it would come as a relief to her that her father did not end his own life? But murdered? Just like her own biological father? Was that so much easier to deal with?

'Have you told Sandra?' she asked.

'Lisa's on her way there now. Bosse is going to contact you. Speak to you later.'

Mette ended the call.

* * *

A grey morning, blackish grey clouds that rode across the sky at a leisurely pace, but no rain yet. It was only a matter of time. Stilton stood by the railings and brushed his teeth: he liked doing that outside, a habit he'd picked up on Rödlöga, a feeling of freedom. He had some water in a plastic cup. Luna was standing some distance away, observing him while she brushed her hair. Stilton worked hard with his toothbrush, for a long time. While he was homeless he hadn't even owned a toothbrush, he'd picked his teeth with his index finger and rinsed his mouth when there was water around. Or coffee. On Rödlöga he'd changed all that. Hygiene had crept up on him. Every morning he'd forced his skinny body into the biting cold seawater, as long as it wasn't frozen, to scrub himself clean with a brush that he'd found behind the enamel tray in the kitchen alcove. As though outward cleanliness would clean up some of his inner mess too.

His teeth were a part of that. Luna saw how feverishly he brushed back and forth, almost compulsively.

'You're very meticulous about your teeth,' she said.

'They're the only ones I have.'

'You had nightmares last night.'

'Really?'

'You were screaming pretty loudly.'

Stilton rinsed his mouth with water from the plastic cup, gurgled for a while and spat over the railings. When he turned around, Luna had disappeared. Good. He didn't have time for small talk: he was stressed, he'd slept far too long, and apparently he'd had nightmares. What did that have to do with her? He wanted to get going. In just over an hour he'd be meeting Mette to talk about Rune Forss. It was time to get things moving.

Then he saw Abbas.

On the path in front of the shipyard.

On his way to the barge.

After one of the missed calls to Abbas the day before, Stilton had left a message mentioning the *Sara la Kali* at the Mälarvarvet shipyard where he'd rented a cabin. Apparently Abbas had listened to his messages. He climbed up the ladder and the first thing that Stilton noticed was that he was unshaven. Stilton had roughly the same experience of Abbas's shaving habits as Agnes Ekholm and couldn't remember ever having seen him unshaven.

'Hello,' said Stilton. 'I came to see you yesterday, but you didn't open. Were you hoovering?'

'No. I have to go away for a while and I want you to come along.'

'Where to?'

'Marseille.'

'Marseille? When?'

'Tonight.'

Stilton looked at Abbas. It wasn't just his facial hair that was odd. Everything was. It's the first time he's been here and he's not asking anything. About the barge. Why I'm living here. Why I'm in the city? Just straight to the point.

Not good.

'What are we going to do in Marseille?'

'Let's talk about that later. Are you coming?'

'You know I am.'

It really didn't fit with Stilton's plans right now. But he owed Abbas.

A great deal.

Moreover, he knew that Abbas would not have been asking him if it hadn't been extremely important.

'Does Mette know about this?' he asked.

'No. Why?'

'She's been trying to get hold of you. Maybe you should get in touch? Are we flying?'

'No, we're going by train.'

'Why?'

'It travels on land.'

Abbas had a fear of flying. Moreover, it was easier for him to keep an eye on the knives on the train – that would have been more difficult on a plane. That was probably the decisive factor.

'When are we going?'

'At around four. Come by my place before.'

'OK.'

Abbas turned around and went back down the ladder. Stilton was watching him. When Abbas was at a safe distance, he slammed his fist into the railings. He'd been building up for some time to come to the city to deal with the things he had to deal with, and now he had to go to Marseille. Without a clue as to why.

All he knew was that it wasn't a holiday.

'Who was that?'

Luna came walking across the deck, dressed in a dark-green lumber jacket and a pair of light washed-out jeans. Her thick hair hung over her shoulders and framed her sharp nose and broad, even eyebrows, much darker than the colour of her hair. It caught Stilton's eye. She reminded him of the women on the melodramatic covers of his beloved crime novels, a bit Rita Hayworth, Katharine Hepburn. He hadn't thought of that until now, now he was on his way to Marseille.

'A friend,' he replied. 'Abbas el Fassi.'

'An Arab?'

'Frenchman, grew up in Marseille. We're going there tonight.'

'To Marseille?!'

'Yes.'

'How long will you be gone?'

'No idea.'

'Is it a holiday?'

'No.'

'What are you going to do?'

'Don't know, I suppose it's something important. I have to pack.'

Stilton walked past Luna and disappeared below deck.

Pack? thought Luna. What are you going to pack? Your little blue bag. Suddenly she became pensive. She had no idea who Stilton was. She hadn't done any checks on him. She'd just accepted what he'd said. She'd felt she could trust him, largely because of her intuition. She'd been around, and learned to read people: she was seldom wrong.

Perhaps she was this time.

Maybe he was a drug dealer? What do I know about that? Suddenly going to Marseille at the drop of a hat? What was that all about? 'I suppose it's something important.' Luna was considering going down to Stilton's cabin to demand some answers. On the other hand she'd been given a month's rent in advance. If there was any crap it wouldn't affect her.

But she was extremely eager to find out what it was all about.

Abbas just got through the door when his mobile rang. He saw that it was Mette and thought about what Tom had said.

So he answered.

'Finally! Hello, Abbas! Has something happened?'

'No. Why?'

'I've called you so many times and you normally always…'

'My mobile died the other day.'

'What do you mean died?'

'How are you?'

'Good. And you?'

'I'm going to Marseille tonight.'

'Tonight. Why? Has something happened?'

'Yes.'

'What?'

'Nothing I want to talk about, it's about the past.'

Mette accepted his answer.

'Anything you need help with?' she said.

'Yes. Tom is coming.'

'Tom?'

'Yes.'

'OK. How are you getting there?'

'By train.'

'Well, let me know when you arrive.'

'I will. Say hi to Mårten and Jolene.'

Abbas ended the call. The conversation was short, but there was sweat running down his forehead. He hated keeping things from Mette. And Mårten. People who meant more to him than his own parents. Who had ultimate faith in him.

It was tough.

But he was in no state to say more than he had.

He picked up the newspaper on the glass table.

It was about the past.

Stilton packed his blue bag. It was the only one he had. As he didn't know how long he'd be gone there was no point planning. Some toiletries, a couple of tops, a mobile charger. Light luggage. He was making his way down the gangway when

79

Mette called. She was quick to get to the point, even by Mette's standards.

'What are you going to do in Marseille?'

'Have you talked to Abbas?'

'Yes.'

'What did he say?'

'That it was about the past.'

'Well, then you know more than me.'

'You're lying!'

Stilton turned around and saw Luna standing by the railings. She waved. He waved back. It crossed his mind that it might be the last time they saw each other. Like in a film, the man leaving from the quayside and the women standing by the railings, waving. Then he dies in a foreign country.

'Hello?! Are you still there?'

'Yes. No, I'm not lying. Abbas has asked me to accompany him to Marseille. He hasn't said why.'

'And you haven't asked?'

'No.'

'God, you're so childish!'

This is where I should say 'We're men,' Stilton thought, but he realised that might well be a little too childish.

'Something has happened, I don't know what, and he wants me to go with him and so I will. You know what he's done for me.'

Mette knew very well what Abbas had done for Stilton. It was Abbas who'd been there during his years on the streets when Stilton was close to death. It was Abbas who took him to various shelters and made sure he came out again, even though Stilton tried to keep him at a distance.

So she didn't have much to counter with.

'So it's your turn to take care of him now?' she asked.

Abbas isn't someone you 'take care of', Stilton thought.

'I don't know. Are you worried?'

'Are you?'

'Yes,' said Stilton.

'Thanks. That was reassuring.'

'Mette. It's a complete waste of time to fear the worst. Just deal with crises when they arise. Who was always telling me that?'

'OK. Promise me that you'll call as soon as you get there!'

Stilton ended the call. When he turned around, he saw that the barge was enveloped by thick November fog.

Luna was gone.

* * *

Olivia was sitting with Bosse Thyrén up at the National Crime Squad headquarters. She liked him. He had a groomed beard and bright eyes, and he didn't offer her any disgusting coffee or talk shit. He was concise. So she told him about her visit to the Sahlmanns' house on the night that he hanged himself. About the missing laptop. About the shadow that she'd seen at their gate, but that she hadn't thought it had any significance. But perhaps now it did?

'You're not sure whether it was a person?'

'No. But if it was it's hardly going to have been the murderer? By that time he or she ought to have been long gone.'

'Yes. But you never know.'

'No.'

She also told him about the man Sandra had walked past in the underpass, a man who didn't live in the neighbourhood.

'But you'd better ask Sandra about that. Have you told her?'

'Lisa's on her way there. Are we going to find your finger-prints in the house?'

'No. I was wearing mittens.'

'Mittens?'

'Then again, I did sit on the sofa for a while, so there might be a hair or something there. Does that make any difference? You know I was in the house after all?'

'Yes, that's true. But you know what the technicians are like.'

'Yes. Are we done?'

'Yes.'

Olivia got up.

'I like Rivera,' Bosse said. 'It suits you.'

'Thanks.'

Olivia left the building with mixed feelings. There was something about the atmosphere in there that enticed her, all those people dedicating their lives to protecting and helping others. Why didn't she want to do that? Of course she did, in one way, but not right now. It was too soon.

So she walked to Customs and Excise on Alströmergatan.

Bengt Sahlmann's workplace.

After a bit of back and forth in the main entrance, she was shown to the department where he worked. Or had worked, rather. As she went in, she was greeted by someone she presumed was a receptionist.

'My name is Olivia Rivera and Bengt Sahlmann's daughter has asked me to see whether their laptop is here. In his office. She needs it for her school projects.'

'You'll have to talk to Gabriella Forsman.'

Olivia was shown into a corridor and to Gabriella Forsman's office. Olivia paused in the doorway. The woman sitting in the chair was not really someone she'd expected to see at Customs and Excise. Some people, men in particular, would have seen a very voluptuous woman with gorgeous reddish hair and a strikingly beautiful face. Olivia saw hair that was too red, breasts that were too large, exaggerated red lips and a skin-tight dress in a bizarre shade of orange.

Like a copy of the secretary in *Mad Men*, she thought.

'Can I help you?' she said in a low, husky voice.

Olivia repeated the reason for her visit, which resulted in an emotional outburst of considerable magnitude from Gabriella Forsman. Her face had already started twitching as soon as

Olivia mentioned Sahlmann's name. When she mentioned his daughter, Gabriella urgently reached for some more tissues.

This woman is really going for it, Olivia thought.

'We're all very shocked,' Gabriella said, trying to regain composure. 'It's just so awful, you can't really believe it's happened! Suddenly he's just gone! You sit here and have a coffee together talking about this and that and then suddenly he's no longer there. It's awful, isn't it?'

'Yes. Did you work together for long?'

'For four years. He was the nicest man in the world and he'd already suffered that catastrophe with his wife dying in the tsunami and then this happens.'

Olivia observed as Gabriella drench a few more tissues.

'His laptop,' she said eventually.

'Yes, of course. Please excuse me, everything is just so up and down. You were wondering whether he had a laptop here?'

'Yes.'

'Not that I know of, but we can go and have a look.'

Gabriella stood up. She was tall, and her slim body elegantly balanced on a pair of red-leather high heels. Olivia wouldn't even have been able to squeeze her little toe into them. They went to the adjacent office together, which was somewhat larger.

'This is Bengt's office.'

Olivia looked at the orderly desk. There was a desktop computer on it. But no laptop and no bag made of cork. She had a look over on the shelves by the wall and the small table by the armchair.

'Did he ever bring his own private laptop to the office? As far as you are aware?'

'No. He had a computer here, it was that one he used for work.'

Olivia nodded. The laptop wasn't here. At least she could tell Sandra that, and that she'd tried. Whatever help that might be. She looked at Sahlmann's desk one more time. Next to the computer there was a file with 'Internal Inquiry' written on it.

'What was Bengt working on at the moment?' she asked.

'Well, the usual.'

'Was he working on an internal inquiry?'

Olivia nodded at the file next to the computer and Forsman followed her gaze.

'Oh that. Well, a large stash of drugs has disappeared here and he was working on that.'

'What do you mean "disappeared"?'

'I'd better not talk about that, if you don't mind.'

Forsman looked rather troubled. Olivia nodded and left the room ahead of her. Suddenly Gabriella grabbed her arm, carefully, and lowered her voice.

'Do you know something about why he killed himself? We're all so shocked here and everyone's sitting around making speculations and no one knows anything. Do you?'

'No.'

'I mean, I know that he felt down about his father's death, he was quite depressed for a while, but it can't be that, can it? You don't commit suicide because your elderly father dies? When you have a seventeen-year-old daughter to look after. Right?'

Suddenly Gabriella was fighting back the tears again, her eyes and nose streaming, and Olivia felt that she'd had enough.

'Bengt Sahlmann didn't commit suicide,' she said. 'He was murdered.'

* * *

His wheeled suitcase stood ready packed in the hallway. He held his passport in his hand and the tickets were in the inside pocket of his jacket. He was basically ready to go when Stilton rang the doorbell.

'Come in.'

Stilton went in and put his blue bag on the floor. Abbas looked at it.

'I'm assuming it's going to be quite a short trip,' Stilton said.

'Yes. Maybe.'

Stilton followed Abbas into the flat. He'd been here a few times. Each time he'd been struck by the simple harmony in the rooms. Each ornament chosen with care, in terms of functionality, colour and design. The Tibetan tapestry on the wall, the wooden chairs, the simple rug. And each time he'd wondered where Abbas, the boy who grew up in a social cul-de-sac in Marseille's poorest neighbourhood, had got his incredible feel for aesthetics. His own home, the one he'd shared with his wife Marianne, had looked like the definition of normality.

This was something else entirely.

'I'm just going to take out the rubbish.'

Abbas walked past him with a couple of grey rubbish bags towards the front door. Stilton nodded. He went into the kitchen and poured himself a glass of cold water. He drank it quite slowly. 'Yes. Maybe' meant that this quite short trip could become something rather different. In the worst-case scenario. Stilton didn't have time for that. He put the empty glass down and turned around. The kitchen was just next door to the bedroom. He went a bit closer. He'd never been in there before, the door had always been closed. Now it was open. He stood in the doorway and a large framed circus poster on a cold white wall caught his eye. It was the only decoration in the room, right opposite the low bed. A very beautiful and decorative circus poster. When he heard Abbas's footsteps he turned around.

'Nice poster.'

'Yes. Shall we go?'

Mette and Bosse were on their way into Customs and Excise. Mette had prepared a strategy to try to elicit as much information as possible about the missing stash of drugs before disclosing that Sahlmann had been murdered. They went up to his former department and headed straight for the receptionist. Mette showed her police ID.

'We're looking for staff in Bengt Sahlmann's department.'

'They're in a crisis meeting unfortunately.'

'Where?'

'Over there, but…'

Mette went straight over to the door she was pointing at. Bosse followed her. Mette opened the door and stepped inside. There were nine people sitting in the room, including Gabriella Forsman. They were all trying to maintain composure. An older man turned to face Mette.

'I'm sorry, but what is this about? We're in the middle of a meeting here.'

'A meeting about what?'

'May I ask who you are?'

'We're from the National Crime Squad. Mette Olsäter.'

Mette showed her police ID again.

'What kind of a crisis meeting is this?' she asked.

'One of our colleagues has been murdered.'

Mette needed a few seconds to digest this information before she said: 'Who has been murdered?'

'Bengt Sahlmann. You didn't know?'

'How do you know about it?'

'I told them,' Gabriella Forsman said and stood up, as if she knew she needed to make herself heard.

'And how did you find out about it?'

Mette stared straight at Gabriella, silently insinuating things. Though hard to interpret, they certainly didn't seem pleasant.

'A family friend was here a while ago asking for Bengt's laptop. She told me.'

'Male or female?'

'Female.'

'What was her name?'

'It… her name… I can't really remember, it sounded a bit Italian.'

'Olivia Rivera?'

'That's it!'

Mette turned on her heels, forcing Bosse to jump out of her way.

'Take over,' she hissed.

Bosse nodded just as Mette slammed the door behind her.

Olivia was down in the laundry room, stuffing in the last bits of dirty washing when Mette called.

'Are you at home?'

'I'm down in the laundry room.'

'I was planning to drop by.'

'What's up?'

'It's about Bengt Sahlmann.'

'OK, I'll be upstairs in five minutes.'

Olivia put the washing on and went back up to the flat. Bengt Sahlmann? Intriguing. Mette had probably already had some news she wanted to share with her. About the perpetrator? Not likely, not that soon. Olivia felt the curiosity bubbling up inside her. It reached boiling point when the doorbell rang. Olivia opened the door and there was Mette.

'Hi,' Olivia just about managed to utter.

'What the hell are you playing at?' Mette snapped.

'What?'

'Who do you think you bloody are?'

Olivia was visibly shocked as she stepped into the hallway. Mette followed her in without even closing the door. Her built-up anger burst out right into Olivia's face.

'How can you be such a fool?!'

'What are you talking…'

'I'm talking about that fact that half of Customs and Excise knew that Sahlmann was murdered before we'd even got there! All thanks to you!'

'But I just said…'

'You've messed up our entire strategy there! Don't you get it? If there are people involved in the murder, you've given them an amazing chance to cover their tracks. So thanks for that!'

'But I didn't think that…'

'No! Precisely! You didn't think at all! How many more people have you blabbed to?'

'I didn't blab, I just…'

'What were you doing there anyway?!'

'Checking whether Sahlmann's computer was there.'

'What were you going to do with it?'

'Give it to Sandra.'

'Take the victim's computer and give it to a relative? In the middle of a murder investigation? Didn't you learn a bloody thing during your training?'

'OK, that's enough now!'

Suddenly it all got too much for Olivia. The first attack had taken her aback, but now she felt that there were things welling up inside her that had been festering since the day before. Since Mette had belittled her for not wanting to carry on with her police career.

'Have you forgotten who told you it could be murder?' she said, pulling the door closed to prevent half her neighbours finding out the same information about Sahlmann from Mette as Olivia had shared with 'half of Customs and Excise'. When she turned around, Mette was gone. She'd gone into the kitchen to get some water to soothe her throat after her outburst.

She drank straight from the tap.

'Mette.'

Mette carried on drinking.

'Mette!'

Mette turned off the tap and turned around. The women glared at each other. One of them was very tall and had just about regained her composure; the other was just about to lose hers.

She started.

'It was wrong of me to talk about it,' Olivia said. 'It was reckless, I'm sorry. Now I think you should apologise.'

'For what?'

'For attacking me as though I was a piece of shit.'

Mette smiled, far from sincerely.

'Dear girl,' she said. 'You know how much I care about you. I know who you are. But if you ever trample on one of my murder investigations again and mess up like you did today, my patience will run out.'

'So you're giving me another chance?'

'Are you being sarcastic?'

'I'm pissed off. OK, I made a mistake, but this whole outburst is actually only about me not wanting to join the police, which actually has bugger all to do with you. I'll do as I please.'

'You made that pretty clear today. From now on I think you should focus on your history of art and not meddle in my work.'

'I think you should go now.'

'Thanks for the water.'

Mette walked past Olivia and out into the hall. When she slammed the door closed, Olivia sank down into a chair. Her anger subsided quickly. She knew that what she'd done was wrong, pure thoughtlessness. She knew that Mette was right in principle. She'd behaved very unprofessionally, and now she had seriously fallen out with one of the few people whom she respected.

Then Sandra called.

She was angry and upset, having been told that her father was murdered and then been asked loads of questions about that awful night. Olivia had to snap out of her mood.

'Was it Lisa Hedqvist who spoke to you?' she asked.

'Yes. She was nice, but those questions were really tough.'

'What did she want to know?'

'All kinds of things. If I'd seen anyone on my way home and stuff...'

'Did you?'

'No. Well, there was that guy in the underpass, and that car.'

'What car?'

'A car drove past when I was on my way towards the woods, and then she asked me what make and colour it was and stuff like that.'

'Do you remember?'

'It was a BMW, a blue one.'

'Are you sure?'

'Yes, Dad rented one like it not so long ago when we went on holiday.'

'Oh right. Where are you now?'

'At Charlotte's.'

'Is she there?'

'Yes.'

'Good.'

There were a few seconds of silence. When Sandra's voice returned, it was desperate, almost breaking.

'Who wanted to kill my dad?'

Olivia wanted to know that too, but she didn't have any answers.

'I don't know, Sandra, but I'm certain that we'll find out.'

'Do you really think so?'

'Yes.'

Just words of comfort. But what was she supposed to say?

'Thank you for calling,' she said. 'I was thinking of ringing you myself. I was at your dad's work today, but there was no sign of the computer there.'

'Oh no, really? Where is it, then?'

'I don't know, maybe it's been stolen.'

'Who by?'

Olivia declined answering that question and in the silence, Sandra formulated the answer herself, and said: 'Imagine if was still been there when I got home.'

Her voice was small and fearful.

With reason.

Olivia hadn't thought of that.

The murderer could well have still been in the house when Sandra came home.

* * *

Mårten felt that something wasn't right. He'd noticed it as soon as Mette walked into the kitchen and sat down. She could hardly look at him or Jolene. She'd just stared at the floor and then got up and left the room. He followed her. She was standing in the African room, the room that was decorated and adorned with sculptures and fabrics and all kinds of weird and wonderful ornaments from their trips to Africa. The room that was generally used whenever someone wanted to disappear into themselves. It was kind of sacred, but Mårten chose to ignore that now. He went towards Mette who was fiddling with a large wooden tube. The tube was filled with bone fragments, so it was said, which created a monotonous rattling noise as they trickled from one side to the other, like tropical rain.

'What's the matter?'

Mette didn't reply. She turned the tube upside down and the contents tipped to the other end.

'Jolene wants to watch *Downton* – we bought the box set,' Mårten said.

Mette loved *Downton Abbey*. If there was anything that could get her out of this state, it was that.

Mette carefully placed the tube against the wall and looked at her husband.

'I love you,' she said.

That was worrying. When said just like that, it was a sign of serious emotional turmoil. What had happened? Mårten took Mette by the hand and walked her out of the African room.

'Two things,' she said. 'We'll talk later.'

So Mårten, Mette and Jolene sank down into the big flowery sofa in front of the flatscreen television and into the programme. Roughly halfway through, Mette turned to Mårten and said: 'I had a go at Olivia today.'

'Why?'

'Shhh!' Jolene hissed. She hated people talking while watching TV. It upset her concentration. So everyone watched the rest of the episode in total silence. Mesmerised. When it was over,

Mårten turned the television off and Mette kissed Jolene on the cheek.

'Go up and brush your teeth and get ready for bed.'

'Are you going to "have a conversation"?'

'No, we're not going to "have a conversation". I'll be there in a minute.'

Jolene gave Mårten a hug and ran up the stairs to her room. Once she'd gone, he turned to Mette.

'So, firstly: Olivia?'

'Yes, the first thing is about Olivia. She did something stupid that messed things up when we tried to question people at Customs and Excise today. So I went to see her and told her that it's not OK to do that.'

'Told her off?'

'Yes.'

'With reason?'

'Yes.'

'But you went a little overboard, because you're still annoyed by her decision.'

'Are you going to start on that too? I told her off because she cocked things up.'

'So why do you feel bad?'

'I don't.'

'Yes, you do, I know it. That's why you love me. Call her.'

'Why would I do that?'

'To put it to bed.'

'Never in a million years.'

Mårten knew there was no point pushing this. He'd said what he thought and he knew it would sink in. Mette always needed some time before she backed down.

'And secondly,' he said.

'Abbas.'

'What about him?'

'He's on his way to Marseille, with Tom.'

'Really?'

Mårten did his best to answer in a normal voice.

'What are they going to do there?'

'No idea.'

'Maybe he wants to show Tom where he grew up?'

Mette looked at Mårten as though he was nuts.

'Did you ask them what they were going to do?' he asked.

'Yes. He just said that it was something about the past.'

'Really?'

That wasn't a normal response and Mette noticed. It was a clear, surprised 'Really?' Mårten stood up. Mette looked at him.

'What do you think?' she said.

'What about? Their trip?'

'Yes.'

'We'll find out in time, I suppose.'

'Yes.'

They both looked at each other. Mårten stroked Mette's arm.

'I'll do the dishes. You go upstairs.'

Mette nodded and headed towards the stairs. Mårten opened the dishwasher and began loading it with some dirty plates. For show. As soon as he heard it was quiet upstairs, he went down into the cellar.

Down to his private cave.

The room he'd furnished just as he wanted it.

It was his spiritual retreat.

The conversation about Abbas had upset him, more than he'd let on. His calm reaction was just for Mette's sake – in actual fact he was seriously worried. He went straight over to the CD player and put a Gram Parsons album on. He wanted Kerouac to keep him company, his special little pet. When the black spider heard the music, it crawled out from its crack in the wall and crept over to its favourite spot in the corner. Mårten sank down into the shabby leather armchair.

Abbas.

He recalled so well the first time they met. Stilton walked over from the gate with a skinny youth who looked away when they greeted each other. And when they talked. And he carried on looking away for a long time after that.

That look became a benchmark for Mårten.

Many years working as a child psychologist had taught him a great deal about people's expressions. Broken children had the same expression on their faces all over the world. The day that Abbas first managed to look him in the eye properly, really held his gaze, he knew that they would succeed.

Almost two years had passed by then.

And much of it was thanks to Jolene. The ten-year-old girl had broken through the iron-clad emotional tank that Abbas had built up since childhood, with her uninhibited hugs and spontaneous kisses. He let her in, eventually, and ever since then he would have been willing to give his life for Jolene.

Mårten knew that.

And now he was worried.

For many reasons.

One was the fact that Abbas was even going to Marseille, a city that was so loaded with traumatic memories – a place where he'd been both physically and emotionally abused for so many years, by his mother and his father and all the people who regarded Moroccan outsiders as fair game. In the end he'd just left. Or fled. With a fake passport and a couple of scary knives in his luggage.

And now he was on his way back there again.

With Tom, a person he'd never have chosen for company, they just didn't spend time together like that. Mårten knew that. They were men who stood up for one another, when necessary. Otherwise they didn't spend a great deal of time together. Now they'd gone to Marseille together.

And that was part of his concern.

He knew what each one was capable of.

When necessary.

But the main thing that Mårten was worried about was what Abbas had replied when Mette asked him about the purpose of the trip.

The past.

Mårten didn't know that many details about Abbas's past, not more than Abbas had chosen to share with him. A chaotic mix of sorrow and hatred, entirely devoid of warmth and love. So he assumed that the trip must be about one or the other: sorrow or hatred.

At worst, both.

* * *

Olivia had calmed down. There wasn't much she could do about her confrontation with Mette. Secretly she hoped that Mette would call and apologise, or at least try to smooth things over. That would be OK, but it was a long shot.

Mette wasn't that kind of person.

So she'd been to Koh Phangan to get some Thai takeaway.

She was now sitting in bed eating Moo Pad King, stir-fried pork with chilli, garlic and ginger. Good food always cheered her up. When she reached for the Coke on the bedside table, her gaze fell on the picture of Elvis, her beloved cat, killed on the orders of escort service owner Jackie Berglund. A real bitch. Olivia enjoyed thinking of bizarre scenarios for this woman to face comeuppance.

Then suddenly her computer made a noise. She wiped her fingers and looked at the screen. It was Ove wanting to skype. The reception was pretty dismal, but eventually she saw his face beaming back at her from the screen, all the way from Guatemala.

'How does it feel being home?' he said.

'Cold, dark and completely wonderful!'

'Seriously?'

'The cold and dark bit is true, it's hideous here at the moment. How about you? How is it there?'

'Warm and light, but it will come to an end soon.'

'Are you coming home?'

'Yes. I've got a job working on the restoration of the Säcken Reef. Cool, huh?'

The Säcken Reef was something that had totally passed by Olivia. She had no idea where it was or why it needed to be restored, but she did her best to hide her ignorance.

'Absolutely! What does it involve?'

'That I can live on Nordkoster and be near my dad.'

Olivia knew that was important to Ove. His father lived in an old people's home in Strömstad and his health had been rather precarious the last year. Ove had found it difficult not being able to be there.

'Good!'

'Good? It's fantastic. And furthermore I'll be able to work on saving my local environment.'

So the Säcken Reef is obviously near Nordkoster, I'll have to google it, Olivia thought. There was no need – Ove enthusiastically described the work involved in saving the last coral reef in Sweden, conveniently located in the Koster Fjord. Olivia watched him on the screen as he explained how deep-water white coral from nearby Norwegian reefs had been successfully planted there. His enthusiasm fascinated her. He was really passionate about what he did.

She envied him.

'It sounds fantastic! Congratulations!'

'Thanks!'

'When are you coming back?'

'I'll be coming to Stockholm in a few days. I'm going to a conference before I leave. I'm not entirely sure when, it's not booked yet, but I'll be in touch. But tell me about you now! What are you up to?'

Well, what do I do? Olivia wondered. Pretending I'm in the police, even though I don't want to be.

'I'm just taking it easy at the moment,' she said. 'I've only just got home. It looks like I'll be able to do some shifts at a video store where Lenni works, to make some money. I'm thinking of studying history of art in the spring. But I told you that last time, right?'

'Yes. Are you sure that's what you want to do?'

'No, but it's what I'm most sure of right now. And I've sort of been dragged into a murder investigation.'

Ove laughed.

'Sort of been dragged into? How does that happen?'

So Olivia explained what 'sort of dragged into' meant. Her version, not Mette's. She kept her blunder and Mette's outburst to herself. It was all a bit too sensitive, even to tell Ove. For now anyway.

'So you're barely home five minutes before you manage to sniff out a murder?'

Olivia was a bit offended by his choice of words.

'I didn't exactly "sniff it out".'

'OK then, but a normal person would just drop it and you won't do that, if I know you correctly. But where…'

The last few words were interrupted by a crackling sound. Small rectangles were rearranging his face.

'Hello?'

The crackling continued and she finally deciphered what he was saying: 'I'll be in touch.' Totally out of sync. Then he was gone. She stared at the screen a while longer, as though she hoped he might reappear. I miss him, she thought, I really do. Not like Lenni thinks, but it's great that he's coming home.

Olivia closed the laptop, resting her hands on it.

The laptop?

Who had stolen Bengt Sahlmann's laptop? The murderer, who else? Why? What was on that laptop that the murderer wanted to keep hidden? Or *murderers*? Or was it something they needed? It wasn't her job to find out, Detective Chief Inspector Mette Olsäter had made that quite clear. And that's precisely why it was enticing. And she had a little trump card, which she hadn't remembered until now and that's why she hadn't told Bosse Thyrén when he talked to her.

The man who called Sahlmann's house on the night of the murder.

Alex Popovic.

The journalist.

She quickly started up her computer again and searched for his name. No problem – a journalist at *Dagens Nyheter*. His phone number and address were there.

She called him, even though it was almost midnight.

'Hello.'

'It's Olivia Rivera here. I was the one who answered at Bengt Sahlmann's the other night. Could we meet up some time tomorrow?'

'Why?'

'Aren't you a journalist?'

'Yeah.'

'Well, you should be wanting to know why Sahlmann was murdered.'

'You said that he committed suicide.'

'I was wrong. Are you free?'

'Yes.'

They arranged a time and a place and ended the call. Olivia had 'blabbed' again about the suicide that was a murder, but she was feeling fine. She'd just seen a news report about the murder about an hour ago. Hadn't Alex Popovic heard? Not much of a journalist, she thought. And what was she going to talk to him about?

Time would tell.

* * *

They changed trains in Copenhagen, onto the City Night Line. Abbas's quick decision to go had meant he'd had to buy a first class ticket in the sleeper carriage – there weren't any second class tickets left. It didn't bother him. He had money enough, and in any case, money was irrelevant at the moment. They sat opposite each other, in their own bunks, with a little window table between them. A rounded lamp was casting a warm yellow light over the table and the carriage smelled of detergent.

The train was to take them to Paris with one change in Cologne.

They would have to change yet again to get to Marseille.

During the journey from Stockholm, Abbas had sunk down into his seat and fallen asleep before they'd reached Södertälje. He seems exhausted, Stilton thought, and picked up a book he'd brought. *Darkness at Noon* by Arthur Koestler. He'd found it among some other books in the lounge on the barge. Stilton liked the title. He thought it might be a crime story. By the time they'd reached Katrineholm, he'd realised his error and fell asleep too. The book was about the author's disillusionment with communism.

'How many did you bring?'

Stilton nodded at the two thin black knives lying on the table. Abbas was busy rubbing one of them with a blackish grey paste from a small metal tin.

'Five,' he said.

'The same kind?'

'Yes.'

Stilton noted that Abbas's slim fingers treated the knives as though they were precious goods found in a treasure chest in the Caribbean. Perhaps they were, Stilton had no idea. He'd seen Abbas use them, several times, and he had great respect for the way he handled them.

'You're really good with knives,' he'd once said.

'Yes.'

The conversation had ended round about then. Abbas had never been particularly talkative and when it came to the knives he was basically mute. So Stilton didn't know much. He assumed that the knives were a necessary accessory out in Castellane, the slum district where Abbas had grown up.

Abbas started polishing the other knife.

'You liked the poster?' he suddenly said, not looking up.

'The poster? The one in your bedroom? The circus poster?'

'I worked there.'

'At the circus?'

'Yes. Cirque Gruss.'

'When?'

'Before I fell into crime.'

Abbas took some more paste from the metal tin.

'My dad took me to the circus when I was thirteen, for the first time. We'd never been able to afford anything like that. I sat almost right at the edge of the ring and felt sorry for the animals being forced to do lots of degrading things. After a while, I felt that I wanted to leave, but I knew what the ticket had cost so I sat still. And that's when he came in.'

Abbas fell silent, put the black knives into his bag and took out two more.

'Who came in?' Stilton asked after a while.

'The Master, Jean Villon, the knife thrower. His performance only lasted fifteen minutes, but it changed my life. I was mesmerised.'

'By knife throwing?'

'By his whole performance. He threw the knives at a girl strapped to a spinning wheel and the knives framed her body. My stomach was churning, almost knotted, throughout the performance. When we left, I asked my dad whether we could go again the following night. We couldn't. So I started saving money, secretly, some of it pinched from my dad's pockets while he slept. But by the time I had enough for a ticket, the circus had left.'

Abbas looked out through the window, into the darkness, as though the memory of the departed circus still pained him.

'But then you started working at a circus?'

'Yes, four years later, when I was seventeen. By then I'd seen a number of performances in various circus tents around Marseille. All of them had knife throwers and none of them came close to Jean Villon.'

'The Master.'

'That's what he was known as among circus people. He was quite famous, but I had no idea. One day I saw that Cirque Gruss was coming to town again, with Jean Villon. And that's when I decided. I'd been practising knife throwing for a couple of years, at home in the backyard and out on the fields. I knew the basics. So I got in touch with Jean Villon and told him that I wanted to be a knife thrower and asked him whether he would consider training me.'

'That was quite cocky.'

'Perhaps, I wasn't so polished in those days. Maybe that's why he listened. Then he asked me to throw a few knives against a plank of wood. It was quite dark outside and hard to judge the distance, but I managed to hit the plank with two of the three knives. At the right angle. "Come back tomorrow at seven," he said. I'd thought he meant in the evening and was there bang on time – he'd meant seven in the morning. But I was given another chance, and the next day I was there at six. He'd already started. He practised with the knives for four hours every morning and two in the afternoon whenever they weren't travelling. I was there for two hours and he showed me all the mistakes I was making. There were plenty. When we'd finished, he asked whether I wanted to go with the circus to Nice. I certainly did.'

'He hired you?'

'I became his apprentice. Board and lodging, that was enough. I shared a little blue circus caravan with a dwarf, Raymond Pujol, the grandson of the great Joseph Pujol. Have you heard of him? Le Pétomane, the "fartomaniac".'

'No. Fartomaniac?'

'He was once a very famous artist. He could fart *La Marseillaise* and blow out a candle three metres away. He married a dwarf and their daughter gave birth to Raymond.'

'With whom you shared a caravan.'

'Yes.'

Abbas held a knife up to the lamp and inspected the blades. Stilton watched him. He'd never heard Abbas give such a long and detailed account about himself, and he realised that this had nothing to do with knife throwing or Abbas's life in the circus. This was the prelude to the unusual trip they had embarked upon. He still had no idea what it was about, but he knew he would find out.

All he needed to do was listen.

'I accompanied Jean Villon for almost two years,' Abbas said. 'Mostly around southern France, Nîmes, Avignon, Perpignan. Each day we practised for several hours and I improved with every hour that passed. Eventually I was able to pin up a five of hearts on a post ten metres away and hit each heart without the knives touching. Then came the really hard part, when you have perfected the technique and it's all just in the mind, to be so focused on the throw that nothing can distract you in the ring – a child screeching, someone coughing or gasping, a balloon suddenly bursting, you know. Being able to shut out everything around you.'

'You learned that too?'

'Gradually. The acid test came in Narbonne. It was our first night there and suddenly the Master became ill, with a fever. I was summoned to his caravan. He was lying under a couple of large tattered blankets. "You're throwing tonight," he said. And that's all he said. It was a sell-out and there was no way of cancelling. When I left his caravan his wife was standing next to one of the wheels. He was married to a much younger woman, a very beautiful Moroccan woman called Samira. She was blind.'

'Blind?'

'Yes. She was the Master's target girl, the one who was attached to the spinning wheel when he threw the knives.'

'And she was blind?'

'Yes.'

'Strange.'

'Perhaps. She heard me stepping out of the caravan and waved at me. I walked towards her. "You'll be throwing at me tonight," she said. "Yes, are you worried?" I asked. "No, Jean says that you're as good as he is." "I'm not," I said. "Tonight you are," she replied.'

Abbas turned over and stuffed the last of the knives into his bag. Stilton saw his eyes straining, it was hard for him to talk about this. Why? So far it had just been about knife throwing, hadn't it?

'We were very attracted to each other.'

He said it while he still had his head turned towards his bag, as though he was revealing a secret.

'You and the woman who was going to be your target girl?'

'We'd been dancing around each other, emotionally, for more than a year. It was easier for me, I could see her. She could only imagine. What, I don't really know, but once she said it was my smell, another time my voice. We'd never touched each other. She was Jean Villon's wife. But we both knew. I dreamed about her at night, stole a glimpse as she washed behind the caravan in the morning. She was a fantastic woman. Fantastically beautiful, in my eyes. I was utterly consumed by her.'

'And now you were about to throw a load of knives at her on a spinning wheel?'

'Yes.'

'How did that work? I mean that total concentration you talked about, being able to shut everything else out. Considering your feelings for her?'

'It worked perfectly. As though whatever was between us was helping. When they dimmed the lights in the packed circus tent and it was only me and her in the ring, it really was only us in there. No one else. Just me and her. And the knives. When the wheel started spinning and I weighed the first knife in my hand and flung it at her, it was like a strange declaration of love. For every knife that landed a couple of centimetres from her body I became more and more aroused, without losing focus. When the final knife was in place and the whole tent started roaring, I collapsed into the sawdust. Pujol ran in and lifted me up and out of the tent. The last thing I saw was her face as she was lifted off the wheel. She looked very sad.'

'Why?'

'I'll get to that presently.'

Stilton nodded. He was trying to tally Abbas's flow the whole time, so as not to interrupt him in the wrong place, not say something that would make him shut off. In some way, the whole tale was connected to what he knew was coming – what Abbas was getting closer to telling him… in his increasingly thinner voice.

'It was almost two o'clock at night, that same night that she'd been my target girl, and I couldn't sleep. I was lying naked in the bed, staring at the strange bells hanging here and there on the ceiling, wondering where Pujol was. Suddenly the door opened and he helped Samira up into the caravan. Then he disappeared. I got up out of bed. The light from one of the tent lamps was shining in through the window, enough for me to see her. She'd wrapped a blanket around her shoulders. When she dropped it on the floor she was naked. I touched her shoulder – it was the first time I touched her. She reached out her hand and touched my waist. I took her hands and guided her down into the bed. Then we made love.'

Abbas fell silent and Stilton didn't dare to say anything. He tried to picture the scene in front of him – the beautiful blind woman and the young knife thrower in a cramped circus caravan somewhere in southern France, aroused following months of dancing around each other, unleashed by knife throwing in a packed circus tent, making love as silently as possible, while the woman's fever-ridden husband lay in a nearby caravan.

He wanted to know more.

'So what happened then?' he dared to ask.

'The last thing I asked her was why she'd looked so sad out in the tent. "Because you and I will never be," she whispered and kissed me. When I woke up she was gone. I fell asleep again and was woken by the Master. He was better and came into the caravan with a thermos of coffee and a bottle of calvados. We drank coffee and some booze. Then he calmly and rather cheerlessly explained that I had to leave the circus that same day. I understood. So an hour or so later I said goodbye to Pujol and a few others I'd got to know and left. As I was walking out through the gate, I turned around and looked back at Samira's caravan, at the oval window. There was no one there – I never saw her again.'

Abbas fell silent. He'd reached an emotional barrier, a very private barrier. The barrier to Samira, to the meeting with her and the scars that it had left him with, scars that were still there, on the other side of the barrier. After a while, he looked up at Stilton again.

'You've never been able to forget her,' Stilton said.

'No, never. Of course I've been with other women, in other ways, but no one has reached that same spot.'

'She's still in there?'

'Yes.'

Abbas pulled a jug towards him and poured a splash of water into a tumbler. He raised the glass to his lips while gazing out through the window. He drank slowly. Stilton watched him. Abbas put the empty glass down and stared into it, for a long time, as though he was looking for what he wanted to say.

'A few years ago, I read in a French newspaper that Jean Villon had died. I got hold of Samira's address and wrote her a few letters. She never replied.'

'So you don't know what happened to her?'

'No, not until now.'

Abbas bent down towards his bag and pulled out a newspaper and another knife. He put the newspaper on the table and unfolded it, while holding the knife in his hand. Stilton looked at the newspaper and saw that it was French.

'What's this?'

'*Libé*, a French newspaper, *Libération*, I subscribe to it. This is what I found a couple of days ago.'

Abbas pointed at a long article on the front page. There was a large photograph of French police officers by a cordoned-off site in a nature reserve.

'What's it about?' Stilton said. 'I don't speak French.'

Abbas steeled himself. His hand holding the knife had slid down around the blade, and he began translating the article. It was about the finding of a butchered female corpse. The body had been found by tourists in Callelongue, in a national park south of Marseille. A wild boar had dug up a dismembered body part, and a tourist had tripped over the gnawed bony remains. Next to the picture of the mangled body was a photograph of the victim, a very beautiful woman. Abbas pointed to it.

'Is that Samira?'

'Yes.'

He suddenly realised what this trip was about. Why Abbas had told him what he'd told him. He suddenly understood what was waiting. He looked at the small photograph again.

'She was beautiful.'

'Lunar beauty.'

Stilton looked up at Abbas.

'That's what her name means. Samira.'

Stilton nodded and saw a little blood trickling from the hand that was gripping the blade.

'Abbas.'

He nodded at the knife. Abbas loosened his grip and wrapped a napkin around his hand. With his other hand he folded up the newspaper and put it back in his bag. As he sat up, Stilton saw that he had tears in his eyes. They looked at each other. They felt the train pounding along the rails and saw lights in the distance as they sped through the darkness. Stilton pulled his blue bag towards him. Luna had slipped in a bottle of whiskey for him. Wise woman. He pulled out the bottle and put it on the table. He knew that Abbas only rarely drank alcohol, but in light of what he'd just told him, Stilton felt that this was one of those rare moments. He poured two glasses and raised his.

Abbas didn't move.

Stilton had a swig.

'You know Jean-Baptiste Fabre, don't you?' Abbas said.

'Yes, I'm assuming that's why I'm here.'

'Yes.'

Jean-Baptiste Fabre was a detective in Marseille. Stilton had had close contact with him during a few joint murder investigations. It was a long time since they'd been in touch. Those years on the streets lay in between.

But Abbas knew about the contact.

'You want information about the French murder investigation?' Stilton asked.

'Yes.'

'Maybe they've already arrested the perpetrator?'

'They haven't, it would have said. I've checked every single online newspaper.'

'So what are you planning to do?'

'What would you do?'

'In your position?'

'Yes.'

'The same as you.'

And Abbas knew that. Stilton would have done the same as him. Done everything he could to catch whoever murdered and butchered Samira.

Simple as that.

'I'm going to get some sleep now.'

Abbas curled up on the bed, turned his face against the wall and turned off his bedside lamp.

His whiskey remained untouched.

Chapter 7

Stilton was standing on the hotel's breakfast terrace, observing an elderly woman dressed in black carrying a metal detector. She was slowly walking back and forth along the narrow beach. Her husband was doing the same a short way out to sea, with water up to his waist. Stilton assumed that they were a couple. They could have been siblings of course, aged unmarried siblings on the hunt for a lost coin or a piece of jewellery. He sipped his bitter espresso and let his gaze wander out over the bay, before it settled on a rocky island.

The island of If.

The famous setting of *The Count of Monte Cristo* to some, a common crossword answer to others.

Stilton watched boats making their way over to the island and sat down on a plastic chair. He had a pain in his groin. The sun was just about rising behind him and Marseille, the rays of sunshine spreading out over the mountains on the other side of the bay, glistening against the large golden statue of the Madonna on the hill. He looked at the long narrow stone pier that seemed to disappear straight out into the Mediterranean. He'd been to the coast down here a couple of times before, on police business. He didn't know about this hotel. Abbas had booked it online – Hotel Richelieu – a flaking stone building built on rocks that jutted out into the sea. The terrace was resting on a few concrete pillars that went right down into the deep. Stilton peered over the edge and saw the dark-blue waves lashing all the way up against the stone balustrade in front of him. He turned back to look at the spartan reception, a blue wooden desk and a Windsor chair. Not much of a welcome. The hotel was cramped and pokey, with a kind of flaking charm, and the porter always stood slightly too close when you talked to him.

Stilton looked at his watch.

Abbas was having a shower, a procedure that could seldom be hurried. From hot to lukewarm to freezing cold. Always the same process – from lassitude to samurai. Sometimes it took half an hour, but he was faster today. Abbas stepped out onto the terrace with a thin jacket in his hand and a piece of fruit. Stilton had no idea what kind of fruit it was. It looked bitter, like the coffee.

'That was where I started.'

Abbas took the fruit out of his mouth and pointed down at the narrow beach next to the hotel. The woman in black and her husband had gone.

'The Catalan Beach – during the summer it's full of locals and tourists. I started selling fake watches, then bags.'

'Did you sell anything?'

'Every so often, not much. Have you called Jean-Baptiste?'

'Yes, we're meeting at ten.'

'Where?'

'Some bar by the police station.'

'Do you know where it is?'

'Not the bar.'

'Come on.'

Abbas had booked what the hotel's website had described as a 'suite' with two separate bedrooms. One of them had a wide bed that stretched from wall to wall, almost. You could just about squeeze in next to it. The other was a window alcove where the owner had managed to fit in a bed at one end. These facilities were complemented with a narrow corridor, a tiled bathroom and a shared wardrobe.

Suite?

'I'll take the alcove,' said Stilton.

He'd been sleeping in all sorts of places for several years and presumed that Abbas was a little more fussy. He was, normally anyway, but at the moment he could have slept on broken glass if he'd had to.

But he took the wide bed.

'There.'

Abbas had put up a large detailed map of Marseille on the wall next to the bed. He pointed at a crossing right in the middle of the city.

'How do I get there?'

'Walk. It'll take half an hour. And it won't be any quicker to take the bus.'

'And what are you going to do?'

'Meet a friend.'

'When will we meet up?'

'I'll call you. If we don't speak, we'll meet at the restaurant next door, at eight.'

'OK.'

'Have you charged your phone?'

'Yes.'

Stilton noted that Abbas took charge in a very natural manner.

Good.

It was his revenge.

Not Stilton's.

Stilton had asked the porter for a simple tourist map, as a back-up. He knew roughly where he was going, but nevertheless, it was quite a distance to the police station. He stepped out onto Boulevard Kennedy and turned left, towards the old port. Just ten minutes later he realised his first mistake – his clothing. He'd left Stockholm in November where the temperature was around zero, and landed in Marseille where it was almost twenty degrees hotter. His thick leather jacket came off straight away. A few blocks later, his newly purchased Timberland boots felt like two walking sauna heaters.

But he couldn't exactly go barefoot.

So it was a rather sweaty Stilton who arrived half an hour later at the enormous grey police building next to the Cathédrale de la Major. The bar was apparently just opposite.

And indeed it was.

There was some outdoor seating with plastic tables and two faded parasols. It was quite unlikely that the rather unkempt smoking men sitting beneath them worked in the building opposite, though they'd probably visited many a time. Stilton crossed the road over to the bar. The men under the parasols followed his movements. He was a new face in the area, with shoes that were far too heavy. It was not yet ten o'clock. Jean-Baptiste would not be here. He was invariably punctual. They'd met as part of a rather gruesome murder investigation in the late nineties, a Frenchman who'd stabbed a couple of Swedish youngsters to death at a seaside resort on the west coast and then disappeared. Jean-Baptiste had found some clues about the man in Marseille and Stilton went down there. Before they had the chance to arrest him, he'd committed another murder in Toulon.

That was the beginning of their friendship.

It had probably begun with what you'd call chemistry. They were both professional. They had the same attitude. They were both from the 'countryside' – Stilton from Stockholm's outer archipelago and Jean-Baptiste from a small mountain village in Provence. They were both loners with an unsentimental attitude towards work. They kept in touch over many years, another couple of their murder investigations interlinked, and their careers advanced at roughly the same pace. But they were very different when it came to punctuality. Though not frequently late, Stilton was not a patch on Jean-Baptiste.

When there were just two minutes to go, Stilton walked into the bar. It was pretty cramped with a dirty stone floor and a stale smell of booze. A black spiral staircase led up to another floor and there were different-coloured pennons criss-crossing the ceiling. One wall was entirely covered with cigarette packets with eye-catching health warnings. There were dark round tables by another wall, with others further in towards the middle. The bar area itself was small. There were only men there and not many of them were drinking anything, just filling in tickets.

'Everyone is playing the lottery, everyone wants to wake up in the land of milk and honey.'

Stilton turned around. It was ten o'clock precisely and Jean-Baptiste was standing in the doorway of the bar, smiling. He was big, bigger than Stilton remembered him, not far off Depardieu both in terms of size and reddish hue. Anyone who didn't know him could have mistaken him as someone who was overfed and phlegmatic.

But Stilton knew better.

That was confirmed when they shook hands. Jean-Baptiste's handshake reminded him of his grandfather, the seal hunter. When your hand went in you were never quite sure how it would come out.

'Let's sit down.'

Jean-Baptiste led the way to a table at the front of the bar. He sat down in a chair and lit a cigarette.

'There's no smoking in the bar,' he said. 'But they make exceptions.'

Stilton looked at his yellowed fingers. He smoked far too much, always Gauloises, as long as Stilton had known him.

'So where have you been, then?' said Jean-Baptiste.

'I went off the rails.'

'Things happen. I got divorced and remarried.'

'Yeah, things happen. Are you happy?'

'On and off. At my age you lower your expectations.'

Jean-Baptiste blew a smoke ring and nodded at a slim dark-haired woman who passed by their table.

'Hi, Claudette, how are you?'

'I can't complain,' the woman replied and disappeared towards the tables further in.

Jean-Baptiste waved at the barman.

'Two Perriers.'

Despite his reddish hue, it looked like he was just on water now. Maybe he enjoyed consuming fine wines in private, Stilton didn't know. They'd never gone boozing together.

'How is it down here nowadays?' he said.

'In Marseille?'

'Yes.'

'Full of contrasts, as always. Calm on the surface and a bloody shambles below. Have you heard about the corruption mess?'

'No.'

'A load of our own people, in the gangsters' pockets. It's been going on for years and it's a major scandal down here right now. But of course there's no sign of it on the surface – everything's being kept spick and span up there. We're set to be the European Capital of Culture for 2013.'

'What does that mean?'

'A load of bloody hassle. Half the city is being renovated and spruced up. And it's hell for the traffic cops. It's chaos everywhere. You must have seen that on your way here?'

'I had other things on my mind.'

Jean-Baptiste laughed and drank half of his Perrier. When he put it down, he lowered his voice a little.

'So how are things with el Fassi?'

'Good. He's a croupier.'

'In Stockholm?'

'Yes.'

'So you got him back on track?'

'Eventually. He's even done some undercover jobs for the police.'

'Who'd have thought it?'

Jean-Baptiste didn't look as surprised as he sounded.

'But at the moment he's here.'

'In need of help?'

That's what he liked about Jean-Baptiste, his intuition.

'A female acquaintance of his has been found dead here,' said Stilton. 'Samira Villon.'

'Did he know her?'

'They once worked at the same circus.'

'She was murdered.'

'We read about it. Do you know any more?'

'No, other guys are dealing with it.'

'Guys you know?'

Jean-Baptiste twiddled the bottle of water between his fingers and looked straight into Stilton's eyes.

'Did he bring any knives?'

'I don't think so.'

Jean-Baptiste observed Stilton and saw that he was lying and Stilton saw that he saw. But it was a necessary white lie to prevent Jean-Baptiste having to lie at a later stage. If they were used in a way that came to the attention of the French police.

That was a potential risk.

'I could ask around,' said Jean-Baptiste. 'But you'll have to tell me a bit more.'

'About?'

'El Fassi's plans.'

'I don't know anything.'

Jean-Baptiste looked down at the table. The solid respect they had for each other emanated from their shared sense of right and wrong, their deep personal morals, which had once guided them into the police force and turned them into successful professionals. Now Stilton had 'lost his way' for a few years and Jean-Baptiste was not entirely sure what that meant. He knew that Stilton no longer worked for the police, he'd heard that following brief contact with Mette Olsäter a couple of years ago. But had he changed? Could he be trusted now?

Stilton observed Jean-Baptiste and guessed what was going on in his head. Entirely understandable. So he felt he needed to go one step further.

'Abbas wants to catch the murderer,' he said.

'That's for the French police to do.'

'I know, but sometimes even the best policemen need some help, right?'

'Sometimes.'

Jean-Baptiste suddenly got up and as he did so he made a decision, entirely based on his former trust in Stilton.

'Where can I get hold of you?' he said.

Stilton gave him his mobile number and the address of the hotel.

'You don't fancy coming to my house for dinner tonight?' Jean-Baptiste asked.

'I can't, I'm sorry.'

'I understand. Send el Fassi my best.'

Jean-Baptiste squeezed his way out of the bar and Stilton sank down a little. One problem fewer. He'd done what Abbas had asked him to do, pretty well actually. The large policeman would be in touch, he knew that. He also knew that he had to find a way of telling Abbas that he needed to be extra discreet with the knives.

That was a considerably greater problem.

Stilton looked around the bar and caught the eye of the beautiful dark-haired woman whom Jean-Baptiste had greeted, Claudette. She sat at a table all the way in, looking at Stilton. He held her gaze. He wasn't sure how long, but he was aware of how it felt. Suddenly he longed for a woman, for sex. He hadn't had sex since he and One-eyed Vera had made love in her caravan just a couple of hours before she was beaten to death. That was more than a year ago. Now he was sitting in a cramped bar in Marseille in the middle of the day, looking at a woman who was looking back in a way that turned him on. Suddenly she got up and went to the bar. He followed her body through the room. She was wearing low-heeled black shoes and a tight green dress. She stood with her back facing him and ordered. After she'd been served, she went straight over to Stilton's table with two small glasses in her hand.

'Do you like pastis?' she asked as she put the glasses down and sank into the chair where the large policemen had been sitting.

'Kind of,' Stilton replied.

'Cheers.'

They sipped on their glasses of pastis and looked at each other, for quite a while. The woman wasn't young – neither was Stilton. He was fifty-six and guessed that she was roughly ten years younger than him, with some first wrinkles around her make-up-free eyes.

'Claudette,' he said when the pastis was almost finished.

'Yes. And your name is?'

'Tom.'

'You know Jean-Baptiste?'

'Yes, and you do too?'

'Everyone in this area knows Jean-Baptiste. He's a good policeman.'

'Yes.'

'Are you a policeman too?'

'No.'

'Your English is good. Where are you from?'

'Sweden.'

'Ibra.'

Stilton smiled. Zlatan Ibrahimović was currently a big star at PSG, in Paris, not Marseille. He ought not to be so popular here.

'But here we think that he's a monster,' Claudette and smiled a little.

She had small, even teeth, not completely white, her arched lips were smooth and painted with a little red lipstick. Stilton smelled her breath over the table, it was pleasant, and then he suddenly thought about his own and hoped that it would be masked by the pastis.

'Are you staying at a hotel?' she asked.

'Yes, the Richelieu.'

'Shall we go there?'

'No, I'm sharing a room with my colleague.'

'Female?'

'No. Where do you live?'

'Rue de la Croix.'

'Is it far?'

'Not in a taxi.'

It took about fifteen minutes for the taxi to navigate its way through the centre before ending up in Claudette's neighbourhood. They sat in the back seat with the windows down. Stilton looked out and saw a barrel organist waving with one hand while the other fed the organ with perforated music. Stilton heard a melancholy tune coming from the wooden contraption and put his hand on Claudette's bare knee. He wanted to feel her skin.

'*The Crying Soldier*,' she said.

Stilton turned towards her.

'That's the name of the tune he's playing. It's an old folksong about a soldier who comes back from the war with no legs.'

'Which war?'

'One of them.'

Claudette put her hand on Stilton's and guided it up her thigh. Stilton felt how warm she was and leant up against her.

'We're here now,' she said.

Claudette paid for the taxi.

* * *

Abbas knew this area like the back of his hand, a rough area, full of poverty, where you weren't supposed to go at the wrong time of day. Some of it had been smartened up, some new buildings here and there, but underneath it was all still the same place. The same suspicion in people's eyes, the same small groups of frustrated men, the same smell. He remembered that smell. He didn't know what it was, only that it had smelled like that his entire childhood. Burned rubbish, exhaust fumes, wet cement. He didn't know. He tried hard to prevent the smell awakening emotions and memories, that's not why he was here. He thought he'd burned his inner album of memories, but there were remnants, it seemed.

He hurried over to the high-rise buildings where Marie apparently lived, eight floors up. He hoped that the lift was working.

It was.

As he stood in front of the battered door with the name that she'd given, he suddenly felt unsure. He didn't ring the doorbell straight away. He looked at the door. Marie had a different surname, of course, she was married with children, that much she'd told him on the phone. She was not the same woman as before, when she performed at Cirque Gruss as Bai She, the white snake woman. It was a spectacular act – the circus director introduced her with a story about a Chinese snake that had taken on human form and then she wreathed her way out of a drum to evocative chimes. She had an exceptional ability to make a human circle with her body, as though she didn't have a skeleton. Abbas never understood how it was possible. Now she was married and had a family and her life in the circus had come to an end. But that was not why he was hesitating in front of her door.

It was because she might tell him.

About Samira.

He knew that Marie and Samira had been close at the circus, maybe even after Marie had left? Maybe until Samira was murdered?

He rang the doorbell.

Marie put some cold iced tea on the kitchen table. It was a small kitchen considering that she had four children and a husband. One wall was full of grey-green glass cupboards and there was a large circus poster on the other.

Cirque Gruss.

Abbas looked at Marie.

It was more than fifteen years since she'd been the white snake woman. It wasn't likely that her body would bend into a circle again.

'It's been a long time,' she said.

As though she knew what Abbas saw. But she was still beautiful, in his eyes. He saw her as she'd once looked. Except the eyes. There was a hint of what he'd seen in his own eyes before he'd stepped into the shower at Dalagatan and emerged with an entirely different expression.

A hint of despair.

Marie sat down right next to Abbas. To him it had already felt like time had stood still when she opened the door and hugged him. They shared a past that was always present. Now they were sitting close as children tend to do. Marie looked at Abbas.

'Are you still…'

'No, I stopped many years ago.'

'I knew things would go well for you.'

'How did you know?'

'You never lied. Everyone else lied when it suited them, you never did. So I decided that if you don't lie, things will go well.'

'A half-truth.'

'I know, but it worked for you.'

'Until now.'

'Yes.'

Then their despair became intertwined, their despair over Samira, and it kept hold of them until Marie reached for her glass and Abbas did the same.

Both of them knew what this moment in the kitchen was all about.

'She grieved for you so long,' Marie said. 'It was agonising. The Master knew how she felt, everyone knew and no one could do anything. It was what it was. She was his wife and target girl.'

'Yes.'

Abbas tried to remain focused. He wanted to get through this as quickly as possible, he wanted to get to the part that would feel much worse, he couldn't crumble yet.

'What happened when the Master died?'

'Samira had to leave. The new knife thrower had his own target girl.'

'So where did she go?'

'At first we were in touch quite a bit, but I was away with the circus and she was here, in Marseille.'

'What did she do?'

'I'm not really sure.'

Abbas felt that Marie was hiding something, but he didn't want to push her. She should say what she wanted and was up to telling him.

'Did you ever meet up?'

'Once, a couple of years after she'd left. She was so sad.'

'Why?'

'She wondered if I'd kept in touch with you.'

Abbas felt a mounting pressure in his chest.

'I wrote a couple of letters,' he said. 'I got hold of the circus director and he gave me an address where he thought Samira lived. But I had no reply. Maybe she never got them.'

'Or maybe her agent ripped them up?'

'Her agent?'

Marie stood up. She went to the window and looked out. Abbas waited. Marie walked towards the sink and took a thin chopping board out of a drawer. When she was about to put it down, Abbas saw that her hands were trembling. He got up and went right up close to her. Marie dropped her head down onto his chest and cried, quietly. He stroked her short blonde hair and let her cry.

As though he was fine.

He was far from fine.

Agent?

Marie lifted her head up from Abbas's chest and reached for some kitchen paper. She wiped her cheeks and looked at Abbas. She said it as directly as she could.

'She made films.'

'What sort of films?'

'Porn films.'

It took a few seconds, perhaps minutes, before Abbas was able to comprehend this difficult news.

'She made porn films?'

'Yes.'

Abbas sat down at the table again and poured himself some more iced tea. Marie stayed by the sink. She knew that Abbas wanted to know. A man who never lied didn't want other people to do so either. Or hide things. The only reason he was here was to get information about Samira. All she could do was tell him what she knew.

Abbas looked at her.

'Why?' he asked.

'I asked her the same thing. She didn't really know what to say. After leaving the circus, she'd met an older man who was supposed to help her and as I understood it he sold her to the agent. She was blind, poor, had to make a living – she was easy prey for people wanting to take advantage of her. And she was so beautiful.'

'And this agent used her to make porn films.'

'I'm not really sure how it works, he was some kind of producer too. Maybe he rented her out?'

Abbas got up and went over to the window. He brushed a finger against the window pane, from one edge to the other. In the distance he saw large swarms of black jackdaws swooping over the houses in undulating formations.

Porn films? Samira?

He carried on looking out through the window and asked, 'Why did she agree to it?'

'Well, why do women agree to it? I reckon he drugged her, or got her hooked on drugs.'

'The agent?'

'Yes. I suppose it makes most people let down their barriers.'

'Presumably.'

Abbas drew a little cross on the windowpane with his index finger and turned to face Marie.

'Do you know the agent's name?'

'Yes.'

He took the stairs down.

The lift was too slow.

* * *

They made love for a long time, in a large peaceful bedroom, on a wide Victorian steel bed. They didn't say a word, both of them had pent-up desires that drove their bodies together. Stilton knew the reason for his own – what drove Claudette was her own business.

Eventually the heat subsided and they lay naked on the soft bed, crossways. Stilton felt the sweat trickle down onto the sheet.

He was empty, drained.

Such a great feeling, he thought, and looked at Claudette. She was lying on his arm with her eyes shut. He let his gaze move along her shiny body and over to the wall. There were several unframed oil paintings hanging on the light-blue wallpaper, some of them looked unfinished. Stilton lifted his head a little to get a better look.

Then his mobile rang.

Claudette opened her eyes. Stilton looked at her. She lifted her head and released his arm. Stilton grabbed his mobile, he assumed that it was Abbas.

'Hi, Tom? Have you arrived?'

It was Mette Olsäter.

'Yes.'

'You promised you'd ring!'

'I haven't had time.'

'Why not?'

'I didn't get a chance. Have you spoken to Abbas?'

'He's not answering.'

'Well, he can probably see it's you calling.'

'And what is that supposed to mean?'

'Nothing. He wants to be left alone.'

'Tom, please… we're adults. We've known each other for donkey's years. What are you up to?!'

Stilton didn't answer directly, partly because he had to say something with some substance, otherwise it would be ridiculous, and partly because Claudette had leant down over his groin and begun caressing his penis.

'It's a long story,' he said. 'Abbas will have to tell you himself. I heard it on the train. It's pretty tragic.'

'But it's about him?'

'Yes.'

'Why are you there, then?'

'I have a few contacts down here.'

'Fabre? Jean-Baptiste Fabre?'

'Yes.'

Mette had never met Fabre, but she knew that Stilton had worked with him some time ago and developed a warm personal acquaintance. They'd also met a few times as part of investigations in which Mette was also involved. So she concluded that the visit to Marseille had something to do with police business.

Which didn't do much to assuage her concern.

'Could it get dangerous?' she asked.

'For whom?' Stilton half-groaned and felt his penis stiffen.

'For you?'

'I hope not. Why would it?'

'Because I know exactly what you two…'

'Mette, I'm sorry. I have to go, there's a taxi waiting for me outside! I'll be in touch!'

Stilton managed to end the call just seconds before he was about to come again. Claudette looked up at him.

'Was that your wife?'

'I'm not married.'

'Me neither.'

And then he came.

* * *

Marie knew the agent's name, Philippe Martin. But she didn't know his address or where Abbas could find him. He had to establish that for himself. However, she did know that he was dangerous. She'd heard his name a couple of times in the last few years in connection with some brutal incidents. Each time, she'd thought about Samira. A couple of times she'd tried to get hold of her, unsuccessfully. Her husband had advised her not to be too persistent.

He'd also heard of this agent.

Abbas just had a name, but he had a pretty good idea of the circles that the man in question probably frequented. Or that he was known in at least. So, feeling extremely frustrated, he had waited for it to be evening and for the place he wanted to visit to open. Le Bar de la Plaine, a place he knew from before and he assumed would still be there. Presumably with the same clientele, a mix of pimps, musicians, gangsters and hookers. And the occasional celebrity.

Abbas went in. The bar had only been open ten minutes, but it was already packed. He elbowed his way to the bar. An older bartender brushed away some non-existent ash in front of him.

'Hi,' Abbas said. 'I'm looking for Philippe Martin, do you know where I can find him?'

'No.'

'I owe him three grand, he'll be annoyed if he doesn't get it.'

'Not just annoyed.'

'No, exactly. So?'

'The bar diagonally opposite the station. He tends to be there at lunchtime. What do you want to drink?'

'I don't drink.'

Abbas turned around and pushed his way towards the exit again. He knew that people had their eyes on him. He just hoped they weren't the bad kind, from before, from the Arab quarter, or the port, the kind that might recognise him.

He knew that would create problems.

* * *

Stilton stopped to catch his breath. He'd been running. It was just gone eight o'clock and he'd reached the restaurant. From the front, from the road, it looked pretty wide, but from the side you could see that it must have been one of the city's narrowest restaurants, Eden Roc, located in one of the city's narrowest buildings, four metres wide and twenty-five metres long, on just one floor, built onto the hotel that Abbas had found online. The restaurant was also on the rock jutting out into the sea, hence the name.

Stilton went inside.

A thin, red-bearded, stressed waiter was standing behind a tiny bar a couple of metres in.

'Une coupe?'

The waiter looked at Stilton while pouring different drinks into different glasses. Stilton didn't know what he meant, so he shook his head and peered into the restaurant. Two of the nine plastic tables were occupied by families, six were empty and Abbas was sitting at the ninth. Right at the back, at a window table looking out at the bay. Stilton went in and sat down opposite him.

'You smell like sex,' Abbas said.

Stilton had only just sat down, but he knew that it was probably true. He'd had no time to shower, he knew that he was soaked in bodily fluids.

'I needed it,' he said.

'Someone you knew?'

'No.'

'What did Jean-Baptiste say?'

Stilton summarised his conversation with Jean-Baptiste, leaving out the bit about the knives.

For now anyway.

He had to do that when he didn't smell of sex.

'When do you think he'll be in touch?' Abbas wondered.

'When he hears something. What are you having?'

The waiter had hurried past with a couple of small chalk-boards with today's menu. Stilton had a look at it – rabbit, fish, seafood risotto, artichoke, calamari fritti.

'Calamari fritti,' Abbas said.

Stilton wasn't too partial to squid so he ordered the risotto. Both of them drank Perrier. Abbas didn't speak. Stilton felt that the current hierarchy demanded him to report back first. The issue of the large policeman was dealt with, but not the large policewoman.

'Mette called,' he said. 'She said she's been trying to reach you.'

'Yes, I saw that. I didn't feel like talking to her.'

'She wants to know what we're doing down here, she's worried.'

'And you think she'd be less worried if she knew why we were here?'

Stilton didn't have to answer as the red-bearded waiter had just placed a plate of thin crispy calamari in front of Abbas and a bowl of black sludge in front of Stilton. Abbas squeezed some lemon over his plate and picked up one of the squid rings with his fingers.

'What did you say to her?' he said as he put the crispy sea creature into his mouth.

'That it was a long story and that it was yours, and that you needed to tell her when you felt ready to.'

'Was she satisfied with that?'

'I ended the call. I had to run to catch a taxi to come and meet you.'

'Did you get lost?'

'No, why?'

'You were running, I saw you through the window.'

Stilton pushed a heaped forkful into his mouth.

'How's the squid?'

'Excellent. And that?'

'That' tasted pretty much how it looked. Stilton had a few more mouthfuls and then realised that he'd clearly ordered tasteless black porridge. The black stuff was made from squid too.

'It's good, a bit spicy perhaps,' he said. 'Did you get hold of your friend?'

'Yes.'

Stilton assumed that Abbas would elaborate. He didn't, not immediately. He finished his food first. When his plate was empty he put it on the empty table next to them and drank up his water. He put that on the other table too. Stilton watched him. He realised that this was some kind of ritual that he was observing, one which demanded that everything around him was cleared away. When the waiter asked whether they would like anything else, Abbas replied: 'It would be great if we weren't interrupted for a while.'

The waiter's body language did the talking – he headed back to his safe haven behind the bar. Then Abbas looked out through the window, at the darkness outside, the sea, the sky and tried to say it as directly as Marie had said it.

'Samira did porn films.'

Abbas let the information sink in, rather like Marie had done, and sink in it did. In a way that surprised Stilton somewhat. He'd never known Samira, and he knew nothing about her other than what Abbas had told him. But it was enough. He knew Abbas. And when Abbas turned away from the window to look him in the eyes he saw everything he needed to know. In particular, he saw the darkness of Abbas's pupils.

'She had an agent,' Abbas began. 'Philippe Martin. An arsehole. I'm thinking of looking him up.'

'I understand. To talk?'

'You coming?'

* * *

Mette sat on the toilet seat and watched her husband brushing his teeth. Mårten had a special technique, he brushed each tooth individually. The front, the back, the chewing surface, and then he flossed both sides. As all his teeth were still in good repair, at the age of sixty-eight, that meant thirty-two individual brushings before Mette was given access to the washbasin. That was one of the reasons why she was nagging him about redoing the bathroom, so that they could have a double washbasin.

'Apparently it's about a murder.'

Mette tried to distract Mårten, who was working on tooth number twenty-six. He pulled out the toothbrush and looked at her.

'The trip to Marseille?'

'Yes. I called a colleague down there I vaguely know. Well, no… It's Tom who knows him, but we've had some contact. He said it was about a murder and that Abbas knew the victim.'

'Oh shit.'

Mårten sank down on the edge of the bath with the toothbrush in his hand and Mette took the opportunity to occupy the washbasin.

'How does that tie in with the past that he talked about?' she said.

'The victim might be someone he knew when he lived in Marseille?'

'I thought that too, at first.'

'But?'

'It's been ages since he lived there and as far as I know he hasn't been in touch with a single person since he left,' Mette said and started brushing her teeth.

'No. Could it be a relative?'

'He's got no family left, you know that.'

'His mother,' Mårten said.

'What about her?'

'She disappeared when he was seven. She might still be alive.'

'And now been murdered?'

'Yes.'

'A mother who abandons her son when he's seven and never makes contact would hardly cause the adult son to rush down to Marseille at zero notice and take someone like Tom with them?' Mette said. 'Even if she'd been murdered.'

'No, perhaps not. I have six teeth to go.'

'I'm almost done.'

Mårten took the opportunity to drift off into thought while he waited. Abbas and Tom in Marseille with a French murder and Abbas knew the victim, a victim from the past, a past he hated. What were they planning to do? He didn't really want to know as he had no chance whatsoever of influencing it.

So he focused on his teeth.

'So have you called Olivia?' he said. 'To apologise?'

Mette turned around with her toothbrush in her mouth, and as she didn't take it out, he didn't understand what she said. But he saw.

She hadn't.

'I think you're being a bit of a wimp,' he said, peering down at the washbasin.

Mette pulled the toothbrush out of her mouth.

'Please can you stop getting involved in things that are nothing to do with you!'

'Absolutely. Sorry.'

Mårten had reclaimed pole position by the washbasin and began working on tooth number twenty-seven. Mette suddenly threw her toothbrush into the bath and left. Mårten watched her go in the mirror. What kind of reaction was that? It couldn't only be about Olivia? Or Abbas and Tom?

That was a sign of imbalance based on something else.

Her heart?

Mette had recently had another check-up. Her heart wasn't in great shape, and the doctor had issued her a couple of serious warnings: minimise all stress and do something about your weight.

She'd ignored both of them.

Chapter 8

Olivia generally kept a healthy distance from journalists. It had not turned into contempt, as it had among some of her colleagues at the Police Academy. She respected the Fourth Estate of the Realm. She'd seen astonishing examples of the value of investigative journalism, but she'd also grown up in a media-obsessed society where journalism often pushed the boundaries. It undermined the credibility that press freedom depends on, often because of certain journalists' total lack of respect for their own profession.

She hoped that Alex Popovic did not belong to that category. He'd asked her to come to the editorial office of *Dagens Nyheter*. He had to be there to monitor something or other.

He'd given no indication as to what.

But he had an interesting voice, Olivia thought, regarding her reflection in the entrance door at Gjörwellsgatan. She pushed her smooth grey knitted hat down on her head. It was a nice hat, not like the one that Maria had forced upon her in Rotebro. She should probably have taken it off as she was going indoors, but she liked the appearance it gave her. Her long black hair fell down over her shoulders. She leant in towards her reflection.

There was something contradictory about her healthy tanned complexion and her winter attire.

Alex Popovic had just turned forty-two and he'd been employed by the large newspaper for the last eight years. His desk was right at the far end of the editorial office. He'd just sent an email to the Swedish embassy in Senegal asking them to confirm that there were no Swedish citizens on the tourist bus that crashed down into a ravine a couple of hours earlier. When he looked up he saw a young woman in a grey hat being escorted in by a man from reception. He also saw that some male colleagues had registered her arrival. A few backs were straightening up behind their screens. The woman carried on in and leant down to talk to a female journalist. She nodded, turned around and pointed straight at him. The young woman started walking towards him. Is that Olivia Rivera? he thought.

Olivia approached Alex. He greeted her with an outstretched hand and gestured towards the chair next to his desk. Both of them sat down.

'Nice tan,' he said and smiled, while removing some nicotine gum from his mouth.

'I'd just got back from Costa Rica when you rang.'

'Bengt's house?'

'Yes.'

'What were you doing there?'

'In Costa Rica?'

'At Bengt's.'

'I wanted to collect a laptop.'

Alex's expression revealed that Olivia needed to clarify certain things, so she told him about her relationship with Bengt Sahlmann and his daughter and why she had gone to collect a laptop.

'I told Sandra that you'd called the house. She said that you'd known Bengt for ages.'

'Yes.'

'How long?'

'We went to Lundsberg together.'

'The boarding school?'

'Yes.'

Alex gestured as though it was not the first time he'd had to explain the fact that he'd gone to Lundsberg.

'Well, we both fitted in equally badly there,' he said with a smile. 'But then we kept in touch over the years. Bengt was a good friend. You gave me a double shock – first that he'd committed suicide and then that he'd been murdered.'

'Both things were true when I said them. Why did you call?'

Alex was an experienced journalist and he was used to asking the questions. Now he found himself being questioned by a total stranger, an attractive one, but nonetheless a stranger. He'd googled her name and found nothing about this Olivia Rivera. Perhaps it wasn't her real name? Why? What did she want?

'Why do you want to know that?' he said.

'Because I'm curious.'

'That's not enough.'

Olivia looked at Alex. She liked him. She didn't know whether it was his voice or attitude or his short dark hair, it was probably just the energy he was radiating.

So she tried to find an acceptable answer.

'Bengt Sahlmann has been murdered. It's a tragedy for Sandra. She's a family friend and I want to do all I can to help her find out what happened. And why.'

'Are you a police officer?'

'Yes and no. I've done my police training, but I don't work there. The National Crime Squad is investigating Bengt's murder.'

'Why them?'

'I don't know. So why were you calling?'

Alex started chewing on some more nicotine gum and saw that it was his last one. He had had far too many. He brushed his hand over the short stubble on his cheek. What should he say?

'Maybe you don't want to say?' said Olivia, as though she'd seen it in his eyes. 'Maybe it's sensitive? Private?'

'It's private.'

'OK.'

A few seconds of silence followed. They both looked at each other. Alex averted his gaze first and looked over Olivia's shoulder to check that there was no one sitting too close. He wanted to answer. He wanted to keep the dialogue going with this alert woman. So he leant over towards Olivia.

'Bengt had got in touch a few days before and said that he had some seriously explosive material he knew I'd be interested in, as a journalist. He didn't want to talk about it over the phone, he was going to send it to me. I was calling to ask whether it was on its way as I hadn't received anything.'

'So you don't know what it was about?'

'No. But I know that he wouldn't call me like that unless it was serious. And he sounded stressed. I asked him whether something had happened and it had, he said, and then he ended the call.'

'Maybe it had something to do with the theft at Customs and Excise.'

'What theft?'

Olivia knew that she should have kept quiet if everything had been as normal. But things weren't normal. Nothing had been normal since Tom Stilton had divulged the truth about her murdered mother. Now everything was abnormal and Olivia didn't really know what she was doing. Right now she was having a semi-private conversation with a journalist she didn't know.

Things hadn't gone very well last time she did that.

Well, that's how life was sometimes, she thought, and told him about the disappeared stash of drugs at Customs and Excise and Bengt Sahlmann's internal inquiry. She didn't know that much, hardly anything.

But of course Alex became more and more interested.

'How large was the stash that disappeared?'

'I don't know.'

'And I thought it was about something completely different.'

'What? I thought you didn't know what kind of material he was talking about.'

'No, if I'd known I wouldn't have said it. I only have assumptions.'

'About?'

Alex understood that she'd disclosed something she probably shouldn't have, about Customs and Excise, so he did the same, because he liked her too.

Her energy in particular.

And moreover, his intuition told him that this contact would come in useful in the future.

'Bengt recently had a violent outburst at a party, well, more of a dinner. There were a few friends from school and he got quite drunk and suddenly started talking about his father's death, in a nursing home, and made loads of accusations and claimed that he'd still be alive today if he'd received proper care. It was really awkward, so we put him in a taxi.'

'And you thought he wanted to give you information about that?'

'It just struck me, considering how upset he was. But that thing about the drugs sounds more solid.'

'Yes, perhaps.'

Suddenly it was time for Alex to leave – he'd been waiting for the press conference with Jimmie Åkesson. A couple of Sweden Democrats had gone around the city centre beating people up with iron bars. Alex excused himself. Olivia got up, took off her grey hat, shook her long hair, wrote down her mobile number on a pad and left. Alex watched her go.

That's the third time I've heard about Bengt's father's death, Olivia thought to herself on the way down. From three different people. He must have been extremely upset about it. She got out her mobile and called Sandra. She answered quickly.

'Hi. Have you found the computer?'

'No, sorry, but I'm sure the police are busy looking for it. How are you?'

'So-so. I'm not sleeping well.'

'You know you can call me any time if you can't sleep.'

'Yes. Are you calling about something in particular?'

'I'm just calling. I'm thinking of you, all the time.'

'Thanks.'

'But there is something I was wondering. What was the name of your grandfather's nursing home?'

'Silvergården, in Nacka. Why?'

'I'm just curious. It sounds like your father was pretty upset after your grandfather died.'

'Yes?'

Yes. And? Olivia felt that she was messing this up.

'So, how is it living at Charlotte's?' she said, changing the subject.

'Fine, I suppose… she said we could move home to Rotebro if I wanted, but I don't. Maybe later…'

'Yes, the most important thing is that you do whatever feels best for you.'

'That's what Charlotte says too. Sorry, can we speak tomorrow? A school friend just arrived.'

'Sure! Call me when's good for you.'

'Thanks, I will.'

Olivia ended the call and felt pretty crap. She'd only been ringing to obtain information, not to see how Sandra was feeling. But she did want to know. We'll talk for longer tomorrow, she thought, and headed towards the glass doors at the entrance. As she looked out she saw people hunched over, trying to make their way through the icy wind and rain.

Horrid.

She put on her knitted hat and stepped outside into the storm.

She took the car out to Nacka.

Thus far she'd used the missing laptop and her relationship with the orphaned Sandra as the reasons for her actions. She could do that a while longer, without 'trampling' on Mette's investigation. The meeting with Alex Popovic had fired her up.

She turned off the motorway and skidded on the corner. The roads were soaked in icy rain and she still had her summer tyres. Time to change those, she thought, and headed towards Jarlaberg.

The nursing home lay at the end of the road, a modern, grey, two-storey building. She parked near the entrance and hoped that she wouldn't need any door codes to get in.

She didn't.

She pushed the glass doors open and walked into a deserted entrance hall. There was no one there, except a small white cat brushing against the wall. A cat? She passed through another glass door, which didn't shut in time to prevent the cat from squeezing through. Shit! Should she take it out again? She couldn't – it had already gone. Was it normal for cats to be in nursing homes? She walked through a short corridor towards yet another glass door. There was still no one to be seen. She pushed the next door open and stepped into a larger corridor with an empty reception to the right. A stark fluorescent light reflected off the white walls, almost dazzling her. She carried on in and was struck by the silence, as though it was sound-proofed. Her own footsteps were hardly audible. She walked a few more metres. Then a strange feeling came over her and she turned her head. There was a man sitting on a wooden chair, in a corner, just behind her. He was wearing grey flannel pyjamas. There was not a hair on his head and his skin was covered in bluish-black spots. His skeletal hands were holding onto the armrests. He sat completely still, his eyes fixed on Olivia. She suppressed her initial shock reaction and approached him.

'Hello, my name is Olivia. Do you know where the staff are?'

The man just sat there, completely still. In fact, his face was entirely motionless, his body frozen. Olivia had seen human statues in both Barcelona and Mexico City, people standing as though they were made of stone, for hours on end, only moving their eyes. This man wasn't even moving his eyes. Was he even breathing?

Olivia turned away and walked on through the deserted corridor. When she'd almost reached the end, she turned around. The fossil in the chair still hadn't moved. Olivia turned the corner into another bright corridor, just as empty as the other one. She passed a number of doors, many of them with a key in the door. She stood still in the middle of the corridor. This was ridiculous. Surely there had to be someone here?

'Hello?!'

She heard her own voice bounce along the walls a couple of times before it faded away. And then it was silent again.

Then she heard the scream, an unpleasant drawn-out scream, like a howling fox in the night. It came from one of the rooms further down. Olivia walked towards it. The door was ajar, so she carefully pushed it open. The room was dark, the blinds were drawn. She saw a woman inside squatting on the floor. The woman was wearing a white coat. Had she been the one screaming? Olivia stepped into the room. The woman looked straight up at her.

'Is the ambulance here?'

'I don't know. What's happened?'

Olivia took another step forward and then she saw a second woman, a very old woman in a white robe. She was lying on the floor. Blood was running from a cut on her forehead. Her legs were moving up and down as though she had cramp. Her hands were thrashing about in the air. The woman in the white coat took hold of her hand and tried to keep her arm still.

'There's help on its way, Hilda, soon...'

The woman let out another scream, this time much longer and more piercing.

'I'm here now, Claire is here... everything will be all right in a moment.'

The old woman, Hilda, started lashing out with her other arm, her body arching like a bow on the floor. The woman in the white coat looked up at Olivia.

'Please help me!'

'What should I do?'

'Take the other hand.'

Olivia sank down onto the floor and took hold of Hilda's other hand. She felt how strong the old woman was, Olivia could hardly hold her flailing arm. Suddenly Hilda turned her body on the side and pulled her head up from the floor. Her eyes were staring straight up at the ceiling, her whole body was screaming, without a sound. Claire tried to stroke her forehead.

'Is there no one else here?' Olivia said.

'No, not in this ward. I've called the ambulance and the doctor.'

But there wasn't much point. Olivia and Claire both realised that life would flow out of Hilda long before that. They held the woman's hands in the dark and saw her frail body slowly stop fighting, her breathing slowly wane and her head bend down to the floor. Seconds later Olivia felt the old woman's hand clasp her own so hard that she felt like screaming and then it went limp.

Hilda was dead.

Olivia sat down on the floor with her back to the bed. Claire had felt for a pulse and noted the time and a few other details. Then she gently brushed the old woman's eyelids shut and neatened her hair, pulled out a cloth from her pocket and wiped away the blood on Hilda's face.

'She probably cut her forehead when she fell out of bed,' she said quietly.

Olivia nodded. She was shaken. It was the first time she'd seen a person die. A person whose hand she held at the moment of death, a complete stranger. She looked around the room, the walls were bare. There was a framed photograph on a shelf next to the bed.

Of a dog.

That was all.

'Could you help me?'

Claire had got up and stood behind Hilda's head.

'Take hold of her calves,' she said.

They were going to lift Hilda up onto the bed. Olivia held her legs and Claire held her under her shoulders. Olivia prepared to lift a human body and was shocked. The body hardly weighed anything at all, it was like lifting a white robe, as though death had taken away all her weight. Carefully they placed Hilda on the bed.

'Thank you,' said Claire.

She sat on the edge of the bed and looked at the dead woman. Olivia could see how incredibly moved she was. Filled with sadness, her hand became moist as she wiped her eyes. Olivia sat down in an armchair. The silence was different in here. It had been frightening out there, not in here.

'It's just hopeless…'

Claire spoke down to the frail body, not looking at Olivia. Her voice was controlled, but resigned, as though she was confirming a recurring tragedy. Olivia sat in silence. She felt there was more to come.

'We struggle on until we reach breaking point, and this still happens. Over and over again. We don't have time to be where we need to be, we don't have time to do what we know we should, it's just hopeless…'

Claire turned to Olivia.

'I came in to see her a couple of hours ago, and then she was just lying in her bed as normal, breathing, and I talked to her a bit and told her that I had to go and check on a couple of other rooms and deal with the food and work on some supply orders. She was to press the emergency button if she needed anything. But she didn't.'

'Why not?'

'She couldn't reach it. It had slid down behind the edge of the bed. If I'd popped in earlier I'd have seen it, but I had all that other stuff to do and I'm on my own here today. What could I do?'

Olivia didn't have an answer. She didn't work here. But she understood that Claire was shaken by what had happened and that she needed to talk about it.

'What do you mean by "over and over again"?' she said. 'Has this happened to you before?'

'Several times, unfortunately.'

Claire looked at Olivia.

'Thanks for your help, by the way. My name is Claire Tingman.'

'Olivia Rivera. I'm a friend of the Sahlmann family. Torsten Sahlmann died here a while ago, am I right?'

'Yes.'

'His son Bengt was very upset about his death.'

'I know. And with reason.'

'Did you speak to him?'

'Yes.'

'What happened?'

'Torsten had a stroke during the night, and the person on night duty was busy with other stuff and she wasn't able to keep an eye on things properly, so he wasn't found until the morning and by that time it was too late.'

'So he could have been saved if they'd found him earlier?'

'Yes.'

'Like Hilda?'

'I don't know. But this kind of thing happens all the time. A couple of weeks ago we had a diabetic woman who didn't get her insulin on time – it wasn't recorded in the notes when the support staff took over. She almost died too.'

'But that's terrible.'

'Yes.'

'Why is it like this, then?'

Olivia saw that Claire was hesitating.

'Because we're constantly short staffed,' she said. 'Because half of us are underqualified. Because of the need to make savings everywhere. Because there's no proper planning, no one knows what anyone else is doing, everyone needs to be everywhere. Several of the elderly people have got terrible bedsores and last summer we found fly larvae in a sore on an old man's back. It was disgusting.'

Claire turned her head away slightly, as though the memory of it was still troubling her.

'I'm always almost in tears when I go home at the end of my shift,' she said. 'It's like they don't get that it's human beings we're dealing with here, as though it was some kind of final storage place for people who are going to die.'

'"They"?'

'The people running the home. It's only about cutting costs and making money. And about…'

Claire stopped abruptly. There was a clacking sound of hard heels in the corridor.

'You probably ought to leave now.'

Olivia stood up. She met a woman with short blonde hair in the doorway. She was dressed in a stiff beige coat and was on her way into the room. She was startled. Olivia walked past her out into the corridor. The woman walked into the room and pulled the door shut. Olivia heard muffled voices inside. A couple of minutes later, the door opened and the woman came out again. She took a couple of steps towards Olivia and reached out her hand.

'Hi. Rakel Welin.'

'Olivia Rivera. Who are you?'

'I am the director of Silvergården. Do you have family here?'

'No.'

'So what are you doing here?'

'I've just helped one of your employees with a dying woman in there. Apparently there's no one else here.'

'Well, I'll have to ask you to leave now.'

'Why?'

Rakel Welin was rather taken aback.

'Because this is a private nursing home. We can't have unauthorised persons running around here.'

'I'm a friend of the Sahlmann family.'

'They no longer have a relative here.'

The women looked at each other. Welin gestured towards the exit. Olivia didn't move.

'How do I get in touch with the company running Silvergården?' she said.

'Are you going to leave or do I have to call the police?'

'And why would you do that? Because I saw what happened in there?'

'That has nothing to do with outsiders.'

'Except that you let an old woman, who could have been saved, die.'

'Are you going to leave?'

'Are you trying to cover up what happened?'

Rakel Welin looked at Olivia and got out a mobile. Olivia turned around and walked towards the door. Halfway there she stopped. Claire was standing in the doorway behind Welin. Their eyes met. Olivia went out through the glass door. Just before it slammed shut, the white cat scurried out after her.

It had probably caught sight of Rakel Welin.

She gripped the steering wheel. The roads were slippery, but more than that, she was extremely upset. The windscreen wipers were flapping to and fro all the way home – she hadn't even realised it wasn't raining.

It hadn't been raining at all.

She was still upset when she got into her flat, both by the experience with Hilda and the meeting with Rakel Welin, but more than anything about what Claire Tingman had told her, about how things were at Silvergården. She suspected that there was a great deal that was covered up out there. She threw her jacket down in the hallway and felt she needed a really hot bath and a cup of tea. Sadly the bath option was no-go as she didn't have a bathtub and a hot shower just wasn't the same. But hot tea was no problem. She put the water on, changed into some comfier clothes, got her laptop and turned it on.

Her feet were tapping the floor, waiting for the screen to load.

By the time it did, the water was boiling. She pulled the saucepan towards her. As she poured the hot liquid she noticed that her hand was shaking slightly. The hand that Hilda had squeezed the moment she died. It was almost as if she could still feel it. And it would be a long time before that feeling went away, she knew that.

Likewise the shock of that weightless body.

She started by googling Silvergården.

Before long she'd found some sort of ownership structure. The home was ultimately owned by a venture capital firm called

Albion. She looked at Albion's website for Silvergården. It was a visual masterpiece, both in terms of design and readability, with a rousing appeal:

Do you want to give your mum and dad what they deserve? Time for love and care? With people who love people? Give them Silvergården – the nursing home that takes care of all the details!

They didn't mention the fly larvae, Olivia thought to herself. But that probably wouldn't sell quite as well.

Two cups of tea later she closed down her laptop and thought about Claire Tingman. She would probably never come forward publicly, but she was there. If need be, maybe Olivia could get her to talk.

Then the doorbell rang.

Olivia jumped and looked at the clock. It was only just gone eight o'clock. She had thought it was the middle of the night. Perhaps it was Mette Olsäter coming to offer a grovelling apology.

It wasn't.

It was an Olsäter, but not Mette. It was Mårten.

'Hello?! Come in!'

Mårten gave Olivia a warm hug and stepped into the flat. He'd never been there before.

'Is this the flat you're renting from your cousin?'

'Yes.'

Mårten had a look around, which did not take long as it was a one-bedroom flat.

'A real bachelor's pad.'

'Stupid expression.'

'Yes, it is.'

'Would you like some tea?'

'I never drink tea.'

'Why not?'

'Because I think it's watery.'

'I don't have any red wine.'

Mårten smiled. There was always wine on offer when they had dinner out in Kummelnäs.

'I'll make do with you,' he said.

'Thanks.'

Mårten and Olivia had developed a special relationship of their own. Mårten had been the one taking care of her when her whole world was crumbling down around her, he'd been the one stitching together her broken mind and keeping her on her feet during the last part of her police training. And he had been the one to support her decision to travel to Mexico.

So he could drink whatever he liked as far as she was concerned.

'Are you finding this thing with Mette and me difficult?' Olivia asked as they sat down at the kitchen table. She wanted to get it out of the way so they could talk about more enjoyable things.

'Yes.'

'I think she should ring and apologise.'

'So do I.'

'But she won't.'

'No,' said Mårten.

'So?'

'I just don't want you to do anything silly.'

'Because I'm angry at her?'

'Yes.'

'Why would I do that?'

'Well yes, why would you do that?'

Mårten gave her a look of amusement. He'd got to know Olivia pretty well by now and he knew that she was just as stubborn as his wife. Neither of them would take the first step. But he also knew what a stern warning Mette had been given at her most recent health check-up.

Olivia didn't know that.

And so she didn't know that Mette needed all the stress relief she could get at the moment. An emotional conflict with Olivia was not what she needed. But Mårten had no intention of talking about that.

Not now.

That's not why he was here.

'Was that why you came here? To make sure that I wasn't going to do something "silly"?' Olivia asked.

'No. I came here for my own sake. Yours and mine. Mette and I have been very symbiotic on many levels, you've probably noticed that, but I'm not Mette. Your conflict with Mette has nothing to do with our relationship. It's ours, no matter what happens. I just want you to know that.'

Olivia reached out her hand and put it on Mårten's. A living hand, she thought.

'I know that,' she said.

'Good.'

They looked at each other, kindly. Then Olivia pulled her hand away.

'So have you heard anything from Abbas?' she asked. 'I've tried to call.'

'He's gone to Marseille. With Tom.'

'What's doing there?'

'Dunno. At worst he'll get dragged into something that isn't very nice.'

'Dangerous?'

'Might be.'

'Good job he has the tramp with him, then.'

Olivia immediately heard how childish it sounded and made a gesture. Mårten gave her a little smile.

'That'll sort itself out.'

Olivia shrugged her shoulders. She wasn't particularly interested in sorting things out with Tom Stilton, so she said: 'Do you know a company called Albion?'

'A venture capital firm. Yes. Why?'

'Do you have a moment?'

'Absolutely.'

Olivia gave a brief account of her experience out at Silvergården a few hours earlier and Mårten noticed how shaken she was.

And upset.

He shared her sentiments, in general. He hated venture capitalists. Mårten had a solid history in various left-wing movements. He'd dropped some of his ideological beliefs over the years, but his basic feelings would never go away.

'Profits in the welfare sector are problematic,' he said. 'There are vultures who are just looking to rob taxpayers of money, and there are ambitious and dedicated people who want to run businesses in a more personal and innovative way than municipalities and county councils are able to do. It's a hard balancing act.'

'Silvergården is run by vultures.'

'You know that?'

'I'm assuming that's the case based on what happened today and what that woman out there told me.'

'Yes, but at the same time it would be tremendously counterproductive if Albion consciously mismanaged its business: it's against the fundamental ideas of venture capitalism.'

'Which are?'

'To take over companies, make them extremely profitable and then sell them at a big profit. That's not really possible if they run an organisation into the ground.'

'But maybe you can push it until it reaches breaking point, to be able to produce some great numbers?'

'That's possible. There's been some rather disturbing evidence of that. How come you ended up at Silvergården?'

'Bengt Sahlmann's father died there. But you mustn't tell Mette.'

'That he died there?'

'That I was there. You saw what happened when I went to Customs and Excise.'

Mårten promised to keep quiet about Silvergården. Olivia accompanied him to the door and got another warm hug. Before pulling the door shut she said: 'I hope that Abbas won't get into trouble down there.'

'We hope so too.'

Olivia closed the door and leant against the wall in the hallway. She thought that Mårten had been a little too vague on the topic of Albion. She wanted to know more about Silvergården, about Bengt Sahlmann's reaction to his father's death. She picked up her mobile and called Alex. It went straight to voicemail.

'Hi, it's Olivia Rivera. Could you give me a ring? There are a couple of things I want to ask you.'

She ended the call and went into her bedroom. And what should I do now? She felt that the energy in her body needed some release. She'd done enough googling. Alex was the next step for Silvergården. And she didn't want to bother Sandra. Maybe I should call Ove? Or Lenni? She lay down on her bed. Eeny, meeny, miny, moe,... She fell asleep before she had the chance to choose. With her clothes on.

Chapter 9

Stilton lay awake most of the night in the cramped window alcove, partly because of the erratically flashing green pharmacy sign shining in through the window above his bed, and partly because he'd been hit by a 'What the hell am I doing here?' feeling, a feeling that kicks in when everything else but the darkness is stripped away and the only thing you can hear is your own breathing and a cockroach scratching on the wall.

But most of all he was lying awake because of the blackness in Abbas's eyes. 'Did he bring any knives?' He had, and he knew what he was capable of doing with them.

In his state.

That kept Stilton awake.

He'd used his personal acquaintance with Jean-Baptiste to get a favour. It was based on trust, on what Stilton had seen in the large policeman's eyes, which meant that Stilton had to take responsibility for Abbas's knives.

In the middle of the night Stilton decided that he would look for the knives and hide them. And as soon as he'd thought it, he abandoned the idea, partly because it was a bloody stupid idea, in general, and partly because Abbas was probably sleeping with them under his pillow.

So Stilton lay there tossing and turning. He stared up at the flashing green light on the wall and listened to the sea eroding the rock underneath him, trying to think about nothing at all.

Which is basically impossible.

Just when he'd finally fallen asleep he was awoken.

The nature reserve was located just south of Marseille. Callelongue was large and beautiful, peaceful and wild at the same time. Cliffs and sea on one side, forest and mountains on the other. For nature lovers it was a real experience to hike there.

For Abbas it was just torture.

They'd taken a taxi from the hotel. Stilton had managed to swallow a couple of pieces of bread and some bitter coffee, before Abbas called him from the street. He had no idea what Abbas had eaten, probably nothing.

He was feeding off something else.

Both of them sat in silence the entire car journey – Stilton because he needed some time to wake up in the morning before he could be moderately sociable, and Abbas because he wasn't really there. He was deep within himself, gathering strength for what he would experience out there.

In Callelongue.

The area where Samira's dismembered body had been found.

On the way they passed a racetrack on the outskirts of a large park. Abbas nodded out through the car window.

'That's where Cirque Gruss used to have its tent.'

'Where the racetrack is?'

'Yes, it wasn't there then.'

It was a blank statement.

Everything changes.

The taxi dropped them on the edge of the nature reserve and the driver wondered how they were going to get back.

'Come and get us in an hour,' Abbas said.

Why only an hour? Stilton didn't want to ask, he assumed that Abbas had determined a finite time that he could handle. Or maybe it was just a guess.

But it was Abbas's trip.

He was the one making the decisions.

So they headed into the beautiful surroundings of Callelongue. Stilton had learned his lesson when it came to clothes and was dressed in just a T-shirt. Abbas was wearing a thin beige jacket that he'd bought in Venice many years ago, which perfectly complemented his skin tone. It was chosen with care. Back then.

Now he didn't care any more.

He could just as well have been wearing a sheet.

Neither of them knew where to go, but both of them knew what they were looking for. Stilton was feeling a bit below par after his sleepless night and found himself admiring the beauty of the place. The scenery of sharp shadows, soft terrain and reflections from the protruding rocks. It was a sensation of something from the past, wistful, ancient times passing by.

'There!'

They'd been wandering around aimlessly for almost half an hour before Abbas caught sight of it, among trees and bushes, a piece of plastic tape that had been left behind by the police after they cordoned off the area. They squeezed through the pretty thorny bushes and saw the first hole. A large hole. Further in between the trees they could see another.

Abbas walked over to the first hole and took out his mobile phone. With surprisingly steady hands, he began taking photographs of the hole. Stilton was standing back, in silence. He didn't know what was going on in that tormented man's head. What pictures were flashing in front of his eyes? Wild boar? Gnawed skeletal remains? Or Samira's face when he threw that last knife at her?

A few minutes passed.

Then Abbas put away his mobile and turned to face Stilton.

'Pourquoi?' he said.

A question that could be referring to a great many things at this point. Why was Samira murdered? Why was she buried here of all places? Why was she dismembered? Why wasn't I there? Stilton felt he was referring to all the above.

So he chose one of them.

'Why was she murdered?'

Abbas was crouching down. Stilton saw the marks from the French technicians' tents over the holes. He could imagine what they'd been looking for. Jean-Baptiste would have to tell them whether or not they'd found anything.

Hopefully.

'Why was she murdered?' Abbas said without looking at Stilton. 'She was blind. Totally defenceless. To whom could she have been a threat?'

It was a rhetorical question and Stilton let it fade away. He felt a warm breeze coming in from the sea, the leaves in the bushes were gently sashaying in it, and the sun cast a shadow over the hole, as though nature wanted to cover up the savagery.

Abbas ran a hand over his face before turning to Stilton.

'Well, there's only one person who can answer that,' he said.

'Her agent?'

Abbas got up. He looked down into the hole, looked over at the other hole further in and turned around.

He was done.

He was going to find Philippe Martin.

The taxi was waiting for them as they returned, and drove them to the port right in the centre of Marseille, the Vieux Port. Abbas didn't want to drive any further, he wanted to take the metro for the last bit of the journey.

'Why?' Stilton wondered.

'To arrive in the right state.'

Abbas was preparing himself for the meeting with Martin. The metro would put him in the right mindset, the metro where he'd lived for many years, when he was young – thieving, pick-pocketing, being chased by guards and white Frenchmen, being heckled and jeered.

He wanted to get back into that state again.

Philippe Martin was a white Frenchman.

'Why did you take pictures of the hole out there?' Stilton asked.

'I don't know.'

Abbas stepped into one of the white carriages. Stilton followed him. They stood by the doors. Almost all the seats were empty. The train started moving and Stilton thought about the knives. He knew that Abbas had brought them. He didn't know how many, but he knew he had them, and Stilton didn't quite know how he'd deal with that. He looked into the next carriage. It was virtually empty, a woman was reading a children's book to a child sitting on her knee. On her way to a place called home, Stilton thought. He, on the other hand, was on his way to meet someone who'd abused Samira.

And maybe even dismembered her.

'So how are we going to approach this?' he said.

They got off at Gare Saint-Charles, the main railway station in Marseille. The bar that Philippe Martin allegedly frequented was just outside. The sun was beating down here as well, onto the stone steps of the central station and onto drugged-up Rasta boys sitting hunched over with their heads between their knees, lost in thought. Onto heavily made-up eastern European women leaning up against stone statues and holding their mobiles up right in front of their eyes, engulfed in a world that wasn't their own. And onto cripples sitting with their rags and plastic cups, hoping for a slice of a world that was not theirs either.

Abbas and Stilton passed by it all pretty quickly.

It took Stilton a little longer though, in his head. It wasn't so long ago since he'd been sitting hunched over like that himself, not begging, but he was there. He was an outcast, homeless, and in many respects destitute. He had lain on old rags. Maybe that's why he stopped in front of a scraggy woman to buy a copy of *Macadam*, Marseille's street newspaper. He wasn't going to be able to read it, but it felt good.

'There it is.'

Abbas pointed at a bar a bit further down the street. Stilton followed his hand and saw a rather ordinary looking bar with a red awning and a couple of empty plastic chairs outside.

'How do you know he's there?' he asked.

Abbas didn't answer and went into the bar, closely followed by Stilton. There was very tall sturdy man in a green blazer sitting at the bar, and a dark-skinned old woman standing behind him.

The man sat with his back towards them. Abbas stopped and let Stilton get by. He approached the man.

'Philippe Martin?'

The man turned around. Before that, it could have been just anyone, an accountant on a short lunch break or a psychologist without any patients.

But it wasn't.

Once he had turned around, it became pretty clear who he was. Or at least what he did. And it wasn't anything to do with balancing books or tending to people's souls. He was no stranger to dodgy business dealings. It was written all over his face, judging by the number of scars on his face and the look in his eyes. Both Abbas and Stilton knew that look very well. It was typical of people who lived in that world. Maybe he had beautifully long piano fingers and five pedicured toes on each foot, but he was up to his eyeballs in dodgy dealings.

So Stilton repeated his question.

'Philippe Martin?'

'Are you the guy who owes me money?'

News travels fast in tight circles, Abbas thought. But it was Stilton who replied.

'Yes.'

'You don't owe me money.'

An old maxim: 'To live outside the law you must be honest.' Stilton didn't owe this man any money, and so he wasn't going to take money from him.

'It was just an excuse,' said Stilton, in his melodic Swedish accent. 'I didn't want to advertise what I really wanted.'

'And what's that?'

The man turned away. Stilton began again.

'I'm from Sweden. I make films and I heard that you work in the same genre down here.'

'Who told you that?'

Jean-Baptiste Fabre was definitely the wrong answer. Stilton rifled through his memory and said: 'Pierre Valdoux.'

'Who the hell is that?'

'He imports films to Sweden. You don't know him?'

The man, who clearly was Philippe Martin, looked at the woman behind the bar.

'Do you know who Pierre Valdoux is?' he asked with a smile.

'No.'

'Does your mother know?'

'I don't think so.'

Martin turned towards Stilton.

'You see? No one knows who Pierre Valdoux is. Did you have bullshit for breakfast?'

'No. Did you?'

Stilton could tolerate a certain amount of provocation. No more. He'd taken a big risk now and didn't know how Martin was going to react. Maybe he was messing it all up now and it would just get worse.

Abbas was standing right behind him.

'You wanna say that again?' Martin said and slid down off his bar stool, a kind of physical warning. He was tall, though not quite as tall as Stilton. But he looked in pretty good shape. Stilton looked him in the eye.

'The thing is, Philippe, I haven't had bullshit for breakfast and neither have you. We work in the same industry. We have attitude. Good. But if you could disengage that for a moment and listen to me, you'll soon find out it's about money. I'm interested in investing in a French film for the Swedish market and I have an established distribution network all over the country. I'm prepared to put up quite a bit of cash and I want some good stuff. Are you interested?'

Maybe it was because Stilton was completely calm when he said it, his way of completely ignoring Martin's physical warning, or maybe something else entirely, but Martin listened to what Stilton had to say. Eyes locked on his face. Then he nodded at Abbas.

'Who's that?'

'A guide. He's taking me around Marseille.'

Martin turned to the woman behind the bar.

'We'll go upstairs.'

The room was right above the bar, quite a big room, furnished like a small lounge, with a wide window facing out to the street. The standard of the furniture was a fraction higher than in the bar. A couple of shabby grey armchairs, a curved sofa and a chequered table in the middle. There was a round glass bowl with a goldfish on a small bureau. The light from the street was shining in between a couple of half-open window shutters made from grey wood. Martin walked over to the bureau, pulled out a box and lifted up a pretty hefty gun. He put it down next to the goldfish bowl. Another warning. He gestured towards Stilton to sit down in one of the armchairs. He completely ignored Abbas. Stilton sat down while Martin hung up his green blazer. He was wearing a short-sleeved blue T-shirt underneath that awarded glimpses of his bulging biceps. It also revealed a rather shoddy tattoo of a kitchen knife on his forearm. Why do criminals have such terrible taste? Stilton thought. He could have had a beautiful dagger instead.

Martin sank down into the other armchair.

'Invest, you said?'

'Yes,' Stilton replied.

'How much money are we talking about?'

'It depends. Do you make your own films or do you buy them?'

'Both. Are you after any particular kind of films?'

'Yes. Back home we're mainly used to white girls, eastern Europeans. I'm looking for something a bit more exotic.'

'Blacks and shit?'

'That sort of thing.'

'That's no problem. Do you want the movie type or just straight-up fucking?'

'Straight-up fucking.'

'Good. That's less trouble.'

'Do you work with some girls in particular?'

'Yes, but we can get hold of anyone.'

'I saw some French porn online a while ago, with a bloody gorgeous girl, quite dark, and I think that she was blind?'

'That Arab whore.'

Abbas was standing right behind Stilton, against the wall, so Stilton couldn't see his reaction. He didn't need to.

'Can you get her?' Stilton asked.

'No, she's dead.'

'Shame.'

'Not really. You just have to accept that there's a churn rate in this industry. But I have girls who fuck just as well as her.'

Stilton nodded and asked how they were going to proceed. It solved itself. In the corner of his eye, he saw Abbas move over to the window to close the shutters. The noise of the traffic outside disappeared, as did much of the light. Martin saw it too and reacted.

'What the hell are you doing?' he said in French.

'Closing the shutters.'

It was the first words Abbas uttered in Martin's presence, and he did it in an obvious song-like Marseille dialect, a dialect from the Castellane slums. Martin recognised it immediately.

'And who the fuck told you to do that?'

Stilton saw how nimbly Abbas moved around the room and how softly he smiled as he sat down on the sofa opposite Martin.

'That Arab whore,' he said tenderly.

Stilton felt what was coming, he recognised the scene, it was like a spider spinning its web.

'Who the fuck is this guy?' Martin said to Stilton. 'He's no fucking guide.'

'No. He's Swedish too. He was friends with Samira Villon.'

The penny dropped and Martin felt that this conversation was going the wrong way. He got up, took a few steps towards the goldfish and put one hand on the gun next to the fish bowl. He was still controlled. He'd been in this sort of situation before.

Many times.

'Get out,' he said calmly. 'Now.'

'Or else?' Abbas said.

'Or else I'll blow your Arab-Swedish brains out.'

'That would be a shame.'

Abbas got up and Stilton followed his lead. Was he planning to leave? Abbas went towards the door and Stilton went after him. Martin had lifted up the gun from the bureau a little and followed their movements with the barrel. Abbas stopped in the doorway and turned to Martin.

'Your goldfish has died.'

Martin peered at the aquarium and then a long black knife went through the top of the hand holding the gun. The gun fell to the floor and Stilton threw himself at him. He'd guessed how strong Martin would be and trusted that he was stronger. A year of island life had given him some real brute strength in his arms.

But it took a while.

Abbas stood still in the doorway and observed the fight. Neither of them was making any noise. When Stilton ducked a hefty punch and got behind Martin, it was basically over. He lifted the Frenchman up off the floor and hurled him over the sofa. His many years of police training stood him in good stead, and he pulled one of Martin's arms up so high behind his back that the Frenchman screamed for the first time.

His arm was about to snap.

Abbas was there in a flash. He'd prepared himself for this situation in many ways, including bringing some blue cable ties. Together they managed to bring the other arm around as well and they tied his wrists so tightly that it was cutting into his flesh. They fastened another one around his ankles.

'Stand him up against the wall.'

Abbas nodded towards the wall next to the bureau. Stilton dragged Martin up and pushed him up against the wall. Martin was just about to headbutt him when he saw the knife. The other black knife. Abbas held it right in front of his face. Martin pressed himself up against the wall.

'Open your mouth,' Abbas said in French.

Martin spat in his face.

Tough guy.

Abbas didn't flinch. He let the spit run down his cheek and onto the floor. And then he raised the knife a little closer to Martin's face and felt its weight in his hands.

'Open your mouth.'

'Who the hell are you?!'

'Open your mouth.'

Martin stared at the knife in front of his nose. He shifted his gaze and saw Abbas's eyes. Then he opened his mouth. Abbas quickly pulled out a small white towel he'd brought with him. He used his free hand to press the towel into Martin's mouth.

Deep inside.

Stilton took a few steps back. This was Abbas's show. He would have liked to leave the room now, not be there, not see, and not have to lie to Jean-Baptiste.

And more than anything, so as not to have to bear witness to a side of Abbas that he knew existed, but always tried to let it slip from memory.

'You can go outside if you want,' Abbas said without looking at Stilton.

'I'll stay.'

Abbas nodded and looked at Martin again. This ruthless porn producer had a different expression on his face. He was clearly the underdog now and was having trouble breathing through his nose. A keen but unhealthy cocaine habit had blocked his nasal passages. He snuffled.

'Close your eyes,' Abbas said.

Martin allowed his gaze to wander past Abbas and over to Stilton, as though he was seeking some kind of help from him. He didn't get any. Stilton said: 'I think you should do as he says.'

Martin closed his eyes. Abbas leant in towards him.

'Now maybe you can imagine what it's like being blind? Not knowing where the knife is? Not being able to see whether I'm raising it to stab you or angling it to cut straight across your cheek? How does it feel?'

A murmur could be heard from behind the towel.

At this stage, Abbas knew whom he was dealing with – a man who wasn't going to talk unless he was forced to, in particular about anything that could tie him to the murder and butchering of Samira. So he carefully placed the tip of the knife onto Martin's left eyelid and pushed it in about a centimetre. The scream could be heard through the towel. Not loud, but the fact that it could be heard at all was indicative of its intensity. Stilton saw that Martin's right leg was shaking uncontrollably. A thin stream of blood was running down his cheek from his eye.

'Now you're half blind,' Abbas said as he moved the tip of the knife and placed it on the other eyelid. 'Now you know who I am. I'm going to remove the towel from your mouth. If you scream, I'll stick the knife in your other eye and you'll be completely blind. OK? I'm going to ask you quite a few things and I want you to answer.'

Abbas pulled the towel out of Martin's mouth without easing the pressure of the knife against his eyelid. Martin breathed in deeply. He was shocked.

'Were you the one who killed Samira?'

It took a few seconds before Martin's voice managed to emerge from the cave of horror that he was in, but it emerged. Broken, hoarse.

'No,' he said.

'Who did it?'

'I don't know.'

Abbas removed the tip of the knife from his eyelid. Martin's head was shaking. He didn't know where the knife was. He had no idea what Abbas was intending to do with it. He chewed his lips until they were bloody.

'Did she get my letters?' Abbas asked.

'What letters?'

'I sent four letters to her, from Sweden, in blue envelopes. Did they get here?'

'Yes.'

'Did you rip them up?'

'No.'

'Did you read them to Samira?'

'Yes.'

'What was the first word in every letter?'

Martin swallowed hard without saying a word.

'You ripped them up.'

Abbas put the tip of the knife back against Martin's uncut eyelid. Martin's jaw was moving up and down.

'How did you get her to take part?' Abbas asked. 'Did you drug her?'

Martin nodded so slightly that it was hardly noticeable.

'You drugged her?'

Another nod.

'What do you know about the murder?'

'I told the police what I know.'

'And what was that?'

Martin was breathing with short heavy breaths, his chest pumping under his T-shirt, the words gushing out of his mouth.

'She was supposed to be part of a film shoot, I wasn't involved in it, I was just renting her out. Someone collected her here and then she never came back.'

'Who collected her?'

'A taxi.'

'Where was the film supposedly being shot?'

'I don't know.'

'Who else was going to be in the film?'

'No idea.'

'Philippe.'

Abbas's voice was still quiet and controlled.

'I think you're lying,' he said.

Abbas carefully wiped away the blood under Martin's eye with the towel.

'I'm almost certain you are,' he said. 'Can you feel the knife against your eye?'

Martin nodded, his head shaking.

'So I'm going to ask you one more time,' Abbas said. 'Who was there at the shooting of the film?'

Martin was silent. What he was going to be forced to say would warrant the death penalty, but he said it nonetheless.

In the end.

'Le Taureau... I don't know his real name.'

'Philippe.'

'I don't know any more...'

'Just Le Taureau?'

'Yes.'

'Did you tell the police that? About Le Taureau?'

'No. I wasn't involved in any of it... I just...'

Martin's voice became weaker and weaker, before long he'd probably pass out. Abbas noticed. He leant forward a little and whispered in Martin's ear.

'My name is Abbas el Fassi.'

Martin sank down against the wall, his jaw still busy moving up and down. Abbas lowered the knife and went towards the door. Martin fell down onto the floor. Stilton walked towards the open door. Martin turned his head, and with his good eye he looked at the door as it slammed shut.

Then he turned up to look at the fish bowl.

The goldfish was lying at the bottom, dead.

Chapter 10

Alex had called Olivia once he'd listened to her voicemail message, later that night. Olivia was already sleeping by then. When in turn she listened to her messages in the morning, he said that he had something to do in the city and suggested meeting for lunch at the Prinsen restaurant. If she was free.

She was.

Not because she thought it was an ideal venue exactly. She didn't like meeting people at restaurants to talk about sensitive matters. There were always people sitting around and then waiters came by and you were forced to order something. Olivia wasn't particularly keen on sitting down to lunch at all, for that matter. She preferred wolfing down a prawn salad, or instant noodles. Everything took such an age in restaurants.

But she was the one who'd requested a meeting, so Prinsen it was.

In a leather booth.

Good.

At least there was some chance of getting some privacy.

Alex was there before her and had ordered a beer. He was wearing a thick grey knitted jumper and was talking on his mobile when Olivia appeared. He nodded at her to sit down opposite him as he finished leaving a message. The last thing she heard him say was: 'Check with Customs and Excise again.'

'Customs and Excise?'

Olivia took her jacket off while she asked the question.

'I must remember to call them after we're done.'

'Why?'

There she was again, he thought. She ought to be a journalist.

'Because I'm working on an article about that missing stash of drugs you tipped me off about.'

'Me. What do you mean *me*? You haven't dragged me into this, have you?!'

'No, you're just a source.'

'What do you mean, *source*?'

Olivia was beginning to get worked up. She knew that she'd told him about the missing drugs and was assuming that he would keep this information to himself. And all of a sudden she was now a 'source'?

'I'm a journalist, Olivia, you're well aware of that. What you tell me off the record remains just that. But if I need to use it I will. Without getting you involved. We do have source protection in this country.'

Olivia was certainly familiar with that and calmed down a little.

'What have you found out about the stash?' she asked.

Alex was under no obligation to answer. Quite the opposite, in fact. But as it Olivia was the one who'd told him about it, he felt he should be offering her something in return.

'It was very large and it was only so-called internet drugs, mainly 5-IT. And it could fetch up to three million on the streets. So I understand that it caused a commotion, as you said, when it disappeared.'

'And it was Bengt Sahlmann who was supposed to be investigating their disappearance?'

'Yes, they've confirmed that.'

'Who's "they"?'

'A woman, among other people. Gabriella Forsman, she was the one who raised the alarm when the drugs went missing.'

'Have you met her?'

'Yes.'

'Did you like her?'

'Overly red hair, overly large breasts, and overly red lips.'

I like this guy, Olivia thought.

'And I've talked to the woman in charge of the murder investigation,' Alex said. 'Mette Olsäter.'

I don't like this guy, Olivia thought.

'Why did you talk to her?!'

'You know her?'

'Why?'

'Your reaction.'

'I know her and would be damn grateful if you would keep me completely out of any chats you have with her. Both as a source and whatever else you bloody call it.'

'Of course. I said that, didn't I? Sources remain anonymous. Mentioning your name would be an offence. Would you like a beer?'

'No.'

Both of them looked at each other. Alex smiled a little. Olivia did not. For the life of her she didn't want to be linked with this journalist Alex Popovic when it came to Customs and Excise or the Sahlmann murder investigation. Things were messy enough with Mette as they were.

'I'll have some mineral water,' she said.

Alex ordered some sort of soup and a mineral water for Olivia. When it arrived, Olivia had cooled off a little and reminded herself it was she who'd requested this meeting.

But it was Alex who changed the subject and starting talking about what she wanted to discuss.

'So you wanted to ask something?' he said.

'Yes.'

Olivia felt that she needed to back down a little and soften up around the edges. She wanted their conversation to have another tone. A private tone. An off-the-record tone, as he said.

'Listen, I'm sorry if I snapped,' she said. 'I have my reasons. I'll tell you about that some other time, somewhere else.'

'Yes, please.'

Alex smiled at her. Olivia smiled back a few seconds later. There, that felt a bit better. He was probably ready now.

'Well,' she began. 'When we met last time, you told me about a private dinner during which Sahlmann had had some outburst over his father's death, right?'

'Yes.'

'Was it directed at anyone in particular?'

'Yes.'

'Who?'

Alex slurped a couple of spoonfuls of soup. Somewhat too carefully. Olivia saw that he was thinking, deliberating. Why? Was he trying to protect someone?

'Is it sensitive?' she asked.

'Yes and no.'

'Was it directed at you?'

'No.'

Alex laughed, as though it was a fairly legitimate question.

'It was directed at a mutual acquaintance,' he said. 'And I'm not that keen on revealing his name.'

'Because?'

'Because it feels like gossip.'

Oh my god, you're a journalist, Olivia thought. Don't you live on gossip? But she didn't say it.

'I understand. But you have source protection,' she said and smiled.

Alex looked at Olivia. Reversed roles. He actually had no problem telling her who this person was, far from it. He just wanted to keep her on her toes. She was pretty full on.

'It won't go any further,' she said. 'I promise.'

'OK. It was Jean Borell.'

'And who's that?'

'You don't know him?'

'No?'

'He's a very successful venture capitalist.'

'Why did Bengt have a go at him?'

'Because his company owns the nursing home where Bengt's father died. Albion.'

Olivia was having a sip of water. She pressed the glass against her lips extra firmly and leant back. If she hadn't had back support she would probably have ended up on the floor. She swallowed the water and hoped that she sounded as she did before.

'Albion?' she said.

'Yes. *Dagens Nyheter* did an investigative series of articles about it a while back, did you read it?'

'No, I was abroad then.'

Why didn't I find it online?

'What was it about?' she said.

'It went through its organisation here in Sweden. Some heavy stuff. I can send it over if you want.'

'Yes, please,' Olivia said. 'How did Borell react to Bengt's outburst?'

'Bengt was quite drunk and Borell is a first-class arsehole. He was bloody condescending and Bengt was close to attacking him. It was really awkward.'

Olivia nodded and smiled.

'So you hang out with some first-class arseholes?'

'Very occasionally. Borell also went to Lundsberg, at the same time as Bengt and me. That's why we had the dinner. A few of us tend to get together for reunion dinners every now and again.'

Alex peered at his watch while popping some nicotine gum into his mouth.

'Thank you for taking the time to meet me,' Olivia said.

'Are we done?'

'I'm done.'

'Why did you want to know who Bengt had had a go at?'

'I was just curious.'

Alex looked at her and Olivia knew that it was the wrong answer. Just like last time.

Even if it was true.

'It's all a bit confused in my mind right now,' she said. 'I need to sort it out. Why don't we have a beer some time?'

That generally worked.

'Absolutely!'

It worked.

She didn't trust Alex. Not after that business with Customs and Excise and Mette. She didn't want to initiate him into her thoughts, she just wanted to use him as a source of information.

Nothing more.

They parted ways just after one o'clock. Alex was heading back to the office and took a taxi. Olivia started walking towards Söder.

Feeling rather overwrought.

Bengt Sahlmann and Albion's owner Jean Borell were personal acquaintances?

Bengt had accused Borell of being responsible his father's death?

Borell had been bloody condescending towards him?

What did that mean?

That's when the thought hit her: Bengt Sahlmann had also talked to Claire Tingman at Silvergården! Had he been told the same things as Olivia? Maybe he'd found out a load more shit about how the nursing home was run? Were Alex's suspicions correct, then? Had Bengt's material been about the negligent care at Silvergården? Had he threatened Jean Borell with publicising it as revenge for his father's death?

It was certainly possible.

Olivia quickly developed a theory: had Borell murdered Sahlmann and stolen his computer? Because it contained explosive material about Silvergården? Could that really be a motive for murder?

How much was at stake? Surely more than just a poorly run nursing home? There had to be more to it.

How could she find out?

Olivia stopped at the quayside and looked out over Stockholm. She knew herself pretty well, and she was all too aware of her tendency towards fanciful theories.

But theories can be proven, she thought. Or disproven. For now, she still wanted to try and prove hers. It could be correct after all.

Then Sandra called.

'Hi! How are you?'

'Yeah, all right,' Sandra said. 'Charlotte and I are sitting with a priest, talking about Dad's funeral and we're wondering when we can have it.'

'I don't know, but I can ask someone who'll know.'

'Thanks. Maybe you can ask about the computer too? Whether they've found it?'

'Will do. Say hi to Charlotte.'

Olivia ended the call and rang Lisa Hedqvist at the National Crime Squad, not Mette. After some small talk about her trip abroad, Olivia asked about the funeral. Lisa promised to get back to Charlotte and Sandra.

'And she asked about the laptop too. Have you found it?' Olivia enquired.

Without thinking about the implications. But Lisa knew. And she'd been there when Mette had bemoaned the occurrences at Customs and Excise, and Lisa knew that Olivia wasn't very high up on Mette's list of favourite people. So she didn't really know what to say. And Olivia picked up on that pretty quickly.

'You don't need to answer that,' she said.

'We haven't found it.'

'Thanks. Bye.'

The laptop was still missing.

It was still possible that Jean Borell had stolen it.

Her theory was still relevant.

Chapter 11

It was dusk in Marseille. The low sun was washing over the magnificent port, reflecting off the hundreds of masts in the bay and up across the bars on the quayside. It was still warm enough to sit outside.

Even though it was November.

I live in the wrong climate, Stilton thought to himself. He was sitting with Abbas at a dark wooden table right at the edge of the quay, soaking up the warm rays of sunshine. It was a fish restaurant. Both of them were hungry even though it was only just five o'clock. When Abbas got the menu he'd commented that they had seafood risotto.

'You liked it, right?'

'Absolutely. Do they have any meat?'

They ordered dorado and a carafe of white wine. Abbas did the ordering. Stilton noted that he'd ordered wine, but he didn't comment on it. It was, as he'd said, Abbas's trip. When they'd got their carafe and glasses and prepared to take their first sip, Stilton said: 'So what was the first word in the letters you wrote to Samira?'

'Hi.'

Abbas tasted the wine. He looked just like anyone else in this town, accompanied by a large pale foreigner. He didn't look like the person Stilton had seen just a couple of hours earlier. He wanted to forget about that person. But Abbas had done what he'd needed to do and he'd done it his way, the way he'd come to know growing up. Now he was sitting sipping a cold glass of white wine, looking out over the beautiful port.

'You probably won't be very popular after this,' Stilton said.

'I never was, that's why I left.'

Stilton nodded. He watched Abbas's eyes shift to the side, over to another table further in. There was a man sitting at the table. Stilton didn't recognise him.

Abbas did.

It was the barman who'd told them where to find Philippe Martin. And then called Martin to blab that Abbas owed him money. Then he watched the barman get up and hide behind a stone pillar. Hidden when viewed from Abbas's direction, without thinking that his reflection could be seen in the window. Abbas watched the barman get out his mobile while quickly glancing over at Abbas's table.

'Someone you know?' Stilton wondered.

'No.'

Abbas looked at Stilton again.

'Le Taureau,' he said. 'The Bull.'

'Yes.'

Abbas had called Marie on the way to the restaurant to check whether she'd ever heard of anyone by that name. She hadn't. He'd made two more calls, to people from before. No one knew who The Bull was.

'Maybe he was lying,' Stilton suggested.

'Do you think so?'

'No.'

Neither did Abbas. He'd been standing close enough to Martin to smell the fear. He knew that Martin hadn't been lying.

'Samira never returned from that film shoot. She was found murdered shortly afterwards. The Bull was there at the shoot.'

'One plus one makes two?'

'Generally, yes.'

'So how do we find The Bull?'

Stilton didn't feel entirely comfortable articulating these words. The Bull. It sounded extremely silly to him, but out of respect for Abbas he took it seriously.

'I don't know,' Abbas said. 'Maybe Jean-Baptiste has a few ideas?'

'Yes.'

Stilton was already feeling uncomfortable about the meeting with Jean-Baptiste. He was convinced that Abbas's actions towards Philippe Martin would spread through certain circles in Marseille like wildfire.

And so it would reach Jean-Baptiste just as quickly.

And then Stilton would have to give some answers.

The fish interrupted his thoughts. It was lightly grilled and deboned, and had a slightly nutty flavour. Both of them ate in silence. Stilton noticed that Abbas was keeping the same pace as him with the wine. He's certainly affected by what happened over there, Stilton thought.

Comfort of some kind.

Even savagery is not seamless.

Once the sun had dipped down into the Mediterranean it turned a little colder. Stilton pulled on an extra jumper. They'd finished the meal, but Abbas sat still. He'd ordered another couple of glasses of wine, not a carafe. Stilton saw that his expression had calmed. The alcohol perhaps, or a reaction to something else? Abbas looked out over the old port, his gaze sweeping over the shabby white houses winding their way up the hill on the other side.

'I lived there for a short time.'

Stilton followed Abbas's pointing hand up to the houses on the other side of the port.

'Is that the Arab quarter?'

'No, I lived there when my old ma disappeared.'

Stilton noted his choice of words. Abbas referred to his father as 'my dad' and his mother as 'the old ma'.

'When did she disappear?'

'When I was seven.'

Stilton thought about Luna's mother, the wind walker. About absconding mothers.

'Where did she go?' he asked.

'Well, if you disappear you disappear. I have no idea. I grew up with my dad.'

Abbas gulped some more wine.

'He couldn't handle me,' he said. 'He just wanted out. Every time he got drunk he told me about the Gulag prisoner.'

'Who was that?'

'A prisoner who woke in the barracks one night, got up without any clothes on and sewed buttons on his chest and took an axe and went out into the winter storm. He'd had enough, Dad said. I think he wanted to do what that guy did, escape from something he was hopelessly trapped in.'

'So did he do it?'

'No, he was trapped in his life. How do you escape that?'

'Commit suicide.'

'He didn't dare. So he took it out on me instead.'

Stilton followed Abbas's gaze over to the quay on the other side again.

There was a black car standing there.

'Is it them?'

'Yes.'

The man who answered was sitting in the passenger seat and had a thick bandage across one eye. The eye that had been cut. His lips were chewed up. The man sitting behind the wheel looked over at the quayside on the other side of the water. At Stilton and Abbas. He gripped the wheel with his large coarse hands, with a half-smoked, unlit cigarette hanging out of the corner of his mouth.

'And they were looking for Samira's murderer?'

'Yes.'

'And they were Swedish?'

'They said they were.'

'Why were they looking for Samira's murderer?'

'How the fuck should I know?'

'How much did you say?'

'Nothing.'

The man behind the wheel peered at Martin, at the bandage across his injured eye.

'Nothing? With what they did to your eye?'

'Well, I didn't bloody know anything.'

'You knew about me.'

'I'd forgotten that.'

The man behind the wheel looked at Martin. They knew each other from the streets, had done business together, neither of them trusted the other. Now one of them was forced to trust the other, that he hadn't disclosed the wrong information. If he had, there were two people who knew the wrong things – the people sitting on the quayside opposite. Could he take that risk? Martin had been tortured.

But he chose to lie low.

'We'll have to watch them,' he said.

'You go ahead. I don't want to be involved.'

'OK.'

'He's lethal with those knives.'

The man behind the wheel saw big Martin look down at his seat with his good eye. Someone had scared the shit out of him, properly. He lit the cigarette and looked out over the water again, at Abbas and Stilton.

Knives?

Their glasses were empty. Abbas's gaze had shifted down to the water below the edge of the quayside. His body had sunk down a little. He suddenly looked very small, Stilton thought. Forlorn. He saw Abbas's head rocking a little. And it wasn't just the wine that was flowing freely – he saw tears streaming down Abbas's face. Stilton stretched out his hand and put it on Abbas's arm. He kept it there a while. He hadn't forgotten that Abbas had been there for him on various occasions, on various side streets in Stockholm.

'Not everything comes back, Abbas, you have to realise that.'

'I know.'

Abbas looked up.

'Shall we go?'

Stilton nodded. As he got up he saw Abbas grabbing a load of sachets of sugar from the table.

'What are you doing?'

'Nicking a few sachets.'

'What are you going to do with them?'

'I'll get the bill.'

Abbas went off. Stilton looked out over the port and felt his mobile vibrating in his pocket. He'd put it on silent.

He took his phone out.

A text, a short one. 'I've fixed a lock for your door. Luna.'

He read it twice, it was like a message from outer space.

Stilton put his phone back in his pocket just as Abbas was coming back.

'Shall we walk back to the hotel?' he said.

Stilton looked up. Dusk had changed to Mediterranean darkness and it was quite a way to walk. Through some equally dark streets.

'OK.'

They walked around the old port to the other side of the quay, both of them caught up in their own thoughts. They passed by a black car with two men sitting inside and carried on past the bars and restaurants with scores of people sitting outside.

Neither of them noticed the car's headlights being turned on.

Stilton assumed that Abbas was taking the fastest route and didn't react when he suddenly turned into a small street. He just followed him. Abbas on the other hand did react once they'd walked a couple of hundred metres. It was a small street without any shops, with tall buildings on either side, and it was dark down on the pavement. That's why Abbas noticed the car lights behind them. When he looked over his shoulder, he saw that the car was moving just as slowly as they were walking. Has the news already spread? he wondered, moving his hand across his body. The knives were where they were supposed to be.

Stilton didn't notice any of this. The wine had dulled his senses. He felt secure with Abbas by his side.

He wouldn't have if he'd known what was going on in Abbas's head: stay and wait for the car and go for a confrontation? Or turn off?

He turned off. Sideways into a narrow alleyway, too tight for a car. Stilton hardly managed to keep up.

'Are we going in here?'

'Yes. Come on!'

Abbas was moving quickly and Stilton followed him. Now all his senses were in gear again. He turned his head and saw a car stop down on the street. Were they being followed? Abbas turned another corner. Stilton ran after him. There were two bins standing against the wall. He had to weave in between them. Then he almost tripped over a black cat that came shooting out from behind one of the bins. He managed to grab hold of a windowsill and stopped himself from falling. He heard a clattering noise a long way behind him.

He had no idea how long they ran between the densely packed houses, but they suddenly emerged through an archway into a small square with some empty vegetable stalls. A young man was wheeling an elderly woman across the square in a wheelchair. The wheels were squeaking loudly. Abbas hailed a taxi that was driving past and jumped in the back seat. Stilton jumped in the front. The driver looked straight ahead and asked: 'Where are we going?'

Stilton gave the hotel address in his heavy Swedish accent, which inspired the taxi driver to try to do a little detour, until Abbas tapped him on the shoulder.

'Take the fastest route,' he said.

In his expressive Marseille dialect.

So the taxi drove straight to Hotel Richelieu. Abbas paid and both of them jumped out. There was a seedy nightclub right opposite the hotel. The music was pounding out onto the street. There were a couple of hefty, drunk Russians standing at the entrance, trying to get in. There'd probably be a fight next. Abbas and Stilton walked in through the hotel doors. They'd already disappeared up the stairs as the black car drove past.

Once it had passed by, the driver put his foot down and disappeared off into the darkness.

* * *

Darkness had fallen outside Olivia's window too, another kind of darkness, heavy Swedish autumnal darkness. It was probably that that prompted her to light the candles on the table. She sat on the small sofa in her living room with her laptop in front of her, the candles just behind it. They weren't creating much light, but all she needed to see was the keyboard.

She'd been reading for quite a while already.

It was both interesting and alarming. It was *Dagens Nyheter*'s series of articles on Albion. A number of journalists had been digging and analysing and checking.

Thoroughly.

They'd turned the company upside down and found some damning information. The cases of negligence at Albion's nursing homes hit them one after the other. They had escalated in the past year. Three different homes in three places around Sweden were subject to external investigations due to negligent care. Several municipalities were currently reviewing their contracts with Albion. The company had been subject to scathing criticism. Various representatives had defended the organisation in different ways.

These did not include Jean Borell.

He was nowhere to be found in any of the articles.

Journalists all over the world had tried to reach him for comments without success. The only person they'd managed to reach was his closest colleague in Sweden, Magnus Thorhed. On one occasion, a journalist had bumped into Borell in Australia, during the Australian Open, more or less by accident. Borell had agreed to a short interview about Albion after the match and had then disappeared.

Olivia started googling Jean Borell but there was hardly anything about him. Born in Danderyd, living in London – she didn't find much more. She hadn't expected to either. It was a typical sign of people at that level, in that world – they were invisible in the media.

So she went back to reading the articles.

What was pretty clear was Albion's precarious situation. It was a company struggling for survival. They'd generated enormous profits over the years. In 2011 alone, municipalities and county councils had bought services from private companies for 71 billion Swedish kronor. She didn't know how much of that had ended up at Albion, but it was probably quite a sizeable chunk. So they weren't talking peanuts. The debate about profits in the welfare sector had hit Albion's reputation hard. But the company had party-political ties – several leading Moderate Party politicians supported the organisation. A multi-million deal was currently under negotiation with the City of Stockholm. A strongly criticised deal. The critics highlighted all the nursing homes that had been mismanaged by Albion. Instead the politicians talked about Silvergården in Nacka, as an example of an exceptionally well-run organisation.

And that's where Olivia found the motive.

That's where her theory crossed the finishing line.

Another scandal, particularly one at Silvergården, would be catastrophic for Albion. It could ruin the entire new multi-million deal.

Olivia leant back on her sofa and rubbed her eyes. She'd been leaning closer and closer to the screen. Now her eyes were really aching.

But it was worth it.

If the material on Bengt Sahlmann's laptop really was about the scandals at Silvergården and was on its way to a journalist at *DN*, then that was a clear motive.

A clear motive to silence him and steal his laptop.

The world had witnessed far lesser murder motives.

So what to do now? I still don't know what Sahlmann's material was about. It could be something completely different. It could have been about the missing stash of drugs at Customs and Excise.

And then Mette appeared.

Not literally, but in her thoughts. Should she call Mette and tell her what she was thinking? She knew that Mette very much respected her 'intuition'. But as things were now? 'Who do you think you bloody are?' The words still stung.

She wasn't going to call Mette.

Not yet.

Not before she knew what Sahlmann's material was about.

She blew out the candles.

Chapter 12

Abbas woke up long before Stilton, for once. It was only half past three and his mouth was all furry. He showered, the whole procedure, and left the hotel. He wandered around for hours, with heavy clouds in the sky, and watched the city come to life. He watched bakeries getting ready for a new day of business, vegetable stalls rolling up to the market near the port, fishing boats coming in to deliver the night's catch, and tired waiters putting out the first tables. But he didn't really see any of it. He was deep in thought. He knew what he had to do and he hated it. But there was no other way right now. He had to move forward.

He had to find out more.

So when the time had come he went into the shop, a porn shop. The man behind the till was quite young. That bothered Abbas. But he could go to more such shops – there were plenty of them in the area where he'd ended up.

'Le Taureau?'

'Yes.'

'Never heard of him.'

So Abbas went to the next shop. There was an older man who had considerably more filth on his conscience. He'd been running the shop for fifteen years.

'What? You mean a porn actor?'

'I don't know, but he's involved in making porn films.'

'Sorry, no one I know of, but there are quite a few people involved in this business.'

The man moved towards the shelves behind Abbas, stuffed full of porn, one of the world's most lucrative industries.

'Why not look to see if you can find something?'

Abbas started perusing the DVDs, hundreds of them. There was hardly any difference between the covers. Naked women, naked genitals, dead eyes. But he carried on looking. He knew what he might find and hoped that he wouldn't.

But he did.

After about fifteen minutes.

A porn film with a cover like all the others, but one clear difference.

The woman on the cover was Samira.

Abbas looked on the back of the DVD. There was a small picture of an oiled man, but no names.

'Have you seen this one?' he asked the man behind the till.

'No, I don't like porn. I mainly watch stuff like Buñuel, Haneke and Kurosawa.'

Abbas bought the film.

Stilton sat on the hotel terrace and wondered where Abbas was. No note. Nothing on his mobile. He'd called but there was no answer. He looked out across the bay and sipped his coffee. It was drizzling, or rather sprinkling. Light, warm sprinkling rain. Stilton didn't take any notice of it. He felt that he was running out of steam and wondered how much longer the trip would last. He'd fulfilled his primary task – making contact with Jean-Baptiste. He hoped that the large policeman would get back to him soon.

But what then?

How long would he have to stay here looking for The Bull? A person they didn't even know existed.

Abbas would stay for a long time, he knew that. And he understood it. This was Abbas's major trauma. But how long did Abbas want him to stay? He could probably go home as soon as he'd been in touch with Jean-Baptiste, if it wasn't for one thing.

Philippe Martin.

And what Abbas had done to him.

Which made Abbas fair game here.

Stilton had come to know that much about this city – Jean-Baptiste had told him enough about it. And he knew that Jean-Baptiste would not be keeping an eye out for Abbas, particularly not after the knife attack on Martin.

So?

A guardian angel?

Was he going to stay as some kind of bodyguard for Abbas?

'Come!'

Stilton turned his head. Abbas was on his way to their 'suite' with a DVD player under his arm. The hotel porter had managed to get hold of one in exchange for some cash. Stilton got up and followed him.

Abbas rigged up the DVD player with the rather outdated television in the room. All this in complete silence. Stilton sat on the edge of the bed.

He sensed what it was about.

When Abbas pulled out the DVD from his jacket it was confirmed.

'It's a film with Samira,' Abbas said.

He put the DVD in and sat on a chair next to Stilton, holding on to the remote control. He didn't turn it on directly. First he took off his shoes and socks. His feet weren't sweating at all even though he'd been walking around for hours. Stilton sat and waited.

Quite a while.

'Do you really want to see this?' Stilton finally asked him.

'No.'

Abbas put on the film.

It was a porn film just like most other porn films. A pokey room, harsh lighting, poor sound. A woman egging a man on, giving him a blow job, playing with herself, before the man finally starts fucking her, in this case from behind against an armchair.

It was a routine.

Or it would have been if it hadn't been for the beautiful Moroccan woman bending over the armchair.

Samira.

Suddenly Abbas stopped the film and wound back a bit. The camera had zoomed in on Samira's face. That's when he saw it. The thin gold necklace. A necklace that he'd once given her at the circus, secretly. Now she was wearing it. He put the film back on. The act continued.

Stilton found it quite uncomfortable to watch, considering the circumstances. What was most uncomfortable is that he got a hard-on, a biological reflex that he couldn't control. He held his hands over his groin so that Abbas wouldn't see.

Suddenly Abbas paused the film again, during a close up of the naked man: robust build, oiled, quite muscular, dark hair.

'Do you think that's The Bull?'

'No idea.'

Abbas turned it off. The screen went black. Stilton felt his erection soften. He looked at Abbas and guessed what was going on in his head.

Then Stilton's mobile rang. He looked at it.

'It's Jean-Baptiste.'

'Can you take the call out there?'

'Sure.'

Stilton got up from the bed and left the room. When the door slammed shut, Abbas went over to the window alcove, Stilton's 'bedroom'. He pulled back the curtain and looked out over the Mediterranean. He stood completely still and let his eyes close. A couple of minutes later, he raised one hand and slowly moved it around in front of him, back and forth, as though he was stroking an invisible shoulder.

All three of them met up at the Beau Rivage bar down in the port. Jean-Baptiste had been the one to suggest it. He was there on time, unlike Stilton and Abbas. Stilton had waited out in the hotel corridor after the conversation with Jean-Baptiste. He felt that Abbas wanted to be in the room alone. More than an hour passed before he came out. And by then they were almost half an hour late already, but Stilton had called to let Jean-Baptiste know. They scurried towards the bar without noticing the black car pulling over to the pavement just behind them.

Jean-Baptiste stood up as they walked in. He had chosen a table in the corner of the outdoor seating area, protected by a small hedge. It had stopped drizzling and the sun had almost reached the table. As Abbas approached, Jean-Baptise gave him a big hug and a smile.

'You've lost weight.'

'And it's ended up on you.'

Both of them smiled and sat down.

'Le Taureau,' said Abbas.

He cut straight to the chase.

'Do you know the name?'

'The Bull? As the name of what?'

'Of the man who may have murdered Samira Villon.'

Jean-Baptiste peered at Stilton. He thought that he was the one who was going to provide information. Stilton gestured with his hand, discreetly.

'No,' said Jean-Baptiste, 'I've never heard that name. The Bull you say?'

'Yes.'

Abbas pulled out the porn film he'd bought and pointed at the picture of the oiled man.

'Could that be him?'

'That's Jacques Messon.'

'Maybe he was known as The Bull?'

'It's possible, but he was shot dead about six months ago outside a bar.'

Abbas looked at the cover of the DVD.

'But I can ask around,' Jean-Baptiste said.

'Thank you. Have you got some information?'

Given that Abbas didn't know Jean-Baptiste very well he was rather forward. But the policeman didn't react, he knew very well what it was about.

So Jean-Baptiste spent a while updating them how far the French investigation had got. He didn't reveal too much internal information, just enough for them to get an idea of the status quo – how she had gone missing during a film shoot, the location of which remained unknown. It could have been a hotel room, a flat, or a house in the countryside – they had no idea. And there was no information about who'd been there at the time either.

And so it went on.

It wasn't very impressive.

'Sadly a dead porn actress isn't really at the top of the agenda right now. I'm sorry,' he said. 'There have been a great deal of internal rumblings of late.'

Stilton saw that Abbas was gritting his teeth.

'So you have no potential suspect?' Stilton asked.

'Not at the moment.'

'Who told you about the film shoot? That it had taken place?'

'I can't tell you that unfortunately.'

'Did she have drugs in her system?' Abbas asked.

'Yes.'

'What did she die of?'

'Do you really want to know?'

'Yes.'

Jean-Baptiste and Stilton exchanged looks again, as though the large policeman was wondering whether Abbas could take this. Stilton nodded almost imperceptibly.

'She was subjected to serious abuse and then she was strangled. That was the cause of death. Then she was cut up into six pieces and buried in a nature reserve.'

'We've been there,' Abbas said.

As though the horrific details had passed him by.

They hadn't, Stilton knew that.

'And you have no idea about a possible motive?' Abbas said.

'No.'

'Clues? DNA? Was there semen inside her?'

'On her body. But that's probably not that strange.'

'Why?'

'Well, she was murdered during or after the making of a porn film, I just said that.'

184

Stilton noted that Jean-Baptiste's tone had changed slightly. Abbas probably shouldn't push this too far. But he continued: 'Has the DNA been matched?'

'Abbas.'

'Yes.'

Jean-Baptiste leant over towards the frustrated man.

'I've told you what I can. And I've done so because Tom asked me to. Don't push me further.'

Abbas looked at Jean-Baptiste and understood that he needed to back down.

'But, that said, we have questioned her agent,' Jean-Baptiste said and leant back again. 'Philippe Martin. Have you met him?'

Here we go, Stilton thought.

'Only briefly,' he said.

'There's a rumour flying around that he had his eye gashed with a knife yesterday.'

'Oh really?'

Jean-Baptiste looked at Abbas.

'And you had nothing to do with it?'

'Is that what he's saying?'

'I don't know. It was just a question.'

'I don't do things like that any more.'

'Good, because if you did, you probably ought to leave Marseille quick smart.'

'Because?'

'Because the man who now only has one eye knows more hitmen in this town than there are flies on a cowpat.'

Abbas shrugged his shoulders, stood up and picked up a few sachets of sugar from the table.

'I'm going for a walk,' he said and left.

When he was out of earshot, Jean-Baptiste looked at Stilton.

'Were you there at Martin's?'

'Yes. Are you going to arrest me?'

'No, no charge has been made.'

'Just rumours.'

Jean-Baptiste nodded gently. Stilton was honest. He'd probably done what he could to control the situation. Without Stilton there would probably have been a corpse in the room above the bar near Gare Saint-Charles, something that would have made things much worse. Jean-Baptiste followed that line of reasoning.

'Martin is an arsehole,' he said.

'Yeah, we got that impression too.'

'But that thing about the hitmen is true. Martin is looking for revenge. I'd prefer it if you didn't have to fish Abbas out of the port.'

'Me too, but you know what he's like. I can't force him to leave.'

'No,' Jean-Baptiste said, rolling his bottle of water between his hands. 'We'll just have to hope for the best.'

'Yes.'

Jean-Baptiste got up. When Stilton reached out his hand, Stilton asked: 'How well do you know Claudette?'

'Well. She worked with us for many years, at the office. Now she's a bit of a drifter.'

'In what way?'

'She doesn't really know what she wants to do. I think she wants to paint. Did you hook up?'

'Yes.'

'She's a good girl.'

They shook hands and Jean-Baptiste starting walking around the hedge. Stilton realised that Jean-Baptiste hadn't smoked, not a single cigarette. Even though he'd said he chose this bar because you could smoke in there.

'An old colleague called for you.' Jean-Baptiste had stopped outside the hedge and leant over towards him.

'For me?'

'Mette Olsäter.'

'What did she want?'

'She wanted to know what you're doing down here.'

'And what did you say?'

'I don't feel comfortable lying, particularly not to people I respect, like Olsäter.'

'So?'

'I said it was about a murder down here and that Abbas knew the victim. Something like that.'

'Was she satisfied with that?'

'No.'

'What else did you say?'

'There wasn't much more to say. Bye.'

The large policeman crossed the road without looking for cars. Quite a few of them beeped him. Stilton remained seated. His gaze wandered down along the hedge – a large brown rat was busy making its way through the thicket.

He felt it was time to go home.

When Stilton left the bar, he was entirely consumed by the meeting with Jean-Baptiste. It hadn't resulted in much more, in terms of concrete facts, than they already knew. But they now knew that the perpetrator was still unknown, and that they didn't even have a suspect.

So far.

He walked past a black car and carried on towards the hotel. Two eyes followed him until he turned the corner, two eyes that belonged to a man with very coarse hands. He'd been sitting in the car the whole time while they had the meeting in the bar. And he'd established something rather disagreeable.

The two Swedes had met the well-known murder investigator Jean-Baptiste Fabre.

One of the ones you couldn't bribe.

Why?

Were they coppers too?

Why would two Swedish coppers be interested in the murder of Samira?

He had an answer to that.

And it scared him.

Stilton was lying on Abbas's hotel bed. He'd presumed that Abbas would get in touch if he was needed. He stared at the black television screen in front of him. The porn film had been disgusting. Mainly to Abbas, of course, but even to Stilton. Not just because of the disgusting content, but because of the associations it triggered.

Associations with Rune Forss.

The detective chief inspector of Stockholm Police who'd been sleeping with prostitutes, pimped out by the escort queen Jackie Berglund.

Stilton knew it, but it still had to be proven, something he intended to do as soon as he got home. For moral reasons, but mainly for personal ones. It was Forss who had manoeuvred Stilton away from a murder investigation in a deeply humiliating way during his psychosis. It was Forss who'd spread the rumours and talked crap behind his back when he came back. It was Forss who made sure that he was more or less frozen out by his colleagues until Stilton had had enough, handed over his service gun and left.

And Forss had done that for one reason alone: he was afraid that Stilton was going to reveal his liaisons with prostitutes. He was afraid that Stilton was going to find something that linked Rune Forss and Jackie Berglund.

That's why.

Stilton closed his eyes. He didn't have a hard time recalling how Forss had treated him when he was homeless. When he'd offered to help solve the case of the mobile murderers, as the media called them.

Forss had treated him like a piece of shit.

Stilton felt a longing to go home.

'Wake up.'

Abbas was standing just inside the door. Stilton sat up in bed, feeling a little dazed. He must have dozed off.

'What's the time?'

'Almost four. Your plane leaves at six.'

'My plane?'

Abbas handed him a piece of paper. Stilton looked at it, a printed boarding pass. Abbas sat down on the chair by the wall.

'You've fixed what you were going to fix,' he said. 'I want to stay on a couple more days. I'll be coming back by train.'

'What about Martin though?'

'What about him?'

'You heard what Abbas said about the hitmen.'

'Yes, but I don't feel very comfortable having a bodyguard. And I don't think you enjoy that role much either.'

'No, but it doesn't feel great leaving you here on your own.'

'You'll just have to accept it.'

Stilton looked at Abbas's emotionless expression and shook his head. This didn't feel good. But what should he do? He got up off the bed.

'What are you planning to do?' Stilton asked.

'Say goodbye.'

Stilton didn't really know what he meant. Say goodbye to Marseille? To Samira? But he knew that Abbas had made up his mind. He didn't want Stilton around.

'Are you coming to the airport?'

'No.'

So Stilton got in a taxi with his blue bag and told the driver where he was going. Ten minutes later he changed his mind.

'The police station?'

'Yes.'

The taxi stopped outside the police building. Stilton paid and got out. He looked up at the gigantic edifice and hoped that Jean-Baptiste wasn't standing by a window smoking. Then he went into the small bar opposite. It was almost empty. He walked towards the barman.

'Lottery ticket?'

'No, I'm looking for Claudette.'

'She left ten minutes ago.'

'Oh right.'

'But she's coming back. Shall I leave a message?'

'No.'

Stilton left the bar.

At roughly the same time as Stilton took off into a clear blue sky, Abbas said goodbye. He crossed a square at the edge of Marseille, on foot, with eyes in the back of his head. He knew these streets, still, not much had changed. From the outside. The people probably had. He didn't know much about that, but the surroundings were just like they had been when he lived here.

He'd lived in many places in this city, moving around with his erratic father, from one shithole to the next. Then he left home and lived in far worse shitholes.

He was not bidding farewell to the city.

He was bidding farewell to himself.

To Jean Villon's young apprentice.

The young knife thrower who met the love of his life at a circus. A man who no longer existed. Who had existed as long as Samira existed, and lived on forlorn hope. The unlikely dream about a man and a woman who would eventually find their way back to one another.

Now Samira was dead and the young apprentice no longer existed.

It was to him that Abbas was bidding farewell.

He was now someone else.

With a very different task in hand.

He crossed over a deserted square, past a merry-go-round spinning around in the middle of it.

When he came back to the hotel it was almost midnight. The porter was sleeping in a room just inside the tiny reception. Abbas went upstairs. It wasn't long before he came back down. He went into the room where the porter was sleeping and whistled. The porter managed to hit his head twice, on the wall behind him and on the bedside lamp above his head, before he got to his feet and came to stand very close to Abbas.

'Yes?'

'Someone's been in my room.'

'Your colleague perhaps?'

'He left before I went. Someone has been here since then.'

'Perhaps it was the maid?'

'Does she generally clean people's washbags?'

The porter couldn't answer that. And he hadn't seen any unfamiliar faces at the hotel either. But, having said that, he had been sleeping for a couple of hours, and quite soundly at that, so...

Abbas went back to his room. What had they been looking for? The knives?

Probably.

Or him.

* * *

Stilton's plane landed just after eleven o'clock at night and he took the airport bus into the city. On the way to the barge, he saw someone selling *Situation Sthlm*, a confused-looking young guy standing outside a Konsum grocery store on Hornsgatan holding up his magazines. The shop had closed several hours ago, but this guy hadn't noticed. Stilton bought a copy from him. He didn't recognise this guy so he refrained from asking questions. About other sellers, friends of his just a year ago. He did tell the guy that the shop was now closed and that he'd have more luck selling magazines if he moved closer towards the underground entrance.

The guy thought that Stilton was a genius.

She's probably asleep, Stilton thought as he climbed aboard the barge. The lights were all off. He headed down into his cabin as quietly as he could. There was a new brass sliding bolt lock on the back of the door. He pushed it closed and lay down on his bunk. It was well after midnight. He sent a short text message to Abbas. He'd call him tomorrow to check how things were.

Then he'd call Mette.

Just the thought of that call put him in touch with the latent magma inside him. Nothing was going to get in his way now, not trips to Marseille, gouged pimps or beautiful French women.

He was going to focus now.

On Rune Forss.

Chapter 13

He raised his voice considerably.

'Why not today?'

'Because I don't have time. There is a world outside your own, you know, Tom.'

Stilton was sitting in his cabin in his underwear. It was just after nine o'clock and Mette didn't have time to meet him today, something he just had to accept. His lowered his voice a little.

'So what time tomorrow, then?'

'Ten. Is Abbas back too?'

'No.'

'Why not?'

'There is a world outside your own, you know, Mette. See you tomorrow.'

Stilton ended the call and threw the mobile on his bunk. He didn't like it when his plans didn't work out. What was he going to do the whole bloody day? Then there was a knock on the door.

'Yes!'

'Welcome home.'

Luna's voice slid in through the wooden doors and Stilton pulled out a pair of trousers. He put them on with one hand while opening the bolt on the door with the other.

'Come in.'

Luna opened the door. There wasn't much space, so she stopped where she was standing. She was wearing her green dungarees.

'How was Marseille?'

'Messy. Thanks for the whiskey.'

'Did it come in useful?'

'All the time. Thanks for fitting that.'

Stilton was pointing at the lock on the door.

'Do you feel safe now?' Luna asked.

'What do you mean? With the door?'

Luna smiled and had a look around the cabin.

'Did you know her?'

She pointed at the little shelf behind Stilton. He turned around. The little photo of One-eyed Vera was the only thing standing on it.

'Yes. Vera Larsson.'

'The one who was beaten to death in a caravan?'

Stilton looked at Luna.

'How do you know that?'

'I remember the murder. Quite a lot was written about it. I saw her headstone.'

'Did you?'

'Yes. At Norra cemetery. I work there, remember.'

'Was she buried at Norra?'

'Yes. Didn't you know that?'

'No.'

'Haven't you ever been there?'

'No.'

Stilton had never been to One-eyed Vera's grave. He'd buried her in his own way.

'But you must have known each other pretty well? If you have a photo of her there, I mean?'

Stilton was sitting on his bunk, looking at the little photo of Vera. Had they known each other well? Yes, in a way, like homeless people know each other, but in many ways no. But he'd made love to her, once, and her murder had dragged him out of his vegetative state and made space for a rage that had taken him far.

In actual fact, off the streets and out to Rödlöga.

And now back here again.

'I want to see her grave,' he suddenly said.

After all, he didn't have plans.

They saw her from a distance, long before they had reached the grave, a haggard creature down on her knees in front of a simple metal plaque in the ground. Next to her was a green plastic bag.

'Someone you know?'

Luna spoke quietly, as is customary in a cemetery.

'I only know her first name,' Stilton said. 'Muriel. She's a druggie from Bagarmossen.'

They approached the grave. Muriel had her hands together in front of her, her thin arms shaking. It was very autumnal weather with low fog and just a few degrees above zero. Muriel was only wearing a short jacket, with sleeves that were too short. Stilton and Luna stopped a couple of metres behind her.

'Hi, Muriel.'

Muriel thrust her upper body around. She assumed it was coppers standing behind her. When she saw Stilton she stared at him for several seconds.

'Is that you?!' she said in a thin, broken voice.

'It's me.'

Muriel scrambled to her feet and flung her arms around Stilton. He hugged her and it almost made him feel sick. There wasn't much body to hold onto. Luna looked down at the floor. Stilton felt Muriel crying, silently, on his shoulder. He let her cry. He looked down at the burial plaque. He knew that One-eyed Vera had been a kind of mother to Muriel, a substitute for her real mother. Vera had tried to keep an eye on her, keep her away from the worst shit. As much as she could. Now Vera was dead and the protective net left was gone. He guessed at how she got by. He carefully peeled Muriel off his shoulder and looked at her.

'Are you feeling OK?'

Muriel shook her head. Her face was full of red and black blotches, her eyelids were swollen and infected, it looked like it might be some kind of disease.

'Have you eaten today?'

'No.'

Stilton turned towards Luna and she nodded. 'It's fine.' He looked down at Vera's grave. There wasn't much to see. Probably a small urn buried in the ground under the metal plaque, nothing more, with some sand around it, and a new metal plaque half a metre away. He regretted coming here.

But he'd found Muriel.

* * *

Olivia pushed the front door closed and put her hands up against the wall. Her whole body was gasping for air. She'd been out running for almost an hour and her clothes were drenched in sweat. Unfit, she thought to herself, so bloody unfit! She pulled off her trainers and saw that her blister from Mexico had become sore again. Shit! During her time at the Police Academy she'd exercised every day and her body was in excellent physical shape when she finished. Then she went to Mexico. And she'd had other things on her mind than keeping fit. That morning she'd woken up and felt how stiff and sluggish she was and she dug out her running gear. She had to get fit again. At least one hour a day, she'd decided. This was day one. She peeled off her clothes and jumped in the shower.

Half an hour later she was sitting in the kitchen in her dressing gown with her laptop in front of her. She drank a rather disgusting sports drink while she clicked her way to a news broadcast on the Swedish TV site. When the business news came on it made her slam down the plastic bottle. The first report was about Jean Borell. He was just arriving at Albion's head office on Skeppsbron and a journalist was standing outside the main entrance hoping to get a comment about Albion's new contract with the City of Stockholm.

'Do you think that it will be approved? Despite all the criticism you've had?'

'No comment.'

Borell disappeared in through the door. Olivia was quite surprised. Is that what he looked like now? After some intensive googling last night she'd finally managed to find a picture of him, but it was an old picture depicting a rather slick and tidy young man with furtive eyes.

This was a very different man.

His hair was long, ash-blond and bushy, his face was tanned and the knitted sweater seemed to be hugging a trim body.

He also had a short, dark, well-groomed beard. That was quite unusual. Men like him in positions of power seldom had beards.

Looks good, she thought. A first-class arsehole according to Alex, but with interesting looks.

What did he know about the murder of Bengt Sahlmann?

Olivia thought about the question while she got dressed and dried her hair. She wondered how she was going to find out whether Borell was involved in the murder, which is what her entire theory was founded upon. That Borell had silenced his angry school friend who was seeking revenge for his father's death by creating a scandal for Borell's company. She went through the theory a few times in her head. She knew that it had major flaws, but flaws are there to be fixed.

Should she get in touch with him?

She let out a burst of laughter, at first, as though it was an extremely bizarre idea. A man whom the media had been chasing all over the world to no avail. How was she going to be able to meet him?

But what if? Imagine if it were possible, one way or another. What would she do then? What would she ask him?

'Listen, your old school friend Bengt has been murdered. Have you got anything to do with it?'

She laughed again, rather more hopelessly. What should she ask?

She sat down at the kitchen table. I'm a police officer, she thought. Not officially, but I am. So how would I act? As Mette? Did she have anything to go on?

Not much.

Nothing, Olivia.

And that's when she gave up on her idea, in ten seconds, before remembering the one thing she did have.

Her intuition.

And there were a number of highly qualified people who greatly respected it, including Mette Olsäter. So why shouldn't she? How many murder cases had been solved because one investigator or other, in a chaos of nothing, had followed their intuition and suddenly uncovered the truth? Many.

She called Albion's Stockholm office and asked to speak to Jean Borell. The woman who answered the phone was very friendly, even though she probably thought the call was a prank. She said Olivia should speak to Magnus Thorhed.

'Who is that?'

'Jean Borell's colleague.'

'Is he there?'

'No, he's at Bukowskis. He'll probably be back in a couple of hours.'

'Can I reach him on his mobile?'

'No.'

And that's where the call ended. She'd tried to reach someone who was being covered for by a person who was himself unreachable.

I'll go to Bukowskis, she thought to herself.

Olivia knew that she often acted before she'd had time to catch up with her thoughts. This time she found time to do so on the bus to Kungsträdgården, largely thanks to Alex and what he'd told her before they left Prinsen, about Jean Borell. Private things. That he only had one eye, for example. He'd lost his right eye as a child. And he had a breathtaking property out on Värmdö and a small château in Antibes.

And he also had an almost legendary art collection.

He was a top-class collector, with a particular penchant for young modern Swedish art. According to Alex, he had the largest private collection of internationally acclaimed contemporary Swedish artists.

Which didn't mean much to Olivia. Yet. She wasn't starting her history of art course until the spring.

But it gave her a foot in the door.

She'd caught up with her thoughts.

It was the final exhibition day for Bukowskis autumn auction of Swedish art. The premises on Arsenalsgatan were overflowing with overflowing wallets. Olivia walked in and grabbed hold of a catalogue while surveying the people in the room. She'd googled Magnus Thorhed. Unlike his boss, he had a strong online presence. He'd written books on widely different topics including derivative analysis and Goethe's Theory of Colours. He was an honorary member of various gentlemen's clubs. For some time he'd run his own gallery on Nybrogatan. Olivia had seen numerous pictures of him. He was thirty-six years old and of Asian origin.

Was he adopted too?

She spotted him further in. He was wearing a mustard-coloured suit. As she pushed her way forward she saw a little plait running down the back of his neck and a little gold ring in his ear – a man careful about the kind of impression he made. When she was almost behind him, she smelled the distinctive aftershave emanating from the man's body. A touch of nutmeg, she thought. He was shorter than her and quite stocky: he gave a powerful impression.

Thorhed was quietly talking into his mobile while studying a painting hanging on the wall in front of him. Olivia looked at the small note next to it: Karin Mamma Andersson. Number 63. She looked it up in the catalogue. The reserve price was two million Swedish kronor. Not likely to be hanging at her place, even though she thought it was very… strange? Suggestive dark colours in the foreground, dull layers of ochre behind, some disconcerting shadows. Olivia pretended to study the painting, while straining to hear what Magnus Thorhed was saying.

'How high will we go?' he said quietly. 'Good.'

He ended the call and adjusted his discreet round glasses. Olivia stepped forward.

'Isn't it fantastic!'

Thorhed turned his head slightly and was greeted with a gentle smile. Olivia nodded at the painting in front of them.

'What suggestive contrasts!'

Thorhed looked at the painting again. He agreed with the young woman with the naturally beautiful eyes. The painting was fantastic.

'Yes,' he said. 'It really is. Are you planning to bid on it?'

'No, not at all, I am interested in it on another level.'

'What level?'

She'd awakened a second of curiosity in Thorhed.

'I'm studying history of art and I don't look at paintings as objects for purchase. I try to put them in a bigger context. Olivia Rivera.'

Olivia extended her hand and the rather taken aback Thorhed shook it. He had a firm handshake.

'Magnus Thorhed.'

'Didn't you own a gallery on Nybrogatan?'

'That was a few years ago.'

'Before you started working with Jean Borell.'

Thorhed looked at Olivia, who quickly flashed another big smile.

'I was trying to reach Jean Borell today and I was told to speak to you. That's why I'm here. I'd like to see him.'

Thorhed's expression stiffened considerably.

'Why?'

'I'm working on a dissertation about modern Swedish artists and their impact on the international art market and I've been reading about Jean Borell's fantastic collection. I'd like to do an interview with him about it. How he's put it together, what criteria he's used, what it is that he finds so interesting about these artists. It's for my undergraduate dissertation.'

Thorhed was still listening so she carried on.

'And I saw on the news this morning that he was coming to Stockholm today.'

'And now he's on his way to Marrakech.'

'Oh. And when's he coming back here?'

'Maybe at the weekend.'

'Do you think he might be interested in meeting me then?'

'I doubt it.'

'Why?'

'Because I'm in charge of his calendar and I know what it's like. But I can certainly ask him. What did you say your name was?'

'Olivia Rivera. I'll give you my number.'

Olivia wrote her number down on the back of the catalogue and handed it over to Thorhed. Not her mobile number, she didn't want to share that, but that of the landline in the flat on Skånegatan.

'It would mean a great deal for my thesis if he'd be willing to do it,' she said.

Thorhed nodded and gently tugged on his plait.

'How long would it take?'

'An hour maybe? Any time, any place. Well, near Stockholm, not Marrakech.'

Olivia smiled that big smile again. Thorhed didn't smile back.

'I'll be in touch.'

He pushed his way over to the door and Olivia exhaled. She waited a few minutes and then made her way out as well. If Borell was coming this weekend and would agree to a meeting, then she had a few days to cram as much as she could about young, contemporary Swedish art.

For an interview.

* * *

Luna watched Muriel lift the spoon to her mouth. She'd made her some hot noodle soup, assuming that Muriel's stomach wasn't up to heavier food. Muriel blew on the spoon and tried to guide it into her mouth without spilling it. Stilton was sitting just on the other side of the lounge.

'So do you see any of the other guys? Pärt? Benseman?'

'We don't see much of Benseman any more, he's got into that "Housing First" scheme and he's got a pad by Skanstull, so he spends a lot of time over at Ronny Redlös's. I think he works there sometimes.'

'And Pärt?'

'He's finished.'

Like you, Stilton thought and turned to Luna.

'It was Pärt who found One-eyed Vera in the caravan, half-dead. He's a nice guy. Does he still sell the magazine?' he asked Muriel.

'No. He had to stop that, some shit about money. Last time I saw him he was lying under the Traneberg Bridge throwing up.

Stilton looked at Luna. Just as well that she got a slice of his past, so he didn't have to speak about it himself.

Muriel finished her soup.

'Would you like some more?'

'Nah, thanks.'

Muriel's arms starting shaking again. Luna sat down next to her and put her arm around her shoulder.

'You're welcome to sleep here if you want.'

'Sweet.'

Muriel pulled her plastic bag towards her, from the wrong end, and some of its contents fell on the floor. Stilton bent down to pick them up. A hairbrush, a small cuddly toy, a packet of condoms and some small square plastic bags filled with tablets. Stilton held one of the bags up.

'What are you taking?'

'5-IT. It's fucking brilliant. Much cheaper than heroin and it's bloody safe too.'

'You think so?'

'Can I have them back?'

Stilton passed the bag of tablets back to Muriel. Luna looked at him. She would have got rid of the bags if it were up to her.

'Where did you get hold of it?' he said.

'Off that guy, Classe Hall. He's a good bloke, sometimes I don't need to pay. He gives me five bags for a shag.'

Stilton looked at Muriel and she averted her gaze. She knew that Stilton had got back on his feet. She knew that he'd got revenge on the people who killed Vera. She knew that he'd left the city. Now he was back and looking at her with that expression that Vera sometimes had.

'What the fuck am I supposed to do?' she said almost inaudibly, trying to get control of her hands.

And then she started crying.

Stilton and Luna let her cry, that would tire her out, and when her tears finally dried up, Luna helped her up from the wooden bench and took her out towards the bow of the barge. Stilton watched them. It was a pretty stark contrast between the short scraggy Muriel and the tall and well-built Luna.

'You're really sweet, you know?' Muriel said to Luna.

'Thanks.'

Stilton saw them disappear down into a narrow corridor. He assumed that there was some extra sleeping area there at the front, where Muriel could get a few hours' rest. Then she'd disappear again, he knew that, out into a world that he did not have any control over.

* * *

Abbas had walked around half of Marseille, alert and focused. He'd scoured all the porn shops he passed. He'd talked to prostitutes along all the places he knew, the eastern European girls by the central station, the transvestites up on the West side, the lot. He'd moved from bars to gambling dens to dealer hangouts.

And he'd asked the same question to everyone: Le Taureau?

No one knew who he was, or dared to tell him. Some of them had reacted in a way that suggested they might know, but no one said a thing and Abbas didn't want to wave his knives about again.

Now he was on his way back to the hotel. Darkness had fallen over the Mediterranean and was mirrored in his thoughts. Had he been wrong? Had Martin been lying to him after all? Should he go and see him again? Pointless. He wasn't going to get any more out of Martin than he already had. He wasn't going to get more out of this city full stop.

He'd failed.

Then Marie rang.

'I just remembered, have you spoken to Samira's sister?' she said.

'Did she have a sister?'

'Didn't you know?'

'No. Where does she live?'

It was late when Abbas turned into the narrow rue Sainte. The door he was trying to find was between a bakery and a small restaurant. Samira's sister worked at the restaurant, La Poule Noire, 'the black hen'. She was due to finish at eleven. Abbas waited on the other side of the road. He'd had no idea that Samira had had a sister. Samira had never mentioned her. There'd been no reason to. Then he saw a short middle-aged woman emerging from the restaurant. She was wearing a grey knitted jumper and dark trousers. She stopped and looked at him.

'Abbas?'

Abbas crossed over the road and held out his hand. They greeted each other. The sister's name was Nidal.

'Shall we go upstairs?'

They went through the door and up two flights of stairs. Nidal lived alone. Her flat was small, and Abbas had to squeeze his way past the furniture in the small living room. When Nidal turned on one of the lamps he saw how poor she was. The furniture was shabby, there were holes in the rug, the wallpaper had loosened at the ceiling skirting and was hanging down. The only thing that stuck out in the room was a large mirror with a shiny gold frame. It was hanging above a small bureau with a statue of Christ. Nidal lit the incense next to the statue.

Abbas sat down on a chair.

'I'm going back to Sweden tomorrow,' he said.

Nidal nodded and placed a bottle of water down on the table in front of him. Abbas poured some water into the old glass while Nidal pulled out a box from the bureau under the mirror. When she turned around she was holding a gold necklace in her hand. Abbas recognised it straight away.

'The police gave me this,' Nidal said. 'Samira once told me that she'd got it from you.'

'Yes.'

'She always wore it. I want you to have it.'

Abbas took the necklace. He didn't know what to say. Nidal was standing almost completely still in front of him. Her thin wrinkled face was almost frozen, as though there was something she didn't dare, or want to, reveal. Abbas wondered how much she knew. About Samira. About what she was doing. He looked at the necklace in his hand. There was so much he wanted to know, about all the time he didn't know anything about, but he felt it wasn't really the right moment to ask. He lifted his head, the incense filled his nose.

'She was sixteen when she ran away from the orphanage.'

Nidal said it without looking at Abbas, her gaze was focused on the wall behind him. He turned around and saw a small photograph, a black-and-white picture of two girls holding hands, one much older than the other.

'Is that you and Samira?'

'Yes. She was three and I was thirteen when we came to the orphanage.'

'Why did you end up there?'

'Our parents died in a fire. I was thrown out of the orphanage when I was eighteen, and Samira stayed on. She was blind and they didn't think that I could take care of her. Every time I went to see her she cried and asked me to take her with me.'

Nidal was still standing, looking at the photograph. She was deep within her past.

'Then she ran away. I still don't understand how. Someone probably helped her. She was so beautiful, there were always boys around her. After a while she got in touch. She'd met an older man who worked at a circus and she was living with him now.'

'Jean Villon.'

'He was a knife thrower and she was his target girl.'

'That's where we met.'

'I know, she told me about you.'

Nidal said it without looking at Abbas. She turned around and went to the statue of Christ and lit some more incense. Abbas understood that she wasn't going to tell him any more.

'Thank you for the necklace,' he said and got up to leave.

Nidal remained seated. Abbas took a few steps towards the door out in the hallway.

'She loved you.'

The voice came from behind. Low. Toneless.

Abbas didn't turn around.

On the way to his hotel, he passed a seafront restaurant, a much nicer one than Eden Roc, with fancy cars parked outside. He saw dressed up people mingling around in the garden inside the stone porch. They all had tall glasses in their hands and the hum of people could be heard all the way out on the street. He passed by the large building and started walking along the low sea wall. Dark rocks crept out into the water below. A lone fisherman sat on one of them. He had a long rod in his hand, a bright red float was bobbing about far out in the water. Abbas looked at the man for a while. He's trying to scrape a meal together, Abbas thought to himself and started walking again.

He didn't turn around.

If he had, he would have seen this lone fisherman pulling out his mobile and holding it up to his mouth.

Abbas carried on walking along the waterside, circumnavigating a drunk who was sitting against the stone wall with a red-and-white traffic cone on his head. His hotel still lay a bit further on. He passed by a dark bus shelter. There were some people standing there waiting for a night bus. Then suddenly he stopped, something was bothering him, something he'd seen.

What though?

Suddenly he remembered.

He had seen the lone fisherman's bright float disappear under the surface, but the man hadn't reacted. He hadn't reeled it in. Why?

Abbas turned around and was hit right across the face.

It was probably an iron bar, wielded by the people standing at the bus shelter. Abbas never had the chance to see. He fell flat against the quayside. When he tried to reach for one of his knives, he was hit over the head again. Blood was spurting out. He curled up on the pavement. Through the blood he saw a large man with coarse hands leaning over him. Two other men were standing next to him. He turned towards the edge of the quay and tried to put one hand up on the wall. Then someone administered a sharp kick to his diaphragm and he collapsed.

They were planning to beat him to death right there.

He was totally defenceless.

It wouldn't have taken many more blows with that iron bar to stop Abbas el Fassi from ever moving again. It was a large police patrol van with flashing lights that interrupted the assault, coming thundering past the fancy restaurant. The men saw it. Two of them grabbed hold of Abbas and hurled him over the sea wall. Seconds before he fell down towards the rocks, he saw the man with the rough hands. The tattoo. On his neck, just below his ear.

A black bull.

His body bounced down the rocks and landed at the water's edge. The men above saw the patrol van roaring past. When it had gone they looked down towards the rocks. Then they left.

Abbas was still conscious when he landed in the water.

A few more seconds.

The second before everything went black, a name flashed through his head.

* * *

Stilton sat on his bunk, agonising. He'd tried to ring Abbas again. He'd called and texted several times in the last few hours and he couldn't understand why there was no reply. Every time it went straight to voicemail the lump in his throat grew, along with the dark thoughts in his head. Where is he? Has something happened? Have those bloody hitmen got hold of him? He called Jean-Baptiste even though it was past midnight.

'No, I haven't heard anything from him. I thought he'd left with you?'

'He stayed on.'

'Oh shit, that's bad news.'

'Yes, thanks. I'll call his hotel. Bye.'

Stilton called the hotel. The comatose porter was able to inform him that Abbas el Fassi wasn't in his room. But where he was, he didn't know. Stilton ended the call and got up and sat down again, there wasn't much space to pace around. He felt the doubts that he'd had on the plane home come creeping over him again. Was it wrong to leave him? Did I bail too soon? But Abbas was the one who'd bought the ticket. He didn't want me to stay. Should I have ignored it and stayed anyway? But he's probably capable of looking after himself. He has the knives, after all.

And so he overcame his bad conscience and put the light out. He was just about to sink into the great darkness when he heard a gentle knock on his door. Muriel? Not likely. He put the light on.

'Yes?'

The door opened slightly, he'd forgotten to lock it.

'Am I disturbing you?'

Luna's face was partly shaded in the doorway.

'I'm trying to sleep,' Stilton said.

'Me too.'

'Standing up?'

Luna smiled and pulled the door halfway open. She was wearing a light-green T-shirt and a pair of grey tracksuit bottoms. She was holding a stuffed bird in her hand.

'Do you know what this is?'

'A dead bird.'

'A sparrowhawk. Sweden's smallest bird of prey. It lives on small birds and pigeons.'

Stilton nodded. He didn't have any great ornithological insight.

'It's pretty bare in here,' Luna said. 'I thought that you might like some company.'

'From a dead bird?'

Luna took one step into the room and put the bird on the table under the porthole.

'Sometimes it blinks,' she said with her back to Stilton. He sank back down into his bunk.

'Thank you for taking care of Muriel,' he said.

'I felt sorry for her. She seems like a good girl.'

'Yes. Is she asleep?'

'Yes. It was her who made me think of this. She looked like a little bird when I put her to bed, just a bag of bones.'

'She's destroying herself.'

'Why didn't you take the tablets from her?'

'Because she'd only go and fuck her way to new ones tomorrow. Anyway, she'd run in the other direction as soon as she saw me next time. I can't drag her out of this shit, both she and I know it.'

Luna looked at Stilton. She'd moved back to the doorway again.

'Sleep well,' she said after a while. 'I hope you won't have any nightmares.'

'You too.'

Luna pulled the door closed behind her.

Chapter 14

It was almost half past nine and Stilton was due to meet Mette at ten. He'd just tried to get hold of Abbas again, without success. He was now standing on deck and looking out at the light veils of mist on the water: the cold air had caused quite a bit of evaporation. A large crane barge floated by further out in the water. There was a lot of crane work going on this side of Slussen. Maybe it will look all right in the end? he thought. Things have to keep moving forward, after all. Even cities. He turned around and saw Luna coming up on deck.

'Is Muriel down there?' he asked.

'No, she'd already gone when I woke up.'

'OK.'

'And she'd nicked five hundred kronor out of my wallet too.'

They looked at each other for a few seconds. Luna shrugged her shoulders.

'I'll pay you back,' Stilton said.

'Why?'

'I was the one who brought her here.'

'It's fine. Maybe she won't need to sell her body today. Are you going somewhere?'

'Yes.'

Finally.

That was what he felt when he went into the National Crime Squad headquarters. He was finally going to get started. He'd finally have the chance to extinguish what was burning inside him.

The last time he'd been in this building he'd been shuffled in through the back and into an interrogation room. He was still homeless then. Now he had a spring in his step, totally indifferent to any looks he got.

He'd got past that.

'Follow me. She's not in her office.'

Stilton followed a female police assistant through a number of corridors, most of which he knew very well, but finally they turned into some newly renovated areas that he'd never been to before, even though he'd spent more than twenty years in the building.

'She's in there.'

The woman pointed at a door and Stilton opened it. There was only one thing inside the room, a ping-pong table. Mette Olsäter was standing on one side of it, Lisa Hedqvist on the other.

'Hi, Tom! We're almost done! Close the door!'

Stilton pulled the door closed and spent about ten minutes watching Mette trying to play table tennis with minimal movements. When the ball slipped off the table so that Lisa couldn't reach it, Mette put her paddle down on the table and grabbed her towel, visibly pleased. She was sweating copiously. Is she going to have a shower now too, Stilton wondered.

'I'll shower later,' Mette said to Lisa and walked towards Stilton. 'Hello there! You look very sprightly! Have you been on the oysters down in Marseille?!'

They went into Mette's room. On the way there, Mette had asked about Marseille and given Stilton an earful for coming home without Abbas.

'It's fine, he can take care of himself,' he said.

'Neither of you can.'

Sometimes he got the feeling that Mette behaved like some kind of übermum. She should take care of herself instead, he thought. But he didn't say it. Mette picked up a large bottle of water and gulped down half of it.

'So you're living on a barge?'

'Temporarily.'

'Everything is temporary with you nowadays. Are you thinking of coming back to the police?'

'No.'

'Then you can join forces with Olivia and open a detective agency. Two masterminds helping cats stuck in trees.'

Stilton waited for her to finish. Mette had been on at him a couple of times in the last year about the police thing. Each time he'd explained that he could never go back and each time it had ended with Mårten having to step in and change the subject. He wasn't here now, so Stilton had to do so himself.

'What's that?'

He pointed at a couple of small square plastic bags that were pinned to a notice board behind Mette's desk. He thought he recognised them.

'Drugs. 5-IT. We're in the middle of a big operation against online drugs at the moment.'

'Muriel had some.'

'And who's Muriel?'

'A homeless druggie, I know her from before. We ran into each other yesterday and she had a few of those.'

'Do you know where she'd got them?'

The tone of Mette's voice had changed considerably.

'From a dealer, Classe Hall or something. Why?'

'A large stash of those drugs was stolen from Customs and Excise. They'd been seized during a raid, and we're trying to find out where they went. Classe Hall?'

'Yes.'

Mette took out her mobile phone and keyed in a number.

'Hi, it's Mette! Can you look up Classe Hall? Or Clas. And talk to the drug guys if they know of someone by that name. Thanks.'

Mette ended the call.

'Where is this Muriel?' she said.

'No idea, in the city.'

Mette nodded and felt it was time.

'Rune Forss,' she said.

'Yes.'

Mette sat down behind her desk and took out a thin plastic file with a couple of white pieces of paper inside.

'This is the list of what we seized at Jackie Berglund's last year. Unbeknownst to her. Her client list. It dates all the way back to the beginnings of her escort service, Red Velvet, in 1999.'

'And Rune Forss's name is on that list.'

'Yes.'

'Which you didn't tell me last time I asked.'

'I didn't deny it either.'

'Is there any information about how many times he used her services?'

'No,' Mette said. 'But his name appears early on, so it must have started some time around 2000.'

'Do you think he's still doing it?'

'No. And moreover it's thought that she's put her business on hold. She was pretty shaken up after we got a bit too close last year.'

Stilton got up. He'd heard what he needed to hear. Forss was on the client list. Now it was time for the next step.

'What are you planning to do now?' Mette asked.

'What I should have done six years ago.'

'Get revenge?'

'Yes.'

'Is that wise?'

'It's necessary.'

He said it without adding any frills, and Mette knew that he meant it. She shook her head a little.

'It might not be so easy,' she said.

'Because?'

'First of all, because his first sexual contacts are outside the statute of limitations. And secondly, we only have this list, which doesn't actually prove anything, substantially. Furthermore, we've got hold of it in an improper way, you know that.'

Stilton knew that Mette was right. Formally there was nothing they could pin on Forss. Today. But informally it would of course make his position at the Stockholm Police impossible if it reached the media, particularly after that scandal with Captain Dress. The private sexual exploits of a high-ranking detective with a prostitute would certainly end up splashed across tabloids.

But for that he needed proof.

Proof that he didn't have.

He needed to find a witness, someone who was willing to come forward and confirm that Rune Forss had bought sex through Jackie Berglund.

'I'll be in touch,' Stilton said.

Then he left. Mette picked up her water bottle again. Abbas adrift in Marseille and Stilton chasing a high-ranking detective in Stockholm.

Not good for her heart.

She was just about to gulp down the rest of the water when Lisa Hedqvist called.

'Clas Hall is on the drugs register, and we've got a great deal on him.'

'Watch him.'

Stilton left the building and crossed the derelict Kronoberg Park. The icy wind had cleared the cold benches and semi-frozen grassy areas: not even homeless people could stand being there. Stilton knew this was a typical hangout for some of them, though not for him, it was a little too close to the building he'd just left. As he was on his way out of the park he passed by a man walking a large dog wrapped in a black fleece jumper. The dog looked sprightly, while the man shivered along in a thin jacket.

'Get revenge?'

Stilton thought about it as he walked down towards Fridhelmsplan. He knew it was right. Both he and Abbas were seeking revenge. For fundamentally rather different reasons, but nevertheless. So what? He didn't like the undertone in Mette's reply, or what it was insinuating. That it was primitive to be seeking revenge. Or 'retaliate an injustice', as they said in the courts. What was wrong with it? What did she think that he could do otherwise? Turn the other cheek? He'd never turned his cheek, he didn't know how to do so now.

So?

He turned into Hantverkargatan and headed to Linas Bar.

Mink's preferred hangout.

Mink, who'd been christened Leif Minkvist, sat at the short bar with a half-drunk beer in front of him. He was very short, balding, and during his forty years of life he'd tried most things you can try and quite a lot more. Nowadays he went easy on the heavy stuff. His pale complexion revealed quite a bit about his habits – he was a man who lived on the shady side of life.

'Hi there.'

Mink spotted Stilton in the bar mirror in front of him. He didn't turn around. Stilton sat down next to him. Mink had been one of his best informants during his years at the police. A bit of a weirdo, but an invaluable source of information in some areas.

Like this one.

'How are things?' Mink said.

'Good. You?'

'I'm quite stressed right now.'

'Why?'

'Haven't you heard? The world is going to end on 21 December according to some bloody American Indian calendar. Of course I'm fucking stressed! Aren't you?'

'No. My thoughts are as follows. It's quite a while until then and perhaps it's best to do something worthy if everything goes tits-up.'

'Smart.'

Mink gulped his beer. That needed to sink in. Stilton waited for him to drink up and then he leant in a little closer.

'I need to get in touch with a prostitute who worked for Jackie Berglund about ten or twelve years ago.'

'OK.'

'You're the first person I'm asking.'

'Wise man.'

Stilton knew that Mink greatly valued respect. He liked to see himself as a professional, as Stilton's equal, a man who could deliver. Mink slid down off the chair.

'I'll be in touch.'

*   *   *

At first she could hardly believe it. She put down the black receiver and sat completely still in her kitchen for several minutes.

Magnus Thorhed had called.

Jean Borell was willing to meet her for a short interview about his art collection, at his house on Värmdö, where a large portion of his Swedish collection was. The day after tomorrow, at six o'clock.

She leapt up from the kitchen table.

Flattery always works!

Intuitively she'd felt that the only way to edge her way to a megamagnate like Jean Borell was to find his weak point. His ego. His passion for art, the thing that made him more than just a shark, a Gordon Gekko, made him a man with deep feelings and emotions.

And then she sat down again.

What am I going to find? Out there? With him? I know what I want to find, I want to know if he murdered Bengt Sahlmann. Or whether he's got something to do with it.

But how?

Intuition, Olivia.

She had to keep telling herself the same thing, over and over again. To build her confidence. You have antennae, Olivia, you can wheedle out the information, read undertones and overtones. He has no idea about why you're actually there. You have the upper hand. You know what's going on at Silvergården. You know how fragile Albion is. You know there's a motive. You just need to get confirmation. Intuitively.

Out there.

She hoped they would be alone at his place, and that that nutmeg-scented little man wouldn't be there, trying to poke his nose in. That would interfere with her antennae.

Then her mobile rang.

'Hi, it's Sandra. Are you at home?'

'Yes.'

'I'm standing outside your building, can I come up?'

'Absolutely!'

Olivia went into the hallway. She had time to think a few quick thoughts. Sandra, here? What time is it? Almost nine. Why is she coming here? When she opened the door she could basically see why. There was a bleary-eyed teenager with swollen eyelids and a nervous expression, wrapped in an unzipped green jacket, standing in front of her. Olivia gave her a big hug in the doorway.

'Come in. Would you like some tea?'

Sandra shrugged her shoulders. Olivia led the way into the kitchen and put the water on to boil. When she turned around, Sandra had gone. She stepped into the living room and saw her standing in the bedroom doorway.

'You don't have any photos.'

Olivia walked towards Sandra and followed her gaze into the room. She didn't have any photographs, neither there nor in the living room. She did have some, several, of herself and Maria and Arne from different places and occasions. She put all of them away about a year ago. Quite childish really looking back at it.

'I have one,' she said and walked towards the bedside table on the other side of the bed. 'This one.'

'A cat.'

'Elvis.'

'Where is it?'

'He went missing.'

'How?'

Olivia didn't feel up to recounting the whole story now. So she said something about the water boiling, put her arm around Sandra and they went into the kitchen. Sandra sat down on a chair without taking her jacket off. Olivia watched her looking down at the table. She feels like shit, she thought, and got out two cups.

'How are things?'

Sandra didn't answer. Olivia let the tea brew and lit a couple of candles on the table.

'You don't know any more about the computer?' Sandra almost whispered.

'No, I'm sorry.'

'Imagine if I never get it back.'

'Well, then I'm sure we can get you a new one.'

'But what about all the photos?'

'You had photos on it?'

'Yes, loads. Imagine if I don't get them back!'

Olivia saw how the idea of the lost photographs was torturing Sandra. She understood her. Perhaps the photographs were the only thing she had left of what she once had. She realised how important it was to get hold of that computer. For several reasons. She poured the tea. Sandra didn't touch her cup, she sat slouched down in the chair. They sat in silence for a while. Olivia was having a hard time finding a way to connect with this closed-off girl. She hardly knew her, after all. She didn't really know what to talk about.

'Shall I tell you about my mum?'

Sandra said it without looking up from the table, almost breathless.

'If you like.'

Perhaps that's why she came here, Olivia thought to herself. Maybe she needs to talk about it, about her mother, like I spoke about mine?

'We were going to ride elephants, Dad had booked it at the hotel and I was really looking forward to it, but Mum didn't fancy it. She wanted to go for a long walk along the beach instead, so she hugged me and off we went. Then that tsunami struck, while we were out. Dad was told about it when we got back with the elephants and we went to the hotel, but we couldn't reach it. There were people everywhere running around and screaming. You couldn't get there by car and Dad went absolutely crazy and we headed straight to the hotel but there wasn't a hotel any more, everything was destroyed, everywhere. I was standing behind the car and didn't really understand anything except that it was terrible. Everything was terrible, everyone was screaming and crying and I just wanted Mum to come…'

Sandra stopped talking and picked up her cup. She held it in her hand for a while and then put it down again. Olivia put her arm around her.

'But she didn't come.'

'No.'

Olivia saw the little eight-year-old girl in front of her, in the middle of that awful chaos, without any chance of understanding what was happening, except that it was terrible and that her mother didn't come.

'Was your mother found?'

'No. She's in the sea.'

Sandra scraped away at a little non-existent mark on the table and took a deep breath.

'And now with Dad in heaven there's only me left and I just don't know how I'm going to cope without them.'

'Is that how you feel? That you can't cope?'

'Yes.'

Sandra's eyes went blank and a tear dropped down into the cup in front of her. She dried her face on her sleeve and looked at Olivia. The tears had dissolved her mascara and she looked very small and helpless. Olivia felt for her so much that her stomach cramped up. But how are you supposed to console someone who's inconsolable? Should she say it as it was, that she still had her whole life in front of her and that it wouldn't be quite so painful one day?

'And everyone keeps telling me that I have my whole life in front of me,' Sandra said. 'That I'll get through this, but it doesn't help me now, does it?'

'No, it probably doesn't.'

'You're actually the only person who understands how I feel, I think.'

Sandra rested her head on Olivia's shoulder. Olivia put her arm around her and thanked her lucky stars that she hadn't spoken before she thought. The best thing she could do was listen, not spout a load of clichés.

'Sometimes I think that if I'd filled up my tank, I wouldn't have run out of petrol and I would have been home earlier and interrupted the murderer and Dad would still be alive. But I couldn't be bothered and took a chance and got there too late.'

Olivia reacted immediately. She took away her arm and turned her whole body towards Sandra to add power to her words.

'That's not true, Sandra. Even if you'd put petrol in your scooter you'd never have been able to prevent your father's murder. His death has nothing to do with you bothering to do something or not. Do you understand?'

Olivia saw Sandra flinch.

'Sorry,' she said and put her hand on Sandra's. 'I didn't mean to sound harsh. But you mustn't feel guilty about this. You have enough to deal with.'

'I know, but these thoughts are racing through my head and I just don't know what to do with them.'

'But you're going to see someone, aren't you?'

'No, I haven't wanted to. I've talked a bit to Tomas, a priest we know, and that's been good, I suppose.'

'And you've got Charlotte too.'

'Yeah, sure, but I can't talk to her like I can talk to you. She's always trying to find fun things to do to cheer me up, but I don't want to be cheered up.'

Olivia recognised that feeling all too well. Too many people around her had tried to cheer her up when things were at their darkest. She'd hated it. Mårten was the only one who'd understood, who'd kept the right distance, close enough to be there when she needed him. Without trying to cheer her up.

Perhaps Sandra should meet Mårten?

And he's a former child psychologist.

Sandra lifted her head a little and looked into Olivia's eyes.

'It feels like all I have is you.'

Her head sank down on her shoulder again. Olivia felt the pit of her stomach tighten. All she has is me? What did she mean? What has she projected on me? Olivia knew that she'd become very personal during their conversation at home at Maria's, that she'd told Sandra things that she hadn't told anyone else, private things, in an attempt to comfort her and be truthful. Had Sandra read too much into it?

'Can I sleep here?'

Sandra said it with her head still resting on Olivia's shoulder and Olivia didn't have a chance of trying to think of a good reason to say no.

'But we'll have to ask Charlotte first,' she said.

Sandra called Charlotte and Charlotte wanted to speak to Olivia and asked whether it was all right for Sandra to stay the night.

'Absolutely.'

'It's not a problem for you?'

'Not at all.'

So they drank up their tea and then Sandra said that she wanted to go to bed. Olivia folded down the covers of the large double bed and tucked Sandra in. Olivia lay down on the covers, fully clothed.

'Do you want the light on?' she asked.

'No, unless you want it on.'

Olivia turned off the bedside lamp. Sandra lay still on her side of the bed, and her voice came out of the darkness.

'What happened to the cat? You never said.'

'I'll tell you tomorrow.'

Sandra turned over. Olivia carried on lying on the bed, she was going to wait until Sandra had fallen asleep. Then she was going to sit in the kitchen and try to establish what she was going to do with Sandra.

She listened to try to hear whether she'd fallen asleep. When her breaths got longer and more even she sat up on the edge of the bed.

'I'm frightened.'

Sandra's voice was directed at the wall but it reached Olivia's back. She turned around and stroked Sandra over the covers.

'There's nothing for you to be afraid of, Sandra. I promise. Sleep now,' she said, as though she were a child.

* * *

It was almost half past eleven at night. Bosse and Lisa were sitting in a dark police car not far from the Riche restaurant. They'd spent a couple of hours watching Clas Hall. They'd found his name, address and lots of useful information in the drugs register, like his workplace, for example. He was a waiter at a big restaurant in Stureplan. A good environment for him to push his drugs – 5-IT perhaps? But it wasn't there they found him. They'd stopped outside his home address on Roslagsgatan and had hardly had time to turn off the engine before he came out through the front door.

Then they'd tailed him. To a clothes shop, a 7-Eleven and then a bookshop. He'd spent quite a while in there. For a while they'd thought he'd seen them, gone out another way and left his car. But finally he came out. They took a couple more pictures. They'd done a good job of filling the memory card at this point.

This wasn't actually their department. They weren't plainclothes police officers, they were murder investigators, but Mette had asked them to take care of this and so they did.

'What do you think is going on?' Bosse said.

'With what?'

'With Mette. There's some shit going on, right? Playing ping pong?'

'She wants to lose weight.'

'Playing ping-pong table? I think this is something else.'

Lisa nodded. Both of them had noticed how Mette had changed. Small things, like needing support when she got up. She didn't need that a few weeks ago. So something was wrong, though nothing either of them dared to ask her. Mette didn't really encourage such conversations. She was caring when it came to others and that's where it stopped.

'There he is!'

Lisa pointed through the large windows out onto the street. Clas Hall had gone inside the restaurant a while ago, sat down at a table and got up again shortly afterwards, probably to go to the toilet. Now he was coming back. But he didn't return to his table, he just got his jacket and headed for a table further in. Lisa picked up some binoculars. She watched Hall sit down at the new table. There was a woman already sitting there.

'He's sitting down with some woman,' Lisa said.

'Is he hitting on her?'

'Maybe.'

'What does she look like?'

'Overly red hair, overly large breasts, overly…'

Bosse grabbed the binoculars. It took a few seconds before he could get the table in focus. Then he saw her.

'It's Gabriella Forsman,' he said.

'Who's that?'

'She's an employee at Customs and Excise. She worked with Bengt Sahlmann.'

Mette was on her way home after working some rather pointless overtime. She'd had a conference call with various police officers across Europe about this big drug operation. Everyone had had a little moan, about the budget, about bureaucracy, about every-thing that had nothing do with the matter in hand: shutting down the online retailers that were supplying drugs. Eventually Mette had managed to bring the call to an end. When she got out her mobile, she saw the text from Lisa and Bosse. Time to go back to the office.

'Gabriella Forsman?!'

Bosse was standing by the wall just inside Mette's office. Lisa was sitting opposite Mette at her desk. All of them were equally baffled, and worked up. Drug dealer Clas Hall had met up with Customs Officer Gabriella Forsman. At a restaurant. It may have been just a normal date, maybe they hung out together, but there were interesting aspects to this.

Gabriella Forsman could well be involved in the stash of drugs that had gone missing from Customs and Excise.

'She was the one who reported them missing.'

'A good way of detracting the attention from oneself.'

Had she been the one supplying Clas Hall with the drugs that he'd apparently sold to that druggie Muriel? 5-IT? The exact same kind as had gone missing?

That was one question.

The other was even more interesting.

If so, did Bengt Sahlmann know about it? Had he discovered that one of his colleagues was involved? And become a danger? To Clas Hall and Gabriella Forsman?

'We've got some work to do tomorrow.'

Mette pulled herself up out of the chair. Bosse was just about to help her when he saw Lisa's discreet gesture: Don't!

* * *

Olivia blew out the candles in the kitchen. She'd been sitting there quite a while, drinking cups of green tea, trying to process the situation. She felt torn. Her enthusiasm over the meeting with Jean Borell had been clouded by Sandra's arrival. The meeting with Borell suited her police instinct. It was concrete: a theory and a murder.

Sandra was about completely different things.

She knew that she could handle the first issue, she was looking forward to it, but the other one was like quicksand to her.

But when she finally crept into bed and felt the body that was lying right next to her, she realised the crux of the matter: this girl's father has been murdered, perhaps by the man I'm going to meet the day after tomorrow.

There's a link.

Chapter 15

Her breasts were still heavy and full, she'd never needed to inflate them artificially. She felt his hands lifting them up, stroking them, her erect nipples sending signals all the way down into her crotch. She put her hands against the wall and braced herself. Her long, gold-painted nails dug into the wallpaper. She was pushing up against it. When he pressed himself inside her she felt how big he was, just like before, nothing had changed there. She held her forehead against the wall and stared down at the floor, moaning. She knew he could go on for a long time and he did. A long time. Right up until she felt a violent orgasm from her pelvis all the way up to her brain. He carried on. Her next orgasm was a bit calmer, it eased off just as he came. She let him pull out before she turned around.

'Thanks,' she said.

He nodded.

'It's me who should be thanking you, my dear.'

He'd grown up just outside Oxford and spoke very proper English. But it wasn't his English she was after, it was his sexual prowess. She'd had a little taster of it many years ago, and now she'd been able to enjoy it to the full. She pulled up her pants and invited him into the flat. He'd rung the doorbell half an hour earlier with a brown suitcase in his hand and she'd let him in without any small talk. They'd looked at each other for a while and then he moved his hand up her thigh. Now they'd done it.

Now they could engage in some small talk.

'What are you doing here?'

'I'm travelling a bit. It's a few years ago since I was in your beautiful city.'

'Rather too many years ago.'

Jackie had missed him. His body. The rest didn't interest her much. But he was nice and had helped her once upon a time, and her door was always open to him. She'd said it and she meant it.

And he knew it.

You could rely on Jackie Berglund. She was in fact ten years older than him, but he had nothing against mature women. They knew what they wanted and they got to it straight away.

'Do you want something to drink?'

'Yes, please. A splash of gin if you've got any.'

It was barely breakfast time, but Mickey Leigh was the way he was. He opted for steady yet balanced consumption. He got his gin and sat on the sofa.

'How long are you staying?' Jackie asked.

'As long as you'll have me.'

Jackie deduced from this that Mickey was planning to stay with her. No problem. She had a large flat on Norr Mälarstrand with a spare bedroom. The idea of having free access to Mickey in one of them was enough to get her going again.

'How is Red Velvet doing?' Mickey wondered.

'I've put that on hold, now I'm just running the interior design shop.'

'Why?'

'It's a long story.'

Well, not that long really, she thought. She'd made the decision just over a year ago, when she was called in for questioning about a murder on Nordkoster. She'd felt that the coppers were circling a little too closely around her, just as they had a few years earlier, when Tom Stilton got it into his head that she was involved in the murder of one of her escort girls, Jill Englund. If it hadn't been for her relations with Detective Chief Inspector Rune Forss it could have ended really badly. Well, relations wasn't quite the word – more like control. But Forss had steered Stilton away from her and she hadn't forgotten that.

Mickey sipped his gin and put his hand on her thigh.

That got her thinking about other things.

* * *

Olivia woke up late. She'd fallen asleep in the early hours of the morning, and when she turned her head, Sandra was gone.

'Sandra!'

She called out through the flat and leapt up. There was no answer. When she went into the kitchen she saw a yellow Post-it note on the kitchen table with a few words scribbled onto it: 'I'm not as strong as you.' Olivia rushed back into the bedroom and grabbed her mobile. She called Sandra and it went straight to voicemail. She asked Sandra to call her as soon as she heard her message. Then she rang Charlotte, who hadn't heard anything from Sandra since the night before.

'Please call me as soon as she gets in touch,' Olivia said.

'Will do.'

Olivia got in the shower. She stood there for a long time, much longer than normal, and after a while she sat down and let the water carry on streaming over her body.

'I'm not as strong as you.'

Why had Sandra written that? She wasn't planning to do anything stupid, was she?

When she finally got out of the shower she called Mårten and told him what had happened, both the night before and about the note on the kitchen table.

'She doesn't seem very stable,' he said.

'No. What shall I do?'

'There's not much you can do right now, hopefully she'll get in touch soon.'

'And if she doesn't?'

'She will. She seems to feel a strong connection with you.'

'Yes. Could you see yourself talking to her if the time comes?'

'Absolutely, I'd be happy to. If she wants to.'

'Thanks.'

Olivia ended the call. She didn't like the word Mårten had used: 'Hopefully.' But what could he say? He couldn't guarantee that Sandra was going to get in touch.

What if she didn't?

* * *

A few people turned their heads, both men and women, as a long shapely body was ushered down the corridor to the interrogation room.

Gabriella Forsman exuded charisma.

When she sat down in the designated chair, she pulled her dress up just enough to allow her to cross her legs. Bosse noticed that. He was standing against a wall next to Lisa. Mette was sitting opposite Forsman. Forsman looked very calm: she'd applied fresh lipstick and tied her hair up so that it resembled a bale of red hay on top of her head. Forsman assumed that the conversation was going to be about the dreadful events concerning Bengt Sahlmann.

If she could help, she was more than willing to do so.

'A large stash of 5-IT went missing at Customs and Excise a while ago,' Mette began. 'It was part of the stash you'd seized earlier during the autumn, right?'

'Right. I was the one who discovered it had gone missing.'

Forsman's deep alto voice filled the room.

'And what did you do then?'

'I told Bengt. He is, he was... responsible for... for...'

Forsman had trouble speaking. She picked up her neat matching handbag and got out a handkerchief. Mette glanced at Lisa and Bosse. Forsman managed to pull herself together.

'...I'm sorry, I haven't... every time I think about him I get... sorry. So yeah, Bengt was the main person in charge of the seized goods, so he was the one I told.'

'And what did Bengt do?'

'He was shocked. It was a large stash that had gone missing. He felt it was very worrying. It wouldn't be very good for us if it came out, right?'

'So he launched an investigation.'

'Yes. We didn't know whether or not it had disappeared during the handling process, internally, and whether it might turn up somewhere. It had happened before.'

'You didn't contact the police?'

'No. Bengt wanted to investigate this himself first. I suppose he thought it wasn't necessary to drag in the police if they'd just got lost somewhere in the building.'

'Do you know what he found out?'

'No.'

'So you don't know if he found out anything about whether anyone on the inside had been part of their disappearance?'

'No. Unfortunately not.'

Forsman smiled a little and crossed her legs the other way, her free leg dangling calmly and rhythmically. She'd done this before.

'Do you know whether he made a written report about his investigation?'

'No, I would have heard about that.'

'What's your relationship with Clas Hall?'

Forsman looked at Mette with very big eyes. Bosse spent a few seconds wondering whether they were always this large. They were certainly beautiful.

'Who's that?' Forsman finally said.

'He's a waiter who's been convicted of numerous drugs charges. At the moment he's selling 5-IT around the city, the same drug that disappeared from Customs and Excise. Do you know Clas Hall?'

'No.'

'You don't hang out?'

'No. Why would I hang out with a drug dealer? Who do you take me for?!'

Forsman had recrossed her legs again. Even her voice had changed. Rather less alto and more soprano. Mette picked up a plastic file and laid out a number of photographs in front of Forsman.

'These pictures were taken at the Riche restaurant last night.'

Forsman remained seated, upright.

'Please could you have a look at them?' Mette said.

Forsman leant forward a little, her voluptuous bosom almost resting on the table. She looked at the enlarged photographs.

'That woman sitting at the table is you, yes?' Mette said.

'Yes.'

'And the man you're sitting with, who's that?'

'That was some guy who approached me and wanted... he wanted to dance.'

'Dance?'

'That's what he said, but there isn't any dancing there, so I just assumed he was trying to chat me up. It happens quite a lot when I go out.'

I wonder why, Lisa thought to herself.

'Who is he?' Forsman asked.

'It's Clas Hall. The guy you claim you don't know.'

'I don't.'

'So his chat didn't work on you?'

'No, I'm not that type of girl.'

Forsman tried to smile again. Mette pulled out a few more photographs. Lisa loved this. Pinning down prey.

'On these pictures, taken outside the restaurant a while later, you're kissing each other. Pretty passionately.'

A few seconds passed before Forsman forced herself to look at the pictures.

'That's what it looks like.'

'Yes, it does.'

Forsman leant back, sat up straight, shook her arms out in front of her and attempted an apologetic smile.

'Forgive me, I lied,' she said. 'I actually fell for his charm. We kissed. But that's hardly illegal? I had no idea who he was.'

Mette and Lisa looked at each other.

*　*　*

The bus driving along Odengatan was forced to brake sharply. A young girl had walked straight out into the road. The bus driver screamed at her from the other side of the windscreen. Sandra didn't hear or see his reaction, all she could see around her were blurry people, blurry buildings and blurry movements. All sounds had gone, she was walking in a dark cloud, first one way and then she turned off in the other direction. Occasionally she looked up at the sky, it was grey and low. Her green jacket was unzipped and she felt the wind blowing against her neck. A while ago she'd been sitting on an iron bench in a park, but then got up again. She didn't know where she was, it was silent in her head. She was now walking along a row of houses, right up close, she brushed the inside of her arm against the rough stone and didn't feel anything except the little flat package she was holding in her clenched fist, deep down inside her pocket.

The feeling calmed her.

* * *

The crackdown was coordinated. Bosse was in charge of the investigations at Roslagsgatan. Clas Hall wasn't there but there were clear signs of drug dealing in the flat.

The technicians were called.

Mette and Lisa organised the raid on Gabriella Forsman's place. She'd been released after questioning. She lived on Sandhamnsgatan. When the police charged through the door, Mette chose to stay on the street. Forsman lived on the third floor and Mette wasn't sure whether there was a lift. She remained in constant communication with Lisa. Just when she heard that they'd got into the flat, a car came driving out from the garage under the house. Mette saw who was sitting in it: Clas Hall at the wheel and Gabriella Forsman next to him. Mette screamed at Lisa as she moved towards the car. It came out onto the street and turned towards Mette. Forsman caught her eye. Mette lifted her arm and stepped out into the street. The car swept right past her. Mette ran after it. Lisa had run back down to the entrance by then and saw what happened from the doorway, she watched as Mette took another few steps, more slowly, as though in slow motion, and then suddenly lost her balance, slammed into a parked car and fell to the ground with a thud.

Hall's car disappeared out of sight.

* * *

It was cold and dark, but that didn't stop Luna. She'd rigged up a strong floodlight that illuminated the entire deck. She'd decided to take a huge chest freezer down to the galley. She'd bought it second-hand on the Internet and had it delivered to the barge. Then she'd waited for Stilton. When he showed up he sensed there were problems as soon as he stepped onto the ladder.

'Hi!' Luna shouted. 'You're so late!'

'Am I?'

Stilton wasn't aware of any curfew. But he went over towards the floodlight and saw the chest freezer. Then he understood.

'Have you bought this?'

'Yes, we need to get it down below deck. Pitch in, will you!'

Stilton didn't like the tone. He was a tenant. He didn't have any obligations. If she wanted help with something then she should use a different tone! But she'd also taken care of Muriel so he had to help her with her freezer.

'How are you going to get it down there?'

'We'll do it. I've got straps. You go first.'

Going first meant going first down the steep and narrow iron steps – backwards.

'Have you taken measurements to…'

'Yes, obviously. Come on now!'

Stilton went towards the freezer and lifted a couple of straps and pulled them over his shoulder. Luna did the same thing on the other side.

'Now let's lift,' she said.

They lifted.

It's not as heavy as I imagined, Stilton thought, and started down the iron steps. After a couple of steps he was shouldering more or less all the weight and he understood why he was supposed to go first. The freezer got heavier and heavier with each step and was almost brushing against the sides of the bulkheads.

But Luna's measurements were correct and they managed to get the freezer below deck with some tinkering and tweaking. Once in place they removed the straps.

'Are you going to deduct that from my rent now?' Stilton wondered aloud.

'No, but I can make you dinner.'

'OK.'

It was the first time she'd offered to make him dinner, so why not? Stilton went to his cabin and changed, which involved him taking off his leather jacket and putting on his woolly socks. There was a cold draught on the floor in the lounge. He went back in and sat down at the oval table. Luna had put some lights and music on.

'Can I do something?' he called, dutifully.

'You can lay the table!' was the response from the kitchen.

Stilton went to the cupboard that he knew contained crockery. He lifted out a couple of fine ivory-coloured plates and two robust glasses, assumed the cutlery was in the galley, put the plates and the glasses on the table and sat down again. The table was laid. A while later he smelled many tempting odours coming from the kitchen and he noticed how hungry he was. Starving. Hopefully she'll come in with a fatted calf, he thought.

She didn't.

The first thing she put in front of him was a plate of asparagus with a knob of butter. This was followed by a number of large and small plates, all filled with vegetables. The last thing she brought in was a jug of water and a large blue casserole dish.

'What's that?' Stilton wondered, hoping that there were a couple of rabbits hidden in there.

'It's carrot soup.'

234

'How delicious.'

Luna started plating up.

'Lots of vegetables,' Stilton said.

'Yes.'

'Are you vegetarian?'

'No, I'm allergic to meat.'

'You don't like it?'

'No, I do, but I'm allergic. I can't eat meat from four-legged animals.'

'But ostrich is fine?'

'Ostrich is fine, it's just quite hard to get hold of.'

'Are you being serious? You're allergic to meat?'

'Yes. Apparently it was caused by a tick bite, or that's what the doctors said anyway. It's quite an unusual allergy. Are there ticks on Rödlöga?'

'Loads.'

Stilton helped himself to carrot soup. It was delicious, nicely seasoned, and certainly superior to seafood risotto. When Luna gave him some more he saw her hand trembling. He assumed that it was the result of all that carrying.

'So, how are things going for you, then?' Luna asked.

'What things?'

'I don't know… you must be doing something?'

He hadn't said a word about what the Marseille trip had been about. She'd asked whether it had gone well and he'd answered 'I don't know'. And changed the subject. So now she was trying again.

'Or do you just roam the streets all day?'

'Basically. How much did you pay for the freezer?'

Luna was tempted to throw a beetroot at Stilton, but she stopped herself. This man doesn't divulge very much, she thought to herself, and she wasn't sure whether she liked it or not.

But the freezer was in at least.

* * *

Olivia was lying in her bed reading. She'd wandered around Moderna Museet, checking out all the artwork by living Swedish artists.

And making notes.

And calling Sandra. Three times without a reply.

She'd also managed to have a proper chat with one of the museum's curators and recorded their conversation. It had provided her with lots of useful information. She also gathered a load of different books and magazines, and borrowed an old printer from Lenni. She'd got masses of material from the Internet – she wanted to be able to scribble all over it.

Once she'd crammed all this she wouldn't need to do a bloody course, she thought.

This is hard core.

But she was going to be well-prepared when she met Jean Borell.

That was important.

She picked up one of the thick art tomes that she'd dragged home from the library in Medborgarhuset.

It was about the golden ratio equation.

She put it down again and thought about Sandra.

Charlotte had called an hour ago. Sandra had come home. She hadn't said much other than that she'd been wandering around the city.

'The whole day?'

'Yes, apparently.'

'Can I speak to her?'

'She's in the bath.'

'Can you ask her to ring me when she's done?'

'Sure.'

Sandra still hadn't called. Olivia looked at the clock, it was almost eleven now. Should she ring again or didn't Sandra want to speak to her? Was she upset or angry? Why should she be?

Olivia brushed her teeth and got undressed. As she was about to creep under the covers, Sandra called.

'Hi,' Olivia said. 'I've been trying to call you!'

'I saw that. I haven't been feeling very well today, I couldn't face picking up.'

'No worries. You'd gone when I woke.'

'I didn't want to wake you.'

'That's sweet. I saw the note you wrote.'

'Yes.'

'So what have you been up to today?'

'Wandering. What have you done?'

Olivia felt that Sandra was distant. She heard it in her voice, in the way she expressed herself, there wasn't any connection any more. Not like yesterday, in the kitchen.

'I'm studying art,' Olivia said.

'I thought you were starting in the spring.'

'I am, I just want to do some preparation.'

'Oh right.'

And then there was silence. Olivia thought about Mårten. How was she going to suggest a meeting with Mårten to Sandra? Should she even mention it? How much should she involve herself in Sandra's situation? But she already was involved, right up to her neck.

'Sleep well.'

It was Sandra who said it and Olivia didn't get the chance to reply before she ended the call. She sat on the edge of her bed for a while with her mobile in her hand, then she sank down on the covers. After a couple of minutes of staring at the ceiling, she'd decided. One thing at a time. Focus on what's next on the agenda. Tomorrow it was Jean Borell.

Then she'd deal with Sandra.

Chapter 16

He opened up the special little plastic box. There were three glass eyes sitting next to each other in a clear fluid, one with a blue iris, one with a brown one and one without an iris. He chose the brown one, it matched his good eye. He carefully rinsed the glass eye under warm running water, washed it with unscented soap, poured over a splash of sterile water and pushed it into the empty eye cavity.

Then he closed the plastic box.

Olivia had looked up the address on her phone and got a good idea of how to get to Jean Borell's house out on Värmdö. It lay far out on Ingarö. By the water. When she turned off from the main road it started to rain. She followed a sign towards Brunn. The whole time she tried to remind herself who she was going to act like, a person who certainly didn't allow their feelings to shine through. She was going to meet a man whom she deeply despised, without ever having met him, a man who intentionally risked other people's wellbeing to increase his own private fortune. A first-class arsehole, as Alex had said.

An arsehole who might actually have killed Sandra's father.

She was going to smile at him.

Her big, charming smile.

She was going to listen to him, compliment him on his exquisite taste in art, praise him for being able to see what so few others could: the depth of expression of great artists.

She was going to massage his ego.

She turned off at Brunn and carried on along a small lane through the forest. There were no road signs. She carried on down the lane for quite a while. The rain got heavier and the forest became tighter and darker. She couldn't see any houses, no lights. He's probably bought up all this land to make it as private as possible. People like him tended to do that sort of thing. They don't want other people around, they want space. Privacy. They want a little kingdom.

Out of sight.

After driving even further through the darkness she started to wonder whether she was going the right way. The windscreen wipers were on full trying to clear the rain and she had more and more trouble seeing where she was going. Then she saw it, in the distance. A large iron gate, hanging on two large marble pillars. She started slowing down. To the right of the gate was a small gravelled area. There was a dark car standing there. She pulled over in her Mustang and turned off the engine.

So this was where he lived?

She got out, locked the car and approached the iron gate. There was a little white box with a button on one of the pillars. She pressed the button. There was a crackling noise. She waited. Then she pressed again and thought the gate might open. It didn't. She leant up to the box and said: 'This is Olivia Rivera. I have a meeting with Jean Borell at six o'clock. I'm standing outside the gate.'

She took a few steps back. Suddenly the gate slid open, without making a sound. No creaking or scraping, it just slid open. Olivia went in. Then she saw lights. A long row of beautiful iron lanterns on tall posts leading the way. She started walking down a wide gravel path in the glow of the lanterns. It's so strangely silent, she thought. The rain had almost stopped and she heard her own breath and a faint noise. Was it water? The house did lie next to the water apparently. But she could see no house and no water. She followed the lanterns. Soon I suppose I'll have dogs barking at me, guard dogs, but she didn't hear any. The lanterns took her round in a curve, and then she saw it.

The house.

Well, Olivia actually thought it looked more like something that had landed, from high up above, from outer space. Various concrete platforms overlapping each other in different directions, poorly lit, from the side, large glistening glass facades, broken up by black angled pieces of metal. A long, hidden bank of lights made it look as though the roof was floating in the air.

She stood still.

Unbelievable, she thought, un-fucking-believable! Do buildings like this really exist? Do people live like this? I wonder how many taxpayers' care sector millions have been ploughed into it. She shook her head and proceeded towards the spaceship. I hope I'll find an entrance, I don't have a remote control. But the lanterns guided her all the way to a gigantic door with silver details. The sound of her knocking would be carried all of about ten centimetres into the wood. So she searched around looking for some kind of doorbell. There was a large copper urn to the right. Perhaps you're supposed to throw this at the door, she thought.

Then it slid open.

Again, without a sound.

There was a man standing, backlit, looking at her. Jean Borell. The man she'd seen on the news. Rather differently dressed now, a nice pair of skinny jeans and a thin beige blazer over a tight black jumper. His artistic attire, Olivia just about managed to think before she remembered who she was supposed to be. The woman with the big smile and the academic interest in art.

'Hi. Olivia Rivera.' She smiled.

'Jean Borell.'

They greeted each other. He had a firm handshake and he hugged pretty hard too. But not as hard as Hilda at Silvergården, she thought.

'Come in,' he said.

Borell stepped to the side and Olivia went in. She noticed a pleasant sober cologne, without a hint of nutmeg. Borell allowed the door to slide closed again before he caught up with Olivia. He stopped just behind her.

'Rivera,' he said. 'Do you have Latin American roots?'

Olivia turned around.

'Yes. Mexico.'

'I can see that. Any relation to Diego?'

'Distantly. What a fabulous house!'

'It was designed by Tomas Sandell. I gave him free reign. Would you like a martini?'

'No, thanks, I'm driving.'

'A Mustang.'

'Yes, how did you know?'

Borell was already walking off.

'Please have a look around in the meantime!'

He gestured towards the inner part of the spaceship.

'Maybe I'll have that martini after all,' Olivia said. 'But not too much gin.'

'Perfect.'

Borell was on his way towards a bar further in. A large well-lit bar area with a fantastic fluorescent creation as a background. Probably a work of art. Olivia racked her brains, but she couldn't think of a possible artist. She started walking around in the first large room. The off-white walls were sparsely decorated with art that she recognised, at least most of them. Marie-Louise Ekman. Ernst Billgren. Cecilia Edefalk. Olle Kåks. Lena Cronqvist. There was a faint sound of music, as though from outer space, electronic sounds swirling around without disturbing one's concentration. This space was built for art, for an art lover, a large roomy space.

'What do you think?' Borell hollered from the bar. Olivia turned towards him. He was busy cutting up small bits of lemon peel.

'I think it's fantastic!' she replied.

'Me too.'

Borell smiled and put some lemon peel in a cocktail glass. Olivia carried on looking around and felt that she was gripped by something almost sacred in the room, the perfectly placed spotlights were carving out the paintings in front of her. This is how I'll live one day, she thought, this beautifully, walking around in a room like this, just enjoying. And the world won't be full of hideousness and bedsores full of fly larvae.

The image brought her back.

Remember why you're here, Olivia! Pull yourself together! Just think how many cut care services these paintings have cost!

'One martini.'

Borell passed the thin, low glass over to her. He raised his glass and they toasted. With his drink in hand, Borell initiated a guided tour through his collection in the room – he really adored his paintings. Once they'd come full circle he stopped and looked at Olivia. Ever since she'd come in she'd avoided looking into Borell's glass eye. She knew he had one. Now she was dodging his gaze. Borell noticed.

'A hunting injury,' he said. 'We were near Mount Kilimanjaro and I had a lion in my sights. I was a little too eager, the breech hit me in the eye. But we got the lion.'

'Oh good.'

A hunting accident? According to Alex he'd lost his eye as a child? And he'd been at school with him. But OK, who hasn't tweaked their CV a little?

'You have a slight squint yourself,' Borell said.

'Yes.'

'Does it bother you?'

'Why?'

'I know a specialist in Lausanne, he could fix that.'

'It isn't something that bothers me.'

Olivia sipped her martini. She didn't like the private nature of this conversation. She didn't feel in control.

Engage your intuition!

'Shall we do the interview here?' she said.

'Let's do it in the bar.'

They went over to the spectacular bar. Olivia pulled herself up onto a leather barstool, and Borell sat on the stool next to her. There was a black object at one end of the bar that immediately caught Olivia's eye.

'What a beautiful violin,' she said.

'Blackbird. Lars Widenfalk. He made it according to Stradivarius's drawings. Touch it.'

Borell handed the beautiful violin to Olivia. She was expecting a light instrument, but she actually almost dropped it. The violin was made from stone. It was heavy.

'What's it made of?' she said.

'Black diabase,' said Borell. 'He made it from an old gravestone. The only violin in the world made from stone.'

'Can you play it?'

Borell reached for the beautifully shiny diabase violin. He picked up a bow from behind the bar and turned off the fluorescent creation in the background. The gentle lighting from the art room shone onto the bar.

They were sitting in the shadows.

'Close your eyes,' he said.

Olivia hesitated for a moment, then she closed her eyes. What am I doing? Then she heard the fragile notes of the violin. The resonance from the stone body was powerful. And then a few more notes that joined together to form a melody. He could play the violin? She opened her eyes. Borell lowered the bow.

'You *can* play it,' he said.

He carefully put the violin down on the bar.

'The interview,' he said.

Olivia took out a little tape recorder and asked him whether it was OK that she recorded their conversation.

He agreed.

She also got out a pad of paper with some questions she'd prepared and started the interview after explaining to Borell what her thesis was going to be about. In a way that made Borell understand that his role in it was going to be very significant.

He appreciated that.

She'd compiled most of the questions using different articles about art and the questions that followed them. Some of them came from interviews with Borell that she'd found on the

Internet, about his passion for art. Largely in English. She also made it clear that she wasn't even close to his level when it came to knowledge about modern Swedish art, but that she hoped he didn't find it too basic.

He didn't. He liked talking about his collection. And about his own relationship with it. About his deep passion for art and how much of his life he dedicated to it.

'Have you ever dreamed of being an artist yourself?' Olivia asked when she reached the end of her list of questions.

'Never. My talents are rather more pecuniary.'

'You're a venture capitalist.'

'Yes.'

'Do you regard your collection as an investment?'

'Yes, but not in financial terms. It's an investment in myself. I think I develop as a person through my art.'

'You become a better venture capitalist?'

'In a way.' Borell smiled.

'So then it is a kind of financial investment?'

Borell looked at Olivia. Does he think I'm being impudent or does he like a challenge? His work involves him taking risks after all.

'Are we done with the interview?' he asked.

'Yes.'

'Then I'll show you my L-room, as a bonus. Come.'

Borell slid down from the barstool. Olivia followed him, through various corridors and smaller rooms with beautiful watercolour paintings on the walls. A short while later they reached a long atrium with a huge glass wall facing out to the dark sea. Olivia peered outside and realised that the whole room had to have been built on a rock over the water. She saw the waves breaking below. Coastal protection laws clearly didn't apply to everyone, she thought to herself and scurried after Borell. Suddenly she stopped. One of the gigantic glass walls had been turned into a narrow floor-to-ceiling aquarium, full of green liquid. The foetal remains of a pair of conjoined twins were floating around inside. Their fused bodies were slowly moving towards one side of the glass.

'That English artist,' he said.

There was only one person this could be. That guy who shocked people with pieces about death. But this…?

She looked at the bizarre aquarium.

'You're not allowed to write about this,' Borell said. 'It's not an official piece of art. He created it specially for this house. On site. For me.'

Olivia was struggling to find words.

'But where did he… where are…'

'Stillborn twins. From Manchester. Their parents received a substantial sum of money. Now the foetuses live on as a work of art.'

Borell carried on into the atrium. Olivia pulled herself away from this macabre piece of 'artwork' and felt a great sense of unease. What's he going to show me over there? In the L-room?

'Here.'

Borell had stopped in front of a metal door at the far end of the hall. He pressed a button on one side. This door slid open without a sound too.

'After you.'

Borell gestured with his hand and Olivia stepped inside, rather hesitantly. The room wasn't very big – square, no windows. All the walls were adorned with paintings, two on each wall. She recognised most of them and she now understood what he'd meant by L-room. There was Lena Cronqvist again, Lars Lerin, Linn Fernström and Lars Kleen.

'Lena, Linn and Lars times two. My favourites.'

First names? Olivia thought to herself. Did he know them? It certainly wasn't unlikely. Or was he just showing off? She looked at the valuable paintings hanging in the room. Profits from neglecting the elderly invested in exquisite artwork, she thought. Complete cynicism. I wonder how many artists have views on where their buyers get their money? Do they even reflect on that? Or does 'money talks' apply here too? Are they only responsible for their own work of art? Not what happens to it? In whose hands it ends up? Their creations being bought with private blood money and hung up in a sealed-off bunker. Don't they give a shit?

She hoped that they did.

Borell went and stood right in the middle of the room with his martini glass in his hand. It was empty.

'This is my treasure chamber,' he said. 'Maybe not in terms of market value, but to me. This is my Shangri-La.'

Olivia peered at Borell. His gaze slowly scanned the walls and she felt that he really meant it. This room was special. To him.

'What's that I can hear?' she said.

The electronic music had stopped, and instead she could hear a gentle buzzing sound, from above, from a ledge running along the ceiling.

'The vacuum system.'

'What's that?'

'The world's most modern way to prevent art theft. It's only available to private buyers so far.'

'How does it work?'

'You're inquisitive.'

'Is it secret?'

Borell smiled.

'Not at all,' he said and gestured up towards the ceiling. 'When the system turns on, the doors slide shut and all the air is sucked out of the room. As you can see, there are no air valves. It gets hermetically sealed and it's impossible to get inside.'

'What happens if someone happens to be in there?'

'It would be pretty excruciating.'

Olivia looked up at the buzzing ledge on the ceiling. Was he lying? Why would he do that? He could probably install whatever high-tech system he wanted with all his money.

She felt that she wanted to get out.

From this room.

From the house.

'Would you like another martini?' Borell said.

'No. Thank you.'

Olivia left the L-room. Borell followed her. The whole way through the atrium, Olivia tried to keep her gaze on the wall opposite the glass facade. She didn't want to see that disgusting formalin aquarium. Borell was silent the entire time. As they passed through a short, poorly lit hallway, Olivia suddenly smelled smoke. Cigarette smoke. They were not alone. There was someone else here too.

She started walking faster.

'You met Magnus Thorhed?'

Borell's voice revealed that he was right behind her.

'Yes, at Bukowskis,' she said. 'He seemed interested in a Karin Mamma Andersson piece. Was that for you?'

'Yes.'

'So he's involved in your art collection?'

'He's involved in everything that concerns me. He's very loyal. Very much at the forefront of things.'

'Did you buy the painting?'

'Yes. I also bought some video art by Ann-Sofi. Would you like to see it?'

'Ann-Sofi Sidén?'

'Yes.'

Olivia had read about Sidén, one of Sweden's most successful international video artists. She had no desire to see this video. What she wanted was to go to her car and back to civilisation.

She'd had enough.

'It's in my office,' said Borell.

His office?

'Yes, please,' she said. 'But then I have to go.'

Olivia followed Borell into his office. She couldn't quite work out where exactly it was in relation to all the other rooms and corridors, suddenly it was just there. On the other side of another door that slid into the wall without a sound. Borell went up to a large flat-screen television, pushed a CD into a player and put on Ann-Sofi Sidén's video.

It started.

Whatever was playing on the screen was probably fine art, a talented woman's attempt to explore the human psyche with the tools available to her. But it just passed her by. She didn't look at the screen. She let her gaze wander around the room without turning her head. She couldn't see much in her field of vision. There was a large beautiful mirror with a gold frame on one wall. On the left was a desk with an open laptop on it. A PC. On one side of the flat screen she saw a large bookshelf full of folders and on the other side was a shelf with random piles of art books. And at the far end, on top of a couple of large books, she saw a thin bag. Closed.

A very special bag made from checked hard-pressed cork.

A laptop bag.

Olivia felt her pulse rise dramatically.

'What do you think?'

Borell looked at her. He'd been looking at her the whole time, ever since the video had started. He hadn't even glanced at the screen. Olivia felt it.

'It's fascinating,' she said.

'Very.'

Borell carried on looking at her with his good eye. Olivia tried to fix her gaze on the screen in front of her. Borell laid his arm around her shoulder and turned off the video. He leant in towards her and almost whispered.

'You're not writing a dissertation,' he said gently. 'Am I right?'

Olivia removed Borell's hand from her shoulder. That gave her a couple of seconds. Then she said: 'Yes, I am.'

'I think you're lying. Why did you come here?'

'To interview you. But now I need to go back to the city. Thanks for letting me come. I'll find my own way out.'

Olivia quickly proceeded towards the door. Borell stood still. Olivia came out into a corridor and she didn't quite know where it led. She turned her head slightly and saw that Borell was looking at her. She started walking faster and heard the electronic sounds bouncing off the walls. When she turned a corner she saw a coloured stream of light a bit further off. The bar? She quickened her step, her heels clicking against the stone floor.

It was the bar. She reached a room that she recognised and hastily headed towards the front door. From the corner of her eye she saw something move and looked back at the bar. A man was sitting there with his back to her. A ring of blue smoke was swirling up in front of him. She immediately knew who it was, she recognised the plait at the back of his neck. Had he been there the whole time? Why didn't he turn around? She reached the hallway and saw the large wooden door. How the hell do I open it? She didn't need to. A couple of metres before she reached it, the door slid open by itself.

She ran out.

She ran along the avenue of lanterns.

She ran through the open gate and jumped in her car and sank down into the seat. Why did I run? she thought. She shook her head a little, started the car, reversed and set off down the dark forest road in front of her. In her rear-view mirror she caught sight of a dark figure coming through the gate. Thorhed? Why weren't her bloody rear windscreen wipers working? She put her foot down and tried to keep the car on the narrow lane. Suddenly she was forced to slam on the brakes. Her headlights had stopped working. It wasn't the first time this had happened, it was a loose cable, she knew that. She got out of the car. As she was about to lift the bonnet she saw a couple of cones of light shining through the forest, far off behind her. I have no desire to meet whoever that might be, she thought, not now, and she jumped back into her car again. I'll have to make do with my parking lights. She put her foot down again and tried to see as far ahead of her as she could. The rain had stopped and the clouds had revealed a cold moon. The greyish-blue moonshine gave her a good few more metres of visibility. She looked in her rear-view mirror and saw two blurry headlights getting closer. She drove as fast as she dared to. Twice she'd almost driven into the ditch, the gravel bouncing off her windscreen.

Suddenly she saw lights. Houses. Street lights. Suddenly she was no longer surrounded by forest. She'd almost reached Brunn. She pulled the car up onto the main road and looked into the rear-view mirror. The headlights behind her were gone. Had he stopped? Whoever the bloody hell it was? Thorhed? She sped out onto an asphalted road and kept her eyes looking straight ahead until she saw a petrol station.

She turned in and parked. There were several people moving around her, filling up their cars, going in and out of the shop. She turned off the motor and took her mobile out while looking at the time. It was only half past eight. She dialled Sandra's number.

'Hi, Sandra! Sorry to bother you, I just wanted to ask you about that bag you used for your computer, what did it look like again?'

'It was some kind of pressed cork, with brown and black checks. Dad bought it in Milan… But apparently you can buy it online too. Have you found the computer?!'

'Maybe. How are you?'

'OK.'

'Good. Listen, I need to head off now, but I'll be in touch tomorrow. Bye!'

Olivia ended the call.

Chapter 17

The first thing he thought was that he was thinking. I think, therefore I live. They didn't beat me to death.

But his face was a dream for a teacher of watercolour painting. He had the whole spectrum there. From deepest cobalt blue to purple and red and bright yellowy orange, connected with black stitches.

'Have you seen your face?'

The question was put to him in French and it was Jean-Baptiste who did the asking. He was sitting on a chair next to Abbas's bed at the Hôpital de la Conception in central Marseille.

'No.'

Abbas had sat up a bit. He hadn't looked in the mirror, he didn't need to, he could feel what he looked like. But he was alive. It was thanks to the waiter at Eden Roc, who'd caught sight of him and called an ambulance, that he was black and blue instead of deathly white.

'I thought you had your knives with you?' Jean-Baptiste said with a smile.

He tried to lighten the mood a little. Abbas did not smile back. He couldn't, otherwise half his face would have split open. But he could speak. Not completely clearly as his nose had been badly clobbered, but he snuffled out what he'd seen. The face of the guy who'd assaulted him, who'd had a little bull tattooed on his neck.

'He must be the guy known as Le Taureau,' Abbas managed to utter.

'Presumably.'

Abbas described the man's face to Jean-Baptiste. He shook his head.

'It doesn't ring any bells.'

'But this has to have something to do with Samira?'

'Or Philippe Martin.'

'Or both.'

'Yes. When are you being discharged?'

'Soon.'

'Are you going to go home?'

'I'll go when I'm done.'

Jean-Baptiste looked at the battered man lying in the bed. What was he planning to do? He'd already viciously attacked one person in this city, admittedly an arsehole, but still. Jean-Baptiste had accepted it, but he wasn't going to accept any more. Stilton was no longer here. He leant forward a little.

'El Fassi.'

'Yes?'

'As soon as you are discharged from this hospital you're going to get out of Marseille. By train or plane. I don't want to have to identify you in some morgue or take you in for whatever shit you do next. I've turned a blind eye once, I never do that twice. Do we understand each other?'

Abbas looked at the large policeman.

* * *

There was another man sitting in another hospital in another country at a similar hospital bed. Mette Olsäter was in the bed, half-sitting, with a thick plaster on her cheek. She'd needed nine stitches.

Her husband was holding her hand.

'It was a heart attack,' Mårten said.

'I know. A mild one.'

'This time. There might be more. You know that.'

The doctors had made that very clear to both of them. It wasn't certain that there'd be more heart attacks, but there could be, unless the detective chief inspector changed a few things: her lifestyle in general and her workload in particular. And to underline the gravity of her situation, Mette was put on sick leave for a while. Which required her to stay at home.

It wasn't something she was looking forward to. Mårten knew that.

'But you have to,' he said.

'I know.'

Lisa and Bosse had visited her a short while earlier to give her an update. Clas Hall and Gabriella Forsman had managed to get out of the city despite a massive police presence. Their car was found outside Södertälje. They'd probably taken another car.

Several bags of 5-IT were also found at Forsman's flat. They were currently trying to establish whether the bags were part of the missing drugs at Customs and Excise. It seemed likely. They'd also seized Forsman's laptop and the computer forensics team was busy working on it.

After Lisa and Bosse had left, Mette realised how much she was longing to go back to the Squad already. Back to work. Instead, she was going to be sitting locked up in Kummelnäs, with a man who was going to be fretting about every step she took. On the stairs. In the cellar. Up in the attic.

'But surely it's going to be nice to come home and have a bit of a rest?' Mårten said.

'Yeah, lovely,' Mette said.

It's going to be unbearable, she thought to herself.

* * *

Stilton was sitting in the lounge on the barge drinking coffee. He found himself in an unbearable void. Mink hadn't got back to him and Abbas still wasn't answering. There was something wrong, seriously wrong – he was increasingly convinced of it. He looked at the screen in front of him. He had borrowed Luna's computer to check for flights to Marseille. There weren't any direct ones, only with stopovers and shit, just like on the way back, so it was going to take quite a while to get there.

Then Mink called. And came through for him.

'Ovette Andersson,' he said.

'Acke's mum?'

'Yes.'

'Has she worked for Jackie Berglund?'

'Apparently. But she stopped eleven years ago, when Acke was born.'

'How did you find that out?'

'Listen, us professionals don't reveal our methods, right?'

'Of course not. Thanks!'

'So where are you planning to be?'

'When?'

'When the world ends?'

'On the moon. Bye!'

Stilton ended the call.

Ovette Andersson? And Jackie Berglund? That was a big surprise.

He looked at the time again and closed the laptop.

Marseille would have to wait.

* * *

There were quite a few pedestrians who turned around as the young woman charged past them on the pavement, at pretty high speed. Exercising in this weather was tantamount to masochism. Olivia realised that too. She was on her way home after a long run in bloody awful weather and she still had a way to go before she reached Skånegatan. The blister she'd got in Mexico was throbbing, but she tried to ignore the pain as best she could. Her adrenalin-fuelled mind tried to get to grips with her visit to Borell's. 'You're not writing a dissertation. Am I right?' Did he know that I was faking the whole time? Had he looked me up? How? So why did he let me come? And why was Thorhed hiding like that? Why didn't he come and say hello? He didn't even turn around in the bar.

She couldn't work it out.

So she thought about the laptop that she'd seen in Borell's office instead. Not the one on his desk, the one lying half-hidden among the art books on a shelf. In a bag made from hard-pressed cork. Unusual, but not unique. Borell could have bought it during one of his countless trips around the world. He could even have ordered it online. But he could have stolen it too. From Bengt Sahlmann, to get hold of any files about the neglect at Silvergården. That would mean he was involved in the murder of Sandra's father.

In that case her theory was correct.

The cold, raw wind blew up from Hammarby and Skanstull and was pressed between the stone buildings. Once it reached Skånegatan it was like a wall of ice. She had to run with her head hunched over to be able to get home.

So what about her intuition? What use had that been? What had the visit to the spaceship out there yielded in that respect? What had she felt?

She'd felt a great many things, both during her visit and in the car on her way home. And during the night that followed. She'd gone through the visit from beginning to end, several times, gone through all the conversations. All the impressions, all that had remained unsaid. The next morning she'd boiled it down to what she'd just been thinking about.

There was a cork bag with a laptop inside in his office.

That had nothing whatsoever to do with her intuition.

On the other hand, she'd established that Jean Borell was a very unique man with very unique inclinations. A man who got what he wanted and probably did so without any scruples. And he was probably willing to go very far to protect what he had.

But how far was he willing to go to protect the millions he made in profits in the welfare sector?

Olivia cogitated about how she was going to find out to whom the laptop in the cork bag belonged. Was it Sahlmann's or Borell's? She couldn't exactly go through Mette and order a search warrant on his house, she didn't have enough to go on for that. In fact, she had nothing, nothing substantial. And, moreover, she didn't want Mette in on this. This was her own theory. And if it was correct, it was certainly going to put Mette in her place.

She was already relishing the thought.

Then Mårten rang, just as she reached her building.

Once he'd finished, the feelings of joy quickly dissipated. Mette's heart attack really shook her up, even though it was a mild one and she was getting better. But what if it hadn't been mild? What if she hadn't made it?

Olivia pushed the door open.

'She's going to be at home for a while in case you want to get in touch.'

That's what Mårten had said. She hoped that he would have heard the shock in her voice, and that he'd communicate her reaction to Mette. But get in touch? Did he mean that she should come over and see her? Be the bigger person?

Of course she would, but not yet.

Tomorrow she was going to Bengt Sahlmann's funeral.

That took precedence.

She went into the stairway and pulled the door closed, rather harder than usual. As she was walking up the last few steps, a little bell started ringing in her mind. She couldn't put her finger on it, but it was something about a car.

She started taking off her running gear.

But why wasn't that bell ringing loud enough?

Chapter 18

Stilton had tried to reach Ovette Andersson a couple of times on her mobile, but each time it went straight to voicemail and she didn't call him back. Eventually he asked Mink to find out how to get hold of her. Mink knew straight away.

'At Qjouren. She works there.'

'Thanks.'

Qjouren was started by a charity called RFHL Stockholm four years ago and it was Sweden's only women's shelter for drug abusers. There were plenty of other women's shelters, but none that took care of women drug abusers subjected to violence, even though it was this group who were most in need of protection.

Stilton knew Qjouren. He'd collected Muriel there once. She'd been assaulted after some casual liaison and sought refuge. Now Ovette Andersson was working there. Stilton waited outside, she'd be coming out sooner or later. It had been a year since he'd seen her – when her eleven-year-old son Acke had helped him pin down the so-called mobile murderers.

So he recognised her when she came out.

And she recognised him.

'I've been trying to call you,' he said.

'I know.'

'Do you have time for a coffee?'

'What do you want?'

'Can we discuss that over coffee?'

Ovette considered the offer for a few seconds. She had reason to. Stilton looked at her. A year ago she'd been a broken woman, selling her body to make a living. Far down the ranks. On the streets. That she'd been part of Jackie Berglund's exclusive escort service many years before had really surprised him. Now he saw a rather different woman standing in front of him. Ovette was still broken, you can't hide a certain kind of physical erosion, but she had a different expression on her face, another look.

She looked alive.

'OK, ten minutes. Then I'm meeting Acke,' she said.

They went and sat down in a suitably empty café. Ovette called Acke and told him where she was. Stilton waited for her to finish and then started asking her about Qjouren, to get her to start talking. She told him about the organisation. She'd stopped working on the streets after Acke was attacked last year, as she'd promised. Now she'd been working at Qjouren for six months. It gave her both purpose and insight about a lot of stuff she'd suppressed when she was vulnerable herself. Her experiences had made her a good contact person for other women at risk.

'Now they'll probably be closing the whole organisation down,' she said.

'Why?'

'Because we no longer get government subsidies and the municipalities don't want to support us. Women drug users suffering abuse have the lowest possible status. It's ridiculous.'

Stilton saw how upset Ovette was. He understood her. It was always like that. Those most in need of help got the least: there were too few of them, they didn't generate any votes. Solidarity had become a special-interest issue.

He thought it was disgusting.

'So what did you want?' Ovette asked.

'To talk about Rune Forss.'

Ovette averted her gaze and looked into her coffee cup. Stilton knew that he didn't have long, but he nevertheless gave some background information. His own. And how it included Rune Forss. He delivered it so passionately that he managed to get her attention again.

Then he asked the question.

'Did Forss buy sex from you when you were working for Jackie Berglund?'

'Yes.'

'So would you be prepared to talk about this publicly?'

'No.'

'Why not?'

'Because I've left that world behind. I don't want to be reminded or dragged into it. And I know what Jackie's like. How do you think she'll react if I snitch on one of her high-ranking clients?'

Stilton understood all of her reasons and he could see that she wasn't going to change her mind. He tried to hide his disappointment.

'Did he use any other escort girls?'

'Yes.'

'Do you know which ones?'

'No.'

Either she knew and didn't want to snitch or she didn't know. But now he knew that there were more girls. He'd have to keep going without Ovette.

So he changed the subject.

'How's Acke doing now?' he said.

'Good. He's well, he's much more stable. That's another reason.'

'Because?'

'He doesn't know who his father is. If I were to drag all that up again it would complicate things.'

'What do you mean complicate things?'

'I have to go now.'

'OK. Take care. Say hi to Acke.'

'Will do.'

Ovette saw Acke walking up the road. She got up and left. Stilton swirled his finger around his coffee cup. Complicate things? How? What did she mean by that? Did she mean that...? He didn't dare to think the thought in full. In one go. He was forced to let it float around some more before he could formulate it in his head. He looked out and saw Ovette walk off with her arm around Acke.

Was Rune Forss Acke's father? Did he knock up a prostitute eleven years ago? And does he have a son with her whom he doesn't know about?

Stilton looked at Ovette's coffee cup. The meeting had confirmed what he knew. Rune Forss had used prostitutes. Although he was never going to be able to prove it with Ovette's help.

Nevertheless, Stilton now had another way of approaching him.

* * *

Olivia sat down on a pew towards the back of Sollentuna Church. Sandra and Charlotte were sitting right at the front. There were quite a few people there, some of whom she recognised. One of them was Alex Popovic. They'd nodded at each other as she snuck in. She quickly ascertained that Jean Borell wasn't there. He might well have been, and that would really have complicated things. She didn't want Borell to know about her connection with Bengt Sahlmann.

Maria, her mother, on the other hand was there. She shook her head when Olivia turned up, late, and sat down in the pew next to her.

The priest who led the ceremony was a thin, upright man with short dark hair. Olivia assumed it was the same priest who'd been to see Sandra and Charlotte a few days ago. He delivered a very heartfelt and touching eulogy. Olivia realised that he'd been very close to Bengt and the family, which was confirmed when Maria whispered: 'He was the one who buried Sandra's mum.'

Olivia nodded. She didn't like funerals. She'd only been to two in her life – her fathers' funerals. First Arne and then Nils Wendt, her biological father.

But now she was here for Sandra's sake.

After the ceremony there was tea and coffee in premises next door. Olivia had a moment to talk to Sandra before they went in. She saw that Sandra was struggling to keep things together. They hugged. Olivia understood all too well what Sandra was going through: there wasn't much to talk about.

'Is there a toilet here somewhere?' Sandra asked and Olivia pointed towards a couple of doors further down. Sandra walked off just as Charlotte approached Olivia. She was dressed in a tasteful black dress and her hair was tied in a tight bun. She looks a bit like Therese, Olivia thought. She remembered Sandra's mother having the same blonde hair and quite unusual eyes, rather too close together. Sandra had said that Charlotte was the eldest of the sisters and had worked as a golf instructor.

Charlotte walked towards her with open arms and they gave each other a little hug. Olivia noticed that Charlotte's mascara had smudged a bit under her eye.

'It's so terribly sad,' Charlotte said quietly.

'Yes.'

'He was such a good person.'

'Did you have much contact?'

'A great deal. I was his sister-in-law, and when Therese died we got even closer, it was a terrible time for both him and Sandra. Being alone with a child in those circumstances, that wasn't easy.'

'I can understand that. And you'd lost your little sister.'

'Yes, but it was harder for him, much harder. There were many evenings and nights when I had to sit and comfort him, once Sandra had fallen asleep, because he didn't want her to see too much of his sorrow.'

'No.'

'So yeah, we got very close, it was a tough period... but gradually things got better, with time. Bengt started functioning again, feeling happy and looking forward. That's why I never believed what Sandra told me, the first time, that Bengt had killed himself. It just didn't make sense to me. Sure, he'd been a bit depressed of late, but to go from there to suicide is a pretty big step.'

'Was it because of what happened to his father? At Silvergården?'

'Yes, that as well.'

'What else?'

Charlotte turned and looked down at the toilet doors. No sign of Sandra.

'I don't think that Sandra knows this,' she whispered. 'And she shouldn't either, but Bengt was very sad.'

'Why?'

'He called me one evening and told me that he'd fallen in love again, for the first time since Therese died.'

'With whom?'

'A woman at work.'

Gabriella Forsman was the name racing through Olivia's mind.

'Do you know her name?'

'No. But Bengt had fallen in love with this woman and then something happened at work that suddenly made him very sad.'

'What happened?'

'I don't know, but apparently it made his relationship with this woman impossible somehow. He didn't say why. But like I said, to go from that to suicide is quite a big step.'

'And then it turned out it wasn't suicide.'

'No.'

Both of them stopped talking when Sandra came back from the toilet. Charlotte walked towards her and gave her a hug. They carried on next door. Olivia stayed where she was, she didn't know what to do. Most of all she just wanted to get out of there, leave. But she couldn't.

So she went next door as well.

Charlotte and Sandra had sat down at a table with Maria and a couple of people whom Olivia didn't know. The table was full. She got herself a cup of coffee and a couple of biscuits and wasn't really sure where to sit. She saw that Alex had sat down next to the priest and a woman she didn't recognise. I'll just stand over here on the side. The room wasn't very large and considering the nature of this event it was pretty quiet. Which is why it was rather clear when Alex raised his voice.

'Because he's a fucking arsehole.'

Who he was calling an arsehole couldn't be heard, as he lowered his voice immediately. But it got Olivia's attention. The only arsehole whom she connected to Alex was Jean Borell. So she discreetly moved closer towards the table.

Now she could hear even more muffled words.

'I think you're exaggerating,' said the woman.

'It's possible,' Alex said. 'In your world. To me it's a bloody cheek not even to turn up. Sending some flashy wreath? To show he can afford it? He's bloody well known Bengt since they were seventeen!'

'Can't you fine-tune your language a bit, Alex?'

The priest was trying to get Alex to tone it down.

'Sorry,' Alex said. 'I just think it's bad form.'

'But maybe he's not in Stockholm?'

'He's here. Why are you defending him?'

The priest smiled.

'Someone has to. People tend to give Jean a pretty tough time.'

'Well, there's probably a reason for that.'

Alex turned his head and spotted Olivia.

'Hi! Come and sit down.'

Alex pulled out a chair, which made it difficult for Olivia to decline. She sat down at the table. Alex introduced everyone.

'Tomas Welander. Agnes von Born. This is Olivia, she knows Sandra.'

'She's talked about you,' Welander said, looking at Olivia inquisitively.

'Has she?'

'Yes. Apparently it was you and your mother who took care of her that awful night.'

'Yes, she stayed over at our house. My mum lives near the Sahlmanns.'

'I heard.'

'Now I have to go,' Alex said and got up.

'Can I get a lift with you?'

263

Agnes von Born wanted him to drive her and he said yes. Both of them left the table and then Alex reminded her about that beer that she'd talked about. Olivia promised to get in touch. She was rather troubled to see Alex and von Born go off.

Leaving her with a priest.

'So how do you think Sandra is now?'

Welander had picked up his cup of coffee as he asked the question. Olivia was rather caught off guard. She felt that her relationship with Sandra was private. And nothing she wanted to talk about with other people. But he was a priest.

And, more than just that, he was also a friend of the family.

'I don't really know,' she said. 'What do you think?'

'I'm worried.'

Welander looked over to Sandra's table.

'Why?'

'Because I see the same signs as before.'

'Before? You mean when her mother died?'

'Yes, she was in a really bad place then. For a long time. She almost became catatonic. I've been very worried that there might be a similar reaction now. I've been in touch with her on a daily basis and I think things are very much up and down.'

'But that's probably not a strange thing.'

'No, absolutely not. She's suffered such terrible tragedies, at such a young age.'

'Yes.'

'She's coming now.'

Welander got up and greeted Sandra with open arms. They hugged. Olivia remained seated alone at the table. She was thinking about what Charlotte had said out there.

Gabriella Forsman? And Bengt Sahlmann? What did that have to do with Silvergården? Nothing. It may well have had something to do with the missing drugs at Customs and Excise.

Was her theory falling apart?

* * *

264

Mette had been waiting for Mårten's archiving day. One day a week, he went into the city to dig into his past. He'd started researching his family history in his old age.

'Why?' she'd asked when he brought it up the first time.

'Because I want to know where I'm from.'

'You're from Tjärhovsgatan on Söder.'

'And before that?'

That's where it had ended. Mette was totally uninterested in her past. Sooner or later you find out that you're related to a murderer or a nutty count in Germany. What was so fun about that? Surely it was enough to know that you were related to yourself.

So when Bosse and Lisa rang the doorbell, she knew that she had a couple of hours. To themselves. In that big house.

'How are you doing?' Bosse had asked as soon as she opened the door.

'Fine. Come in.'

And that was all that was said about Mette's condition.

There was all the more talk about Clas Hall and Gabriella Forsman, particularly Forsman. The forensics team had basically given her computer an enema and found some rather mind-blowing information. Emails in particular. Both to and from Bengt Sahlmann. The email conversations revealed that they had had some sort of private relationship, a relationship with strong emotions, largely Sahlmann's.

'She got him on the hook,' Lisa said.

'You think that's how it was?'

Bosse wasn't entirely convinced. That Sahlmann had harboured strong feelings for Forsman was pretty clear, but to what extent they were reciprocated was unclear as far as he was concerned. She might well have been in love with him too.

Lisa didn't think so.

'I think she used him. I think she wrapped him around her red fingernails and consciously seduced him.'

'To do what?' Mette asked.

'To engage in criminal activities behind his back.'

'Is there any evidence of that?'

'Yes.'

Lisa took out a couple of printed documents from Forsman's computer detailing an email conversation between Forsman and Sahlmann. The first email was from Sahlmann:

Maybe you can't understand how unbelievably painful it is to have to discover this. But I can't close my eyes to it. I know what you've done.

Dear darling Bengt! It's not what you think. You have to believe me. I've been forced into it! I'll call you tonight! My body is yours.

'My body is yours'?

Mette had to read the email with her own eyes. She had of course met Gabriella Forsman and was fully aware of this woman's ways, but 'My body is yours'?

'What soap does she think she is she living in?'

The next brief exchange of emails suggested that Sahlmann and Forsman had met up and that some kind of agreement had been made. Sahlmann used a rather different tone this time.

Unless it's all back by next Sunday evening, I'm going to report this to the police on Monday morning. You know I have to. Then the police will deal with Hall and you'll have to face the consequences. B.

It was Mette who summarised the information. She was the boss.

Heart attack or no heart attack.

'So Sahlmann had discovered that Forsman had stolen the missing stash of drugs. She'd confessed and blamed it on Hall. Sahlmann had given her an ultimatum, probably because of his feelings for her: unless the stolen drugs were back at Customs and Excise on Sunday at the latest he'd go to the police on Monday.'

'Which he did not do as he was murdered on Sunday night,' Bosse said.

'By Clas Hall?'

'Or Forsman?'

'Or both?'

'Good work!' Mette said.

Lisa and Bosse thanked her. They hadn't done very much, it was the computer technicians who'd got all the information. But they revelled in Mette's praise.

'So now we just have two problems,' she said. 'The first one is that our suspects remain at large. They won't be much longer, they're amateurs. The second, and rather more tricky one, is Sahlmann's laptop. The one that was stolen. Where is it? Not at Hall's or Forsman's, right?'

'No,' Lisa said. 'But if they stole it because they thought that Sahlmann could have information on it about the theft then they probably wouldn't have just dumped it somewhere.'

Mette was just about to counter this with a couple of objections when she saw Mårten's car outside the kitchen window. Now? He'd only been gone an hour. Mette jumped up, without leaning on the table for support, something that both Bosse and Lisa noticed.

'You have to go now. Mårten's coming.'

Bosse and Lisa had just managed to pack up and open the front door when Mårten came in through the gate.

'Hello?!' he said. 'What are you doing here?'

'They brought me some flowers!' Mette shouted from the hallway. 'They're such sweethearts!'

She waved at Bosse and Lisa who slid past Mårten and towards the gate. Mårten watched them. 'Sweethearts'? He walked up the steps and gave Mette a kiss on the cheek.

'What kind of flowers did they bring?'

* * *

As usual the central station was full of people. Olivia was standing by the so-called 'spittoon', Stig Lindberg's beautiful metal ring in the middle where you can look down at people rushing to and from the commuter trains one floor down. When she travelled on those trains she always avoided walking right underneath: that was ingrained in her after growing up in suburbia. Of course it was Lenni who'd taught her. The first time they'd gone into the city together, Lenni had grabbed her by the arm as she was about to walk straight into the line of fire.

'Are you crazy? Are you going to walk under that?!'

'Why not?'

'Can't you see people standing up there loading up?'

'Loading up with what?'

'Spit! Everyone knows that! Those people up there are spitting pros. They use chewing gum like a performance-enhancing drug to get their saliva production going and then they choose their victim. It's bloody revolting!'

Olivia had looked up, but didn't see anyone looking down, or even chewing, but ever since that day she'd avoided walking underneath the spittoon. Now she was standing there watching who had learned about this potential hazard and who had no idea. There were quite a few. She looked at the clock. Ove had called in the morning and was on a stopover in Stockholm on his way to Koster: there was some lecture in the afternoon and a conference in the morning, but if he had time he would meet up with her for a little while. Around about now in fact.

'Hi!'

Olivia turned around. There he was. Tanned, bleach-blond hair and crumpled clothes. Seriously hot actually, as Lenni would have said.

'Oh hi! I didn't see you!'

Much to her annoyance, Olivia felt herself blushing under her tan. Why was she doing that? She also felt a bit uncertain about whether to hug him or not.

So Ove got in there first.

'It's great to see you again! In real life!'

Olivia manage to utter 'You too' during the hug and cursed Lenni. If Lenni hadn't talked about Ove as some kind of presumptive boyfriend she wouldn't suddenly have started blushing or feeling awkward in his presence.

She never had done before.

'Where are we going?' he said.

Ove had about an hour to spare before he had to head off to his lecture so they decided to have a beer at the Royal Viking Hotel just next door to the station, where they'd met for the first time a year and a half ago.

As they sat down at one of the long tables in the lobby with a beer each, Olivia suddenly stopped feeling nervous. Good. It was entirely groundless. Those other feelings were only there in Lenni's imagination. Now it was all back to normal and they were talking and laughing. Ove told her about his arduous journey home and that he was looking forward to getting back to Nordkoster. She talked about what had happened since they last skyped, about her experiences at Silvergården and that it had something to do with Bengt Sahlmann's murder.

But she didn't mention her visit to Borell's.

'There's something I want to tell you,' Ove suddenly said.

Olivia looked at him. The corner of his mouth was twitching a little. It always did when he was a bit nervous.

'Oh right, sounds serious? It's nothing to do with your dad, is it?'

'No, no, it's something completely different.'

Now he was twisting and turning in his seat as well. What was it that was so difficult?

'I've met a girl,' he said.

A bombshell. Olivia had just put the beer glass to her mouth and a few shameful drops came spluttering out. She immediately wiped them away.

'Oh right, how cool!' she said.

She heard herself how fake it sounded and focused on putting her glass down without spilling any more.

'She's a marine biologist too, American, Maggie's her name. You'll like her. We worked together in Guatemala.'

Ove carried on talking while the images started racing around in Olivia's head without a chance for her to stop them. Ove and this Maggie on a beach, hand in hand, engaged in lively discussions about the problems of the dying coral reefs in the world's seas. The perfect couple. She cursed herself for not going to meet up with Ove when she was on her long trip. He'd wanted her to stop by in Guatemala on her way from Mexico to Costa Rica. She'd said no, she wanted to be alone during this cathartic trip. Now she regretted it. If she'd said yes then maybe it would have been her walking hand in hand down the beach with Ove. But then again that was not something she wanted. Or was it? It was all running through her mind. What did she actually feel? Was Lenni right after all?

No, she wasn't!

Olivia got a grip of herself after this chaotic burst of emotion. She was just surprised. She hadn't had any idea. He could have prepared her for this! They were bloody well supposed to be friends and friends tell each other everything! Then Ove started talking again.

'She's going to be at the conference here and I would love for you to meet her,' he said.

'Me? Why?'

Was he going to force her to meet this Maggie now as well?

'Because I've told her about you, of course.'

'Why?'

'What's the matter with you? Are you annoyed that I didn't tell you before?'

'No, not at all.'

'Yes, you are, I can see it written all over your face. But we've only just met. Me and her. I wanted to tell you about her last time we skyped, but then we got cut off.'

'Oh right.'

'And it doesn't change anything between us, does it?'

Olivia looked at Ove. He looked at her pleadingly, as though he didn't really believe what he was saying himself. She certainly did not.

'Really?'

'No. Maggie has loads of male friends. She has no problem with us spending time together.'

She didn't give a shit whether Maggie had 'male friends', which actually sounded bloody ridiculous. Olivia felt that she wanted to leave. She had no desire whatsoever to listen to Ove talking about his newfound love. They hadn't been friends long enough for that, she thought. So she looked at her watch, as though it could save her.

'I'm sorry, but I don't have time to meet her.'

'But I didn't mean now. She's not arriving until tomorrow. Can we come and meet you then?'

Olivia stopped studying her watch and moved onto her nails. 'We.' It was 'we'.

Already.

'Sorry, I'm going away. Tomorrow. With my mum.'

Ove leant back in his armchair.

'Tell me the truth instead. You don't want to?' he said.

Olivia looked up and met Ove's gaze. Why should she lie to him?

'No, I actually don't. And now you need to go if you're going to make it.'

Olivia got up. Rather too quickly. A wave of disappointment swept over Ove's eyes as he looked at her.

'Please, Olivia, sit down.'

'You're in a rush.'

'Not that much. Sit down, please?'

Olivia sank back down into the armchair and stared out through the window.

'We've become very good friends, right?' Ove said.

'Yes.'

'And there's never been talk of anything else?'

'No.'

'Particularly not from your side. You've been very clear about that the whole time.'

What did he mean by that? Had he had feelings for her? Had she missed that?

'Yes,' she said.

'And it has to happen some time. That one of us meets someone, I mean.'

'Of course. It could just as well have been me. Well, it has already. I met a guy in Mexico. Ramón. I fell head over heels in love. Or rather: we did.'

And then she started laughing. Very unnaturally. Why did she say that? To get her own back? She hadn't told anyone about Ramón except for Lenni. And she definitely hadn't planned on telling Ove. But then again she saw that Ove sank down a little in his chair and she noticed that she enjoyed it. She had got her own back.

'Ramón?'

'Yes, but then I moved on and that was that, but we're in touch.'

Which was also a lie. Just like that head over heels bit. The relationship with Ramón was simply about an exchange of bodily fluids.

For both parties.

'OK,' Ove said.

Reversed roles. Now you're the one who's bothered and it feels much better, Olivia thought.

'I can make sure that you meet if you're on your way past Cuatro Ciénegas,' she said.

Now she was almost going overboard, she realised that. Ove looked at her quizzically and she felt she had to leave. Quickly. Before she said anything even more ridiculous.

'I'm sorry, but I really have to go now. I'm meeting Lenni and I'm late already.'

Ove got up. Just as she was about to go past him, he grabbed hold of her and pulled her towards him. And just at that moment she admitted to herself that she wished that everything was just a bluff, even on his part.

'You mean a great deal to me,' he said. 'I really don't want this to destroy anything between us.'

'Of course it won't,' she lied. 'It was just a bit sudden. But I actually don't want to meet her, if that's all right with you. Maybe another time.'

Olivia freed herself from Ove and attempted a smile.

'Let's stay in touch! Take care!'

Olivia stepped out onto the rain-soaked street. Through the window she watched Ove put on his coat and proceed to the exit. She thought he seemed sad. Not that strange perhaps. Olivia was convinced that things could never be as they were between them. She'd lost a good friend and she would miss their confidential chats and perhaps a little more. She quickly started walking towards the tube station so that Ove wouldn't have a chance to catch up with her. Once she'd got down the stairs and through the barriers she got out her mobile and called Lenni.

'You're right. Ove Gardman is a fucking ugly name!'

She heard that her voice sounded overly brisk. And Lenni heard it too.

'What's happened?'

'He's met a girl.'

'Oh dear… And that's when you realised I was right!'

'No, not like that, but it doesn't exactly feel great. Can we meet at Kristallen in a bit?'

'Of course! I'm in Skrapan at the moment. I'm just going to buy some rain clothes, and then we'll go and drown your sorrows!'

* * *

Stilton was out wandering through the streets again, this time on Kungsholmen. He had to process his meeting with Ovette Andersson. She'd admitted that Rune Forss had bought sex from her, but she would never testify. Stilton knew that he couldn't force her. He didn't want to either. He turned from Fleminggatan down towards Norr Mälarstrand and called Mette. She summed up the situation straight away.

'Well, then we know that he wasn't just a name on her client list. He actually bought sex from prostitutes.'

'Yes.'

'But because Ovette doesn't want to come forward, it's not much use to you.'

'No. But she confirmed that there were more people he bought sex from.'

'But you didn't get any names?'

'No.'

'Back to square one.'

'Thanks.'

Stilton ended the call and stepped over a puddle. Square one? Hell no! He was going to go through this town with a fine-tooth-comb to find another witness. A witness who wanted to speak. Who wasn't as vulnerable as Ovette. That might take time, but if there was something he did have, it was time. For things like this – getting revenge.

In one way or another.

He peered at some baffling graffiti art on the building opposite. For some reason Abbas popped into his head. He called him. No answer this time either. His general level of irritation grew even higher. When he got hold of Jean-Baptiste he sounded more angry than worried.

'I've tried to reach him like a million times and he doesn't answer! What the hell is he playing at?! Have you been in touch with him at all?'

'Yes, hasn't he called you?'

'No.'

'He's in hospital.'

Stilton froze. He didn't want to hear this. This was definitely not something he needed in his current state.

'What's happened?' he said.

'Some horrible bastards kicked the shit out of him.'

'Badly?'

'Yes.'

'How badly?'

'Enough for it to be visible for quite a while. But he's coming home as soon as he's discharged.'

'How do you know that?'

'I'm a policeman.'

Stilton interpreted his answer correctly: Jean-Baptiste had given Abbas an ultimatum. Good. Then he'll come home. Stilton ended the call and headed down to the City Hall. In hospital? He felt his stomach tighten again. I should have stayed in Marseille. I should have stuffed that bloody ticket down his throat and stayed. But I didn't.

He sat on a damp bench and looked out at the water at Riddarfjärden.

Dark, cold water.

So, Abbas had been beaten up and he had no witnesses to pin down Rune Forss.

He drummed his feet against the paving stones.

And what about Jackie Berglund? Could he get anywhere with her? Get her to admit that she'd hooked Rune Forss up with sex workers? How would that work? By scaring her? Jackie wasn't a woman you scared.

He looked towards Norr Mälarstrand. He knew that she lived there, he knew her address. He'd been there to collect her for questioning many years ago, as part of an investigation into the murder of a pregnant prostitute who'd been part of Jackie's stable. He assumed that she still lived there.

Stilton got up and walked along the quayside. He stayed on the far side of the trees. He couldn't remember what number it was, but he knew what the building looked like. As he got closer, a taxi stopped outside a house. He saw two people getting out. First Jackie Berglund and then a large man. He didn't recognise the man. Had she got herself a bodyguard? Just before the couple disappeared in through the front door he saw that Jackie turned in his direction.

He hid behind a tree.

'There. You see?'

Jackie was standing by one of her large windows. The lights were off. She pointed down the street and Mickey Leigh followed her gaze. There was a man standing alone by a tree.

'Who's that?'

'Tom Stilton. A former detective who's been on my case quite a bit over the years.'

'And now?'

'I guess so. Why else would he be standing down there staring?'

Jackie went to pour some gin.

Mickey carried on looking down at the man by the tree.

* * *

Abbas was discharged from hospital at six o'clock in the evening. He was in a rush. He had taken Jean-Baptiste's warning very seriously. He'd looked into the large policeman's eyes and understood that his time in Marseille was running out. But he would have time for one more visit. To the high-rise building, to see Marie.

He took a taxi there.

'What have you done?!'

Marie looked shocked, justifiably so. Abbas looked horrific. He leant towards the side of the door and hoped that none of her children was near. He didn't want to scare the life out of them.

'Are you alone?' he asked.

'At the moment, yes. Come in. What happened?'

Abbas gave an even shorter account of what had happened than he'd told Jean-Baptiste. When he'd finished Marie tried to give him a hug. She stopped herself when she saw that he flinched after she barely touched his chest.

'Do you have a computer?' he asked.

'Paul has one. It's in there.'

Marie pointed into the living room and Abbas went in. The computer was on. He opened the browser straight away.

'What are you going to do?'

Marie was standing in the kitchen making the coffee. She looked at Abbas over her shoulder.

'Looking for information.'

'Oh right.'

Marie didn't want to ask any more, she didn't want to get involved. She had a husband and children and could see the state Abbas was in. She was happy for him to use the computer, but she didn't want to know what for. She hoped that no one had followed him here. She made a couple of cups of strong coffee and gave one to Abbas.

'Thanks.'

'I'll sit in the kitchen. The kids will be home in fifteen minutes. Do you think you'll…'

'I hope so.'

Abbas feverishly scrolled down through various websites. He was looking for actors' lists. Of agencies that managed actors, who also appeared in 'adult films'. He found two. It took quite a while to scroll through the first one. The other one went more quickly. After just a couple of pages he saw it, the picture of the man who'd assaulted him. A colour photograph of a smiling man with an oiled body and a long CV next to it.

'Do you have a printer?' he called out to Marie.

'Yes, it's connected.'

Abbas printed three pictures from the agency site.

The printouts were black-and-white, but it didn't matter.

They would serve their purpose.

Once again he took the stairs on the way down.

* * *

When Olivia stepped into the venerable Pelikan restaurant on Söder, Lenni had already got a table and ordered her a beer. It was still early and the bar section, Kristallen, was only half-full. Good, Olivia thought, it was still possible to have a conversation.

'So tell me. Who's this girl he's met?' Lenni said.

Olivia told her about the meeting with Ove and her reaction, which she hadn't really expected.

'But if you told him how you felt, don't you think he would realise it too? That he's in love with you as well?'

'What do you mean as well?'

'Jesus, Olivia! Stop! Can't you hear yourself? It's time to face facts. How can you be so slow about some things and so quick about other stuff?'

But Olivia was stubbornly refusing to face these 'facts'. It wasn't about love, it was about friendship. A very special friendship that she'd never had before with a guy.

And now she was grieving that it was over.

Nothing more.

And Lenni, as the trusted friend she was, stopped pointing out how wrong Olivia was. Even though she had to bite her tongue when Olivia kept going on about how much Ove had meant to her the past year and still didn't see why. They only paused to get more beer.

After three large beers, Olivia's head began to spin. She hadn't eaten anything since breakfast. Now she was having a liquid dinner. Not so great. The place had really started filling up and the noise level was high. Lenni had just gone to the toilet and Olivia was sitting alone at the table thinking that it was time to go home.

Definitely.

'Oh my god! Hello!'

The voice came from behind and Olivia turned around. Her movements were not entirely coordinated at this stage and she had to grab hold of the chair so as not to lose her balance. Alex Popovic was standing behind her smiling.

'Oh my god, hi!' she said.

'Are you here on your own?'

'No, with a friend. She's in the loo.'

'Can I sit down?'

Olivia cast a glance towards the toilets. Lenni was just coming out and was heading to the bar to greet a mutual friend who was waving at her.

Lenni wasn't going to want to leave.

Not yet.

'Sure,' she said.

So Alex sat down.

'We can have that beer now if you want,' he said.

'What beer?'

For a flat in Stockholm it could certainly be considered to be spectacular. If it had been in the old Meatpacking District in New York it would have been pretty ordinary, but not here. It was a converted loft of almost two hundred square metres in an old industrial building, with a dark pine floor and raw, white-chalked brick walls. Heavy wooden beams criss-crossed the ceiling of this huge open space. A black fireplace exploded upwards in the middle of the room.

Alex had a nice place.

But nowhere near Borell's standard, Olivia thought as she dropped her jacket on the floor.

'Shall we light a fire?'

'No.'

Olivia didn't want a fire. She wanted to have sex, now, preferably with the lights off. She was drunk and she knew that she was going to pass out soon.

'Something to drink?'

'No, thanks.'

'Some music, then?'

Olivia shrugged her shoulders. If he wanted music then it was fine by her.

'You put it on,' he said. 'I'm just going to hang up my jacket.'

Alex gestured towards the huge CD rack on one side of the wall and disappeared in through a dark doorway on the other side. Olivia approached the CD rack. CDs? Didn't everyone use Spotify these days? Not Alex apparently. Olivia peered at the pile of CDs in front of her and felt the titles spinning around in her head, she had a hard time focusing. She took out a CD and tried to see what it was.

'Find something?'

Alex came in from the other side. She'd hoped that he'd be wearing a dressing gown or be naked, but he was dressed in jeans and a T-shirt just like before. He walked towards her. Olivia pulled off her jumper and undid her bra. Alex stood still a couple of metres in front of her. The contrast between her firm white breasts and her extremely tanned upper body was striking. She never sunbathed topless.

'Shall we go to bed?' she asked.

* * *

It had taken a while to find The Bull's address. The information on his CV had helped. The telephone number and address had led him to an area that he wasn't very familiar with. In the centre, but outside Abbas's former radar, on the eastern side, a rather posher neighbourhood. His flat was at the top of an old stone building. There was no problem getting in – there was a gap between the old wooden door and the lintel. He climbed the stairs to the top and reached a heavy iron door. There was no name on the letterbox, but he knew that he'd come to the right place. He caught his breath and felt across his body with his hands. Everything was where it should be. He took out one of the black knives and prised open the letterbox with the tip of the blade, quietly and carefully. He couldn't see any lights. He released the metal slot again and rang the bell.

'I've turned a blind eye once, I never do that twice.'

Abbas heard the large policeman's cold calm voice in his head. He recalled what else he'd said: 'Sadly a dead porn actress isn't really at the top of the agenda right now.'

It was pretty high up on Abbas's agenda.

He rang the bell again. Nothing. He put his ear against the door and listened. Nothing.

He headed back down the stairs and onto the street. There were some stone steps further down the street that led up to a square and he sat down. He could see both the front door and the windows of the top-floor flat from there. There was no light to be seen.

He planned to wait until The Bull came home.

* * *

Mickey Leigh had dedicated himself to his duty as Jackie Berglund's houseguest. He was standing in the shower now and she stuffed some toilet paper in her crotch to protect her pants. She'd gone through the menopause a couple of years ago, so there was no cause for concern about the sperm, but she didn't want semen in her pants. She sat on the toilet and watched the man standing in her shower. The glass was frosted so she couldn't see any details. She didn't need to. She looked at the silhouette of his body and thought back to bygone years. A long time ago. When they'd spent time together on the continent, both of them in the same industry. She'd been a sought-after escort girl and he was good at what men like him are good at. They'd had fun. On many levels.

It had been intense.

Then she'd settled in Stockholm and got involved in the more administrative part of the escort business, eventually starting out on her own.

And Mickey Leigh had stayed on the continent.

The occasional phone call, a few letters and later emails, some rather risqué photographs every now and then. Not much more. But enough to keep in touch.

And now he was here and they were having fun again.

Mickey opened the shower doors and reached for a towel. Jackie smiled at him. He smiled back and dried himself.

He didn't have that back then, Jackie thought. That tattoo.

A small black bull on his neck.

I wonder when he got that?

Chapter 19

A newspaper page was fluttering about across the pavement. The light morning breeze was sweeping in through the blocks of flats. Abbas stretched his stiff body. He'd sat on the stone steps the whole night, his gaze focused on The Bull's front door. A couple of people had gone in and out – none of them were him. Now it was dawn and there was still no light to be seen in the windows at the top of the building. He looked at his watch. Jean-Baptiste might well be calling the hospital soon to check whether he'd been discharged. He climbed down the steps and waited for a taxi.

When it stopped outside the Richelieu he'd made a decision. He would check out and go underground. He still knew quite a few places in this city, where Jean-Baptiste was unlikely to find him. The only thing worrying him was Tom. He knew he'd taken advantage of Tom's relationship with Jean-Baptiste and going behind the large policeman's back was not going to go down too well with Tom.

But this was a peripheral problem in the grand scheme of things – finding The Bull.

Abbas walked past the comatose porter. He had the room key in his pocket, unlocked the door and went inside.

'On your way home?'

Jean-Baptiste was sitting on the edge of the bed, smoking. Smoking was not permitted at the hotel, but Jean-Baptiste didn't take any notice. Abbas felt a sudden urge to flee.

'You'll have a private escort to the central station.'

Jean-Baptiste smiled as he said it, not spitefully, but somewhat dejectedly, rather.

It was just after nine o'clock. Jean-Baptiste was on his third Gauloise at the station. He was standing by platform four observing the movements of a plump pigeon. It had just swallowed a sizeable piece of baguette lying on the floor and was trying to fly up to the high vaulted iron construction in the central station. It didn't seem to go very well as it was forced to have a rest on one of the silver engines. Jean-Baptiste looked away and out over the noisy platform. The train was due to depart in twelve minutes and Abbas still hadn't said a word about where he'd spent the night. It wasn't that important any more. He was being put on a train to Paris. If he got off there it was the Parisian police's problem.

'Here.'

Jean-Baptiste turned around. Abbas was holding out a white envelope.

'What's this?' Jean-Baptiste said, taking the envelope.

'A picture of the guy who assaulted me. It was probably him who murdered Samira.'

Jean-Baptiste opened the envelope and partially pulled out the picture.

'His name is Mickey Leigh,' Abbas said. 'His contact details are on the back. He's The Bull.'

'How do you know?'

'He has a bull tattooed on his neck. Do you recognise him?'

'No, but I'll check him out.'

'Can't I just hang around until you've done it?'

'No. Did you try and get hold of him last night?'

'Yes.'

'But?'

'He has a flat on rue Protis, but he didn't come back there.'

'That was lucky.'

They looked at each other. This was torturing Abbas. He'd just found the man who could potentially have murdered Samira and he was being forced to leave Marseille, sit on a train back to Sweden and surrender the hunt for Mickey Leigh to Jean-Baptiste.

'But I'll do everything I can to get hold of him, you can be sure of that.'

Abbas nodded, took hold of his wheeled suitcase and looked over towards the tracks. His train had arrived. He started walking onto the platform with Jean-Baptiste by his side. Both of them stopped outside an open carriage door. Jean-Baptiste reached out his hand. Abbas shook it and Jean-Baptiste held it for a few seconds.

'If he's here we'll catch him, you know that.'

'Good.'

Abbas climbed up into the carriage.

Jean-Baptiste waited until the train had rolled out from the station. Finally, the thought. Then he decided to take a restorative walk back to the police station. But he didn't go in. He went to the little bar opposite and sat down at his favourite table next to the wall. The bartender was quick to serve him his Perrier. As he lit his second cigarette, Claudette came in. He knew she'd turn up here sooner or later. She spotted Jean-Baptiste and sat down at his table. They looked at each other for a few seconds.

'Tom Stilton has left,' Jean-Baptiste said.

'They always do.'

Jean-Baptiste put his hand on Claudette's.

And completely covered it.

* * *

At first she didn't know where she was. White-painted brick walls? She lay there, motionless, trying to centre in on what was burning inside her head. A few seconds later she succeeded.

Alex. I'm at Alex Popovic's. I'm lying in his bed. He's probably lying next to me. She didn't turn her head. We had sex. I wanted to have sex. We fucked in a large bed right in the middle of this room. It's the one I'm lying in now. I came. It was rather unexpected. But how much did I actually drink? Three beers before he arrived, or was it four? And then I insisted on having a couple of shots. Shots? Why the hell did I want shots? She still hadn't moved. If I move now he'll wake up. If he's lying in the bed. What do I say then? Hi. And then? Can you call a taxi?

'Hi.'

Olivia jumped. He was lying in the bed. He turned around a little. Alex was just lifting his head from a stripy pillow, trying to separate his eyelids. He'd also had a few shots, it seemed.

'Hi,' she said. 'Do you have a shower?'

'Yes. Are you getting up?'

'Yes?'

What did he think? That they were going to have sex again? She hated hangover sex. She wanted to get up and rinse it all off. She pulled off the thick duvet, put her feet down on the floor and stood up. She shouldn't have done that. Not so quickly. Her head was really spinning. She lost her balance and half-sat down on the bed again. Alex laughed and put his hand on her back. That helped her get up.

'Where's the shower?'

'In there, on the right. Do you want some coffee?'

'Yes, please.'

Olivia fished up her top from the floor. She couldn't see her trousers. Had he hidden them under the pillow? She disappeared off towards the door on the other side.

When she came back he'd laid the table, next to a large window facing out onto some water. He'd put her trousers on a chair. She pulled her towel off and put on her trousers. Her pants were probably in her pocket, she thought, and looked out through the window.

'Where are we?' she said.

'Liljeholmen. On the Gröndal side. Don't you remember how we…'

'No.'

She couldn't remember how they'd got here and she was totally uninterested in it. She took hold of the cup he passed over to her.

'Are you hungover?' he asked.

'Yes, horribly.'

'Me too. But it was nice.'

What was 'nice'? What they'd been up to in bed? What was 'nice' about that? Two drunken idiots who were barely in control of their libidos? Olivia felt herself getting irritated. Calm down, she thought, you were the one who wanted this. Don't give him shit, he was there for you and he's a nice guy. Smile a bit.

'Yes, it was nice,' she smiled and swallowed a big gulp of strong coffee.

'What are you going to do today?'

'Sober up.'

Alex smiled back. He thought he had a pretty good feeler for this woman and her temperament. He liked some bite, and he was clear about what the night had meant. Not much to her, perhaps, but rather more to him. It was OK. He wasn't going to whisper sweet nothings in her ear. It wasn't the right approach with Olivia.

But there were other ways.

'So what did you think of the funeral?' he said.

'Tough. I don't like funerals.'

'Neither do I.'

'Why did you get so upset?'

'Over what? You mean Borell?'

'Yes?'

'You heard, did you? He's an arsehole.'

Probably, Olivia thought. She was just on the point of telling him about her trip out to Värmdö. But she managed to keep silent. She didn't want to drag Alex into this, just as little now as before.

'Who was that woman?' she said. 'What was her name, Agnes von...?'

'Born. She's a doctor.'

'Did she know Bengt from school too?'

'Yes.'

'Was she there when he had that outburst at Borell?'

'Yes, why?'

'I don't know. I'm hungover. And there's a phone ringing.'

It was a mobile, over by the bed.

'It's not mine,' Alex said.

Olivia got up. It was her ringtone. She could hear it now. She went over to the bed and tried to locate her mobile. It was lying under the sheet. Under the sheet? How had it got there? She'd got hold of her phone and was just about to answer when she saw the display.

It was Ove.

She didn't answer. She picked up her jacket from the floor and looked over at Alex.

'I'm off now.'

'Keep in touch?'

'Absolutely. Bye!'

Olivia thought that she was going to make a swift exit until she realised that she had no idea where the front door was.

'It's through there and to the left.'

Alex pointed at a door and tried to hide his smile.

Olivia got out onto the road and felt that she needed oceans of water topped off with a kilo of paracetamol. To make matters worse, the sun was shining for once and the cold hard light was torturing her eyes. She'd put her phone on silent, but it was still on vibrate. She felt it massaging her thigh in her right-hand pocket. A short massage. Not a call, a text. She assumed that it must be Ove again. It wasn't. It was a text from Sandra. Olivia started walking towards the underground station and had a look at the message.

It wasn't very long.

Hi, Olivia. Thanks for taking care of me. You're the best. Please think of me sometimes. What I wrote on that note was true. Hugs. Sandra xx

Olivia read these few words a few times before she reacted, before panic pushed her up against a wall. She called Sandra's mobile number and didn't know what she was going to hear. Voicemail. She called Charlotte.

'No, she's not here. She said she was going into the city to meet a classmate.'

'Has she sent you a text?'

'No, why do you ask that?'

'Don't worry. Bye.'

Olivia ended the call. She was standing on a windy, deserted road out in Gröndal and had no idea what to do. She read Sandra's message again. It was so simple and clear, so definitive. A cry for help? She didn't know. But she knew she had to try to get hold of Sandra.

Quickly.

But she had no idea how.

The only thing she could do was send a reply: 'Please call me!'

* * *

Stilton was standing on the rear deck letting the wind blow onto his face. He'd had a good night's sleep. He also faced the sudden sunlight, but he always carried a pair of sunglasses in his leather jacket and was able to get quick relief from the cascade of sunshine. Not the wind, however. He buttoned up his jacket just as Mette called.

'Hi, Tom!'

'Has Abbas been in touch?'

'No. Why, has something happened?!'

So Mette didn't know. Good. They could talk about that when Abbas got back. He didn't want to do this alone and be harangued by Mette about how he'd failed Abbas by leaving him on his own down there.

'What did you want?' he said.

'I was thinking about what Ovette Andersson said – that Forss had bought sex from other girls too.'

'Yes, but she didn't know which ones, she claimed.'

'Have you asked Olivia?'

'Olivia?'

'She contacted quite a lot of the girls that had links to Jackie Berglund when she was digging around last year.'

'Did she?'

'Yes, she might know someone from back then.'

'Oh right…'

There were a few seconds of silence.

'But you don't want to?' Mette said.

'Talk to Olivia?'

'Yes.'

'She didn't want to talk to me.'

'Nor me either.'

'Well, then. How are you anyway?' Stilton realised he should ask.

'Fine. In fact very well today. We've just arrested two people we've been looking for in relation to that drug investigation I told you about. And maybe a murder too.'

'Congratulations.'

'Thanks.'

Mette ended the call. Stilton leant against the railings. Olivia? Who hadn't been in touch for more than a year? Not since she'd called him a cowardly bastard and stormed out of the Olsäters' kitchen. Nevertheless he'd tried to call, several times. She never answered. He no longer existed as far as she was concerned. Mårten had broached the subject a couple of times. In his diplomatic way, he'd tried to explain Olivia's feelings and that these would subside with time.

He thought.

Stilton didn't.

The little contact he'd had with Olivia led him to think otherwise. She cherished grievances. He was one of them. And now Mette thought that he should contact her?

And get a pile of shit thrown in his face?

* * *

Albion was having a meeting right at the top of the building on Skeppsbron. The view over the inlet and Skeppsholmen was magnificent. The building had a long history dating back to the early eighteenth century, with a slightly sloping floor and a rather low ceiling. Jean Borell had tried to charm the city council into letting him raise it by a couple of metres, but so far they'd said no due to cultural heritage considerations.

But he was going to fix that soon.

He had connections.

He sat at one end of the long oval teak table. A large framed photograph of himself shaking hands with Henry Kravis was hanging above his head.

The photograph had been taken on a helipad in New York.

The other four people gathered around the table, three men and a woman, held different positions in the company. They were all members of the inner steering committee. They'd been summoned to a strategy meeting about the near future. It looked problematic. As things were looking now, the debate about profits in the welfare sector would be high up on the political agenda ahead of the 2014 election. It was still too early to predict the outcome, but what they could predict was what would happen if there were a red–green majority. Stefan Löfven and the Social Democratic Party Congress had made that quite clear. If they won the election, private companies would be subject to tough regulations. And the Swedish Trade Union Confederation actually wanted to limit profits to the equivalent of the state interest rate plus one per cent of total capital, which would make the business totally uninteresting to Albion.

'So how do we deal with that risk?' Borell said.

'By signing as many contracts as possible before the election,' said a young, brisk man called Olof Block. He continued: 'Which highlights the importance of our contract with Stockholm, it's absolutely essential.'

'Why?'

'Because several of the municipalities across the country are waiting to see what Stockholm does. If they sign, then the rest of them will dare to do so as well, and then it looks stable.'

Borell knew that Block was completely right. If they had enough large long-term contracts in place they would still be able to sell the organisation.

'How are we doing with the Stockholm contract?' asked Siri Anrén, a dark-haired woman sitting at the end of the table.

'We're doing quite well,' Borell said. 'It should be sorted soon.'

'Is there anything that could jeopardise that?'

Everyone sitting around the table knew what she was getting at. Everyone knew that Albion had been portrayed in rather unfavourable light in the media during the past year. There had been strong criticism from various quarters. Now there were several opposition politicians questioning whether the City of Stockholm was really going to sign another multi-million contract with a company like Albion. The politicians defending the contract were pointing to the fact that most parts of Albion's operations in Stockholm were being run extremely well. Silvergården was one of the nursing homes being used as an argument in favour of a new contract.

'I can't see anything that could jeopardise it,' Borell replied.

'Jean.'

'Yes?'

One of the men at the table leant over towards Borell.

'Unfortunately there's been an incident that I think we need to deal with,' he said.

'What?'

The man got up and went to the door behind Borell. He opened it and made way for a woman to come in.

Rakel Welin stepped into the room.

The man presented her to the group.

'Rakel Welin, director of Silvergården.'

He then gave the floor to Welin. She clearly and concisely provided an account of Hilda Högberg's recent death at the nursing home. Everyone understood the sensitive nature of this incident.

'Are there any relatives who could cause trouble?'

'No, no one,' Welin said. 'And the carer who was present knows that she's not covered by whistleblower protection. She won't be a problem.'

'So why are we talking about this?'

Borell asked the question, sounding rather impatient, while drawing some abstract figures on the notepad in front of him.

'Because an unauthorised person witnessed the incident.'

'Who?' Olof Block asked.

'Her name was Olivia Rivera.'

Borell's pen froze. He stared straight at Welin.

'What was she doing there?' he said, trying to maintain a neutral tone.

'I don't really know, she claimed that she knew someone who'd died at the home. Unfortunately she was in the room where Hilda Högberg died. I wanted to report this, because she behaved very arrogantly when I asked her to leave the premises.'

'Arrogant in what way?'

'She insinuated that we were hiding things, and she asked who was in charge of the nursing home. She was quite unpleasant.'

Welin stopped talking when she saw looks being exchanged across the table, by all except Borell. He'd drawn a big 'O' on his notepad with a question mark inside.

At quarter past one he walked into an exclusive restaurant in the Old Town. He'd booked the table more than a month ago, for two, to have a nice long lunch with Carina Bermann, one of the Moderate Party's big names in the City of Stockholm. They'd discuss the new contract while enjoying a seven-course lunch, he thought to himself. But not now. Straight after his meeting at Albion, he'd called Bermann and explained that there was an emergency he had to deal with. She understood without asking any questions: at Borell's level, schedules could change in a flash.

'We'll do it when you have time,' she said.

'Absolutely. How are things looking otherwise? With the contract?'

'It looks good. I think we have most people on board. Most of the probing has stopped now, so I'm sure we can slip this through without too much trouble.'

'Good. I want you to know how much I appreciate your efforts.'

'Thanks.'

'So what did you think about the Karin Mamma painting?'

'It's amazing, thank you! Absolutely amazing! We've actually hung it in our dining room, it's perfect in there. You'll see when you come over next!'

'Sounds great. Take care of yourself!'

'You too. Bye!'

Borell looked up at the waitress. She was just about to launch into a presentation of the menu when Borell interrupted her.

'I don't have much of an appetite today. I'll just have the vendace roe.'

'Of course. Are you expecting a guest?'

'Yes.'

The waitress left to give Borell a few minutes before his guest arrived. He was still feeling rather off balance following Rakel Welin's revelations. Olivia Rivera? At Silvergården? Did her visiting his house have something to do with that? It had to, it couldn't have been a coincidence. What the hell was she after? Was she a journalist? He mulled it over some more without finding any plausible answers. He'd have to discuss the situation in more detail with his guest.

After another few minutes he appeared.

'Hi. Sit down.'

Magnus Thorhed nodded, pulled off his short coat and sat down on the chair opposite Borell. He took off his glasses and started polishing them with a grey silk cloth. Borell watched him. He knew that Thorhed followed strict rituals. One of them was to always polish his glasses when he sat down at a restaurant table. Borell didn't know why, but he didn't want to interrupt the procedure. When Thorhed had finished, he put on his glasses and looked at Borell.

'What are you having?'

'Vendace roe.'

'Do they have lobster here?'

'I'm sure they do. You don't want the set lunch?'

'No.'

So Borell had to trouble the poor waitress with another special order. This was very much not in line with the Michelin-starred restaurant's routines, but considering the number of times Borell and his business associates had frequented the restaurant and paid staggering bills, they were flexible. It was in everyone's interests.

When they were alone again Borell got straight to the point.

'We have a problem.'

'OK, what?'

'Olivia Rivera.'

'Her surname is Rönning, not Rivera,' Thorhed said. 'And she's renting a flat on Skånegatan from a relative. One of her female friends works in a video shop.'

'How do you know that?'

'I followed her the other day from her flat and saw them meet up in the shop.'

Borell looked at Thorhed and was reminded why he'd chosen him as his closest colleague. It wasn't just because of his financial skills, but a number of others too, such as this. They'd discussed Olivia Rivera's visit to Värmdö after she'd left, and decided that they needed to follow up on it. Thorhed clearly had, in his way. Borell rarely needed to tell him what he wanted done: Thorhed was always one step ahead. A strange man, Borell thought, re-calling the time that Thorhed had intervened when some drunk guy was about to launch an unprovoked attack on Borell's Jaguar. The man was large and violent, but he was lying bundled up on the floor just a few seconds later. In the car on the way back Thorhed had mentioned his black belt in karate. Now he was looking at Borell with his calm Asian eyes.

'In what way is Rivera Rönning a problem?' he asked. 'Except for the fact that she's lying about writing a dissertation?'

Borell waited until they had been served. A large, egg-shaped dollop of vendace roe on a stone slab and a boiled lobster. He took a teaspoon of the salty roe and directed it into his mouth, without polluting it with lemon or the like. Once he'd swallowed it he told him what Olivia had witnessed at Silvergården. Thorhed immediately understood the situation. He was well aware of Silvergården's importance as a flagship for Albion in the ongoing contract negotiations with the City of Stockholm. And consequently he realised the potentially devastating consequences if Rivera Rönning decided to contact the media about what she'd seen.

'So how are we going to prevent it?' he said.

'She's hardly the type to be muted.'

'No.'

Thorhed broke off one of the thick lobster claws.

'Do you want me to speak to her?' he said.

'Yes.'

'OK, I will.'

Thorhed cracked the lobster claw with his teeth.

* * *

Olivia had almost reached Skånegatan when her mother Maria called. She was sitting on the commuter train in from Rotebro.

'Has Sandra moved back home again?' she asked.

'No, not as far as I know. Why?'

'I thought I saw her at the station.'

Olivia starting running towards her car, which was parked around the corner. She managed to knock over a young guy wearing headphones and apologised as she scurried on. When she reached it she couldn't find her keys. Fuck! Had they dropped out of her jacket at Alex's? She started looking around for a taxi when she suddenly felt her keys in the wrong pocket. She pulled open the car door.

Normally Sandra took the bus from the train station, but this time she wanted to walk. She wasn't properly dressed for the time of year, but the raw November chill didn't bother her, she was totally absorbed in herself. She walked quickly with her gaze rooted in the ground. She was clutching a small, flat tin in her hand which was planted in her jacket pocket.

When she reached her old school, Gillboskolan, where she'd spent nine years, she slowed down and decided to go through the school grounds. She didn't know why, it wasn't a shortcut, but it was part of the ceremony. She'd spent both happy and unhappy years here. Happy as long as her mum was alive and unhappy after she'd died. But they'd got through it, her and her dad.

Together.

He'd been there and supported her even though he was out of his mind with grief himself. They'd had each other in this worst of worlds. Now she was alone in it. No one she loved was left. She didn't have anyone to fight for her, no one to cheer her on at volleyball matches, no one who got excited over an 'A' in an exam, no one who cared the way her father had. How could life be so horrendously unfair? All of her friends still had both their parents and they took it for granted. Their lives were focused on trivialities typical of a seventeen-year-old, things that her life should have been focused on too. But it wasn't.

Any more.

She looked at the dark school buildings, there were still lights on in some of the windows, but everywhere else the school day had come to an end. All the children were at home with their parents and would be having dinner soon. The tears welling up in her eyes blurred her vision, she blinked, pulled her open jacket shut and increased her pace again.

As she approached the house she stopped. Just a month ago, she and her father had picked apples in the garden and made apple sauce together for the first time. They'd had a lot of fun. The whole kitchen was sticky afterwards. Now the scraggy apple trees were just standing there, naked and lifeless, framing the yellow wooden house. The beautiful old house adorned with gingerbread-style carvings. She'd lived there her whole life. It was her home. Now all she saw was a large empty shell. She took a few quick steps across the road and went in through the gate. She shut it firmly, as she had always done, and carried on up the gravelled path towards the front door. Before she reached the steps, she saw that one side of the tarpaulin covering the large outdoor barbeque had become unfastened. She went over and covered it up again. Her father had always taken great care of that barbeque. It was some fancy brand and had cost a fortune.

When she put the key in the lock she suddenly felt sick. She quickly opened the door, went into the hallway and sat down on a stool. She remained seated there, in the dark, with her head in her hands, looking down at the floor. She didn't want to look up at the ceiling.

Definitely not.

After a while, the gagging feeling subsided, she stood up and took a few steps into the living room. She sank down into the sofa. She kicked off her shoes and saw that she'd made a real mess on the living room floor, her shoes were terribly muddy. But it didn't matter! And why had she even bothered to cover up the barbeque? Nothing mattered.

Any more.

Her eyes scanned the room. The floor lamp was still standing where it always had, the soft rug looked no different. Everything looked the same, even though nothing was. She put her hands in her jacket pocket and pulled out the little tin – she'd been clasping it tightly the whole way. She opened it and took out a small object. Carefully she unwrapped the paper and looked at the blank, grey razor blade. She held it in her hand as she went over to close the curtains. Suddenly it was completely dark in the room and she had to put on one of the lamps by the sofa. She saw that one of her father's DVDs had fallen down on the floor. She went over and picked it up: *Wings of Desire*. One of her father's favourite films. It was about angels. Why had that been the one to fall on the floor? She opened the case, took out the DVD and put it in the player. She moved the razor blade from one hand to the other as the film started. The beginning was very strange: someone writing on a piece of paper: *'Als das Kind Kind war...'* *'When the child was a child...'* As the gentle voice in the film alternately read and sung the text, Sandra's thoughts turned inwards. When she looked up at the television again she saw a winged man, standing at the top of some kind of church, looking down at the people below. He could hear all their thoughts. But only the children looked up and saw him. She turned it off. She didn't want to imagine that her father could see her now. It just complicated things. She wanted to remain in her emotional state to be able to do what she'd intended. What she'd decided to do. Then she saw some blood seeping from her hand. She hadn't felt the blade cutting her. Strange. Was it the case that when you feel such tremendous pain inside you, you don't feel normal physical pain? There's something soothing about that. She got up from the sofa and went over to the bookshelf. The photograph was there where it had always been, the photograph of her family. Her and her dad and her mum. It was taken on her seventh birthday and they all looked very happy. *'Als das Kind Kind war...'* Sandra took the photograph and headed towards the bathroom. She wanted to be in the bath, so as not to bleed all over the place. After she went in, she threw off her jacket and took off all her clothes except her vest top and pants. Then she looked at the white bathtub for a while. She put the photograph on the edge and climbed in. At one point she thought about filling it with water.

She decided against it.

Olivia exceeded all imaginable speed limits. As she approached the house, she almost hit a fat Rottweiler. The owner came running out behind it shouting something Olivia couldn't hear. Keep your bloody dog on the lead then, she thought, and turned in towards the Sahlmanns' house. She slammed on the brakes outside the gate and ran towards the house without even closing her car door. When she approached the front door she hesitated for a second. Should she ring the bell? She felt the handle. The door wasn't locked. She went into the hallway.

'Sandra!'

She carried on into the living room. The lamp next to the sofa was on.

'Sandra! It's Olivia! Are you here?'

Silence.

Olivia rushed between the office and the kitchen and on to the bedrooms. As she came into the dark hallway she saw that there was light coming from the bathroom. Maybe she's having a bath? Like she did last time she went missing? Olivia felt her throat tighten as she approached the bathroom door. It was slightly ajar.

'Sandra?'

Olivia pushed the door open. Sandra was lying in the bath, virtually naked. Her forearms were covered in blood, there was blood streaming across her thighs, and the white bath tiles were covered in trickles of red. Olivia screamed. Then Sandra turned her head and looked at her. Slowly she held up a bloody razor blade in her right hand.

Olivia rode in the ambulance to A&E. She sat and watched the ambulance staff take care of Sandra. When they arrived at A&E, other staff stepped in and wheeled her in on a stretcher. Olivia followed them. A little way down the hospital corridor they disappeared into a room with the stretcher. A nurse told Olivia to stay put and wait. She sat down on a chair, leant against the green wall and closed her eyes. She saw the bathroom in front of her, the white tiles, the red lines, the bloody young girl in the bath, her eyes looking for Olivia's, it was horrible.

'Hi, Olivia.'

It was Charlotte's voice. Olivia opened her eyes. She'd called Charlotte from the ambulance and explained what had happened. Charlotte had actually been sitting at home with Tomas Welander talking about Sandra. Now both of them were standing in front of her in the corridor. Olivia got up just as a nurse came out through the door that Sandra had disappeared behind. Everyone turned to face her.

'She's cut herself badly,' the nurse said. 'But she's conscious and she probably needs someone to talk to. Are any of you relatives?'

'Yes,' Charlotte said. 'I'm her aunt.'

Olivia and Welander left the hospital together. They hadn't had the chance to see Sandra: she was very drained and Charlotte was going to stay with her. A female doctor had spoken to them about the 'next step', as she put it. The patient had actively attempted to commit suicide and almost succeeded. She would be transferred to a juvenile psychiatric unit where they would decide on a course of treatment. The doctor had expressed herself as empathetically as she could in relation to the clinical circumstances. The doctor had gained Olivia's trust.

Welander's too.

Both of them were upset and tired as they walked down towards the bus stop. There wasn't much to say. Both of them had suspected that this might happen. Both of them knew how fragile Sandra was.

Both of them felt inadequate.

'At least she'll be getting help from people who are a little more knowledgeable about this than us,' Welander said.

'Yes, I hope so.'

Olivia felt saddened. She knew that she'd burst into Sandra's world in a way that she hadn't intended to. In a way that she hadn't been able to deal with. She'd extended her hand and a very broken young girl had landed in her lap.

'You've done your best,' Welander said, as though he'd read her thoughts. 'So have Charlotte and I. Sometimes you just don't have the right tools. You want to, but you're not able to.'

'Yes, that's probably how it is.'

They stood in silence waiting for the bus. Olivia felt that she wanted to talk about something else, something that could release the pressure on her eyes. She started talking about the funeral, about Alex Popovic's unexpected outburst against Jean Borell.

'It didn't come as much of a surprise to me,' Welander said.

'No?'

'Alex has really disliked Jean for many years.'

'Generally a bit of an arsehole, then?'

'Well, there are other things too. He and Jean and Bengt were very – how do you say – close for a while, as I understood it. Then something happened, I don't know what, they never talked about it, but after that Alex's attitude towards Jean completely changed. He could get very aggressive at the mention of Jean's name, as you heard.'

'And you've never asked what happened between them?'

'I asked Bengt once but he just glossed over it, as though he didn't want to – I don't know – gossip maybe.'

Shame I didn't know about this yesterday, Olivia thought.

Alex might have told her a thing or two in bed.

On the other hand, she probably wouldn't have been able to remember a single word of it today.

Olivia went straight into her living room and flopped down on the sofa. She'd collected the car from Rotebro and driven straight home, and now she was absolutely exhausted. The past twenty-four hours, with everything from the news about Ove's girlfriend to the drunken night at Kristallen, the night with Alex and then Sandra's attempted suicide – it had worn her out. She was lying thinking about Sandra while watching a gently swaying spider's web hanging down from the stucco ceiling. Poor Sandra, what was going to happen with her now? Would she finally get proper help? She, Charlotte and the priest hadn't done a very good job. Suddenly her mobile started vibrating. She picked it up and saw that it was a text message. 'Please call me!' It was from Ove. He'd rung her several times during the day, but she had neither wanted to nor had the time to answer. Now he was clearly trying a new tactic. She couldn't understand what he wanted. She'd been very clear about not wanting to meet that Maggie person. Olivia closed the message.

Then her phone rang again, but this time it was Lenni, so she answered. She could do with some cheering up.

'You sound tired!'

'I'm shattered. It's been a supremely shit day. You have no idea what I've been through.'

'Yeah, you woke up in the wrong bed for a start. What the hell are you playing at?'

Olivia's heart sank when she heard the tone of Lenni's voice. She didn't normally tend to sound so disapproving.

'It's one thing to drown your sorrows and quite another to grab hold of the first available guy who comes your way!'

This wasn't what Olivia wanted to hear at all. She wanted a softly-softly approach, not to be criticised.

'It wasn't like that,' she said.

'So how was it, then?'

'We know each other from before.'

'I got that bit. And now you know each other even better?'

'Why do you sound so pissed off? You're generally not one to preach.'

'Why don't you pick up the phone when Ove calls?'

'Because I neither want to nor have the energy to do so... How do you know he's called?'

'Because he's called me.'

'You?!'

'Yes, and he sounded very upset.'

Now Olivia was sitting upright on her sofa. Ove had been complaining to Lenni. Just because she didn't want to meet his girlfriend. She felt her claws begin to come out.

'Well, he can go and cry on Maggie's shoulder then.'

'She didn't come. She changed her mind and stayed in the US. Apparently she had another boyfriend there.'

Her tired head was really starting to spin now. Did Maggie have another boyfriend in the US?

'Oh right, so he's counting on me to be there to comfort him straight away, then?'

'I have no idea what he's counting on, but he sounded very sad that he'd upset you, more so than about Maggie not turning up. It sounded more like her chasing him than the other way around and he'd mostly just been flattered.'

'He hasn't spared any details.'

'Yes, and he would have told you all this too if you'd bothered to answer his calls. But you were too busy with that Alex person!'

That made Olivia angry. Lenni had no right to judge her and make it sound like she was cheating on Ove – because she wasn't.

'The only person you're lying to is yourself.'

'Stop it now, Lenni! You're talking about stuff you have no idea about.'

Lenni laughed. Not in amusement.

'Listen,' Lenni said. 'I sat there listening to you for hours yesterday, so I know quite a bit. If *you* can remember, that is?'

Suddenly Olivia felt nervous. She wasn't used to Lenni having a go at her like this. Lenni was the most loyal person Olivia knew, but even the people you like the most could go behind your back. Bitter experience had taught Olivia that.

'You haven't blabbed to Ove about yesterday?'

'Blabbed?'

'Yes, about what we talked about. You didn't tell him about Alex or what I said?'

'Have I ever "blabbed" anything about you?'

'How should I know?'

Silence. And then Lenni answered.

'You really don't know that? Shame.'

Olivia heard how hurt Lenni was and she regretted what she'd said. Why was she so annoyed that Ove and Lenni had spoken? She liked them both so much.

'Sorry, Lenni. Of course I know. It's just been a bit much today. I've just got back from A&E. Sandra, the girl I told you about, she tried to kill herself. Everything's just a mess right now.'

Silence.

'Lenni? Hello?'

But Lenni had already hung up before Olivia had even said sorry. OK. So now she'd fallen out with Lenni too. A great end to a great day! Olivia threw her mobile down on the sofa. Now all she wanted to do was sleep.

Then the doorbell rang.

Olivia got up, went out into the hallway and opened the door.

'Hi,' Stilton said.

A few seconds passed before Olivia replied.

'Are you going to ask to borrow the shower again?'

Stilton had come knocking on her door once before, about a year ago. When he was still living on the streets. Olivia had let him in. Two minutes later he'd asked where the shower was and got right in without being embarrassed, even though they barely knew each other. It took quite a while for Olivia to get over that.

'I have my own shower now,' Stilton said. 'Rivera?'

'How did you know?'

'It says Rivera Rönning on the door. Can I come in?'

'Why?'

'Because I need your help.'

Olivia looked at him. There was a very different man standing in front of her, but he had that same frank attitude. She was not planning to let him in. Turning up a year later to say hello? Who did he think he was?

'Why do you think I'd help you?'

'Because it's about Jackie Berglund.'

Jackie Berglund? That nasty bitch? Was he after her? She stepped aside and let Stilton in.

'You have five minutes.'

'Perfect.'

Stilton went straight into the kitchen and sat down. The last time he sat there he was half-dead and had just saved himself from a burning caravan. Olivia had found him down by the entrance. This time she stopped in the kitchen doorway.

'One minute's almost up,' she said.

'Aren't you going to sit down?'

'No.'

Stilton had prepared himself for this. He knew how she'd react. But he'd still managed to get into her kitchen. Now it was just a matter of keeping her hooked.

'I want to take down a policeman who's been using prostitutes,' he said. 'Jackie Berglund arranged the meetings.'

'Why do you want to take him down?'

Stupid question, Olivia thought to herself, but she wanted to maintain a distance.

'For personal reasons. He's the reason I left the Squad.'

'So you think I'm going to help you with a personal matter.'

'I hope so. You don't have any coffee, do you?'

'No.'

Stilton looked at her completely expressionless face.

'It's not only about helping me,' he continued. 'For you, it's also a chance to get to a person who's been fucking awful to you.'

'Like you.'

She said it without affect, calmly and matter-of-factly. Stilton felt they'd reached a turning point, one he'd sincerely hoped he wouldn't have to address.

That's how naive he was.

He assessed the situation. He could get up and go. Empty handed. Then he'd be back to square one with Rune Forss again.

Or he could just face the music.

'Like me,' he said. 'What I did to you is something that I've regretted every day for a whole year, when of course I haven't been wondering what I could have done instead. I've got no excuse. I was cowardly and selfish and I never put myself in your shoes. I'm no expert when it comes to empathy, but that's no excuse. If I could make it undone I would. But I can't.'

He was really going for it, he realised that, but there was a great deal of truth in what he was saying. He'd chosen not to tell Olivia that the murder case that she obsessed with last year had been about her own mother. That it was her mother who was the victim on the beach, even though he'd known it the whole time. Once she'd realised that he'd misled her, she'd reacted as she had. And that feeling was still there.

'But what hurts me the most is that I made a promise to Arne,' Stilton said.

'What was that? What promise did you make to my dad?'

Olivia sat down on a chair opposite Stilton and tried to hide how surprised she was. And interested. This wasn't something she knew about.

'To always look out for you, no matter what happened to him. It was only me and him and a couple more people who knew the truth about you. If something happened to him I promised to always be by your side, as long as you needed me. I broke that promise.'

'You went off the rails.'

'As much as anyone can. And there was no room for you there, not for anyone.'

Stilton looked down at the table. Olivia watched him. She was having a hard time doing as she'd set out to do, maintaining a distance, she felt it slowly fading away. She'd already realised in Mexico how Stilton had borne the brunt of her anger towards Arne, how she'd passed on all the blame to Stilton. Arne was dead, Stilton was alive. Now he was sitting opposite her, suffering for what he'd done to her.

Wasn't that enough?

'How can I help you with that policeman?' she finally said.

Stilton looked up from the table and caught her gaze. He saw the change. He saw that he'd broken through. He saw that she was looking at him as Arne's daughter and he felt his stomach tighten. He was close to extending his hand to her, but he didn't. It was too early. Too fragile. He'd do that when she laughed.

When that time came.

So he told her what he was looking for. Prostitutes working for Jackie Berglund ten to twelve years ago. He told her about his meeting with Ovette. He didn't say that it was Mette who'd advised him to contact Olivia. He didn't need to.

She probably suspected that herself.

'I can't recall any names off hand,' she said. 'But I have a few folders where I collected everything I found. I can go through them later. Do you want some coffee?'

'That would be nice.'

'What did you do in Marseille?' Olivia asked while getting up to make the coffee. And Stilton started telling her. For some reason, he wanted to tell her. Everything. About Abbas and Samira. About the murder and the dismemberment. About everything that had happened down there. The only thing he didn't mention was what Jean-Baptiste had told him. About Abbas being in hospital. He didn't want Olivia to worry about that, he knew that she was very attached to Abbas.

'So when's he coming home, then?'

'He's on his way. He's travelling by train. He's so bloody scared of flying.'

There came the first smile from Olivia. Not a laugh, they weren't quite there yet, but a smile. She knew how afraid Abbas was of flying.

'So what are you up to now?' Stilton asked.

He'd felt that that smile had paved the way for that question. He wouldn't have dared to ask it a little while ago. If

308

he'd known the answer he was going to get, he might even have waited a while longer.

'I'm going behind Mette's back,' Olivia said.

She put the coffee down on the table and poured it. Stilton waited. He drank almost three cups before Olivia had finished talking. She also felt that she wanted to talk. About everything. Even about Sandra.

When she stopped talking, Stilton looked at her. She'd changed. So had he. But he'd had six years to do so, she'd only had one. Nevertheless he recognised something of himself in her: she wanted to choose her own path and no one was to stand in her way.

Least of all Mette Olsäter.

'So how are you going to find out if it's Sahlmann's laptop out there at Borell's place?'

'I don't know.'

'Wouldn't it be wise to contact Mette after all? She has very different resources available to her.'

'What's she going to do? She can hardly order a search warrant based on my suspicions? Not when it's someone like Borell.'

'No.'

Stilton knew that she was right. But he didn't like what he saw in her eyes, they foreshadowed dangerous things. That Olivia might act single-handedly, in a way that definitely wasn't advisable.

'Please can I help?' he said.

'I don't know. I need to think about how I'm going to do this. But I'm not going to involve Mette.'

'Because?'

Stilton understood that there was a conflict. He realised quite how serious it was once Olivia had described it. How hurt she still was. Now it's Mette's turn to be in the firing line, he thought, just when he'd escaped. He got up. Olivia accompanied him to the door. Before he left they looked at each other.

'Olivia Rivera,' he said.

'Tom Stilton.'

She pushed the door closed and leant against the wall. There were many questions going through her mind. How did this happen? All of a sudden she'd been sitting with Tom Stilton telling him things that she hadn't told anyone else. Him, of all people? How had that happened? So quickly?

She stood in the hallway for a while.

Chapter 20

Gabriella Forsman and Clas Hall had been arrested at a deserted campsite just outside Flen, and they'd been taken straight to the National Crime Squad headquarters. The local police had seized a stash of the 5-IT from their car. Mette presumed that it came from the Customs and Excise haul.

Bosse Thyrén had questioned Hall. He would have preferred to take Forsman, but Lisa Hedqvist had been pretty adamant about that.

'I'll take her.'

'Why?'

Lisa felt it went without saying.

So Bosse questioned Hall. It went quite quickly. Hall knew the routine – he denied everything and demanded to speak to a lawyer.

Forsman was not quite so experienced. This was the first time she'd been arrested, and she behaved accordingly. She spent the first ten minutes in the interrogation room crying. Floods of tears. Lisa just let her cry. Once she'd calmed down a bit, Lisa started asking her questions. First about the missing stash of drugs. Forsman didn't know anything about it. Absolutely nothing! When Lisa showed her the email conversation between Forsman and Sahlmann, a couple of emails at a time, taken from Forsman's own computer, the flamboyant woman broke down again. It took another ten minutes for her to regain composure. Lisa just sat there and watched with a blank look on her face. Thank God she'd managed to prevent Bosse from leading this interview. She wasn't quite sure how he would have handled it.

Gabriella Forsman was pulling out all the stops.

'So you were the one who stole the drugs from your workplace?' said Lisa.

Forsman nodded. Her long, red hair was hanging down over her face. She flicked it aside with a small movement – it was a damn shame that she wasn't being questioned by that young man she'd met last time. He would no doubt have understood her much better. Particularly the part she was about to explain.

'I was tricked,' she said.

'By whom?'

'Clas Hall.'

Forsman was going to give it her best shot – it might work.

'He took advantage of my feelings,' she said.

'In what way?'

Forsman explained how she'd fallen in love with Hall. How he'd seduced her and manipulated her and got her to do what he wanted.

'He was just like that pastor involved in the Knutby murders! That's just what he was like!'

'He tricked you into stealing drugs?'

'Yes! He said he was going to end it and throw me out if I didn't help him. He needed money. He said that it was completely without risk. All I needed to do was take a few drugs from work and give them to him and we'd get money to go to the Caribbean.'

'And you fell for that?'

'What was I supposed to do? I was a victim of my own emotions!'

Victim, my arse, Lisa thought. But she was still satisfied with how things were going. Forsman had confessed that she was the one who'd stolen the drugs. The motive was irrelevant.

To Lisa at least.

The next step was the Bengt Sahlmann murder. Forsman denied any involvement in that. She'd never stepped foot inside his house.

'Never?'

'No.'

'But weren't you two having a relationship?'

'Me and him?'

Forsman looked as though she'd been accused of having an STD until Lisa showed her the email that said: 'My body is yours.'

'Do you always write that sort of thing to your colleagues?'

At this point Gabriella Forsman felt that she'd had enough. The tears hadn't worked very well and she wasn't sure about the Knutby pastor thing. So she opted for the Clas Hall approach.

'I want a lawyer.'

'We'll fix that. We'll also be taking some swabs.'

'What? Why?'

'To see whether your DNA matches the DNA in the skin cells we found under Bengt Sahlmann's nails.'

Forsman's big eyes clearly revealed her feelings about Lisa Hedqvist.

* * *

It was that bell inside her head that got her to make a decision, the one that hadn't been ringing loudly enough. Suddenly it did, as she sat on the toilet: the car! There was a dark car parked by Borell's gate, close to where she'd parked her Mustang. A BMW. Sandra had seen a dark-blue BMW by the house when her father was murdered. Was the car by the gate dark blue? She had a feeling that it was.

That was it.

She made a decision that had probably been formulated in her subconscious long before that. Out of pure frustration, when she felt that she wasn't getting any further with her main conviction: that the cork bag at Borell's belonged to Bengt Sahlmann. And more than anything, when she thought about what had happened to Sandra. She could still see her bloody forearms in front of her. She wanted to do everything she could to take down the person who'd driven Sandra to cut herself. Her father's murderer. She felt she owed her that much.

The car was just the trigger.

Her decision was easy: she was going to get into Jean Borell's house. She was going to photograph the laptop in the cork bag, there, in his office. If she had the chance she'd look inside the bag and open up the computer to check whether it really was Sahlmann's. Then she'd contact Mette and give her enough material to order a search warrant.

She called Sandra and hoped that she'd answer. Charlotte had been in touch that morning and said that Sandra was due to come home tomorrow, so she was probably still at the hospital.

Sandra didn't answer, but she sent a text message shortly afterwards: 'Sitting talking to some people at the hospital, can't speak now.' Olivia texted her back. All she needed was the password for the computer. A couple of seconds later she got it.

She went out into the hallway.

He loved that car, German quality through and through. This was the fourth BMW he'd owned. He turned into Folkungagatan and almost ran over a drunk man wearing a football shirt on the crossing by Östgötagatan. In his rear view mirror he saw the guy stumble and fall down in the road. He turned the music down on his CD player, he would shortly be arriving at Skånegatan. He was actually on his way to a meeting with the management team in Vaxholm, but he thought he'd pay Olivia Rivera Rönning a visit before. He pulled on his soft, black calf-leather gloves and hoped that she was alone. Jean had been very clear about this: the young woman had wheedled her way into his private home under false pretences and she'd witnessed an incident at Silvergården that simply could not come out. There was too much at stake for that.

It's my job to make sure that doesn't happen, Thorhed thought. It's my task to clean up around Jean. I've been doing that for a couple of years now, successfully, and it's been well worth it. The money was good. The only thing worrying me is Jean's weakness. Sooner or later he'll run into problems with that.

Thorhed turned into Skånegatan and noted that there wasn't a parking space near the front door he was headed for, so he had to squeeze in between two old bangers on Bondegatan. He got out and started walking towards the building.

Olivia was still there. She had what she needed and she knew what she had to do. She walked out through the door and decided to take the stairs. Halfway down she passed the lift on its way up. She carried on down and went out through the main door. But just a couple of metres down the street she realised that she hadn't brought any extra batteries for the torch. There was no way she could risk it not working! She walked back towards the front door and was just about to open it when she realised that she didn't have any spare batteries in her flat anyway. I'll buy some on the way, she thought, and started walking along Östgötagatan. Just as she turned the corner, Thorhed came out of her building. He pulled off his calfskin gloves.

Olivia went straight to the Värmdö municipal building and requested the floorplans for Borell's house. They were public documents. When she went through them she saw that he'd blasted space for a boathouse in the rock directly under the space-ship-like house. There was a stairway leading up to the ground floor from the boathouse.

So far it was easy.

The first issue was whether he had an alarm in the boathouse. She thought she'd seen CCTV when she came to the entrance last time. But did he have that all the way round the house? He'd told her that all the artwork had been burglar-proofed. Each individual object had a separate alarm and nothing could be taken from the house. And he also had his vacuum room. But an alarm in the boathouse?

Maybe. Maybe not.

Probably.

The second issue was how she was supposed to know whether he was in the house. That issue was resolved more easily than she'd dared to hope. She called the Albion office and asked to speak to Magnus Thorhed. She was planning to try to find out where Borell was. But there was no need. The woman on the phone explained that Magnus Thorhed was at the Vaxholms

Hotel with the management team and was not expected back at the office until tomorrow afternoon.

'So he's staying overnight?'

'Probably.'

'Is Jean Borell there too?'

'Yes, can I take a message?'

She could not.

So Borell was at some conference or another out in Vaxholm. She had no guarantees that he'd stay there overnight, but it seemed plausible that he'd be there all evening.

The third issue was a boat. The easiest way to get into the boathouse was by boat. She didn't have a boat and she couldn't think of a realistic way of getting hold of one now. Not at this time of year. Let alone steering it into Borell's house on Ingarö in the dark.

She abandoned that idea.

There were other ways of getting into the house.

She turned off the main road at Brunn and started driving along the narrow forest lane. She was firmly gripping the wheel as she sped along. She was going to do what she'd set out to do and nothing was going to stop her.

There was some light snowfall, but she had no problem seeing the road. And, moreover, she'd fixed her headlights.

She'd decided to park the car a long way away from the gate, down a little logging track. She'd spotted a couple of those when she'd driven along that way last time. She found one not too far away from Borell's house, drove some way down it and parked her car.

She got out of the car with the torch in her hand. She'd put on dark clothes and a pair of leather boots. And thin gloves, not mittens. She locked the car and started walking. She navigated the first stretch through the forest using her inner compass, she knew roughly in what direction the house was. She made her way past vast pine trees and scraggy dead branches, as quietly as possible.

Even though she was assuming that there wasn't anyone in the house.

There wasn't.

Well, it was completely dark anyway. Inside. She could see that when she came up onto the rock just at the edge of the plot. All she could see was the lantern-lined path.

And she wouldn't be going that way.

She thought about the CCTV by the porch.

She made her way through some more thick forest before she saw it. The wall that ran around the property from the pillar. A high stone wall. Probably edged with some barbed wire and splinters of glass if she had the measure of Borell. She followed the wall down to the water: sooner or later it had to end.

It did, just at the edge of the water, with an additional iron extension far out into the water. Olivia shone her torch along it. If she was going to get past it she was going to have to wade out quite a way into the water and then pull herself around to the other side. She didn't know how deep it was out there. She shone the torch down into the water. Were there any stones she could stand on? She could see something dark under the surface, just where the iron extension ended. She hoped it was a stone. Carefully she stepped out into the freezing cold water and felt how quickly the water reached her knees. But she still had quite a way to go. She grabbed the iron trellis, stretched her leg out and tried to feel the dark object under the surface with her boot. She put her foot down onto it, held on with one hand and pulled herself further out. It was a stone, but it was covered in algae and terribly slippery. Her foot almost slipped off and she had to grab the black trellis with both hands. The movement twisted her body around and caused her to fall over to the other side. Straight into the water. She got up, quick as a flash, and floundered her way back to dry land. She flopped down at the edge of the beach and tried to catch her breath. She'd done it! She'd got around the edge. Then she thought about the torch. The torch?! She must have dropped it when she slipped. It had ended up way out in the water at the far end of the iron trellis.

It was gone.

Stilton sat in his cabin staring at the stuffed bird. He thought about Olivia. He couldn't forget the look in her eyes when she'd talked about Sandra Sahlmann. And Borell. And the laptop that she thought was in his house. He couldn't forget the strain in her voice, the expression on her face. The dangerous clarity as she explained that she did not plan on involving Mette in this. She was going to deal with this herself.

How the hell was she going to do that?

He'd called her twice, but there was no reply. He'd called Mette as well, a long shot.

'Has Olivia been in touch with you?'

'No. Have you talked to her?'

'Yes. It went well. We can talk about that later. Bye.'

A while ago he'd passed by her flat. No sign of Olivia. No Mustang parked on the street. It didn't mean anything, really. She could have been anywhere. At the cinema. But she wasn't, he didn't think. And he didn't just want to take a chance.

'Luna?'

Stilton went into the lounge.

'Yes?'

Luna was sitting at the oval table with hundreds of stamps spread out in front of her. She was holding a magnifying glass in one hand. Stilton looked at the table.

'What are you doing?'

'Trying to separate the wheat from the chaff. I got my dad's collection, some of them are worth quite a bit but the rest is just crap.'

'I have an album with ones like that out on Rödlöga. I think they were my grandmother's.'

'It would be great to see them some time.'

'Yes, maybe. Could I borrow your car for a while?'

'Do you have a driver's licence?'

But she was smiling as she handed over the car keys.

'Where are you going?'

'Out and about.'

'Out and about?'

'Yes.'

And off he went. Luna put down her magnifying glass and ran her hand through her thick hair. She was beginning to tire of Stilton's attitude.

He didn't give an inch.

Olivia peered along the edge of the beach. Not many minutes passed before she remembered the torch app on her phone. Fortunately her mobile was in her jacket and it hadn't been affected by her floundering. She moved a few metres away from the wall towards the house, her phone lighting up the way ahead. She didn't dare to face it upwards. She knew that she had to walk along the water for a bit before she reached the carved-out boathouse, but she had no idea how far. She went up a couple of metres and started walking. She stepped over driftwood and a washed-up piece of plastic. It couldn't be far. She saw the large unlit house towering above her. The carved-out space should have been somewhere in the middle of the outer wall. The one with the glass. With the twin foetuses floating in it. She peered up and saw reflections in the large windows. Almost straight above her. I must be here now. She shone the light over the stones in front of her and she saw it. A low brick wall leading out of the water. One side of the entrance to the boathouse. She climbed up on the wall and shone the torch in front of her into a large cave. It stretched far into the rock. She couldn't see a boat in there. Carefully she crept forward along one side of the rocky wall. A little way in, the wall was covered in wood. Tarred wood. She crept in a bit further and reached some wooden decking, which she saw ran along all three walls inside the boathouse.

This was a critical moment.

She was inside the carved-out rock now.

Did he have an alarm in here or not?

Slowly she moved the phone torch to scan the ceiling of the cave, the corners, the edges. No CCTV camera. Not that she could see anyway. It could have been hidden of course, but at least she couldn't see one now. She did, however, see the door that was supposed to lead up to the ground floor.

According to the floorplans.

It was on the other side.

She started walking towards the door. Right in the middle of the narrow decking was a wooden cupboard that forced her to squeeze along the rocky wall. When she was halfway in behind the cupboard she saw the first one. A couple of centimetres from her face. A gigantic cave spider. Black. With thick bent legs. When she turned her phone around she saw the rest. All over the wall. Most of them were moving, disturbed by the light. She quickly made her way through and shook off a few of these crawling beasts from her hair.

Sayonara Kerouac, she thought to herself.

She was only a few steps from the door now. She shone her torch on it. An ordinary handle, an ordinary wooden door, not a metal one. Would she be able to open it? Or was it another one of those that only slid open on command?

It wasn't.

But it was locked.

She'd expected that. But what kind of lock was it? If it was a seven-pin tumbler lock she was in trouble. She wasn't going to be able to pick one of those. If it wasn't, she could make use of her training. Thanks to those of her classmates who thought that picking door locks should be part of elementary police training. Without breaking them down as they did in films.

They'd taught Olivia how to do this, with the help of some small dangling tools. She took out the metal cluster and began working on the spikes in the door lock.

Borell was furious. The meeting had hit a wall. At first everyone agreed that the time period leading up to the next election needed to be milked to the max. Up to that point, things were running smoothly. Then came the conflict. There were two camps in the management team. One that wanted to expand and another that wanted to improve the organisation they were already running. Borell was part of the first group. After half an hour of discussion it was clear that they had reached a stalemate. So Borell ended the meeting. It came quite abruptly. Everyone had expected to be staying at the hotel overnight.

But the plans were changed.

Idiots, Borell thought to himself as he drove down the dark forest lane. Of course we need to expand as much as possible. That's what this whole thing is about. He was so annoyed that he almost missed them, the tyre marks in the snow that turned off into the narrow logging road. First he just drove past them, then he put the brakes on, reversed and stopped. The tracks continued right in. Who the hell has been driving here? At this time? He carried on further down the narrow track and put his headlights on full beam. The tracks carried on further towards a small bend. He drove on a little further and stopped. His headlights were shining straight onto a white car that was standing just next to the road.

A Mustang.

Olivia managed to open the lock. It took a while, but she did it. Before she opened the door she thought about the alarm again. If there is one it's probably connected to a security centre, and then I'll have about twenty minutes before the security guards arrive, she thought to herself and opened the door. Silence. No alarm after all. Good. She climbed up the stairs and knew where she'd emerge. Roughly. She'd memorised the floorplans as best she could, and photographed parts of them with her mobile. She'd be coming out onto the ground floor and then she'd go up the stairs to the right. Once at the top she'd be back on the floor where she'd been a couple of days ago.

The office floor.

She found the stairs. She held the mobile torch straight onto the steps in front of her, she didn't want it casting too much of a beam. She didn't want to risk it being seen from outside. Whoever might be out there. When she got upstairs she saw that she was in the right place. The only thing shining in the whole house was the aquarium in the large glass wall. The green light shone all the way over to the staircase where she stood. She quickly moved away. She knew where the office was. It's so quiet, she thought, when that strange music isn't on. She scurried through a narrow passageway and arrived at the office door. There was a small button on the wall. She pressed it. The door slid open just as silently as it had done last time. She stepped into the room and went straight over to the shelf where she'd seen the cork bag with the laptop and held her mobile up.

The bag wasn't there.

On the art books.

Where it had been before.

Damn it!

Had he taken it with him? Have I come here for nothing?! She scanned the room with the torch.

There!

The cork bag was lying on the edge of the desk. She switched on the camera on her mobile and took several pictures of the bag. Then she used the video function to show her location, slowly moving the mobile around the room. She focused on a large painting by Jan Håfström on one of the walls for a few seconds.

She relished the moment.

He carefully rubbed his thumb over his glass eye. The other one was watching Olivia. She was moving just a couple of metres in front of him, in his office. Every time she faced the mirror with the large golden frame, he was able to look straight into her eyes. He was standing in the narrow room behind the mirror. He'd had it built last year, secretly. It wasn't on the floorplans. He relished standing behind the mirror watching his guests in his office. Some just sat and waited, others inspected the bookshelves or cast discreet glances over the desk. Most of them went up to the mirror to correct this and that, their hair or lipstick, right in front of him. He loved that.

Now he was watching the young and beautiful Olivia Rivera in front of him, the woman who had become a troublesome witness to the incident at Silvergården and had then sought to get in touch with him under false pretences. Now she'd broken into his house and was busy documenting his room with her mobile, in particular the laptop bag. The one made of cork.

I should have got rid of that, he thought.

It was too late now.

He spent a few seconds deliberating about what to do. This was more Thorhed's domain, but he wasn't here. Not this time. He'd have to deal with this himself.

Olivia lowered her phone, went towards the cork bag on the desk and unzipped it. There was a MacBook Pro inside it. She opened it up. On the right under the keyboard was a pink heart. Sandra's sticker.

This is it!

Suddenly she heard a clicking noise behind her. She turned around. The door was about to slide shut! She lurched forward just as it closed. She scanned the walls next to the door with her mobile. No door button. What the fuck had happened?! Was it deadlocked? Was there a motion detector in here? She tried to push the door to the side.

It didn't budge.

Stilton saw the same thing that Borell had seen just a short while before, clear tyre marks just as he approached the logging track. He took a chance and suddenly saw his headlights shining onto Olivia's car. What was it doing here? Why wasn't it parked up by the gate? Olivia had told him about the gate, about the lantern-lined path, about the spaceship down by the water. But she'd parked the car here. Down a little logging track.

Stilton could imagine why and it was hardly a reassuring thought.

She's trying to sneak into that house.

She's nuts.

He looked in Luna's glovebox and found a torch. He grabbed it and got out of the car. Which way had she gone?

Olivia was standing pressed up against a wall in the office. Her brain was in overdrive. Just a minute ago she'd realised that the battery on her mobile was running out. It was about to die and she was locked in the office of one of Sweden's richest financiers.

She was trapped.

Borell was probably spending the night in Vaxholm. Was she going to be stuck in here until he got back tomorrow? She scanned the room with her mobile torch again and tried to find something to pry the door open with, her mind racing. What will he do if he finds me here tomorrow? Ring the police? But if the police come then I can explain what I'm doing here, I can show them the laptop, I can say that Borell has to be involved in the murder of Bengt Sahlmann, and that he's stolen his laptop!

So he's unlikely to call the police, she thought.

Maybe he'll build a new green aquarium with a naked woman's body floating around in formalin.

Then her mobile died.

She tried to edge her way forward in the dark.

Suddenly she heard another clicking noise. Behind her. The door was about to open. She ran towards it and squeezed through before it was halfway open, out into the corridor. Now it was really dark. Pitch black. She remembered that she'd come from the right. She felt her way along the wall. Then it was left, wasn't it? She tried to recollect the floorplans in her head. Or was it right? Then she saw a faint light at the other end of the corridor. A light that was moving along the door, slowly. He's home! Olivia fumbled her way along in the other direction as quickly as she dared. She knew that there were small sculptures and vases all over the place, she could easily have tripped. She turned around a corner and pressed herself up against a wall. Silence. Deadly silence. She could no longer see the light. She strained to hear footsteps. She couldn't hear any.

Then the music started.

That electronic music, in the speakers, not loud.

She moved away from the wall and continued straight ahead. The whole time she held her hand up against the wall to try to feel where she was going. Then the light returned. In front of her. The cone of light was just moving around a corner and down the corridor, towards her. She turned around. She couldn't see anything. She stepped across onto the other side of the corridor and thought she would reach another wall, but she didn't. She found herself in a room. She pressed herself up against the wall inside the door and held her breath. She didn't dare to look out. From the corner of her eye she could see the cone of light on the floor moving along outside past the room. She exhaled. Then she heard a faint clicking noise again. The door she'd come in through slid shut. A couple of seconds later she heard the whirring noise coming from the ceiling ledge.

She was locked in the vacuum room.

Stilton had taken roughly the same route as Olivia through the forest. Towards the wall. Through darkness and marshy terrain. He presumed that she'd have tried to get over the wall and into the house. Completely insane, but it wasn't his idea. He'd tried to call her twice. Either she'd turned her phone off or put it on flight mode. Or maybe she'd lost it? Perhaps she couldn't talk right now? The last option was the most positive. That would mean that she was somewhere over there, in control.

But she wasn't in control. She'd sunk down onto the floor a while ago. Now she was slowly crawling along the cold concrete floor, in the dark, towards the door. The oxygen in the room had almost run out, she struggled to inhale the air, her lungs were being compressed, her throat was a thin, wheezing hole. She clawed the floor with her hands, her head was spinning, eight silent works of art looking down at her cramping body. Finally she turned over onto her back just by the door, gently scratching at the skirting, her eyes closed. Just a second away from going numb, she opened them again. The whirring sound coming from the ceiling had suddenly stopped. The door started to open. Slowly, one centimetre at a time. The room was about to be filled with air again.

Too late.

Her head sank down onto the floor.

Jean Borell was standing in the doorway. He was very pleased. The vacuum system had cost a fortune, but it worked.

Perfectly.

He leant over the lifeless body and fished out a mobile phone.

Stilton had reached the wall. He shone the torch onto it. It was high. Too high for Olivia to have been able to get over. So he followed it out towards the water. When he reached the end of the wall he stood still. He could have waded out and made his way around the iron trellis, he assumed, but he didn't know where Olivia was. He didn't know what the fuck she was doing. Bloody fool! He turned off the torch and looked out over the gently rocking sea. Suddenly he saw a flickering light, far off along the edge of the shore.

Then his reflexes kicked in.

He waded out into the water. Some way out he used the strength in his arms to heave himself along the iron trellis, until he finally managed to swing around the far edge. When he reached firm ground he started moving towards the light. He didn't dare switch on his torch, which meant that he didn't see the dry plank of wood. It broke right off as he stepped on it, causing a loud creak. Suddenly the light went off. Stilton stopped, and listened. He thought he heard a faint splashing sound. He pulled out his torch. He didn't give a shit whether anyone saw him. As fast as he could, he went over to where the light had been shining. He reached a low brick wall leading up to a carved-out opening in the rock. He couldn't see in very far, so he shone the torch down towards the water instead and saw a body floating on the surface.

Borell was standing in the doorway of the vacuum room, drying his forearms with a small towel. He'd been interrupted out there by a noisy creaking sound over by the wall. Probably just a deer, but nevertheless. He'd dumped Olivia's body in the water and hurried back to the boathouse. She'd be found, drowned – there were no outer injuries on her body. If the discovery of her body was linked to his house he could claim that it was attempted burglary, the door to the boathouse had been open when he came home. Picked open. Unfortunately the alarm down there had been temporarily disabled due to some minor reconstruction work. The woman had probably made her way in and out through the boathouse, slipped out by the edge of the quay because it was so dark and drowned. It wasn't up to him to explain that.

If the body was even found.

He took out the mobile he'd taken off Olivia. He was curious. He knew there were incriminating pictures of Sahlmann's laptop on it, but maybe there were even more things of interest. More about what this young lady had gathered together? Maybe pictures taken at Silvergården? Of the woman who died there? Unfortunately, he wasn't able to turn it on. He'd seen that it died in the office and assumed that the battery must have been flat.

But he had a few chargers in the house.

Stilton staggered out into the water and felt the panic rising in his chest. He saw the body and the long hair floating on the surface. It was facing upwards.

'OLIVIA!'

Once he reached her he tried to lift her out of the water. He took hold of her under her arms and dragged her back to dry land. He pulled off his jacket and wrapped it around her body. He shone the torch on her face, leant down over her mouth, trying to see if she was breathing. He let go of the torch and started giving her mouth-to-mouth in the dark. A few seconds later he sat up and started pumping her chest with all his strength. He knew there was life in her, he just needed to get her system going again. He leant down and pressed his mouth against hers. At that very moment came the first gasp, a deep inhalation that almost screamed out of her body. Stilton sat up. He carried on pumping her chest to help her breathe, but now he knew that he'd succeeded. A few seconds later her eyes opened, she saw him, and then they closed shut again. Stilton took the torch in one hand, lifted Olivia up under her arms and started carrying her along the edge of the shore. He both felt and heard her breathing. He was stumbling around in the dark, trying to avoid all the driftwood. He knew he had to get around the iron trellis by the wall, all the way out, with her in his arms.

How would he manage?

Once he got there he did the only thing that was possible. He lifted Olivia's body up onto his shoulder and started wading out. He was almost waist deep. When he got all the way out to the edge of the fencing, he took hold of the railings with his right hand and swung himself out into the water and around. For a few seconds the iron dug so far into his hand with the heavy weight that he felt the pain rush all the way up into his arms and into his brain.

But he did it.

Borell put the lights out in the house. A couple of minutes ago he'd heard something sounding like a scream. A man's scream. He couldn't understand where it was coming from or who it could have been. He went around looking out through different windows. No movements on the outside. He half-ran to the large kitchen and unlocked one of the back doors. The wind was blowing through the forest on the other side of the wall. He stepped outside and closed the door behind him.

Stilton was carrying Olivia in his arms through the forest towards the cars. He didn't know exactly where they were, he had to follow his instincts, worrying about that lunatic in the house behind them the whole time. Had he seen them?

Finally he saw the cars.

Once he reached them, he tried to open the door to the back seat of Luna's car with one hand. Just as he'd managed to open it, Olivia slid out of his arms and onto the ground. Onto her feet. She gasped. He gasped. They looked at each other for a few seconds.

'Jump in,' Stilton said, a rather strange choice of words in this situation. 'Jump in' wasn't really something that Olivia was capable of at the moment. But she managed to get onto the back seat with Stilton's help and he pushed the door closed. Then he noticed the blood seeping from his right hand. The iron trellis had slashed a deep cut into his palm. He took off his T-shirt and wrapped it around his hand, and pulled his jacket back over his bare upper body. Olivia would be warm enough now with the car heaters on.

Then he reversed the car out from the logging track.

Half an hour later he was helping Olivia up the ladder. She felt her chilled body trembling. She'd perked up on the way back to the city. Her lungs were hurting and Stilton had wanted to drive her to Söder Hospital. She didn't want that, so he drove her to the barge instead.

He'd called Luna and explained. Not in detail, Luna didn't demand any details. She'd put the lights on in the lounge and made some hot drinks. She didn't know what Olivia wanted, they'd never met.

Stilton helped Olivia down into the lounge. She lay down on one of the benches. Luna was just about to put a blanket over her when she noticed that her clothes were completely soaked.

'You'll have to take those off,' she said.

Olivia got up. Luna helped her peel off her wet clothes. Stilton crept off into his cabin, he didn't want Olivia to feel uncomfortable. And he needed to tend to his hand, he'd driven the car with his left. As he unwrapped the bloody T-shirt he saw that the cut was deep.

'We're done now!'

Stilton wrapped his T-shirt around his hand again, put on another T-shirt and a dry pair of trousers, went out and sat down next to Olivia. Luna had lent her some clothes and she'd been wrapped up in a big yellow dressing gown.

'Thank you for coming,' Olivia said.

Her throat still hurt, her voice was thin.

'You're nuts, you know that?' Stilton said.

'Now I know.'

Olivia sank down onto her back. Borell had caught her. He'd tried to kill her. And Stilton had saved her. He'd done what he once promised her father he'd do – watched out for her. It was thanks to that that she'd survived. But she'd done what she'd set out to do. Photographed the cork bag and filmed the office. She'd found some rather incriminating evidence. She turned to face Luna.

'Could you pass me my trousers?'

Luna gave Olivia her trousers. She put one hand in her pocket. And in the other pocket. No phone. She sank back down onto the bench again.

'That fucking bastard,' she whispered.

'What's the matter?' Stilton said.

'He's stolen my phone.'

'That's not the end of the world, is it?' Luna said.

'Yes, it is end of the world,' Olivia said. 'The stuff on there was going to prove it all. That's why he stole it.'

Olivia rubbed her eyes.

'Are you up to talking about what happened out there?' Stilton said.

She wasn't really, but considering Stilton's efforts, she felt that she ought to. So she told the whole story. From the moment she stepped into the boathouse, to the office and vacuum room.

When she'd finished, she blinked for few seconds and fell asleep.

Luna covered her up with a couple of thick blankets and put an extra heater in the lounge. Stilton did nothing, but inside he was full of rage. He looked at the young woman sleeping on the bench. Olivia. That fucking monster had tried to kill her. On the way back from Värmdö he'd tried to make Olivia realise that this was attempted murder and that she should contact the police. Olivia didn't want to. She'd broken into his house, after all. Stilton hadn't pressured her, he didn't know what state she was in. Maybe she'd think differently once she'd recovered a bit. But he wasn't sure now. He saw her tossing and turning under the blankets and recalled the feeling of panic in his chest.

He stood up.

'I'm going out for a while,' he told Luna.

'Where?'

'To Värmdö.'

'What are you going to do there?'

'Get her mobile.'

Luna looked at him. Get her mobile?

'Then I'm coming too,' she said.

'Why?'

'Her car's still out there, isn't it? Are you going to drive both of them back?'

Stilton had forgotten about that.

He pulled Olivia's wet trousers towards him and got her car keys out. Luna walked over to a little curtain and pulled it to one side, revealing a safe. She opened it and took out a gun. Stilton looked at it.

'Have you got a licence for that?'

'Yes, do you want to see it?'

'No.'

Stilton looked at Olivia. She was snoring. She was OK. He'd just go and get her mobile.

They set off and sat in silence for a while. Luna had put a gauze bandage and a plaster on Stilton's hand.

'That'll need stitches.'

'Yes.'

They were occupied by their own thoughts. Stilton was thinking about Abbas. He tried as best he could not to think ahead. To Borell. He wanted to remain in his state of fury when he got there. Not plan anything. He was just going to fetch a mobile.

Abbas?

He ought to be on his way home now. By train, of course, that would take a while. I wonder how he looks? He knew that Jean-Baptiste hadn't wanted to go into detail about his injuries, so it was hard to know what to expect.

But he's alive.

He's on his way home.

Luna on the other hand *was* thinking ahead. To Borell. She was preparing for trouble. Based on the little she knew of the man who lived on her barge, she understood that he wouldn't be showing mercy. She'd brought the gun just in case.

She hoped there would be no need for it.

Just before they reached Brunn, Luna broke the silence in the car.

'What was it like being homeless?'

'Lonely.'

'Did you take drugs?'

'No.'

Stilton's responses were truncated and Luna felt that he didn't want to delve into this any further, so she tried another approach.

'You're not that interested in other people, are you?' she said.

'No?'

'You've lived with me for a while now. What do you know about me?'

'Your father's a captain.'

'Exactly, and that's about it.'

'Yes, what's wrong with that?'

'It's quite revealing.'

Stilton turned off towards Brunn and felt the irritation rising in him. What did she want? He'd rented a cabin on her barge. She'd got paid in advance.

'I'm quite tired of other people,' he said.

'In general?'

'Yes.'

'Thanks.'

Stilton heard the undertone.

'What do you want me to say?' he said.

'Nothing. You've been very clear.'

Stilton didn't reply. He drove down the dark, narrow forest lane as fast as he dared and felt that the conversation had taken a bad turn. He had nothing against Luna, quite the contrary, she'd been there for him and Muriel and Olivia. There was also something about her, something he didn't want to feel. Perhaps it was that he was trying to protect himself against?

'There it is.'

Stilton had driven down the narrow logging track and was pointing over at the Mustang.

'Can you drive it back?' he said.

'OK.'

Stilton passed her Olivia's car keys.

'You needn't wait.'

'Is it a long way to the house?'

'Quite a way, yeah.'

Luna got out and Stilton drove off. Luna got in the Mustang, reversed out and followed Stilton. Keeping a distance. With only her parking lights on.

Stilton slowed down as he approached the large iron gate. It was open. He wondered whether he should park and walk down. Why? He drove through the gate and sped up to the lit-up pathway and slammed the brakes on outside the spectacular entrance. Just as he was getting out of the car he saw Luna's gun. She'd put it on the passenger seat. He hesitated a moment. Then he stuffed it into the inside pocket of his leather jacket.

He leapt up the front steps in a couple of strides. When he reached the large wooden door he saw that it was ajar. First the gate and now the door? He noted this in his subconscious and pulled the heavy door open.

'Hello!' he shouted into the hallway. No answer. Just strange music. He headed in towards a lit-up room. To the right he saw a bar. Not a soul in sight.

'HELLO! IS THERE ANYONE HERE?'

Total silence, except for the music. Stilton looked around. Until now he'd just been running on rage. He'd expected to be meeting a person whom he was going to deal with as necessary. And now there wasn't anyone here. Even though the lights were on everywhere. Is he hiding? Where? Perhaps in that bloody vacuum room?

Stilton started walking through the house.

Luna had stopped at the gate. She didn't want to drive in. She was standing outside the car looking down towards where she thought the house must be. She couldn't hear anything from over there. But she did hear something that sounded like a motorboat. She knew that the house was situated by the water, although she couldn't see any. But she recognised that sound. She tried to listen harder.

It was a motorboat.

In November, in the middle of the night?

Stilton went through another room, smaller, full of artwork. He didn't take note of what was on the walls, he just went straight through. Further down he saw another corridor. He went over towards it. It was dark but Stilton still had Luna's torch in his pocket. He put it on and carried on down the corridor.

'Hello!'

Silence. Strange. Was there no one in the house? The lights are on out there. Where the hell is Borell? He stood still in the darkest spot. Suddenly he heard a strange sound of something rolling on the floor, like a marble. He pointed the cone of light towards the sound and caught sight of the rolling object. It was a glass eye. Stilton stared at it, allowing the cone of light to follow its path across the floor until it hit a wall. He took a couple of steps towards an open door and shone the torch into a dark room.

It was Borell.

He was sitting in his office chair, facing the door, leaning back slightly. The empty eye cavity revealed a bullet hole. It had carried on out through the back of his head, splattering brain matter over a painting on the wall behind. It was still trickling down. Stilton hesitated in the doorway. Borell had been murdered. Olivia's mobile was there. It should certainly not be there when the police came. Stilton went into the room. He shone around with the torch, the light reflecting in the large mirror on the wall and onto the desk. No mobile. He pointed the torch at Borell, bent down over the corpse and felt his pockets from outside. There was something in his right-hand pocket. He put his hand in and pulled out a mobile. Olivia's. He recognised it. Suddenly Borell's stomach started gurgling. Stilton stood up straight and ran out of the room.

Through the house.

Down the steps and into the car. He started the engine and sped out through the gate. He saw that Luna was standing by the Mustang a short distance away. He drove past her at full speed. Luna jumped in the car and tried to follow him. While they were still on the forest lane, she was more or less able to keep up with him. Suddenly she saw another car approaching on a short straight bit of the lane and just about managed to move over to the side of the road. It was a blue BMW racing along towards Borell's house. Driving that fast on a road like this? she thought and caught up with Stilton's car further down. When they turned off onto the main road Stilton disappeared into the distance.

He drove until he reached a petrol station, the same one that Olivia had stopped at. He turned in, stopped some distance away from the pumps, took out his mobile and called 112.

'Jean Borell has been murdered at his house on Ingarö.'

Then he ended the call. He always used pay-as-you-go phones. The call would not be traceable to him.

Olivia was tossing and turning under the blankets. She was not sleeping well. As she turned over to face the wall, she came to a little and thought she heard voices, quiet voices. She lay still, facing the wall. They were Stilton and Luna's voices. It reassured her and she closed her eyes. Then she heard Stilton make a very strange comment. He raised his voice a little.

'But I called the police!'

His voice quietened again. Olivia turned her head and she saw Stilton and Luna standing over in the lounge, very close to one another. Called the police? Had he called the police and told them what she'd been doing out at Borell's? He couldn't have. Olivia propped herself up with her arms to hear better. The wooden bench was half-hidden in darkness.

'And you're sure he was dead?'

It was Luna's voice.

'Stone-cold dead.'

'Who?'

Olivia had sat up properly now. Stilton and Luna turned around towards her.

'Who's stone cold?'

'Jean Borell.'

Stilton started walking towards Olivia as he said it. He knew that he had to tell Olivia as well. He wanted to tell her. He was still shaken up himself. Not about the murder itself, but over the fact that he'd been at the murder scene.

On the way back to the barge he'd gone over the macabre sight in the office. The bullet hole where his eye had been. The trickling matter on the painting behind. The murder must have happened just before he got to the house. The murderer may well still have been at the house when he was running in and out.

He didn't know.

What he also didn't know was whether the murderer had arrived after he'd saved Olivia or been in the house the whole time, when Olivia went into the office. He hoped that Olivia wasn't going to think along those lines.

'Imagine if the murderer was there when I was there?' she said once he'd finished.

She was thinking along those lines.

But there was no answer to that.

Yet.

When Stilton had finished, Luna told them what she'd seen and heard while standing at the gate.

'I heard a motorboat.'

'While I was in the house?' Stilton asked.

'Yes. Perhaps it was the murderer getting away?'

There was no answer to that either.

Luna went over to her simple drinks cabinet and got out a bottle of whiskey. She presumed that Stilton would be in need of some.

'Do you want some too?'

Luna turned towards Olivia. She pulled a blanket around herself.

'Yes, please,' she said.

There were three small glasses on the table and a couple of minutes of silent sipping. After Olivia had swallowed the liquid with a controlled grimace she turned towards Stilton.

'What were you doing going back there again?'

Stilton put his hand in his inside pocket.

'Getting this.'

He handed over the mobile phone to Olivia. She took it and didn't really know what to say. Had he just gone there to get her phone? And ended up with a corpse on his hands?

'You're nuts, you know that?' she said.

'I do, now.'

Both of them smiled at each other. Olivia turned towards Luna.

'Do you have a charger?'

'Absolutely.'

Luna went to get a charger and when it was plugged in Olivia turned the phone on. The pictures from the office and the laptop were still there. Borell hadn't deleted them. Other things must have got in the way.

'Did you see the laptop?' she asked Stilton.

'I didn't think about it. I had other things on my mind.'

'I understand.'

'I'm going to hit the sack now,' Luna said and got up. 'You're going to stay over, right, Olivia?'

'Yes, please.'

'There's a small cabin up next door to mine, in there.'

'Thanks. I'll go there in a while.'

She didn't want to go to sleep yet. She wanted to sit and talk to Stilton a while longer. Luna walked around the table and held her hand out towards him.

'What's the matter?'

'The gun.'

Stilton had forgotten about that. He pulled the gun out of his jacket and passed it over to Luna. She went over to her little safe behind the curtain. Just before she was about to put it in she turned her back towards Stilton. But he saw what she did – she checked the magazine. Then she closed the safe again, waved at Olivia and off she went. The bottle was still on the table and Stilton poured himself another splash of whiskey. Olivia shook her head, she'd had enough, she didn't need much in her state.

She looked at Stilton. It wasn't that long ago since she'd felt rather bitter thoughts whenever his name popped up. Now he was sitting opposite her and she felt very differently.

'There's going to be a hell of a commotion with all of this,' he said quietly.

'Yes.'

'Mette's going to get dragged into it.'

'Yes.'

'You and I will get dragged in too.'

'Probably.'

'How are we going to handle that?'

'Do we have to talk about this now?'

'No.'

They didn't have to, not tonight. They'd done enough for one day. Stilton sipped his whiskey. They sat in silence. A couple of minutes later, Stilton looked at Olivia.

'Do you miss Elvis?'

She did. Often. Why was he thinking about that now?

'Yes, very much,' she said.

Stilton nodded. Olivia looked at his sinewy hands holding the glass. The plaster that Luna had put on his right hand was turning red. Suddenly she felt the need to ask him something. Perhaps it was that very special atmosphere in the dimly lit lounge, or the whiskey, or the dramatic events that had unfurled that night, she didn't know, maybe all of the above. But she felt that she wanted to ask him what she'd asked once before and never got a proper answer to: what was it that made you go off the rails?

But she decided against.

He didn't know how long he'd slept, it felt like just a minute, but a second knock on the door of his cabin caused him to sit up. He put the light on and saw that it was half past seven in the morning.

'Tom, can you open the door?'

It was Luna's voice. Had something happened? He pulled on a pair of trousers, got up and undid the lock. Luna opened the door from outside. She stepped aside. There were two men in plain clothes standing in the corridor.

One of them was holding up his police ID.

Chapter 21

There was quite some tension during *Dagens Nyheter*'s morning meeting. The murder of venture capitalist Jean Borell at his house in Värmdö the night before was big news, and there were plenty of different angles to the story. The room was full of adrenaline-pumped journalists.

One of them was Alex Popovic.

His situation was unique. The victim was a personal acquaintance of his. Not a close friend, not now, but close enough that he had information that none of his colleagues had. That's why he kept a low profile when the speculation started. About the motive and the perpetrator. Art theft gone wrong? International links? The police had provided very little information so far. The investigation had entered a sensitive stage, so they said. There were no suspects at the moment. Details about what had happened out at Borell's house would be released later, those that could be made public at least.

So Alex crept off to his desk.

Was this murder linked to Bengt's? How? Why? He felt that he wanted to get in touch with Olivia. He'd called a couple of times after the night at his place. She hadn't called back. She must have heard about the murder by now. Why wasn't she calling? She'd been pretty full on the whole time, pressurising him to tell her that it was Borell whom Bengt had had a go at during that dinner? Why did she want to know that? He'd never got an answer to that. Perhaps he should ask the question again.

Now.

He called Olivia again and got through to her voicemail. He didn't leave a message. When he ended the call, he noticed the hum of the heated discussions taking place among his colleagues.

Who had murdered venture capitalist Jean Borell?

There hadn't been that kind of a hum when it was confirmed that Customs Officer Bengt Sahlmann had been murdered.

Not all men are equal, it seemed.

* * *

One of the investigators working on the Jean Borell murder was Rune Forss. He'd asked to lead the upcoming questioning of a man who'd been brought in earlier that morning. Tom Stilton. His request was approved. It was almost one o'clock now. Stilton had been sitting in a cell at Kronobergsgatan for more than five hours by this time.

'I need to collect some more details for the interrogation,' Forss said to the rest of the group.

He left the building. He'd planned to go bowling at half past one. He wasn't going to miss that. The idea of the man sitting alone in the cell waiting a while longer put him in a particularly good mood.

* * *

Luna hadn't wanted to wake Olivia, she wanted her to sleep. There wasn't much she could do about what had happened. When Olivia did wake up, the news came as quite a shock to her.

'They took him?!'

'Yes.'

Olivia put on her dried clothes, her mind racing. Luna laid out some breakfast, but Olivia couldn't stomach more than a glass of freshly pressed juice.

'Don't you want some fruit?'

'No, thanks. But why?'

'Why did they take him?'

'Yes! How did they know that Stilton had been at the house? It has to have something to do with that, right?'

'Yes, probably.'

'Did someone see him there?'

'He said the house was empty.'

Luna topped up Olivia's glass.

'How do you and Tom know each other?' she said.

'It's a long story.'

'OK.'

Luna felt that Olivia's response was reminiscent of Stilton's way of ending a discussion. But she was curious. Stilton had acted both impulsively and violently, he'd revealed a side of himself that Luna didn't know about. She'd suspected it existed, but there was a pressure in this man that people should not stand up against when it got too great, and now she'd seen a glimpse of it. And he'd done it for Olivia. She had to be very special to him, she thought to herself.

'Thanks for the juice,' Olivia said. 'I need to go.'

She went up on deck and called Lisa Hedqvist.

'Do you know that the police have arrested Tom?'

'Yes.'

'Why?'

'I don't know much, it's something to do with the murder of Jean Borell. Have you heard?'

'Yes.'

'There's a rumour that Tom was caught on one of the surveillance cameras at Borell's house.'

Olivia ended the call and looked out over the water. The CCTV at the entrance. Of course! That was the one he'd been captured on. Now he'd been arrested for going to collect her mobile and finding a corpse instead. He was in the house and ran out and got caught on some bloody camera. Her hands grabbed the railing so tightly, they almost turned white with cramp. When she finally let go she knew what she had to do.

* * *

Stilton had fallen asleep on the narrow bench in the cell. A police officer had questioned him briefly when he was brought in. There'd be a longer interview later. Exactly when 'later' would be was never stipulated.

And neither was the name of the person leading it.

When the cell door opened it was three o'clock. Stilton had just woken up. A young police assistant was to take him to the interrogation room. It wasn't far. When Stilton stepped into the room there was a man already sitting down at the table.

Rune Forss.

Stilton had known it was a possibility. He knew that Forss would enjoy this. It still gave him a bit of a jolt though.

'Sit down.'

Forss pointed at a chair opposite him without looking up. Stilton sat down. Forss started the tape recorder and went through the formalities, including his name, Tom Stilton. Then he opened a file in front of him and started reading. Stilton noted his shiny, balding head and his shoulders, covered in dandruff.

'Jean Borell is the principal owner of the venture capital firm Albion that has its headquarters in London,' Forss read. 'He owns a private property on Ingarö, Värmdö. The entrance is fitted with a surveillance camera. The film shows a car braking in front of the entrance at 00.22 last night. A man was seen getting out of the car, going into the house, coming out again and driving off in the car. Unfortunately, the registration plates are not visible on the film, but the man's face can be seen very clearly.'

Forss looked up for the first time.

'It was you. Correct?'

'Yes.'

'What were you doing in the house?'

'I was due to meet Borell.'

'Did you?'

'No. He wasn't there. I own some land in the archipelago, he was interested in buying some of it.'

'Was he now?'

'Yes.'

'So you drove out to see him in the middle of the night to talk about selling your land.'

'Yes. Call and ask him if you don't believe me.'

Forss looked at Stilton. Ice-cold son of a bitch.

'So you never actually saw Borell?'

'No.'

'On the film you're seen storming into the house and then running back out again. Why?'

'I was in a rush. Can you please explain to me why I'm sitting here?'

'Because Jean Borell was murdered in his house last night. At around about the same time as you were seen storming in and out of it. That's why.'

'So he's dead?'

'You had no idea?'

'No.'

Forss turned off the tape recorder and leant forward.

'This is how it is, Stilton. You know that I know that you're lying. I've been counting on that. Scum like you can't spell the word "truth". In a while I'm going to be showing the surveillance film to a prosecutor. So you can bet your bottom dollar that you'll be remanded in custody.'

'Are you still into bowling?'

Forss closed the file and left the room.

* * *

Olivia's stomach was already in knots when she got in the car. It hadn't got any better by the time she turned into Kummelnäs and approached the large green dilapidated old mansion. But there wasn't much else she could do, she had to tell Mette.

Tell her everything.

They sat alone in a room next to the kitchen. A small, gloomy room with drawn curtains. Mette was wearing a dressing gown. She was on sick leave. She'd made some tea and brought in a large pot. Mårten was off studying his deceased family. Mette poured them both some tea. She hadn't said much when Olivia came in. It was written all over her face that this was not a courtesy call to see how Mette was feeling.

'Something's happened,' Mette said.

'Yes.'

'Something to do with Tom's arrest.'

'You know about it?'

'A detective called me at six-thirty wondering where to find Tom. He was to be taken in for questioning about Borell's murder. How do you know about it?'

Mette's voice was intentionally distant, not too personal, not too cold. She'd been waiting for this meeting a long time. She'd have preferred it to be under different circumstances, but Olivia was here now and they had to take it from there.

'It's because of me,' Olivia said.

'That Tom's been arrested?'

'Yes.'

Olivia hesitated for a moment. She didn't really know how far back she should begin. It actually all started with her visit to Customs and Excise, but that was rather too far back. Then she'd have to address the scolding Mette gave her in the kitchen and she wanted to avoid that. So she began with her visit to Silvergården, and her growing suspicions about Bengt's laptop.

And then it all came out.

Mette interjected with a few short questions.

Olivia answered them all.

Once she'd told her about her own visit to Borell's place and Stilton's little adventure there, Mette asked another question.

'What was he planning to do there?'

'He was going to get my phone. He went there for me.'

The knot in Olivia's stomach tightened. She'd recounted the whole tale with great shame and worry. Worry about how Mette would react. So far there hadn't been any personal reaction from Mette at all.

Then it came.

'So you've finally found each other.'

That was an unexpected reaction. Olivia had been bracing herself for a lecture. A Mette lecture. That Tom had put himself at great risk just to collect a mobile phone and now he'd been arrested for a murder he seemingly hadn't committed.

And it was all Olivia's fault.

She digested Mette's words: 'So you've finally found each other.'

Olivia felt a lump rising in her throat. Mette put her arm around her.

'We'll fix this,' she said. 'Trust me.'

And Olivia did.

In order to fix things as she'd promised, Mette both had to get dressed and write a note to Mårten saying that she was going for a long, restorative walk.

Olivia gave her a lift into the city. On their way in Mette called Oskar Molin, an old colleague from the National Crime Squad.

'Who's in charge of the preliminary investigation in the Borell case?'

'Karnerud, I think. And Forss.'

'Forss?'

'Yes.'

'What technicians have they brought in?'

'I don't know. Aren't you on sick leave?'

'Yeah. Speak to you soon.'

Olivia dropped Mette off at police headquarters on Polhemsgatan. Before they parted ways, Olivia asked Mette whether she knew about Sandra Sahlmann's attempted suicide.

'No, when did that happen?'

'The other day. I found her in their house. In the bath.'

Mette let out a heavy sigh and looked at Olivia. She saw the sadness in her eyes and regretted shouting at her. Perhaps I should apologise after all, she thought. When the time comes.

'I'll be in touch,' she said and pushed the car door closed.

Olivia drove off and Mette went into the building. It didn't take long for her to find out which technicians were working on the case out on Ingarö. She called and explained that the Borell murder may have links to a murder that was being investigated at the National Crime Squad. Bengt Sahlmann's.

'How far have you got?'

'The preliminary report is almost done.'

'Can you give me a quick rundown of it?'

Then she went looking for Rune Forss and asked to speak to him in private. Forss tried to get out of it, but Mette was already there. He was forced into it. In the corridor.

Mette was standing quite close to him.

'You've arrested Tom Stilton,' she said.

'Detained.'

'Because he was out at Jean Borell's place last night.'

'Yes. He was caught on CCTV. I'm about to speak to a prosecutor about remanding him in custody.'

'Have you read the technical report?'

'It's not finished yet.'

'It was finished about fifteen minutes ago. I know what's in it.'

'And?'

'The interesting part is the finding of the murder weapon. In the boathouse, two floors below the office where Borell was shot. A Luger, with the same calibre as the bullet on the wall behind the body. How did the gun end up in the boathouse?'

'How the hell do I know?'

'The murderer dropping it there would be my suggestion.'

'What are you getting at?'

'Based on the times on the surveillance film, Stilton was in Borell's house for just over four minutes, right?'

Forss looked at Mette. He understood what she was getting at. He didn't like it. But what was he supposed to do? A fact is a fact.

'Yes,' he said.

'In that time he is supposed to have gone inside, found Borell upstairs in his office, shot him, gone down to the boathouse, two floors down – whatever he was planning to do there when he had the car by the entrance – then dumped the murder weapon in the boathouse, gone back up two floors, gone out of the house and driven off. In just over four minutes.'

Forss's face was expressionless.

'There were fingerprints on the weapon,' Mette said. 'I'd be very surprised if they were Stilton's.'

Forss went straight back into his office.

* * *

Olivia found a parking space on Tjärhovsgatan near the Kvarnen restaurant, and walked over to Coffice on the corner of Östgötagatan, a café with a separate room where you could sit and work in peace. She sank down into one of the worn armchairs, connected to the WiFi and ordered a large cappuccino. She didn't drink coffee very often, but there was something special about the beans they used here. She accessed the *Dagens Nyheter* site and skimmed through the articles about the murder of Jean Borell. She wanted to check whether Alex had written anything. He hadn't. Perhaps I should give him a ring, she thought to herself. Or maybe not, he was probably rushed off his feet. She hadn't bothered to answer his calls, she wanted to distance herself from that drunken night. She'd ring him soon, about Borell, a murder that may have links to the murder of Sandra's father. Mette had reacted strongly when she showed her the pictures of Borell's office on her phone. Mette knew that the missing laptop had been in an unusual cork bag.

Just like the one in Borell's office.

'But can we be absolutely sure that it's Sahlmann's laptop in there?' she'd asked.

'Yes, I opened it. Sandra had stuck a sticker on the inside, a pink heart. I took a picture of that too.'

'Good.'

Olivia put the newspaper down and sipped her cappuccino. She should probably have called Sandra to tell her she found her computer, but she felt that it would be difficult to explain the situation. And the police technicians were probably busy with it at present.

So she waited with that.

Perhaps she should call Alex after all?

* * *

The fingerprints on the murder weapon were not Stilton's. That was confirmed quite quickly. Once that was done the prosecutor had a brief chat with Karnerud and Forss: he saw no reason to keep Stilton any longer.

Stilton was sitting on the bench thinking about Abbas. He'd be home soon, unless of course he got off somewhere along the way. I wonder how he'll react when he hears what's happened, that I'm sitting here and that Olivia has been subjected to attempted murder by a now-murdered man? He was deep in thought, wondering how Abbas might react, when Rune Forss opened the cell door. Stilton got up. Forss took a couple of steps back out through the open door. Stilton followed him.

'More questioning?' he said.

'There will be more questions, but not now.'

'So I can go?'

Forss didn't answer. Stilton saw the expression on his face. It wasn't Forss's decision, he'd been forced into it. How? Mette? Had Olivia explained? As he walked past Forss he lowered his voice slightly.

'I've been talking to one of your old girlfriends from Red Velvet.'

He saw that this shocked Forss. Not much, but he certainly reacted. And it was enough. Stilton relished this moment. It may have been hasty to say it, but he'd said it now. He was happy to let Forss sweat for a while.

He deserved it.

He didn't just sweat. He was both furious and frightened. As soon as Stilton had gone, he left the building and took out his mobile. He stood outside police headquarters in the drizzling rain and called Jackie Berglund. He was so hasty that she hardly had time to answer.

'Is there any way Stilton can have found out about my old contacts?'

'I don't think so.'

'Is my name still on your list?'

'No, I've deleted it.'

'When?'

'About a year ago, after they called me in for questioning. Why? Why do you think that…'

'Do you think any of the women have blabbed to him?'

'Only one of them is still alive.'

'Who's that?'

'Ovette Andersson. But she won't blab.'

'How do you know?'

'She isn't the type.'

'Have you got an address for her?'

Jackie did.

* * *

It was late by the time Stilton got back to the barge. He'd spent the last hour sitting at a café on Hornsgatan, because of the weather. He was used to bad weather and it seldom bothered him, but this was a bit much. It wasn't just a storm, it was an absolutely unbelievable downpour that exploded across the skies and came pouring down in drops the size of golf balls. People leapt into doorways and cars had to pull over, their windscreen wipers unable to cope with the sheer amount of water.

Eventually it eased off enough for him to be able to finish his coffee and head back to the barge. Wet, but in good spirits. He'd certainly shocked Forss, not enough for him to lose his balance, but a clear riposte. He stood outside his cabin and shook off the worst of the rain.

'Were you out in that?'

Stilton turned around. Luna was sitting over in the lounge watching him.

'No.'

'What happened with the police?'

'They took me in and let me go.'

Stilton walked towards the lounge. There was something he wanted to ask Luna and it was a good idea to do so straight away.

'Can I sit down?' he said.

That alone seemed strange. He was asking whether he could sit down. That wasn't like Stilton. Had something happened? But she gestured and Stilton sat down.

'Would you like a towel?' she said.

'Why?'

'Your hair.'

Stilton hadn't cut his hair since returning from Rödlöga and it had grown quite a bit. Enough to look wet, it seemed.

'It's fine,' he said.

'OK.'

Stilton looked at Luna. When he was lying in his cell, half-asleep, he'd thought about her quite a lot, more or less willingly. She just popped into his thoughts. Now he could partly understand why. There was something about that woman sitting there, looking like she always did, calm and collected, that attracted him to her. Not in the same way as Claudette, that was about something else, Luna was Luna. He leant over towards her.

'I saw that you checked the magazine before you put the gun back,' he said.

'Yes.'

'To check whether there was a bullet missing.'

'Yes.'

'If there had been, it would have been me who shot Borell, right?'

'Well, that would have been a reasonable assumption.'

'So that possibility crossed your mind? That I could have done that?'

'Yes.'

'OK.'

So he'd asked what he had to ask. Luna had made sure that he hadn't shot Borell. So she believed that he was actually capable of it. He looked down at his wounded hand, the one that Luna had kindly tended to.

'But all the bullets were there,' said Luna.

Stilton nodded. So they'd sorted it out. We know where we're at, he thought, and asked: 'Why do you have a gun?'

'It's just stuck around.'

'Since?'

'Since I needed it.'

She gave him a taste of his own medicine.

* * *

The music hadn't helped.

He'd been standing right in the middle of the room for more than an hour, naked, and it hadn't helped. He was just as afraid now as when he'd got the call.

'Jean Borell has been shot.'

Now he was sitting hunched over at the round table next to the alabaster lamp. He'd just watched a cigarillo burn out in the ashtray, he'd hardly smoked it. There was a glass on the table. He filled it with port, right up to the brim – as he moved it towards his lips, half of it spilled out. He put it down again and turned towards the large room, his gaze resting on the beautiful wall opposite.

Was it his turn now? It was only him left now.

He looked down at his arms, the scratch scars were clearly visible. Would they stay or disappear?

He sat down on the floor, his legs crossed, and closed his eyes. His hands were tightly gripping the table legs in front of him. He tried to disappear, tried to dive into the darkness, away from this world he no longer wanted to be part of.

He couldn't.

He lifted his head and felt the tears run down onto his hairless chest. He got up and went over to the bookshelf. With a trembling hand he pulled out a thick book, a German dictionary, hardcover. There was a gun lying behind it.

He looked at it.

He'd used it once before.

He could use it again.

Chapter 22

It was bitterly cold. The kind of cold that's not really about temperature, but lashing, icy, penetrating winds that forced people from open spaces to seek shelter. So there was no way Olivia could walk to the barge. At first she'd thought she would, when Stilton rang, take a nice walk and get some fresh air. She still felt the effects of that vacuum room.

'Mette's on her way here, it's probably a good idea if you come as well,' he'd said.

It probably was.

Things were actually rather muddled in her head. She could do with listening to Mette's more analytical view of the situation to get an idea of what she should be doing herself. Because she was involved in this murder in several ways, some good and some decidedly less good.

But as soon as she got out of the door and almost got blown back in, she decided to take the car. She didn't need that much fresh air.

She ran up the ladder so as not to be blown off and crept down into the lounge. Stilton and Mette were already sitting there. Luna was at the cemetery.

'Hi,' said Stilton. 'Sit down.'

Olivia pulled her jacket off and sat down. Mette got going straight away.

'We've taken over the Borell investigation,' she said. 'There was a fair amount of grumbling, but there always is. I went through all the material this morning and got our team up to speed. The autopsy report confirms what it says in the preliminary report. Borell was murdered. The murder must have occurred at some point after he left you, Olivia, down by the water, and before you, Tom, came back to the house. How long do you think that was?'

Stilton looked at Olivia.

'What do you think? Just over two hours? I found you, carried you up to the car, we drove here, you changed, we talked for a while, you fell asleep and I drove back.'

'Two hours sounds reasonable.'

'So we have a timeframe within which the murder must have taken place,' Mette said. 'Did you see anything at all at the house other than the body?'

'No,' Stilton said. 'I ran in and out.'

'In just over four minutes, according to the surveillance camera. Good job you didn't loiter about, that would have complicated things for you.'

'When have you ever seen me loiter?'

Mette let the comment slip. She didn't want to remind him of the five, six years that he didn't do much else other than just that.

'But Luna did hear a motorboat,' Stilton said.

'Was she there too?'

'She came with me to collect Olivia's car. She was standing by the gate while I was in the house.'

'And that's where she heard the motorboat?'

'Yes.'

'Interesting. Could have been the murderer getting away. The camera outside hadn't registered anything until Tom turned up in his car. That means the murderer must have gone in another way. Maybe the same way as you, through the boathouse, into the office, down again and then off in that motorboat. After dropping the murder weapon in the boathouse.'

'Then I must just have missed him,' Stilton said.

'Probably. The next bit of interesting information came from the technical report. There was no laptop in a cork bag in Borell's office. In fact, nowhere in the house at all.'

Stilton and Olivia looked at each other.

'But it was there when I was there,' Olivia said. 'You saw that yourself on the pictures.'

'Yes. Which means that the murderer must have taken it. Unless you did, Tom?'

Stilton gave Mette a rather fed-up look.

'So the murderer stole Sahlmann's laptop?' Olivia said.

'Apparently.'

'Why?'

'Do you think I have an answer to that?' Mette said. 'I don't. And I don't know who the murderer was either. I don't know his or her motive. What I do know is that there was a man at the murder scene when the police arrived, after you'd left your anonymous tip-off, Tom.'

'Who was that?' Stilton asked.

'His name is Magnus Thorhed and he seems to have been working for Borell.'

'Was he there?!'

Olivia sat up.

'You know of him?'

'I've met him.'

'It must have been his car we drove past,' Stilton said. 'He came racing through the forest like a madman.'

'What was he going to do at Borell's in the middle of the night?' Olivia wondered.

'He claims that he went there because Borell wasn't answering his mobile,' Mette said. 'He knew that Borell had gone home. They been at some conference, and there was something he urgently needed to discuss with him.'

'At that time?'

'We asked him that,' Mette said. 'And he said that their company operates all over the world: when it's night here it's day in Boston. That was the explanation he gave. I'll deal with him later.'

'Aren't you on sick leave?' Stilton said with a smile.

Mette ignored the comment.

'So now we have two connected murders. Via Sahlmann's missing laptop. Is it the same murderer?'

'Doubtful,' said Stilton.

'Because?'

'Sahlmann's murder was arranged to look like suicide. To disguise the fact that it was murder. Borell was just shot. Rather different approaches.'

'True.'

'Which means that Borell could have killed Sahlmann and then been murdered himself,' Olivia said. 'It must have been Borell who stole the laptop the first time, at Sahlmann's, considering that it ended up in his office?'

'He may not have stolen it himself,' Mette said.

Magnus Thorhed? Olivia immediately thought. The man very much at the forefront of things? But suddenly she had other things to think about.

Abbas had stepped into the lounge.

'Hi.'

He didn't say any more than that. Nevertheless it took a few seconds before anyone in the room reacted. For several reasons. His sudden appearance was one. His actual physical appearance was another.

'What happened to you!?!'

A question that both Mette and Olivia had good reason to ask. Mette got there first. But Olivia was first to get up and give him a big hug. He didn't let on whether or not it hurt. He hugged her back. He'd been longing for it. Perhaps not from Olivia in particular, but from someone like her, who meant something to him.

Who was alive.

Stilton and Mette also got on their feet to greet Abbas.

'What happened to *you*?'

Abbas pointed at Mette's cheek. The nine stitches were still visible.

'Let's talk about that later.'

Stilton went to get another chair and Abbas sat down.

'I've come straight from the train station,' he said. 'Don't worry about my face, it'll be fine. I was assaulted and my nose took a beating.'

'Who did this?'

Abbas opened his wheeled suitcase and pulled out a plastic file containing a black-and-white picture.

'This guy.'

Olivia had a look first. All she saw was a slimy-looking man with an oiled face.

'Who's that?'

'Mickey Leigh. A porn actor.'

When Stilton looked at the picture he saw something very different, something that gave him quite a shock. He saw the man who'd disappeared in through the door with Jackie Berglund. Two days ago. Here in Stockholm.

'This is the guy who's known as The Bull,' Abbas said, looking at Stilton.

'Were you the one who found this out?'

'Yes.'

'How?'

Stilton was trying to buy some time. When Abbas started explaining how he'd found Mickey Leigh, Stilton went through various options in his head. He knew what Abbas had done to Philippe Martin to get him to talk and could just imagine what he'd do to Jackie Berglund to get hold of Mickey Leigh. Jean-Baptiste had overlooked the matter. Mette would not.

He needed to keep Abbas calm.

So he kept quiet.

'It's so bloody frustrating,' Abbas said. 'Just when I find the right guy they throw me out of Marseille.'

'Who?' Mette asked.

'The police!'

'Jean-Baptiste?'

'Yes.'

'Perhaps he had his reasons?' Stilton said carefully.

Abbas didn't reply. He didn't want to clash with Tom over Jean-Baptiste. He put the picture back in the plastic file. Mette watched Stilton. She'd seen his reaction when he saw the picture of Mickey Leigh. She didn't understand why. She'd ask him when they were alone. For now she asked Abbas about what he'd been up to in Marseille, other than what she already knew from Jean-Baptiste. Abbas gave her a short summary, excluding the part about Martin. When he'd finished he wanted to go.

'I can drive you home,' Olivia said.

'Thanks.'

Olivia and Abbas left the lounge.

Stilton followed them up onto deck and watched them leave. He wanted to make sure they'd gone.

When he turned around to share what he'd been hiding from Abbas with Mette, she said: 'You recognised that man on the photo. Mickey Leigh.'

'Yes. He's in Stockholm. He's hanging out with Jackie Berglund. I saw them outside her building the other day.'

'And why didn't you want to tell Abbas?'

'Well, you saw how he looked…'

Mette understood. She knew Abbas too.

'Do you think that Mickey is wanted?' she said.

'I can check.'

Stilton called Jean-Baptiste. Mickey Leigh was indeed wanted, for grievous bodily harm and possible involvement in a dismemberment killing. The French police had just released information via Interpol as Mickey Leigh was registered as having left the country.

'He's in Stockholm,' Stilton said. 'I've informed Mette Olsäter.'

'Good,' Jean-Baptiste said. 'Please ask her to keep in touch with us.'

Stilton ended the call. Mette had understood the implications of this conversation and got out her mobile. She called Bosse Thyrén and had Jackie Berglund's building put under surveillance.

'You can find his picture on an Interpol wanted list,' she said.

'OK,' Bosse said. 'Oh and by the way –'

'Yes?'

'There's no match with Gabriella Forsman and Clas Hall's DNA.'

'Now we know.'

Mette ended the call and looked at Stilton. He looked troubled. He felt that the whole Marseille adventure had just landed in Stockholm.

And it didn't feel good.

*　*　*

Ovette Andersson didn't have many friends. Not many she could trust. Her colleagues were colleagues, and her friends from before were dead, most of them at least.

But she still had Mink.

They went back a long way – they'd grown up in the same suburb, Kärrtorp. Mink was the one she'd turned to when her son Acke had got into trouble last year, and Mink was the one she was turning to now.

'Did he threaten you?'

Mink looked genuinely appalled. Not because he thought much of police integrity – that was pretty much in line with his view of the rest of the world – it was the fact that a detective chief inspector was personally engaged in threatening a single woman that provoked a reaction in him.

'Yes,' Ovette said. 'He was bloody unpleasant.'

They'd meet in a narrow side street off Hornsgatan. Ovette had chosen this meeting place, out of sight of glares and cars. She was afraid, her weary eyes made plain that she'd had a sleepless night.

'He was outside my front door yesterday,' she said.

'What did he want?'

'He was wondering whether I'd been in touch with Tom Stilton. I said I hadn't, but he kept going on about it. In the end he pulled me off into a dark corner and told me what he'd do to me and Acke if I breathed a word to Stilton about him buying sex.'

Ovette swallowed several times and Mink saw tears welling up in her eyes.

'What did he say he'd do to you?' he asked.

'Take care of us.'

'OK, and by that he didn't mean a package holiday to Mallorca or a new flat.'

'No. His eyes were black as hell.'

'What an arsehole.'

Ovette swallowed again and Mink saw how fragile she was. He put his arm around her. If the world was ending in December it didn't matter all that much what that copper had threatened her with, but he also thought about what Stilton had said. It may be worth doing good until then, it might well pay off.

'I think you should talk to Stilton again,' he said.

'Why?'

'Because he's a very smart guy. Who also happens to know that arsehole Forss. He might be able to arrange some protection for you? And he knows Acke too.'

Ovette didn't reply. She started walking, with Mink's arm around her shoulders.

* * *

Mette just managed to get into her office when she took the call. It was from one of the guys keeping an eye on Jackie Berglund's building. They'd just seen Berglund go in through the front door accompanied by Mickey Leigh.

Mette reacted quickly.

Rather too quickly for someone who'd had a mild heart attack.

But she ignored that.

She immediately sent Bosse Thyrén and Lisa Hedqvist over to Berglund's place on Norr Mälarstrand. With backup.

'He's wanted for grievous bodily harm in Marseille. And he might have murdered a woman as well.'

Bosse and Lisa took Mette's warning about Mickey Leigh very seriously. They arrived with a police patrol van. Had they not done so, and instead opted to take their unmarked police car, they might have gone unnoticed. But a patrol van is quite hard to miss on an open street like Norr Mälarstrand. Jackie saw it through the window straight away. After spotting Stilton down on the street a few days ago, she'd been looking out through her windows more or less subconsciously several times a day.

She'd been gripped by a sense of paranoia.

She saw the patrol van as soon as it stopped outside her building.

'The coppers are here.'

She largely said it as a statement of fact. It needn't have been her they were coming to see, but it was certainly possible. She had no idea what they wanted, but she didn't feel particularly concerned.

Unlike Mickey Leigh.

He leapt over to the window to catch a glimpse of the uniformed police on their way towards the building.

'Do you have a back door?' he asked.

'What? What's the matter with you? Why do you think they…'

'Back door?!'

She did. Without an understanding of what this was about, other than that it was a matter of urgency, she ran through the flat towards the kitchen door that led down to the garden. Mickey disappeared just as her doorbell rang. Jackie wondered whether she should open the door. Special operations police? They'd probably kick the door in if she didn't. She stood in the hallway for a minute or so to give Mickey a chance to escape.

Then she opened.

'Jackie Berglund?' Lisa asked, holding up her police ID. Bosse and a couple of police officers were standing just behind her.

'Yes?'

'I'm from the National Crime Squad. We're looking for Mickey Leigh.'

'Who's that?'

Lisa held up a picture of Mickey Leigh.

'He's wanted by Interpol. A short while ago he walked into this building with you. Is he in the flat?'

'No.'

'We'd like to take a look, please.'

Jackie stepped aside. She didn't let on what she was thinking. Wanted by Interpol? Had he been hiding? Was that why he turned up here unannounced? What a fucking arsehole!

Lisa moved aside to let the police officers proceed into the flat. She and Bosse remained in the hallway with Jackie.

'Is he staying with you?' Bosse asked.

'The man on the picture you showed me, the guy – I don't know… What's his name?'

'Mickey Leigh.'

'He's just visiting Stockholm, we're slightly acquainted, I had no idea that he was wanted.'

'But he's been staying here?'

'No.'

A police officer came back out to the hallway to tell them about the back door and that the man they were looking for had probably escaped out through it. A couple of officers had headed off to look for him.

'Whose is that?'

Lisa pointed at a brown suitcase in the hallway. There was a little leather name tag attached to it.

'That's his,' Jackie said.

'We'll be taking care of that then. You can accompany us to the station.'

'Why?'

Lisa didn't reply.

Stilton sat in his cabin, trying to sort things out. He had not engaged his brain for several years and now it was being bombarded non-stop since Abbas had come to the barge wanting to go to Marseille. He tried to make sense of what had happened since then. There were positive developments, such as his relationship with Olivia. He was extremely happy about that. And there had been Claudette, another positive development. The barge and Luna? He peered at the stuffed bird. Yeah, that was good too.

Then there were things that were rather less good.

Borell's attempt to murder Olivia and the meeting with Forss in the interrogation room, for example. Although the look of fear that flashed across Forss's eyes when he mentioned his old sex contacts was certainly on the plus side.

Abbas's assault was not.

And Mickey Leigh's arrival in Stockholm certainly wasn't good.

Although, on the other hand, it might help to pin something on Jackie Berglund. In that case it would certainly be on the plus side.

What was most negative, for his own part, was the news he'd just received from Olivia. She'd gone through her old material on Berglund and she couldn't find any prostitute whom Forss may have had contact with.

His only hope of nailing Rune Forss.

But he'd forgotten about Mink.

That little snitch.

He called right in the middle of Stilton's mental summary.

'I think you should talk to Ovette again,' he said.

'Why?'

When Mink told him about Forss harassing Ovette the night before. Stilton felt his blood pumping. This was both good and bad. Bad because he felt sorry for Ovette and what Forss had done to her. And indirectly also Acke. Good because it might give him another chance.

With Ovette.

Maybe.

Just when he was about to end the call, Mink said: 'You know, in the old days, people paid good money for this sort of work. Do you remember?'

'Yes. What do you want?'

'A donkey.'

Mink ended the call. Stilton looked at his mobile. A donkey? He knew that Mink was no stranger to indulging in the dark side of sexual desire. Maybe he was horny? Or perhaps it was some new code word he didn't know? He hadn't been on the streets for a while.

* * *

Jackie was questioned by Lisa and Bosse about her relationship with Mickey Leigh. He'd obviously been in her flat, his suitcase was there. But as she didn't actually know that he was wanted, she had no trouble parrying most of their questions. She'd met him in good faith. She hadn't overheard any of his telephone conversations. She didn't even know whether he had a mobile.

She lied.

Although she didn't actually know where he'd gone, or whether he knew other people in Stockholm.

'No idea.'

But she called him as soon as she was released from police headquarters. Furious. And she made it quite clear that he was never to come anywhere near her again.

'Do you have any idea what you've dragged me into, you fucking idiot?'

Mickey Leigh knew.

'Just one question,' he said. 'Then I'll leave you in peace. That guy standing down on the street outside your place, how do I get hold of him?'

'Go to hell!'

Jackie ended the call.

That was the end of all that amazing sex.

* * *

Olivia drove Abbas back to Dalagatan. She hoped that he was going to invite her up for tea, but he just gave her a kiss on the cheek and got out.

He seemed pretty exhausted.

On her way back she started thinking about Magnus Thorhed.

The man who'd been creeping around the house when she visited Borell the first time, and then sat smoking in the bar without turning around when she left.

The man who turned up at the murder scene, just like that, in the middle of the night.

She felt instinctively repulsed at the thought of him. There was something evasive and calculating that she couldn't put her finger on. She called Stilton.

'You know that car we drove past in the woods, on the way back from Borell's place, did you see what make it was?'

'A BMW.'

'Dark blue?'

'Maybe, I don't know. It was travelling so bloody fast. Why?'

Olivia ended the call. A BMW? The car parked next to Borell's gate when she was there the first time, was it Thorhed's and not Borell's? What if he was the one at the Sahlmanns' house the night of the murder?

She called Alex as soon as she reached the next red light. There were a few things she wanted to ask him, but he was in the middle of a heated news meeting and whispered: 'Come over to mine tonight.'

'Can't we meet at Kristallen?'

'We'll just get drunk if we go there.'

He had a point.

So Olivia listened to herself arranging a time to meet at Alex's. In his flat. A place that, just ten seconds ago, she'd never thought she'd return to.

* * *

The brown suitcase had been put in Mette's office, on her orders. She felt personally responsible for everything to do with Mickey Leigh right now. She'd heard Abbas's story.

Bosse and Lisa took care of Jackie Berglund. Mette took care of the suitcase.

She put on a pair of rubber gloves and opened the suitcase.

What she saw in there was lightyears away from what she expected. Clothes at the bottom and two computers on the top. One computer was a silvery-grey colour, the other one was in a bag made from pressed cork.

She sat down at her desk. A cork bag? That sent her head spinning. She just waited, unable to make sense of her thoughts.

Eventually she picked up the cork bag and lifted out a Mac-Book Pro. When she opened it up, she saw the little pink heart. Sandra's sticker.

It was Bengt Sahlmann's laptop that had first been stolen from Sahlmann and then Borell. Now it was lying in a suitcase belonging to this wanted English porn actor.

Mickey Leigh.

Mette's analytical ability was pretty legendary at the National Crime Squad. It had seen her advance to become one of Sweden's best murder detectives. Now it was off course – all she could muster were elementary questions.

Had Mickey Leigh murdered Jean Borell? Had he murdered Bengt Sahlmann too? But he'd been in Marseille then? Or hadn't he? What would his motive have been anyway?

And then her analytical ability got a hold over her thoughts.

If Mickey Leigh had murdered Sahlmann and stolen the laptop, it wouldn't have been lying in Borell's office that long afterwards. Which it clearly was when Olivia was there. It would have been in the suitcase by then.

Then Bosse and Lisa stepped into the office.

'Was that in the suitcase?' Bosse asked, pointing at the laptop in front of Mette.

'Yes.'

Then Lisa spotted the laptop bag lying next to it.

'Is that Sahlmann's?!'

'Yes.'

Mette immediately sensed where this was going.

'So was it Mickey Leigh who stole it from Sahlmann?!'

'Did he murder Sahlmann?!' Lisa asked.

'I don't think so,' Mette replied. 'He was probably in Marseille then.'

'So where the hell did he got hold of the laptop, then?' Bosse said.

Mette looked at her two talented, young murder investigators. She had complete faith in them. And she knew that it was one hundred per cent reciprocated.

They'd get there after chipping away at it for a couple of minutes.

'I think that Mickey Leigh stole the bag from Jean Borell,' she said.

'Why do you think that?'

'It was in Borell's office just before he was murdered.'

'And how the hell do you know that?' Bosse said.

And now Mette had to tell them.

'Because Olivia saw it there.'

Just how much of the faith they had in her dissipated at that moment was hard to tell, but Mette knew that it was quite a considerable amount.

When she'd finished telling them about Olivia breaking into Borell's house, the attempted murder, and how she'd intentionally kept this information from her colleagues there was quite a long silence.

'Poor Olivia.'

It was Bosse who said it. It probably reflected what Lisa felt too. Both of them knew Olivia. Both of them also knew how close she and Mette were.

Both of them got it.

And returned to work mode.

'So you think that this Mickey Leigh was in the house when Borell was murdered, is that what you're saying?' Lisa said.

'The theft of the computers certainly points to that.'

'And do you think he murdered him as well?'

'Well, it's not unlikely.'

Lisa sat down on the edge of the table and shook her head a little.

'Why would an English porn actor based in Marseille come up here to murder Jean Borell?'

'Maybe he's a hitman?' Bosse said.

'Maybe.'

'On whose orders would he have shot Borell then?'

'No idea. We'll have the computer guys go through the laptops, maybe they'll find some clues.'

Mette took out her mobile.

* * *

Olivia had decided to lie low, take it easy. She'd been rather prickly towards Alex last time she was here and she hadn't been answering his calls since then. This time she needed him for something very different. And she actually liked him too. It wasn't his fault they'd ended up in bed. It was hers. Well, not a 'fault' as such – the sex had been good even though she was so drunk.

She wasn't now.

She even declined his offer of a martini. It didn't resonate particularly well with her.

'But a Coke would be great.'

'Sure.'

Alex got a Coke from the fridge and made himself a martini. He claimed that he needed it. Things had been pretty manic at the office, there was some climate summit in Doha that had presented some rather alarming information about the effects of global warming.

Olivia just listened with one ear. But she did listen, smiling occasionally. When he'd finished he lit a couple of tealights. They sat at the kitchen table in the large hangar-like space. She could smell a gentle waft of aftershave. Olivia noticed a packet of cigarillos at the other end of the table.

'Don't you use nicotine gum?'

'Yes, but I cheat every now and again. You had some questions for me?'

'Yes, thanks for the other night, by the way.'

Alex didn't really know how to interpret that. What was she thanking him for? The whole visit? Or was she trying to smooth over her terrible mood the next morning?

'Well, thank *you*.'

Then he waited. He knew she wanted something and that it wasn't what she'd come for last time. She was just as fired up as she was when she came up to the office the first time. He could see it in her eyes. What was she after?

'Magnus Thorhed,' Olivia said.

'What about him?'

'Do you know him?'

'No.'

'But you know *of* him?'

'He's Jean's personal arse-licker.'

'Have you met him?'

'Yes.'

'Was he there at the dinner when Bengt had his outburst?'

'Yes.'

What was she getting at?

'Do you know whether he was personally acquainted with Bengt?' Olivia said.

'Yes, I think so. Through Jean. Now it's my turn.'

'For what?'

'To ask questions. One. Why are you interested in Thorhed?'

'He smells of nutmeg.'

'Olivia.'

'He has a blue BMW. Sandra saw one at the house the night that Bengt was murdered.'

'Interesting.'

'I think so too. Any more questions?'

'Yes.'

Alex reached for the little packet on the table and lit a cigarillo. He tried not to blow the smoke at Olivia. Then he asked: 'Do you know how the investigations are progressing?'

'Into the murders?'

'Yes.'

'Why would I know that?'

'I get the feeling that you have plenty of conveniently placed sources, am I right?'

'Yes and no.'

'Has any connection been made between the murders?'

'Why?'

'Because you're interested in Thorhed, who's a link between Jean and Bengt. Who've both been murdered.'

Olivia didn't reply.

'Have they got any suspects yet?' Alex said.

'I don't know.'

'Don't know or don't want to say?'

Suddenly there was a harder undertone in Alex's voice, which Olivia noticed. One of the tealights went out. She saw Alex's face in the dark behind the other candle. He held the cigarillo in front of him. Now she was the one left wondering what he was getting at. Is this the journalist asking?

'Do you think I'm lying?' she said.

'Everyone lies when they need to.'

'You included?'

'Me included. Would you like another Coke?'

'No, thanks.'

Olivia got up. She felt that she wanted to get out of there, she'd heard what she needed to hear, she didn't want to continue this conversation. She put on her jacket hanging on the back of the chair.

'Are you going to go already?'

'Yes.'

'Shall we keep in touch?'

'Yes, let's do that. Call me.'

'I have.'

Olivia waved at him.

'I'll show myself out.'

In the dim light she saw Alex get up and stub out his cigarillo. Olivia started walking towards the door she knew led outside. Alex walked behind her. She didn't turn around. When she reached the front door she heard the gigantic loft behind her fill with booming classical music.

She stumbled out onto the street and leant up against the wall. She'd felt stressed and tired. A wet dog was scurrying along on the other side of the road. The owner was nowhere to be seen. When the dog disappeared around a corner she got out her mobile and called Ove Gardman. Impulsively. He didn't answer. When she heard the beep, she didn't know what to say so she ended the call.

'I miss you,' she could have said.

* * *

Abbas sat in his flat and felt empty. The long train journey was still making itself felt, but he wasn't tired. It had felt OK seeing everyone at the barge. Now he was alone again.

The Marseille trip was over.

He didn't have the energy to think about its possible results. He tried to move on and stop thinking about Samira. He had to. He had to force himself back into everyday life.

Whatever that was going to be like.

On the train home he'd sat holding Samira's necklace, pulling his fingers through it like a rosary, contemplating. His own situation. His reaction when he'd read about Samira's murder. Why had he reacted so strongly? They'd been passionately in love, yes, but it was a very brief encounter and it was many years ago. Then Jean Villon died and he had sent a few letters to her without getting a reply.

But then?

He hadn't gone to France to try and find her. Why hadn't he done that? If she meant so much to him? He had no answer to that. He'd read about her murder and something had exploded, deep inside him, beyond his control. He had reacted and acted. Now he didn't really know why. Now it was all over.

That increased the feeling of emptiness.

He put his wheeled bag in the bedroom, took down the large circus poster from the wall, rolled it up and put it in a wardrobe. The area where it had hung was much whiter than the rest of the wall. It would have to be repainted. He went out to buy some paint.

When he got down onto the street, he didn't know which way to go. A paint shop? He walked towards Odenplan in the evening darkness. No rain, just biting wind between the houses.

Repaint? Why did he have to do that tonight? He turned back and started walking towards Valhallavägen. He'd repaint tomorrow. Where should he go? For the first time ever, he felt that he didn't want to go back to his flat, the place he normally so loved coming home to. The silence. The books. The peace. Now he didn't want to go there. Not yet. He didn't want to ring Stilton either. Or the Olsäters. He didn't have the energy. To talk. When he reached Valhallavägen he saw a poster. A circus poster. Not the like one he'd just taken down from his wall. A simpler one, more modern. Uglier.

CIRCUS BRILLOS.

That night's performance was due to start at eight o'clock, down by the tennis club on Lidingövägen. Abbas looked at his watch. It was just gone eight.

Circus?

He hadn't been to the circus since he'd left through the gates of Cirque Gruss in Marseille all those years ago.

Twenty minutes later he'd reached the circus. The girl in the ticket booth said that the performance had started half an hour ago. Abbas bought a ticket and went into the tent. He sat on a wooden bench towards the top. There were acrobats performing in the ring. He thought about Marie.

The snake woman.

This didn't come close.

He looked at the audience. They were captivated by the events unfolding below. He looked up at the construction of the tent. It was made from steel, rather like Cirque Gruss. When a clown came in, he felt his stomach tighten. Pujol. What had happened to him? Did he know what had happened to Samira? Pujol had loved Samira too, secretly, he'd confessed it to Abbas one night when he was drunk.

Was Pujol still alive?

Abbas felt difficult memories popping back into his head. The voices. The smells. Strokes of laughter, tears. Life at the circus. He was about to get up when he heard the announcement of the next act.

It was knife throwing.

With a spinning wheel.

He sank back down onto the wooden bench. A little boy in front of him was waving about a large ball of candyfloss. It obscured his view slightly. Abbas leant over to one side when they dimmed the lights. The knife thrower was a woman. Abbas didn't hear her name. Her target boy was tied to the wheel. He looked very young. The drum roll started as soon as the wheel started spinning. Abbas felt how tense he was.

His whole body was frozen.

When the first knife hit the wheel Abbas got up and left.

On his way out he heard the audience scream every time a knife hit the wheel right next to the young boy's body.

He regretted going.

* * *

They sat in Ovette's kitchen. She and Acke lived in a one-bedroom flat in Flemingsberg. Acke had just gone to sleep. Stilton had waited. He didn't want to talk about the things he needed to talk about while Acke was still awake. He waited for Ovette to return from the bedroom.

'Do you want something?' she asked.

'What have you got?'

'Water and box wine. White.'

'I'll have some water, please.'

Ovette poured a couple of glasses of water. Stilton lowered his voice a little.

'How did he threaten you?' he said.

'He said he'd take care of us.'

'And you felt that he meant it?'

'Yes. Not exactly what he said, but that there'd be consequences. His eyes were all black.'

'And no one heard this, I assume, other than you two.'

'No.'

Stilton twirled the glass around in his hand. He'd been thinking about this new situation a great deal. Even if he could get Ovette to tell a journalist about Forss buying sex, it wasn't certain that it would be enough. Forss would claim that these were the words of some delusional old hooker. If he even responded to them. The risk was that he'd go off bowling and let it all fizzle out.

Stilton wasn't going to take that risk.

So he started from another angle.

'When we had coffee the other day, you said something about Acke that I haven't been able to forget,' he said.

Ovette looked over at the bedroom door. Then she had a sip of water. Stilton waited. Ovette put the glass down.

'Rune Forss is Acke's father.'

She said it as casually as she was drinking the water. Calm and controlled. Stilton was about to ask: 'Are you sure about that?' But of course she was sure. Why else would she say it?

'Does Forss know?' he asked instead.

'No.'

'So he threatened his own son.'

'In a way.'

Now it was Stilton drinking water. Not quite as calm and controlled. Ovette had confirmed what he'd suspected. Good. This was going to be part of the puzzle when it came to the Rune Forss case.

If everything went as planned.

When he got back to the barge it was dark, both inside and out. The lights were off in the lounge and there was light snowfall over Stockholm. The first snow, he thought, and went down into his cabin. He put on the little lamp on the wall and sat on his bunk. The stuffed bird was looking at him with its peculiar dead eyes. He leant back onto the wooden panelling. He felt the pain in his groin again. A dash of whiskey? He'd bought a bottle for Luna. He'd almost finished off the other one the other night. But whiskey meant going into the lounge and that meant there was a risk of Luna turning up in the dark. She did that sometimes. Not that he minded, just not tonight. So he decided against the whiskey and started taking off his trousers. Mette had called on his way to the barge and told him about the hunt for Mickey Leigh. How he'd fled, hot-foot, from Jackie's flat, leaving behind the laptop that Olivia had seen at Borell's place. The laptop belonging to the murdered Bengt Sahlmann.

He couldn't quite put the pieces together.

Mette would get back to him on that, he was sure of it.

But he couldn't really let it go.

So it could have been that bloody Bull at Borell's almost at the same time as him. After he'd shot Borell. And now he was on the loose in Stockholm.

He wondered whether Mette had told Abbas.

He'd forgotten to ask that.

Sooner or later he'd have to bring it up – tell him about Mickey Leigh and Jackie Berglund. It wasn't something he was looking forward to. Having to explain why he'd gone behind his back, after all they'd been through in Marseille. But maybe Abbas would understand? He generally did and a few words later it was forgotten. But he might not forget quite as readily this time.

It was about Samira.

Stilton turned off the light and was about to lie down when he heard it. A scraping sound. He put the light on again. Was it Luna? But the sound wasn't coming from that direction, it came from above, from the deck. He listened. It was silent now. He turned the light off again and lay in darkness for a few seconds. Then he turned the light on and pulled his trousers back on. He didn't fancy lying there allowing his imagination to get him all worked up. Before leaving the cabin he turned the light off again.

He headed down the corridor towards the steps up to the deck. He stopped and listened. He couldn't hear anything. Instinctively he grabbed a wooden basket lying on a shelf. He held it in his hand as he climbed up the steps. He stopped in the opening before he got out on deck. It was dark out there. The city lights were casting something of a glow, but most of the deck was in darkness. It had stopped snowing.

He went up on deck.

Even in the dark, he could guess the contours of the railings. He knew this part of the barge well. He hunched over, walked

378

a bit further and looked from one side to the other. He didn't see a thing. Or anyone. He stood up straight and listened. All he heard was the sound of traffic in the distance. He turned back towards the steps. He was just about to climb down them when he caught sight of something just to left of the stairs.

Footprints.

In the light, white snow.

Large footsteps leading over towards the steps and then back again to the ladder. Stilton quickly walked over to them and looked down at the quayside. It was empty. There were a few cars standing a bit further away. All of them had their lights off. He followed the footsteps back to the steps. Whoever had made them had been heading below deck and then turned around. Because he heard me? But how did he get off the boat? Stilton just presumed that it was a man, judging by the size of the footprints.

But who?

Mickey Leigh was the first name to pop into his head. But how could he have found him? Did Jackie Berglund know about him? Why should she? And why would he come looking for me? Did he see me at Borell's place? Does he think I saw him?

Stilton conjured up several more questions in his head as he went back down to the lounge. He was going to have that whiskey now. In the dark, in silence – he wouldn't be able to go to sleep now.

Not for a long time.

He'd just poured himself a small helping when he heard footsteps coming from behind. He jumped and turned around. It was Luna. She took a few steps into the moonlight from one of the portholes, dressed in a yellow strappy nightie.

'Have you been having nightmares?' she said, quietly, as though the situation and the darkness muted her voice.

'Yes, I needed a stiff drink. I'll buy some more.'

'It's fine.'

Luna reached for a blanket and sat down on the bench by Stilton. Just as she was about to wrap it around her shoulders,

Stilton saw it. The tattoo that went down from her neck over one shoulder. He'd seen a glimpse of it before, of the little off-shoot running up her neck. But now he saw the whole tattoo. He recognised it. He'd seen one just like it, or a similar one, before, but he couldn't remember where. It was unique.

'Would you like some?'

Stilton held up the bottle of whiskey.

'No, thanks. I'm getting up early.'

'Off to the cemetery?'

'No.'

She didn't say any more than that.

Chapter 23

Lisa Hedqvist rubbed her eyes, she was tired, it was well after midnight. And she'd also spent many hours staring at computer screens. She admired the two guys sitting next to her.

Computer forensics technicians.

How did they do it?

Mette didn't want to lose time. She had two murders on her plate and at least one murderer on the loose. She'd requested Bengt Sahlmann's laptop be stripped down at once. She assumed that it would reveal essential information about the murders, considering that it had been stolen from two murder scenes.

But she'd also asked Lisa to help them in determining what could be regarded as relevant information for their investigations.

Moreover, she'd explicitly said that they should call her any time of night if they uncovered anything of interest.

Lisa sipped yet another cup of coffee.

So far they hadn't found anything that was worth waking Mette for.

They wouldn't have woken her anyway. Mette was wide awake. She'd tried getting some sleep, without success. Lying down, staring into the darkness, wondering whether she should take a sleeping pill. But that might mean she wouldn't wake if Lisa called. Eventually she'd got up as quietly as she could.

'Can't you sleep?'

She was caught by Mårten's voice.

'No. And neither can you apparently.'

'No. Shall we go down to the kitchen?'

It was a tried and tested method in their family. Go down and have a little something in the kitchen. To settle any hunger pangs and calm anything that needed calming.

They sat down in the kitchen and lit a candelabra. Gentle light for weary eyes. Mårten heated some milk and poured in a dash of honey. No miracle drug exactly, but sometimes it did the trick.

'It's not your heart, is it?' he dared to ask.

He knew that Mette was extremely tired of his constant anxiety. But he was asking because he cared.

'Thanks for your concern,' she said. 'But it's not my heart. When it is I'll tell you. You'll be the first to know.'

'So what is it, then?'

'What about you? Your heart?'

Mårten laughed a little. His heart was strong as an ox. It wouldn't stop beating until something else gave up. He knew that.

'No, it's my family,' he said.

'What's wrong with it?'

'They're nuts.'

'Do you mean the deceased or current members?'

'The deceased ones.'

And so Mårten started telling her about his ancestral research and finally Mette felt that she could sleep. Immediately. Sitting down. She felt her eyelids closing and they were almost shut when the phone rang.

It was Lisa.

That was the first call.

There would be two more that night.

After the third one, Mette made three calls of her own. To Stilton, Abbas and Olivia.

Olivia was asleep.

Stilton was up drinking whiskey.

Abbas didn't say what he was doing.

But all of them received the same instructions from Mette.

'Eight o'clock tomorrow morning at my place.'

Chapter 24

Olivia picked up both Stilton and Abbas in her car. Stilton looked pretty haggard, but Olivia had seen him looking far worse. But his breath reminded her of that homeless guy.

Abbas smelled freshly showered.

Not much was said in the car on the way to Mette's. Everyone understood that something decisive had happened. Stilton knew about Mickcy Leigh and presumed that it was about him, in one way or another.

So did Olivia.

She'd received a call from Mette after the raid on Jackie Berglund's flat and the discovery of Sahlmann's laptop. It had taken a while for her to digest the fact that Mette had told Lisa and Bosse about her break-in. But she'd understood.

Abbas was the one who knew the least. So, on the way to Mette's, Stilton did what he'd been dreading. But he wasn't entirely sober.

'Mickey Leigh is in Stockholm,' he said.

They were near Orminge and not too far from Mette's house. Stilton knew that, so he could keep the conversation short.

It was to be very short.

'I know,' Abbas said.

'How do you know that?'

'I called Jean-Baptiste yesterday and asked how things were going. He'd said you'd spoken.'

'Yes, I didn't want to tell you just then.'

'Well, you probably had your reasons.'

'Yes.'

So it was forgotten. Stilton hoped. But you could never be sure with Abbas, maybe he stored things up in a corner of his secretive brain for later when he needed them.

But now it was said.

Olivia parked some distance away from Mette's house. There were already a few other cars there.

'Who do you think is here?' she said.

She soon found out as she approached the gate and a group of people came trooping out through Mette's front door. Lisa Hedqvist, Bosse Thyrén and four other people. Mette's core investigation team. They'd met two hours ago. When Lisa hugged Olivia she saw how tired she was.

'You look tired.'

'I'm going to go home and sleep now,' Lisa said.

The larger delegation proceeded on down towards their cars, while the smaller one headed onwards towards the open front door. No one was there to greet them so they carried on into the kitchen. The mood had been more cheery all the other times they'd been to the house.

Mårten was standing in the kitchen in a dark-blue dressing gown. Alone. When they came in, he gestured towards another room without saying a word. He looked tired too. When they went in, they saw Mette standing in front of a large dining table. She was wearing a light, airy top and a pair of black silk trousers. There were piles of paper on the table. Emails. Faxes. Reports. Everything looked orderly, just as Mette liked it when she worked.

'Hi,' she said. 'Sit down.'

The trio sat down on various pieces of furniture. Stilton ended up in a dark armchair that had lost its padding around about the time of the Korean War. Mette picked up a virtually empty water jug from the middle of the table.

'Mårten!' she shouted towards the kitchen and Mårten appeared in the doorway. Mette held out the jug towards him without a word. He took it and disappeared again.

'We went through Bengt Sahlmann's laptop last night,' Mette began. 'I will be summarising what we found. You are welcome to ask questions, but only ones of substance.'

The trio peered at each other. Who would dare to ask anything after that?

'Firstly, some technical information. I don't know how up-to-date you all are. Olivia might be pretty au fait with this having been on her way to becoming a police officer, but I'm not sure how much Tom remembers – it probably wasn't common back then. And I'm not sure that Abbas knows much about this in particular.'

Mette maintained a very strict tone. It was clear that she wanted their full attention. Olivia also noted the 'on her way to becoming a police officer'.

But she let it go.

'So, here are the details,' Mette continued. 'Via a chat tool, such as Yahoo Messenger, someone in Sweden makes contact with people in another country who provide various sexual services. Let's say that person is called Bengt. He orders what he'd like and then he makes use of the service via a webcam. In real time. This is a practice that has been growing in recent years. A couple of months ago, a man from Malmö was found guilty of ordering sexual abuse of children in the Philippines that he accessed online.'

'Disgusting.'

Olivia made the comment. It wasn't a question, but she couldn't help herself. Mette continued.

'This Bengt can also communicate via the webcam about what is going on at the other end. For this service, he pays a certain sum to an American money transfer service called XOOM, which then sends the money on to the people performing the sexual services.'

'So you can sit in your own country watching live porn being streamed from another country?'

Stilton wasn't sure whether this was a question of substance – it was rather more rhetorical. But Mette was kind enough to say yes. She knew that Stilton had been out of the game for a few years.

'If the police get tipped off about such activities, and they turn out to be criminal, they can follow the transfers from Bengt's account to XOOM and on to the end recipient. Thus far, the theoretical part. Now let's turn our attention to the real-life Bengt Sahlmann and his laptop.'

Mette was still standing up. She hadn't lost her tempo for a second. Everyone started suspecting where this was going and was grateful for the freshly refilled water jug that Mårten brought in.

'We have found transfers to the United States using XOOM on Sahlmann's laptop. We've also found email conversations between him and Jean Borell confirming that the payments have been for orders of sexual services abroad.'

Mette picked up a piece of paper from the table.

'This is an email reply from Sahlmann to Borell: "Hi, Jean. Ordered a BDSM session as per request."'

'BDSM?'

'It's an abbreviation of bondage, discipline and sadomasochism, a very particular type of sexual practice. One party is dominant while the other is submissive. The end point for the last transfer was to an account in Marseille.'

Everyone looked over at Abbas, as discreetly as they could. He just carried on staring straight into Mette's eyes.

'So we can surmise that these two gentlemen ordered and witnessed a pornographic act streamed live from Marseille, a so-called BDSM session.'

Mette had agonised over this during the night. How was she going to present this to Abbas? She knew she had to do it. She'd woken Jean-Baptiste and asked for some information without going into detail about why she wanted it. Finally she'd decided to be as factual as possible. Facts. The truth. She knew that Abbas would respect that.

And accept it.

And he did.

Thus far.

'So now let's leave Sahlmann's laptop for a moment and look at what we know about the murder of Samira Villon,' Mette continued.

She picked up a couple of pieces of paper from the table.

Emails from the French police.

'Mickey Leigh is an English porn actor living in Marseille. He is apparently known as The Bull. According to Jean-Baptiste, you are the one who found this information, Abbas?'

Abbas nodded almost imperceptibly. Stilton hoped that Mette didn't know how Abbas had got this information.

'Mickey Leigh engaged in some sort of pornographic act together with Samira Villon. It took place the day after Sahlmann's payment reached Marseille. After said act, Samira disappeared. Some time later, Mickey Leigh shows up here. He has been arrested in absentia.'

Mette reached for the water jug for the first time. A few beads of sweat had started to form on her face. Olivia hoped that she was going to sit down soon. She did not want to witness her having another heart attack.

'Summing up, then,' Mette said and sat down. 'This can lead to a number of possible theories. I will present the one I believe is most plausible.'

Suddenly her tone had changed. The magisterial sternness had eased off: she'd trundled through the facts and now it would be more personal, less speculative. Now she'd discuss the situation with a group of people to whom she accorded a great deal of respect.

For different reasons.

'I think that Bengt Sahlmann and Jean Borell witnessed the killing of Samira Villon, in real time, during the sexual act they'd ordered in Marseille.'

The room fell silent.

Mette brushed her hand over the tablecloth. She understood the silence. She knew it was necessary. She herself had sat quietly for several minutes with her team of investigators at dawn – perplexed, stunned, repulsed. She knew it might take some time.

It was Stilton who finally broke the silence.

'You think they sat and watched a murder being committed? Right in front of their eyes?'

'Yes.'

'And kept schtum about it?'

'Yes.'

'Maybe they'd even ordered the murder?' he said.

'We've discussed that. There are rumours flying about on the Internet about something called "death sex online", allowing people to order and watch murders in real time, but there haven't been any reports of such cases so far.'

'This might be the first?'

'No. The payment made by Sahlmann is within the normal range for online porn. There would certainly have been a different sum for online sexual murder.'

Olivia poured herself some water. She thought about the sick situation they were discussing – as though it was a question of money. Mette continued.

'I think it's more likely that something went very wrong during the sexual act and that they became witnesses to a murder. Involuntarily.'

'And that means they've also seen the murderer,' Stilton said. 'Mickey Leigh.'

'Something he knows, of course,' Olivia said.

'He also sent a very threatening email to Bengt Sahlmann, in English. It was found in the trash folder. Leigh was very clear about what he would do to Sahlmann and Borell if they contacted the Swedish police.'

'So they didn't?' Olivia said.

'No, and there were probably more reasons for that than Leigh's threats. Not least for Jean Borell. It would hardly benefit his organisation if it came out that he'd witnessed a murder during a sex act that he himself had ordered.'

'But how does Mickey Leigh know about Sahlmann and Borell? How could he send an email to them?'

A question of substance, Stilton thought to himself. And Mette agreed.

'We asked ourselves that too but I don't have any answer to that yet. He might have been able to access their names with the account details in some way. Shall I continue with my theory?'

'Yes,' Abbas said.

That was the first word he'd uttered since they'd stepped into the house.

He wanted to know.

'I think the following happened – and please, take this for what it is, just what I think. I've got proof of some things, not all. After Samira is murdered, Leigh dismembers her body and hides the different parts outside Marseille. She's found. But there are no clues leading to Leigh. Then Abbas and Stilton arrive in Marseille and start asking questions about the murder. To whom, I don't know.'

'Philippe Martin.' Abbas said it like just any other name and went on: 'He told me about that act you mentioned and who was there other than Samira.'

'Mickey Leigh,' Mette said.

'Yes.'

'So you said you were from Sweden?'

'Yes.'

'OK. So if we assume that Leigh finds out about your meeting with Martin and then discovers that you are meeting with the French police – you met Jean-Baptiste, I assume?'

'Yes.'

'In the city.'

'Yes.'

'So you can assume that Mickey Leigh suspects you are also from the police and starts thinking that those gentlemen in Sweden who witnessed Samira's murder went to the police anyway. Despite his threatening email. So then he acts.'

'And travels to Stockholm?' Olivia said.

'Yes, to get rid of the two witnesses. When he arrives, he discovers that one of the witnesses has already been murdered. Sahlmann. So he murders the other witness, Jean Borell. And in addition to that, he stole a couple of computers from

Borell's office to get rid of any information about what Borell had witnessed.'

Suddenly Mette looked very tired. Olivia presumed that she hadn't slept much more than Lisa.

'You're tired, Mette,' she said.

'Yes, but we're almost done. There is only this left.'

Mette picked up a small bundle of paper.

'What's that?'

'Emails from Sahlmann to Borell threatening him with two things. One was to bring down Albion, his company, by publicising things about the Silvergården nursing home.'

'I knew it!'

Olivia almost leapt up from her chair. She'd been correct! At least in part!

'Yes,' Mette said. 'You were certainly on the right track. Sahlmann was incredibly upset about his father's death and threatened to disgrace Borell.'

'But you said he threatened him with two things,' Stilton said.

'The other was to reveal what they'd seen online.'

'Samira's murder?'

'Presumably. Which just shows how desperate he was.'

'And in so doing gave Borell a real motive to kill him,' Stilton said.

'Yes,' Mette said. 'Absolutely. There's just one problem. Borell was in India when Sahlmann was murdered. We've checked his travel schedule. Flights, hotel, meetings. He was in Delhi that night.'

'He needn't have committed the murder himself,' Stilton said. 'He may have hired someone to do it for him.'

Or been protected by someone very alert. Very much at the forefront of things. Very concerned about his master's love, Olivia thought to herself.

They discussed Mette's theory a while longer, seeing that it might well be correct.

'Now I'm exhausted,' Mette suddenly said.

She got up from the table with some effort. Olivia was close to helping her up. Everyone went out into the hallway. Mårten joined them and put an arm around his wife. Olivia and Abbas went out through the front door. As Stilton was on his way out, Mette pulled him aside. She waited until Olivia and Abbas had gone out into the garden.

'Now he knows that Mickey Leigh is in town,' she said quietly.

'Abbas?'

'Yes. What's he going to do?'

'No idea.'

'Can you try and keep an eye on him?'

She sounded like Jean-Baptiste.

Stilton hated this situation.

Olivia drove onto the motorway towards the city. Stilton was sitting next to her. Abbas was sitting in the back seat. So far they'd all been silent, consumed by their own thoughts.

Olivia was wrestling with how to deal with Sandra.

Her father had ordered and watched porn, live porn. And he'd probably seen a woman be murdered during one such session. Without informing the police. How could she tell Sandra that? Tell her that, about her beloved father, this broken girl who'd just tried to kill herself? Did she need to tell her? Would what Sahlmann and Borell did need to come out?

Maybe not.

But she wasn't sure.

In any case, she had to tell her that her computer had been found and that alone would prompt a stream of questions. Where? When? How? When can I have it?

It wouldn't be a fun conversation.

Stilton thought about Abbas.

About how Mette had mercilessly, yet necessarily, presented what she knew and believed had happened. How two Swedish men had ordered a sex act during which Samira Villon was murdered in front of their eyes by Mickey Leigh.

If Mette was correct.

Abbas was convinced that she was right.

He'd steeled himself from the moment he realised what Mette was going to tell them. All the details were branded into his mind. The consequences were unbearable. Samira had died because a couple of Swedes had wanted to sit and have a wank.

He leant forward towards Stilton.

'Where did you see him?'

'Who?'

'Mickey Leigh?'

'It was at Jackie Berglund's, right?' Olivia said to Stilton before he had a chance to respond. Now it was too late.

'Yes.'

'Does he know her?' Abbas asked.

'Apparently.'

Abbas sank back down into his seat. Stilton tried to peer at him in the rear-view mirror to catch a glimpse of his face.

'Can you try and keep an eye on him?' Mette had said.

Stilton turned his head to look at the cars whizzing by.

Olivia dropped Abbas off at Dalagatan. He left without a word. She watched him go and pulled away from the curb. 'Maybe it was stupid of me to say that,' she said.

'About what? Jackie Berglund?' Stilton said.

'Yes.'

'I don't know. It was the truth, after all.'

'I just hope he doesn't go and do something stupid now.'

'He's a grown man. He has to take responsibility for his own actions.'

And how did that go last time? he thought, but kept quiet. Olivia nodded a little.

'How's it going with Rune Forss and Jackie?' she said.

'Forss has a son with Ovette Andersson, a prostitute he used. A son he doesn't even know about.'

'Is that something you can use?'

'I think so.'

'Great.'

Olivia glanced over and saw Stilton looking at the long red gash on his right palm.

'How's your hand?' she said.

'It's healing. Luna put some ointment on it.'

'I like her.'

'She's allergic to meat.'

'I still like her. Is she going out with anyone?'

'Not sure. I don't think so.'

'You haven't asked her?'

'No.'

'Don't you care?'

Stilton didn't reply and Olivia didn't want to push him, she didn't really know how much their defrosted relationship could tolerate yet. She turned into Söder Mälarstrand.

'You want to go to the barge, right?'

'Yes.'

Stilton wanted to go to the barge. It was almost lunchtime but he wanted to go to bed: he hadn't slept many hours the night before. He wanted to be moderately refreshed if Ovette called.

* * *

Ovette was standing in a doorway opposite police headquarters. She'd been standing there for a while. First she'd called asking about Rune Forss and was told that he was expected back after lunch.

Now it was after lunch.

She stood there in the only coat she owned and felt her armpits fill with sweat. Not because she was warm, but because she was afraid. She held her hands tightly in her coat pockets. She wanted to hide the fact that she was shaking. She knew she had to do this, she had to get through it, she had to put the past behind her.

With Rune Forss.

He came on foot from Pipersgatan. He was carrying a bowling ball in a shabby leather bag in his hand. He'd almost reached the entrance when he saw her. In a doorway opposite. Ovette Andersson? She waved at him. Forss had a quick look around before he crossed the road and walked towards Ovette.

'What the hell are you doing here?' he hissed.

'I want to talk to you.'

Forss took hold of her arm and dragged her further down the street, around a corner and a good way into Celsiusgatan, a much smaller street. Out of sight of police headquarters. Ovette felt as if her heart was about to explode out of her chest. Forss let go of her arm and put his face very close to hers.

'Didn't I make myself bloody clear the other day?' he said. 'Didn't I?!'

'Yes.'

'So what the hell are you doing turning up here?! Get the fuck out of here and never come anywhere near me again, you fucking whore!'

Forss turned around and managed to take a couple of steps before Ovette said: 'I met Tom Stilton.'

Forss stopped dead. It took a few seconds before he turned around. The bowling ball was swinging in his hand.

'Stilton?'

'Yes.'

Forss took a few steps back towards Ovette.

'What have you said to him?'

'What happened. That you bought sex from me and that you were a regular at Red Velvet.'

Forss looked at Ovette. It was hard to read what was going through his head. Ovette didn't know.

But she saw that he was swinging his bowling ball down by his thigh.

'Do you know that you are the only girl from whom I bought sex who's still alive?' he said.

'Yes. Jill was murdered and Laura died of an overdose.'

'Yes, that's right.'

Ovette peered down the street. There was no one in sight.

'That's why I want to talk about it,' Ovette said.

'Talk about it? To whom? To Stilton?'

'No. To the newspapers.'

Forss looked at Ovette for a few seconds and smiled.

'An old expired hooker? Are you mad? Do you know who I am? I'm a detective chief inspector. Why the hell do you even think that anyone will believe you?'

'I don't know.'

'No. Because you're a complete and utter moron. I should probably give you a good beating, but you have a son. Maybe it's better if something happens to him. What do you think?'

'You're going to harm your own son?'

'...what did you say?'

'Acke is your son. I got pregnant the last time we were together and I didn't want to have an abortion. That's why Jackie kicked me out of Red Velvet.'

'Bullshit.'

'Do you want to do a paternity test?'

Forss was caught off balance. He wasn't the sharpest of policemen and he couldn't really get his head round what this whore was telling him. Father of her son?

'Does Jackie know about it?' he finally said. 'That I'm supposedly the father of your fucking son?'

'Yes.'

'Have you told Stilton?'

'Yes. We'll be in touch.'

Ovette pushed her way past Forss just as a taxi turned into the street.

Maybe it was luck.

Forss had poor impulse control and this situation was pushing him to the limit. But he let her go. He took out his mobile and rang Jackie Berglund. She answered from her shop. She claimed that she had customers, but Forss didn't give a shit about that. He was so incensed that she gave in after a while.

'Yes,' she said.

'I have a child with her!'

'Yes.'

'And you've known this the whole time!'

'Yes. But calm down. She's not going to try and palm him off on you.'

Forss was anything but calm when he ended the call. He threw his bowling bag halfway across the street.

* * *

Mickey Leigh had done what he'd come for. There were no more witnesses to the murder of that Arab chick. Now he'd go underground for a while, perhaps in the Ukraine. He didn't think it would be a problem making a living: the porn industry in eastern Europe was booming. The only problem was the suitcase. With the laptops in it. There could be dangerous information stored on them.

About him and the murder.

Maybe pictures too, he didn't know.

What he did know was that he'd left the suitcase at Jackie's when he ran off through the kitchen door. He'd tried calling her a few times, but she hadn't picked up.

So he'd have to go and collect the bag himself.

He knew that Jackie kept the shop open until eight o'clock. She cared about her customers. That's why he knew she wouldn't be at home now, just before seven. Then again, he didn't know whether the coppers were watching her front door, so better safe than sorry, he went through the back.

In the dark.

It wasn't difficult to pick the lock on the back door.

When he went into the dark flat, he turned the wrong way at first and ended up in the bedroom. It smelled of heavy, sweet perfume in there. He hated that kind of perfume. He went out again and into the hallway. He switched his torch on and looked around. No suitcase. Had she hidden it somewhere? He started looking. All over the flat. It took quite a while. But still no suitcase. Had the coppers taken it? He went to the window facing out onto the street and looked at the cars driving past below. What do I do now? Stay and ask Jackie? She won't like that I broke in through the back door.

He decided to wait down in the back garden until the lights went on in the flat. Then he'd go upstairs. He pulled the back door closed and walked down the steps. When he opened the gate, he was hit. From behind. Hard and heavily, right in the back of his skull. He fell down onto the concrete.

He was probably already unconscious when Abbas covered his mouth with duct tape and tied his hands behind his back with blue cable ties.

* * *

It was Mårten who'd insisted, in a way that made Mette think there were other reasons than just wanting to take her out for a nice dinner.

She knew her husband.

When they sat down at the round table at the Stazione restaurant in Saltsjö-Duvnäs, Mette's favourite private eatery, she asked him outright.

'If you have something to say, please do so now, before we order. I want to be able to enjoy my food in peace.'

Mårten asked the waitress to bring them two glasses of house red wine and wait a while before she took their order. Then he looked at Mette. 'I love you,' he said.

'I should hope so too.'

'But you're pushing it now.'

'Pushing what?'

'What I'm willing to put up with.'

The waitress put their glasses down and slipped away. Mette picked up her glass and gulped down half of it. Mårten's tone and expression dissolved away any of her attitude: he was planning to say something that she didn't want to hear and he meant it.

He waited until she'd put her glass down again.

'This is how it is, Mette,' he said. 'You are who you are, and you do what you feel you need to do. I can respect that, and always have. Until now. I'm not OK with what you're doing now. It's extremely inconsiderate towards all those who love you. Me, your children, your grandchildren. You have rational motives for doing so, I know that, but you do so without thinking about us. You subject yourself to things you know you should absolutely not be subjecting yourself to, if you want to avoid having another heart attack. My conclusion is that you are only thinking about yourself, or that you feel you have to. You don't think about us. We don't seem to be worth living for.'

Mårten averted his eyes and reached for his glass of wine. Now he'd said it. Now it was up to her to process it. It might take a while or sink in very quickly.

Mette sat in silence, staring into her glass. A few minutes later she waved over the waitress and ordered a fillet steak with lobster risotto.

'What are you going to have?' she asked Mårten.

'I'll have the same. And some more wine, please,' he said to the waitress.

When they were alone again Mette took a piece of warm bread and spread some flavoured butter onto it. When she'd finished, she rested her hand holding the bread down on the table.

'Do you remember when we met?' she said.

'Yes. Like it was yesterday.'

Mette smiled thinking about it. She'd done a night shift and had been dealing with a number of left-wing protestors in Kungsträdgården, one of whom was Mårten. A couple of weeks later they'd ended up at the same restaurant on Söder. Mårten had chatted her up, not remembering who she was, and later that night they'd ended up in bed. In the morning she'd told him that she was a police officer and then Mårten recognised her. A few years later they had four children.

And now they were sitting here.

Mette put her hand on Mårten's. He noticed the thick blue veins on his hand – Mårten was approaching seventy.

'You're the only thing that makes life worth living,' she said. 'You and the family. You know that. The rest is just an occupational disease. Sometimes it obstructs my vision, like now. I know I shouldn't be doing what I'm doing. It's selfish. There's too much at risk here, with my heart and stuff. I'm sorry, I should have thought about that.'

'Yes.'

Mette pulled her hand away and picked up her glass, as did Mårten.

'But for now you're still here,' he said.

Mette nodded, without raising her glass.

* * *

Olivia lay in bed trying to sleep. She was close a couple of times, but just as she was about to drift off, those words popped into her head again: 'He needn't have committed the murder himself. He may have hired someone to do it for him.'

And then she was wide awake again.

Eventually she got up and sat in the kitchen. She didn't have the energy to make tea. She lit a candle on the table and stared out into the darkness. Maybe I should go out for a run? To physically exhaust myself? She turned to have a look through the window above the sink and saw drops of rain splashing up from the windowsill outside. I won't, she thought and turned around again. Her gaze landed on the yellow Post-it note from Sandra. It was still on the table, she read the text again: 'I'm not as strong as you.'

She hadn't called Sandra yet. She was putting it off. How much of the truth should she share with Sandra? In her fragile state? How would she react to her father falling off the pedestal she'd placed him on? Just like Arne had? Would she react like her? Hate him? Run away? Disappear? Or try to kill herself again?

However she reacted, the truth would torture her.

For a long time.

Olivia blew out the candle and went back to bed.

'He may have hired someone to do it for him.'

Olivia pulled the covers up to her chin.

Thorhed?

Then she finally drifted off.

* * *

Abbas was not in a rush. He waited until the middle of the night. He wanted to be sure that everyone had left the area. The people asleep in the caravans didn't bother him, he would sneak in through the back of the tent. Where it was pitch dark.

When he pulled the body under the canvas of the tent, he still hadn't switched his torch on. He remembered how it looked, he'd been there the night before. And the large hole at the top of the pole let in some light as well.

Moonlight.

He carried on as quietly as he could. He heard the traffic on Lidingövägen in the distance and knew that it would drown out quite a bit of the noise. He dumped the body once he'd got further into the ring and dragged out the spinning wheel.

The knife-throwing wheel.

He placed it at the edge of the ring and pulled out the cables for the power switch and speed control.

Then he took off all of Mickey Leigh's clothes and lifted him up. It took quite a while to tie his large body onto the wooden wheel with the leather straps. By his hands and feet.

But he did it.

He looked at the wheel. A streak of moonlight poured over the naked body on the wheel. The man was still out of it, but he wasn't completely unconscious.

Very soon he'd be very awake.

Abbas moved back from the wheel a few metres and switched his torch on. He put it down on the yellow plastic in the ring, angled directly up towards the body.

He stared at the wheel in front of him.

This tanned man.

The Bull.

Then he turned the switch and started the wheel. Slowly.

After just the first rotating lap, Mickey lifted his head and tried to focus his gaze. Not very successfully. All he saw was a torch shining straight into his face.

But he heard the voice.

It came out of the shadows behind the light, quiet and calm.

'My name is Abbas el Fassi. It was me you assaulted in Marseille. I loved Samira Villon, the woman you murdered and dismembered.'

Mickey made a sound from under the duct tape. He tried to make out the shadow in the dark as he spun around.

It was hard.

'Many years ago I was a knife thrower,' Abbas said out of the darkness. 'I was pretty good. But it's quite an art. Particularly throwing at rotating targets. Particularly in the dark. I haven't practised this sort of knife throwing for a long time. Tonight I'm going to try again. I've got five knives with me. Two for your head. Two for your middle and one for the most difficult one. The knife that I'll aim at your crotch. A perfectly executed throw will mean that the knife ends up just below your balls. But like I said, it's not easy.'

Mickey stared out into the darkness. Every time his head ended up in an upright position, he tried to catch a glimpse of the shadow. There was a profuse amount of sweat running over his face.

'I'm going to increase the speed of the wheel now,' Abbas said. 'It mustn't go too fast, but not too slowly either. That would be cheating.'

Abbas increased the speed of the wheel. He knew that there was a point at which the person spinning around would faint, when the brain could no longer cope with the rotation. He didn't want to risk that. When he'd reached an optimum speed, he took out the first long, black knife. He weighed it in his hand. He had not been lying – neither about how long ago it was since he'd done this, nor about how difficult it was.

It was difficult.

When he raised his hand, he was extremely focused.

All the noise of the traffic was gone.

The smell of animals and their droppings was gone.

Everything was gone.

All except the body on the spinning wheel.

The first knife landed just where it was supposed to. So close to Mickey Leigh's cheek that he could feel it. There was a deep roar from behind the duct tape, but it didn't reach more than a few metres.

No one would hear that.

The other knife landed perfectly too. Right next to the other cheek.

The third one did not.

It pierced the wooden wheel about five centimetres too far to the right. It startled Abbas. Had it been on the other side, it would have punctured The Bull's abdomen. That would have ruined everything.

So he weighed the fourth knife an extra few seconds before he flung it.

It landed exactly right, beside his naked waist, so close to the skin that the man on the wheel could feel it.

Again.

Abbas saw brown liquid running from The Bull's nether regions – he heard muffled sounds coming from behind the duct tape and he saw his wide-open eyes filled with terror.

'Now it's just one more knife left,' he said quietly. 'I've called it Samira. Did you know that her name means "lunar beauty"?'

Abbas looked up at the hole in the tent at the top of the pole, towards the moonlight. Then he increased the speed of the wheel one more notch. The body was rotating faster. He could hardly focus on the limbs.

It was all about this knife. The one that could hit his balls and the penis that had penetrated Samira.

For money.

It was a difficult task.

He lifted the knife in the dark, balanced it, felt the weight and pulled his arm back.

Just as he was about to throw it, the sharp bray of a horse filled the tent.

Chapter 25

The text message arrived at ten past four in the morning. Mårten was the one who woke hearing the vibration. He gently tugged at Mette's black eye mask.

'Darling.'

Then Mette heard the mobile on her bedside table, picked it up. The message was short: 'You can collect The Bull from the tent at Circus Brillos.'

'Who is that?' Mårten wondered.

'Abbas.'

'What does he want?'

Mette pulled the mask up onto her forehead and sat on the edge of the bed. Her fingers wearily typed in a number to dispatch a police patrol to Circus Brillos.

'He has avenged Samira Villon.'

Mette sat with her back towards Mårten when she said it. He saw her slouch down a little. He understood why. He stroked her shoulder.

Both of them feared what neither of them dared to articulate.

She was still sitting in the same position when the patrol police called back, twenty minutes later. Her mobile was still in her hand. Mårten tried to hear what was being said, even though he was lying down on the other side. He could only decipher individual words but he saw that she sat up straight during the short conversation.

She was not slouching down any further.

'How bad was it?' he dared to ask when she'd ended the call.

'The man had no physical injuries whatsoever, except a large bump on the back of his head and marks from the straps,' Mette said. 'That said, he was "a gibbering wreck", as they put it.'

'The straps?'

Mette told him how the patrol had found Mickey Leigh. Tied to a knife-throwing wheel. Naked. Then she sent a short text message to Jean-Baptiste Fabre in Marseille: 'Mickey Leigh has been arrested. I'll be in touch.' She did not intend to release any details and she doubted whether Mickey Leigh would do so himself.

Then she pulled her eye mask back over her eyes and lay down.

Stilton and Olivia could wait.

Chapter 26

Olivia had a long shower. She'd finally fallen asleep, well into the night, and now she was trying to kickstart her system. It wasn't going very well. She hadn't slept enough. When she realised that she was washing her hair a second time, she pushed open the shower doors and put her dressing gown on. She put the tea water on in the kitchen and went to get her mobile. One missed call. From Alex, fifteen minutes ago. She wondered whether she should focus her energy on her hairdryer or the journalist. Then he called again. And got straight to the point.

'Hi! Are you still interested in Magnus Thorhed?'

'Yes? Why are you asking that?'

'I spoke to Tomas yesterday, the priest you met. I wanted to apologise for the outburst at the funeral, it was rather unnecessary. Well, anyway, we started talking about Bengt's murder and then he mentioned that Thorhed had called him the same night that Bengt was murdered.'

'Really! What did he want?'

'I don't know. Tomas didn't want to go into detail.'

'Why not?'

'No idea, but he knows I'm a journalist, so it might have been a sensitive matter.'

'Such as?'

'Do you want me to guess?'

'Yes.'

'Stop it, I have no idea. I just thought about you and your interest in Thorhed. You'll have to do your own guesswork.'

'OK. Just a minute!'

Olivia got up and pulled the furiously boiling tea water from the stove, splashing a few drops onto her hand in the process. Her short yelp could be heard loud and clear at Alex's end.

'Hello? What's happening? Olivia!'

'Yes, sorry! I bloody well burned myself with boiling water. Just a second!'

Olivia held her hand under cold running water. A few seconds later, she held the mobile back up to her ear again.

'It's all right now. Listen, thank you for calling.'

'Well, I look after my sources.'

'What do you mean by sources?'

'Nothing. Relax.'

Alex laughed a little.

'Dare I ask how things are going?' he said.

'Fine. With what?'

'I don't know, you don't say much. You mainly ask questions.'

'Maybe I should be a journalist?'

'Maybe indeed. Bye!'

Alex laughed again and ended the call. Olivia took her hand from the running water and looked at it. The skin was covered in tiny red spots. She made herself a cup of tea and sat down at the kitchen table. Why did Thorhed ring Welander on the night of the murder? Was it just a coincidence? Not likely. What did he want? To confess to someone sworn to secrecy? Why am I sitting here guessing, she thought. I can go and ask Welander myself. I'm no journalist, after all.

As she raised the warm cup to her lips, the previous night's ruminations popped back into her head. She felt that she needed to share these with someone.

That someone turned out to be Stilton.

'Hi, Tom, are you awake?'

'I am now.'

'Sorry, can you talk?'

'Do I have a choice?'

'You can always hang up.'

'What do you want?'

'I just have all these thoughts running through my head. I felt I needed to talk to someone, and as you were the one to set them off, I thought I'd ring you.'

'Set what off?'

'"He needn't have committed the murder himself. He may have hired someone to do it for him." That's what you said yesterday.'

'Yes, and?'

Olivia told him about Magnus Thorhed. About his blue BMW, the same make of car that had been seen at the Sahlmanns' house the night of the murder and was parked outside Borell's house the first time she was there. A man whom Borell himself had described as 'very much at the forefront of things', insinuating that Thorhed dealt with most things for him.

'Was he the one who was at Borell's when the police came?' Stilton wondered.

'Yes.'

'And you think he's involved in this?'

'I don't know, it's just a theory, but it's not inconceivable that Thorhed could have stolen Sahlmann's laptop on the orders of Borell, while he was in India.'

'It is indeed conceivable.'

'And that means it's also possible that he murdered Sahlmann.'

'On behalf of Borell?'

'On his behalf or on his own initiative. To protect Borell. According to this guy I know, Thorhed was a supreme arse-licker.'

'But murder?'

'I know, it's just a thought.'

'A thought that you'll be pursuing, if I know you correctly.'

'Yes.'

'How?'

'The same night that Sahlmann was murdered, Thorhed rang a priest Sahlmann knew. I reckon the conversation was about the murder.'

'But you don't know for sure?'

'No.'

'So how are you going to find out?'

'Ask the priest. I know him a little.'

'OK.'

There was silence.

'Well, so that's that, then,' Olivia said. 'Thanks for listening.'

'Thanks for calling.'

Olivia ended the call and started getting dressed. She'd called Stilton just like that, to have a chat.

That felt good.

She'd just got in the car when Mette called and told her about Mickey Leigh. Again, Mette didn't go into detail. Abbas could do that if he wanted to.

'So one of the murderers has been caught,' Olivia said and drove out to Skånegatan.

'I'm presuming so, yes.'

'So it's just the Sahlmann murder left.'

'I'm not sure it is a matter of "just".'

'No.'

'What are you doing?'

Olivia thought for a few seconds. Not long ago she probably wouldn't have told her what she was doing, or where she was going. But a great deal had happened since then.

'I'm on my way to see a guy, who I hope will tell me something about Magnus Thorhed.'

'Borell's colleague?'

'Yes, have you questioned him?'

'Yes.'

'About the Sahlmann murder as well?'

'No. Do you think he might have something to do with it?'

'Not sure. I couldn't sleep last night and lay awake cogitating about this and that, and his name popped into my head.'

'OK. So how's the history of art going?'

Olivia didn't know whether Mette was trying to be funny or whether it was a dig. She clearly was spending a great deal of time on everything but history of art. Not least, digging around in Mette's murder investigation.

'I'm not starting until after Christmas,' she said. 'Please say if you don't want me involved in this.'

And had it been a while ago, Mette would have given her a lecture and told her that she should spend her time doing things that she thought were much more important than making a difference, but a great deal had happened since then, even for Mette.

'Do whatever you like,' she said. 'Just no more Borell adventures.'

A double-edged admonition, Mette thought. She was well aware of the importance of Olivia's 'Borell adventure'. It was thanks to her discovery of Sahlmann's laptop in Borell's office that Mickey Leigh could be linked to the murder scene. Without it they would have had no idea where he'd got hold of the stolen computer.

'I promise,' Olivia said.

Mette ended the call. Mårten had of course been right the whole time. Just go with the flow when it comes to people like Olivia and Tom. Sooner or later they'll end up where they belong. Olivia would come back to her eventually, she felt it.

She sat in the kitchen in her dressing gown. It had become an enjoyable habit, not getting dressed. Showering, freshening up and then getting back into her dressing gown. That urgent desire to be at the Squad had dwindled a little. It both concerned and consoled her. She'd be retiring soon. It might not be as traumatic as she'd imagined. She might get really into pottery... She had her own oven in the cellar and a husband who loved any kind of deformed eggcup she produced.

Then Lisa Hedqvist rang, full of excitement.

'Can we come over?'

Half an hour later, Lisa and Bosse came through the door. Mette was still in her dressing gown.

Lisa opened up her laptop.

'This came half an hour ago. It's a file from the French police.'

'Fabre?'

'Yes.'

'What is it?'

'It's an email attachment. Here.'

Mette leant forward and read Fabre's email. He and his colleagues had searched Mickey Leigh's flat. Among the things they'd seized there was a special film. Fabre had uploaded the film onto a server and emailed them the password. He thought that the film would be of interest to Mette's investigation.

Lisa clicked on the downloaded film and pressed play.

It was a porn film. Ineptly filmed in a cramped room. There were just two actors. They were engaged in BDSM sex.

It was an extremely unpleasant film.

The whole way through.

The end was most unpleasant of all, when something went wrong during the 'asphyxiation', a key part of a BDSM session. The woman being strangled suddenly tried to free herself, she was about to suffocate, the straps around her neck were being pulled too tight. She screamed. The man tried to silence her. She got hold of a glass ashtray and hit the man in the face with it. The man went crazy. He grabbed the ashtray from her hand and hit her with it, several times, blood squirting from her face. He carried on hitting her until she sank down and lay completely still. Then he turned towards the camera and it went black.

Lisa and Bosse had seen the film at police headquarters. They knew what it contained, but it came as a shock to Mette. She dropped down onto the chair just next to her.

So that's how it happened.

How Mickey Leigh killed Samira Villon.

She would make sure that Abbas never saw the film.

'Did you hear the voices?' Bosse asked.

'Voices?'

Mette had been totally focused on what was happening in the film. She hadn't heard any voices.

'No.'

Bosse played the film again.

Now she could hear the voices. In the background, a mix of Swedish and English voices, spurring on the sex act taking place in the bed, spurring the man on to do more and more depraved things to the woman.

Mette felt sick.

'Sahlmann and Borell?' she said.

'That's a reasonable assumption,' Lisa said. 'Their voices must be audible through the webcam.'

'Yes.'

'But there's another one.'

It was Bosse who said it. Mette looked at him.

'Another one?'

'There are three voices.'

Mette hadn't been thinking about the number of voices. She'd just heard them. The voices spurring on the man.

'Three?' she said.

'Yes, you can hear them if you listen carefully. There were three men watching this.'

So Mette was forced to endure the film once more. This time she closed her eyes, so that she could hear better, and she realised that Bosse was correct.

There were three voices spurring on the act.

Two of which probably belonged to Bengt Sahlmann and Jean Borell.

* * *

Magnus Thorhed was on his way to Arlanda airport in a taxi. He was going to the head office in London. Borell's murder had sent shockwaves through the financial world; now it was a matter of keeping the empire together.

Business as usual.

He had all the necessary information about Albion's plans in Sweden with him. Nothing would mess this up. The big contract with the City of Stockholm was virtually complete, it would not be affected by Borell's death. Although he certainly was the figurehead in the organisation, there were others who could take over.

Like Thorhed, for example.

At least the Scandinavian division. He was just as au fait with the company's operations in the Nordics as Borell had been, he knew it like the back of his hand. It was now a matter of convincing the board of directors. Of course, this had to be done without discrediting the recently deceased emperor.

But he partly had himself to blame, Thorhed thought. Without knowing exactly what the motive had been, he was sure that it had been something to do with Borell's weakness, a weakness that he knew about. But never understood. Borell had an impeccable social life, he was respected and appreciated and he had an enormous network throughout the financial world, yet still he had this weakness. That need to delve into really nasty pornography every now and again, as though it was the only thing that could titillate him on a deeply private level. Thorhed couldn't get his head around it.

But now Borell was dead and it was time to move on. Thorhed adjusted the mourning band on his arm. He liked to observe certain traditions.

When he was dropped off at the international terminal, there was a journalist standing there. Someone he knew.

Alex Popovic.

'Hi! I called the office and I heard that you were on your way to London.'

'Yes.'

Thorhed proceeded towards the entrance with his wheeled suitcase. Alex followed him.

'Shocking about Jean,' he said.

'Yes, absolutely.'

'What's going to happen now?'

'Are you asking me personally or is this an interview?'

'That particular question was not personal.'

'I'm on my way to a board meeting in London. We're going to assess the situation.'

'So what do you think?'

'About what?'

'Why he was killed. That's a personal question.'

'I have no idea.'

'Could it have something to do with the murder of Bengt Sahlmann?'

Thorhed controlled himself and looked at Alex.

'Why would it?'

'I don't know. Haven't the police asked you about that?'

'No.'

'Why did you call Tomas Welander?'

'When?'

'The night that Bengt was murdered?'

'I have to check in now. Bye.'

Thorhed disappeared off into the departures hall.

Alex popped some nicotine gum into his mouth.

* * *

Olivia parked just off Banérgatan and went to Welander's front door. She'd been given the door code for the main entrance a short while ago. His flat was on the second floor and Welander opened the door as soon as she rang the bell. He was dressed in an elegant but worn dark smoking jacket.

'Please excuse my attire, I'm in between a christening and a funeral, but we have half an hour. Come in!'

Welander proceeded into a large, beautiful room and gestured towards the curved dark-green sofa. Olivia sat down.

'So you wanted to talk about Sandra?' Welander said and sat down in an armchair next to the round coffee table. 'I do hope nothing's happened?'

'No, actually it's not her I came to talk to you about.'

'No?'

'No. I received a call from Alex Popovic this morning. He told me that Magnus Thorhed called you the same night that Bengt Sahlmann was murdered. Is that correct?'

'Yes. But why would Alex call you to tell you about that?'

'Because I'd asked him about Thorhed before.'

'And why did you do that?'

Olivia had been expecting that question, that they'd end up there. She knew that she'd have to explain certain things, otherwise she probably wouldn't get Welander to talk. So she opted for the same approach as she had taken with Alex the first time.

'Because I'm trying to find out who killed Sandra's father.'

'But you're not a police officer, are you?'

'No, not officially, although I have police training. But this is a purely personal matter. For Sandra.'

'I understand. And why are you interested in Magnus Thorhed?'

'For several reasons. He drives the same make of car that was seen at Bengt's house the night he was murdered, for example.'

'You think Thorhed might have something to do with the murder?'

'I don't know. I was hoping you might know more.'

'Because of that phone call.'

'Yes.'

Welander looked at Olivia. He saw that she was serious about this, he had no reason to doubt her intentions. She wanted to help Sandra.

'It was a very short conversation,' he said. 'All Thorhed said was that Bengt Sahlmann had hanged himself.'

'How did he know that?'

'I wondered that too, but he put the phone down before I had the chance to ask him.'

'Why did he call to tell you that?'

'He knew that I knew Bengt and that I'm a priest. Perhaps he just wanted to let me know?'

'Or confess.'

'He didn't say that he killed Bengt.'

'No.'

'Would you like some tea?'

'Yes, please.'

Welander got up and left the room. Olivia tapped her feet on the ground, feeling wired. If Thorhed had called and said that Sahlmann had hanged himself, the same night that it happened, a simulated suicide, then he must have been there? The police hadn't released any information about that.

She was close to calling Mette.

* * *

Mette was just walking into police headquarters with Lisa and Bosse. She'd swapped her dressing gown for a black dress and left Mårten a note in the kitchen: 'National Crime Squad. Emergency.'

He'd just have to accept that.

They went straight to the room where the two murder investigations were underway. There were a few older investigators sitting there. Mette briefly informed them about the film they'd received from France and how they could access it. She asked them to be extremely discreet about the contents. The important part, for the Swedish investigators, were the three voices.

'They need to be identified. We're guessing that two of them belong to Bengt Sahlmann and Jean Borell. We have no idea whose the third is. How shall we proceed?'

'We'll start by extracting a sound file from the film that will allow us just to hear the voices,' Bosse said. 'I'll fix that.'

He disappeared through the door with Lisa's laptop.

When it came to identifying Sahlmann's voice, Mette most certainly did not want to drag in the people closest to him, his daughter and her aunt. They'd sort that out with Customs and Excise. Gabriella Forsman might oblige? She was being held in custody, after all.

'What about Borell then?' Lisa wondered. 'Shall we contact his colleague?'

'Magnus Thorhed?'

'Yes.'

Mette did not respond straight away, due to a number of thoughts she'd had while in the car on the way in. About the things Olivia was looking into. Her interest in Magnus Thorhed. Just imagine if the third voice was his? There was a risk of that. Then it wouldn't be particularly clever to ask him to listen to the sound file. She nodded at the door and walked towards it. Lisa followed her. Mette pulled the door closed and stood outside in the corridor. For some reason she didn't want the entire investigation team knowing what Olivia was up to. A lay person who had absolutely nothing to do with their work.

It was different with Lisa.

Mette quickly explained why she didn't want to contact Thorhed. Lisa understood.

'But can she do it then?' she said.

'Who?'

'Olivia has met this Thorhed, hasn't she?'

'Yes?'

'Well, then, we can start with her? She might be able to hear whether it's his voice on the recording? If it isn't, then we can contact him?'

Mette hadn't thought of that. But she was on sick leave, she'd had a heart attack, she wasn't on the ball. Olivia could identify Borell's voice too!

'Good, Lisa. I'll call her as soon as we have the sound file.'

* * *

Welander poured Olivia a cup of tea from an extremely beautiful, blue teapot. She held the cup between her hands and had a sip. Welander sat down next to her on the sofa and poured himself a cup as well.

'I was thinking about Sandra out there,' he said. 'She rang me yesterday and she sounded a bit more cheerful. Do you think so too?'

'I don't know. I think it's pretty up and down.'

'Well, yes, I suppose, mood swings are common at that age.'

Mood swings, Olivia thought. She'd tried to commit suicide!

'But you're a great support to her,' Welander said. 'I can tell.'

'I hope so.'

Olivia looked down at the floor. She certainly was a great support to Sandra, for now. But that might not be enough. If she was forced to tell her what she needed to tell her. She felt the anxiety rising up inside her.

'Are you all right?'

Welander bent down a little and caught Olivia's gaze.

'You look a bit sad.'

'I have a problem.'

Olivia had not prepared herself for this situation, this wasn't why she was here. Her anxiety over Sandra had been churning away inside her. There was no one she could share this with, no one she could talk to.

Or was there?

She looked at Welander, his eyes were gentle and steady. Maybe she could tell him? Get some guidance? He knew Sandra too.

'Something's happened that concerns Sandra,' she said.

'Something bad?'

'Something that I'm not sure she can handle finding out about at the moment.'

'Because she's so fragile?'

'Yes.'

'Does she need to be told, then?'

'I don't know. It may be unavoidable and then I would want her to hear it from me.'

'It sounds serious. What's happened?'

Olivia wrung her hands. It really was serious. It was horrendous. And it would come out sooner or later, in one way or another, she was sure of that. Perhaps through the media, which would be worst of all.

For everyone.

Suddenly it struck her that Tomas Welander had known Bengt Sahlmann for ages. He was a friend. She hadn't thought of that. She'd only been thinking about Sandra. What had happened would certainly shock Welander just as much as everyone else. When he found out.

Now or later.

'You are bound by an oath of secrecy, am I right?' she finally said.

'Yes, you can tell me whatever you like.'

'Sandra's father was watching online porn.'

Welander looked at Olivia, rather quizzically.

'Why did you have to tell me that?'

'Because something happened while he was doing it.'

'Watching pornography?'

'He was watching a live session on a private webcam.'

'I understand. That certainly is objectionable, though hardly criminal? It's nothing that would involve the police? If that's why you think you need to tell Sandra?'

'No.'

'So?'

Olivia clenched her hands, tightly, looking down at the floor when she finally said it, quietly.

'A very brutal murder was committed during that session. I don't know whether it will be made public, but there is a great risk that it will be once the preliminary investigation is complete.'

'And then Sandra will find out?'

'Well, it concerns her father.'

'I understand. That is troubling.'

Welander got up and started pacing in front of the coffee table. Olivia watched him. Had she said too much? But he'd be finding out about everything anyway. It was unavoidable that it would come out.

Welander turned towards her.

'I understand your dilemma, and I agree with you. The way Sandra is feeling now, it would be devastating if she found out about this.'

'Yes. So what should I do?'

Welander carried on pacing around in front of the table. Then he stopped.

'I don't know,' he said. 'But if you decide that you need to tell her, then we can do it together. If you think it might offer some support having me there.'

'I don't know. But thank you.'

Then her mobile rang.

It was Mette.

'Excuse me,' Olivia said.

She got up and went over to the large windows. She knew how loud Mette's voice could be and she didn't want Welander to hear. It might be something about Sahlmann.

It was.

Among other things.

Mette quickly explained that they needed help identifying a couple of male voices on a film depicting the murder of Samira Villon. The men had witnessed the murder. But she didn't want to discuss any more details over the phone. So she played the first voice.

'Do you recognise it?' Mette said.

'Yes, it's Jean Borell's voice.'

'Good! Thanks!'

Welander had sat down on the sofa and looked at Olivia. She was standing with her back to him, but her voice was clear, even though it was quiet. When she said 'Jean Borell' he got up.

'Here's the next voice!'

Olivia pressed the phone against her ear to be able to hear properly, the sound quality wasn't great. She hunched over the windowsill. Welander went towards the door.

'Hello! Are you still there?' Mette said.

'Yes.'

'Is it Magnus Thorhed?'

'No. But I recognise the voice.'

'So who is it, then?'

'I'll be in touch.'

Olivia ended the call. She saw that her hand holding the phone was trembling. She stood still for a few seconds to regain composure.

Tomas Welander.

It was his voice.

She felt her cheeks going red. She saw his face in front of her, his gentle eyes, his soft voice, how he'd been sitting there, lying straight to her face. Trying to mislead her. Completely. Playing on her feelings for Sandra and getting her to reveal deeply personal information.

He's used you, Olivia, as you promised yourself never to be used again.

She turned around.

The veins were pumping in her forehead, her jaw was clenched, her cheeks tight. Welander was coming towards her.

'Was that a difficult conversation?' he asked.

'Yes.'

'I see that. You're shaking. Was it about Sandra?'

'No, it was about you.'

'Me?'

Olivia took two steps forward and gave Welander a big slap straight across his face. He tripped over the table, and fell onto an alabaster lamp and straight into the wall. The lamp crashed onto the floor without going out. Welander slid along the wall and ended up on all fours. There was blood running from his nose, down over his mouth, down onto the floor, he was gasping heavily.

Olivia didn't move.

A number of seconds passed, perhaps a minute. Finally Welander turned up to face her.

'I understand you,' he sniffled.

'What exactly is it you understand?'

'I should have told you.'

'Yes. Get up.'

'What are you going to do?'

'Get up.'

Welander was still on all fours.

He knew he'd locked the door.

He knew what he kept hidden behind one of the old books on the shelf.

* * *

Mette was still holding her mobile in her hand. She was standing by the desk in her office. Lisa was sitting on a chair and Bosse was leaning up against a wall.

'Did she recognise the voice?' he said.

'Yes.'

'Was it Magnus Thorhed?'

'No.'

'So who was it, then?!' Lisa said and got up.

'She didn't say. She just said, "I'll be in touch." Then she ended the call. She sounded...'

Mette fell silent. Bosse and Lisa looked at her.

'How did she sound?'

'I don't know, strange? Tense?'

They looked at each other. Olivia must have understood how important it was that they found out whose voice it was.

How urgent this was. All she needed to do was say the name. Yet nevertheless she ended the call. Why did she do that?

They all thought the same thing.

Maybe she was with the person in question?

'Where is she?' Bosse said.

'I don't know.'

'Call her again!'

Mette had already set about calling Olivia. She waited. Voice-mail.

'She's not answering. I talked to her about an hour ago and she was on her way to someone who might have information about Magnus Thorhed. She didn't say who.'

'Might someone else know?'

'No idea,' Mette said.

But she picked up her mobile and tried the only person she could think of.

'Hi, Tom, it's Mette. Do you know where Olivia is?'

'No. She was going to talk to someone, maybe she's still there?'

'Who was it?'

'A priest. Someone Bengt Sahlmann knew.'

'Thanks.'

'What is it?'

Mette had already ended the call and rung Sandra's aunt, Charlotte Pram.

* * *

Welander had got up, eventually. Now he was standing leaning up against the bookshelf, wiping the blood off his face with his smoking jacket. The alabaster sheen from the floor lit up his pitiable figure. Olivia was still standing in the middle of the room. Her rage had not subsided.

'Where are we going?'

Welander's voice was hoarse and broken.

'To the police.'

'Because you recognised my voice?'

'Because you have witnessed a crime.'

'It wasn't intentional.'

'You'll have to explain that to the police.'

'But don't you understand what that will mean?'

Olivia saw tears running down Welander's cheeks.

She was repulsed.

'Don't you understand what will happen if this gets out?'

'I couldn't give a shit about that.'

'But my congregation does! I am their shepherd! I am the one who comforts and supports them! Many of them live miserable lives and the only thing that keeps them going is my words! I am the one who gives their lives hope and love.'

'Maybe you should have thought of that before indulging in hardcore pornography.'

Welander stared at Olivia. He was breathing heavily. His eyes narrowed. His voice became lower, tighter.

'And who are you to pass moral judgement over me?' he hissed. 'You come to me asking for help, because you can't cope with telling Sandra the truth. You're a coward.'

'Shall we go now?'

'The door is locked.'

Olivia looked at Welander. She took a couple of steps towards the door and pressed down the handle. It was locked.

'Open it,' she said.

'Do you like music? Classical music?'

'Open the door!'

Welander reached over to his music player on the bookshelf and turned it on. The music came blaring out, the whole room was reverberating. Olivia hunched over and got out her mobile. Welander was standing over by the bookshelf watching her.

'It's *Scheherazade*!!' he screamed through the blaring music. 'My favourite piece!'

Olivia called Mette.

While she was waiting for her to answer, she saw Welander pulling out a thick book from the bookshelf.

* * *

Charlotte had given them Tomas Welander's address.

Mette and Bosse held on tightly as Lisa sped past a bus. Mette had tried to call Olivia again. She wasn't answering. In the middle of a crossroads, she received a call. The number display was clear: OLIVIA RÖNNING. When Mette picked up, all she could hear was blaring music and Olivia's voice shouting: 'I NEED HELP!' Then the voice disappeared, but the music carried on.

The line wasn't broken.

Mette tried to shout into the phone.

No response.

* * *

It was a small gun. It didn't take up much space behind the book. As he held it in his hand it felt almost light, but he knew what it could do. He had inherited it from his father and had used it a couple of times at Lundsberg. To scare those in need of a good scare, teach them a lesson. One time he'd fired it, just after midnight, somewhere not too far from the school, during a punishment ritual. One of the younger boys had not been following the rules, and had actually even threatened to go to the housemaster. That could not be tolerated. He was taken out to an old stone cairn and stripped naked. He liked animals. Jean had got hold of a little white rabbit. He held it up by its ears in front of the young pupil. It was squirming. Then it was shot through the head right in front of the terrified, wayward little boy.

After that he followed the rules.

The woman facing him now was not following the rules. She was making her own. She was disregarding a divine messenger. She was a Pharisee, consumed by arrogance.

A wayward little girl.

'Sit down!!' he yelled, pointing at the armchair with the little gun.

Welander shouted so loudly that his voice could be heard above the music. Olivia tried to assess the situation. The music was roaring in her ears and she realised that the man in front of her was probably very unwell. Or at least totally off balance.

She sat down in the armchair.

Welander went and stood right in the middle of the room, a couple of metres away from her, in the middle of the acoustic intersection. He took off his smoking jacket with the gun pointing at the armchair.

He was naked underneath.

'If you move I'll shoot you!' he screamed. 'Like a rabbit!'

Olivia looked at his white, wrinkly body. Online porn? It's men like him who pay to see women being degraded and sexually exploited. Men with bodies like that. She knew that she was generalising. Sadly men with far more lithe bodies did the same thing.

Like Borell.

Why?

She followed Welander's movements across the floor. She saw that the music permeated his body, consuming him, his naked, bony body writhing as the music escalated. She saw that he had scratch marks on his forearms, the gun in his hand was pointing at her chest. His head started moving, back and forth, searching, as though looking for more music.

Then it stopped, in the middle of a crescendo, and his eyes closed shut.

* * *

When Lisa slammed the brakes on outside the building on Banérgatan, Bosse jumped out first. They'd got hold of the door code and he was in the stairway just seconds later. Lisa rushed in after him. Mette moved as quickly as she could. She recalled when she stayed outside Forsman's building and what had happened then.

Now she wanted to go inside!

Upstairs!

Bosse had stopped outside Welander's front door. The music was blaring out into the stairway. Nevertheless he rang the doorbell.

Pointless.

'What do we do now?!'

Lisa had made her way up the stairs.

'The caretaker?'

'A locksmith!'

'That'll take for ever,' Mette said.

She was gasping as she walked up the last step and stopped outside the door. All three of them realised that none of them would be able to break it down. The police only did that in films. And none of them were keen on shooting the lock off either.

Suddenly the music stopped. The noise of a gunshot broke the silence.

Followed by a muffled scream.

Bosse pulled out his gun. Mette and Lisa backed off. Just as he raised the gun and pointed it at the lock the door opened. A naked man was standing in the doorway. A dark smoking jacket was hanging over his shoulders and his hands were holding his crotch. He was obviously in pain, as though he'd been kicked. His hair was hanging down over his eyes. Bosse pointed the gun at this head.

'Where is Olivia?!'

'Here.'

The voice came from behind Tomas Welander. It was Olivia's. She pushed past the man standing in the doorway. He stumbled out a couple of steps into the stairway. Lisa got out some handcuffs. Olivia stepped forward holding a little gun in her hand.

'We were just on our way,' she said.

Chapter 27

Tomas Welander was wearing a clean white shirt and a pair of dark of trousers. The collar was unbuttoned and exposed a thin chain with a gold cross around his neck. Mette and Lisa sat opposite him in an interrogation room at the National Crime Squad headquarters. There was a laptop on the table. Bosse was following the interrogation from an adjoining room.

They'd gone through the formalities.

Mette went through the sequence of events in Welander's flat. She'd heard Olivia's version, and now she wanted the man sitting opposite her to confirm it. He did not object to her description as such, but he did react to Mette's interpretation of the situation.

'I never threatened Olivia,' he said.

'You pointed a gun at her and said that you'd kill her if she moved. "Like a rabbit."' Mette had to contain a smile, it sounded quite ridiculous. 'Is that incorrect?' she said.

'It is correct that I pointed a gun at her, but she's fabricated the rest.'

'Why did you point the gun at her?'

'Because I was afraid. She'd attacked me. I was acting in defence.'

'In what way had she assaulted you?'

'She knocked me down.'

Mette knew that this was true, Olivia had admitted that. She also knew why it had happened and had a certain understanding of why Olivia had reacted the way she did.

But it was indeed assault.

And without any witnesses there was nothing that contradicted Welander's version.

So she let it go.

For now.

'I'm going to show you a film,' she said.

Lisa opened up the laptop and started the film that Jean-Baptiste had sent them. Welander reacted strongly after a few seconds. He realised what he would be forced to watch. The murder he'd witnessed via the webcam. He held up a hand to cover his face. Mette paused the film.

'Take your hand down,' she said. 'You are going to watch this film from beginning to end.'

Mette's voice signalled that there was no room for objections. Welander lowered his hand. Mette started the film again. Welander squinted, he knew what was coming, and when it did he was forced to avert his eyes. But he could not avoid the woman's piercing scream. It bounced off the walls of the small interrogation room. Welander clenched his hands on his lap, his arms were shaking all the way up to his shoulders. Mette and Lisa were watching him the whole time. Welander looked up again.

'There are three voices to be heard on the film,' Mette said. 'Two of them belong to Bengt Sahlmann and Jean Borell, the third one belongs to you, is that correct?'

Welander nodded.

'I want you to answer the question loud and clear.'

'That's correct,' Welander said.

His voice was hardly audible, very thin and dry, as though he'd swallowed a load of altar bread. Lisa poured him a glass of water and passed it to him. He drank half of it.

'Can you tell me about the background to this?' Mette said.

'To what?'

'To what we've just seen?'

Welander's body sank down in his seat. He knew he'd have to tell them, he knew he wouldn't get out of this room until he had.

'It started at Lundsberg. Jean and I and Bengt had a very strong connection there. We stuck together. We had lots of fun. Then we went our separate ways, but we stayed in touch.'

'You met up?'

'Yes, but only once a year or so.'

'What did you do then?'

'We relived some of the happy times at school. We drank alcohol and talked about old memories.'

'And watched porn on the Internet?'

'It was something of a tradition, from the old school days, to watch pornography, quite innocent, the online porn thing came later. It was – I don't know how to describe it – some kind of forbidden male thrill, as though we were young again.'

Mette and Lisa peered at each other.

Welander drank up the rest of the water.

'The last few years we'd been using a service called porn-online,' he said.

'Livestreamed pornography,' Lisa said.

'Yes.'

'Like the one we just looked at.'

'Yes. It was Jean who'd asked Bengt to order it.'

'A BDSM session.'

'Yes.'

'Did you order a recording of the session too?'

'Yes. Jean wanted it. He is – he was interested in that sort of thing.'

'BDSM?'

'Yes. Like in that film there, I believe?' Welander pointed at the laptop.

'Yes,' Mette said. 'What happened that night?'

Welander was breathing heavily. He tried to recall the night it happened. How they had all met up out at Jean's house on Värmdö, drunk booze, hooked up to the online session at the agreed time and started watching. More and more aroused, more and more drunk. How they had spurred them on more and more to perform more advanced and perverted sex acts. Finally the naked, tied-up woman in the room had reacted, started screaming, but the act continued.

'Even though she didn't want it to?' Mette said.

'Yes.'

'So, in practice, it turned into rape?'

'It could be described that way.'

Mette and Lisa looked at each other. Their thoughts were clearly visible in their expressions.

'Then that awful thing happened that you saw in the film,' Welander said.

'The man in the room killed the woman.'

'Yes.'

'How did you react to that?' Mette asked. 'You'd just witnessed a sex act that you had ordered and paid for ending up as murder?'

'We were terribly shocked. We just sat there. When we came to our senses we started discussing what to do, whether we should call the police.'

'But you didn't.'

'No.'

'Why not?'

'We didn't know what to say. We couldn't do anything about what we'd seen, we didn't know who the people in the room were, we didn't know where it had taken place, just a room somewhere in the world.'

'Hypocrites,' Mette said calmly.

'Sorry?'

'The only thing you worried about was making sure that no one found out about what you'd been doing.'

Welander didn't reply.

'So you decided to keep quiet?' Lisa said.

'Yes, but it was very tortuous, I felt absolutely terrible afterwards.'

'You did?'

'Yes, absolutely.'

Mette looked at Welander in disgust. She'd talked to many people with different crimes on their conscience. This man was one of the most pitiful she'd seen. She opened a brown file in front of her.

'I want to spend some time talking about the murder of Bengt Sahlmann,' she said. 'How did you find out about it?'

432

'First I heard that it was suicide.'

'Who told you?'

'Jean. He rang me at lunchtime and said that Bengt had been totally off balance and was threatening to go to the police and tell them about the irregularities in Jean's company and about what had happened that night. Jean was freaked out. Then he rang later that evening and said that he'd been to Bengt's house to talk some sense into him and that he'd hanged himself. Then I found out that Bengt had been murdered.'

'What did you think then?'

'I was shocked. At first I didn't want to believe it. Then I got scared and started thinking about Jean.'

'Whether he was the one who murdered Bengt?'

'Yes, it was an unbearable thought. That one of my friends would have murdered another of my friends? It was awful.'

'I understand. But you received two phone calls from Borell that same day, first one telling you about Bengt's threats and then one stating that he'd been to Bengt's home. Is that correct?'

'Yes.'

Mette looked in the brown file.

'We've been going through Borell's call lists for that day,' she said. 'It was indeed the case that he rang you twice that day.'

'Like I said.'

'The only problem is that he was in India.'

'India?'

'Yes.'

'I don't get it?'

'Neither do I. Unless of course you're lying.'

'I'm not lying. I'm a priest. Jean made those calls.'

'We know that. But he was not at Bengt's house that night, we know that too.'

'So how did he know that Bengt had hanged himself?'

'What do you think?'

'I have no idea. It sounds very strange? How could he have known that?' He paused.

433

'Yes?'

'Maybe he found out about it from someone else?'

'Who'd been at Bengt's house?'

'Yes. And then called Jean in India?'

'Who might that have been?'

'I don't know, I have no idea. Yes! Magnus Thorhed perhaps?'

'Why him?'

'I saw his blue BMW there!'

'At Bengt's house?'

'Yes! It must have been him! Who saw Bengt hanging there and then called Jean and then Jean called me!? From India?'

'That's possible.'

'Yes.'

'The only thing I'm wondering is how come you were there?'

'Where?'

'At Sahlmann's house? Where you saw Thorhed's car?'

Lisa couldn't help but admire Mette's interrogation technique. She'd intentionally increased the pace of the dialogue so that Welander didn't have time to think before he spoke. And then he'd tripped up without even realising what he'd said.

Now it was caught on tape.

He was at Sahlmann's house himself the night of the murder.

'What were you doing there?' Mette asked again.

'I got worried after Jean's phone call and wanted to hear how Bengt was doing myself.'

'And how was he then?'

'No one opened the door, so I left.'

'And that's when you saw Thorhed's car.'

'Yes.'

Mette opened up the file in front of her. Lisa gave her a look. Welander was fiddling with the gold cross hanging around his neck. He assumed there'd be some kind of legal penalty due to the murder he'd witnessed and his failure to inform the police about it. A penalty he was willing to accept. He hoped it could all be handled discreetly, with his congregation in mind.

'Are we done with the questioning?'

'Yes,' Mette said. 'You've told me what we needed to hear. Now we'll take some swabs and then you'll be done.'

'Swabs? From my mouth?'

'Yes.'

'Why are you going to do that?'

'Do you have anything against it?'

'No, I'm just wondering why.'

'To compare your DNA to the DNA of skin fragments found under Bengt Sahlmann's nails. He struggled for his life and scraped off quite a bit of skin from the person he wrestled with. It's a routine procedure. You're a priest and you don't lie, so there won't be a match, of course.'

Mette and Lisa got up. Welander remained seated. Mette picked up the file from the table and looked at him. His white shirt had sweat stains all the way down to his waist.

'By the way, Olivia told me that you had some pretty nasty scratch marks on your arms?' Mette said.

It was dark by the time Mette left police headquarters, satisfied, but not done. She could have listened to her body's signals and gone home, but she wanted to finish what she needed to. She called Olivia and Abbas, and asked them to come to the barge where Stilton was staying. She didn't want them all up at the National Crime Squad headquarters.

They all gathered in the lounge.

The three of them were very impatient. Curious, excited. The interrogation of Welander affected them all, in one way or another. They knew Mette and that she wouldn't want to tell the story more than once.

When she'd finished, Olivia asked the first surprised question.

'He confessed?'

'Yes.'

'Just like that?'

435

'No. Not until we told him about the fragments of skin found under Sahlmann's nails. He realised that it was over and just collapsed into a pathetic, blubbering mess on the floor.'

'What a creep.'

'But he did see Magnus Thorhed's car at Sahlmann's house?' Stilton asked.

'Yes, he claims so. As he was leaving. Thorhed had presumably been sent there to do the same thing that Welander had set out to do.'

'To bring Sahlmann to his senses.'

'Yes. And then he found Sahlmann hanging from the ceiling and took the laptop to ensure that any dangerous information on it would be kept hidden.'

'But why did Welander lie about that telephone conversation?' Olivia said. 'That Thorhed had called and told him that Sahlmann had hanged himself. When it was Borell who called?'

'I don't know, maybe he wanted to lay the blame on Thorhed? He'd just seen his car there, after all.'

'Not very clever.'

'Murderers are seldom as clever as they think.'

'What was his motive?' Stilton asked.

'Partly to prevent the scandal that would come out of what these gentlemen had been up to at Borell's, and partly because he was afraid of the murderer in Marseille, as he called him. He knew that he'd sent a threatening email detailing what he intended to do if they snitched to the police. And Sahlmann had just threatened Borell with doing just that.'

'Going to the police?'

'Yes. Welander was terrified that Mickey Leigh would find out somehow.'

'So he murdered Sahlmann to try to prevent that from happening.'

'According to Welander it was manslaughter. An argument that spiralled out of control.'

'And ended up with him hanging Sandra's dad from the ceiling and her finding him when she got home,' Olivia said. 'And then he pretended to care about how bad she was feeling and she almost ended up taking her own life. Fucking hideous!"

Olivia got up, she couldn't sit still. The thought of that empathetic priest spending sleepless nights worrying about that poor young Sandra made her feel sick. The memory of that deeply moved priest by the coffin, who'd expressed himself so fondly about a person he himself had killed made her tremble with rage.

She regretted not kicking the shit out of him in the flat.

Everyone looked at her, everyone understood what she felt.

Welander really was a loathsome human being.

'We've run some checks on him,' Mette said. 'He was expelled from Lundsberg, because of some serious incident, and then he tried to kill himself and ended up in a psych ward, and when he got out he started training to be a priest. He seems to be a pretty broken individual. But now he's locked up. Is there anything else you want to know?'

'How did you come to think about him? Welander?' Abbas asked.

It was a question all three, but Mette in particular, had wanted to avoid. She'd hoped that Abbas wouldn't dig any further into it. She'd intentionally avoided mentioning the film from Jean-Baptiste, the film with the three voices. She didn't want him to know that it existed.

And neither did Stilton nor Olivia.

But she also knew that Abbas could decide to ring Jean-Baptiste himself at any time, like he did when he found out about Mickey Leigh.

She didn't want to keep quiet or tell half-truths. Not to Abbas. So she told him about that hideous film and the murder.

Just like that.

When she'd finished, Abbas got up and looked at her.

'Could you drive me home?'

'Absolutely.'

Mette got up.

'Mette.'

Mette turned around. Olivia took a few steps towards her and lowered her voice.

'I would like to have a USB stick with the contents of Sahlmann's laptop, with the stuff about the scandal at Silvergården, is that all right?'

'I'll fix that... and listen.'

'Yes?'

'You still made a difference.'

'Without being a police officer.'

'You are a police officer, you've just gone AWOL for a while.'

Mette smiled and left the lounge with Abbas. On the way from the barge, Mette asked Abbas about what had actually happened in the circus tent. With Mickey Leigh. So Abbas told her. He finished just as they got to the car.

'Imagine if one of the knives had missed,' Mette said.

'Hit him, you mean?'

'Yes?'

'They didn't.'

Abbas got in the car. Mette sat down behind the wheel and rolled the car out onto the street.

'We've tied him to Borell's murder. They were his fingerprints on the murder weapon in the boathouse.'

'Great.'

Then they basically sat in silence until Abbas got out of the car near Dalagatan. Just before he slammed the door shut, he leant over towards Mette.

'Thank you for telling me about the film.'

'I assume that you don't want to see it.'

'No. Can you give these to Jolene?'

Abbas took several French sachets of sugar out of his pocket and handed them over. Jolene collected sugar sachets, she had a couple of large glass jars full of different sachets from all over the world.

'She'll be really happy!'

'I know.'

'But do you want to come and see her yourself?'

'No, I want to give my handsome face a bit more time to recover before that.'

Abbas closed the car door and walked towards the building.

Mette watched him go.

Stilton and Olivia were still sitting in the lounge. He'd made her a cup of tea. He himself was sitting munching a large carrot, his stomach was rumbling a bit. Both of them felt relieved after Mette's briefing. Most of it had fallen into place and each one of them had contributed in their own way. Abbas had found pictures of Mickey Leigh, Tom had recognised him, Mette had been able to move in on Jackie and find Sahlmann's laptop. Olivia had photographed it out at Borell's and given Mette a link between Mickey and Borell, which had led to Tomas Welander. The third voice.

So far so good.

Now there were just two things remaining. A simpler, more satisfying task for Stilton. And a rather more difficult one for Olivia, namely Sandra. Tomas Welander had killed her father, this family friend and priest was a murderer. The motive was that her father threatened to reveal that he had witnessed a brutal murder during a sex act that he had ordered.

And she'd be telling that to a young girl who'd just tried to commit suicide?

She felt a longing to go back to Mexico.

To the solitude and isolation.

Or maybe to Nordkoster?

Then he called, as though she'd placed an order. Olivia's mobile vibrated on the table and Ove Gardman's name lit up on the display. She glanced over at Stilton. He was half-lying down on the bench, in his own world, a world of revenge. She picked up her mobile, got up and went towards the corridor. She took a deep breath before she answered, she didn't really know what to say. Should she apologise? Say that she was missing him? Or just act as though nothing had happened?

'Hi, Ove, how are you doing?'

She tried to sound averagely flippant.

'So-so.'

His voice sounded subdued and sad. Olivia felt herself getting irritated. Is he going to play the martyr? To make me feel bad? Just because I haven't been touch there's no need for him to sound like the world has ended. He was actually the one who'd been rather insensitive last time we met up? But OK, I'll give in and apologise, I have nothing to lose.

She took a deep breath. Saying sorry wasn't her strong point. She needed a run-up, rather like Mette.

'Hello?' Ove said.

'I'm still here. It's just quite bad reception.'

A white lie that comes in handy when you need to buy time.

'Listen, I'm sorry I haven't been in touch,' she said. 'But I've had a lot on my plate recently, you know, with that case I told you about, and I haven't had time, well, once I did actually call your mobile, but it was switched off. I heard what happened with Maggie. Lenni told me. It was…'

'My dad's died.'

Ove's voice almost broke when he interrupted Olivia babbling on. Abruptly. A pang of guilt flashed through her head. She became painfully aware that not everything was about her. She crouched down, her back sliding against Stilton's cabin door, before it suddenly opened and Olivia fell back straight into the cabin. She hit her head on his bunk, but still managed to keep her mobile pressed against her ear.

'Oh, I'm so sorry,' she said. 'When did it happen?'

'Last night.'

'Oh, I'm sorry, Ove, I didn't know he was so bad.'

She heard Ove sighing before he starting telling her. His father had caught some kind of virus that resulted in pneumonia and then he just got worse. His body couldn't cope.

'The shittiest thing of all is that I wasn't there. I've been sitting there day and night since I came home, and I just went to get some new clothes. That's when he died. Alone. Not a single fucking soul was there!'

'Was he in hospital?'

'No, but he should have been. It seems like they didn't grasp how ill he was, even though I tried to tell them. And there was no doctor available either. They promised me they'd watch him while I went off for a few hours, but then some-one fell and fractured their hip and my dad was left alone. It's fucking awful. No one should have to die alone, I get so angry thinking about it. It's so undignified! It's all just about cash.'

Olivia recognised this, all too well.

'I can come down and see you,' she said. 'I just need to deal with something here tomorrow.'

'I'm not sure if I'm that fun to hang with right now. There's a lot to deal with. The funeral and stuff.'

'I'll come anyway.'

'OK, thanks... And listen!'

'Yes?'

'I've missed you.'

'I've missed you too.'

It was true. She really had been missing Ove.

She ended the call and carried on sitting on the floor for a while. She thought about Ove's dead father and Hilda at Silvergården, and Claire Tingman. If Claire hadn't told Olivia about everything, things would have been very different. More people should speak out, she thought. When she came back into the lounge, she saw that Stilton was still lying on the bench, his eyes half-closed. She sat down at the table.

'Hi, there!'

It was Luna coming down the iron steps with a couple of grocery bags.

'You haven't eaten yet, have you?'

They hadn't, so both gladly accepted when Luna suggested having dinner together. Stilton rather more enthusiastically than Olivia, which Luna noticed.

'I've bought you some rib-eye,' she said and disappeared into the kitchen.

It was a long and chatty dinner, with several vegetarian specialities that Olivia thought were great. Stilton was very happy with his piece of meat. The food was accompanied by a couple of well-aerated bottles of ripasso wine. They were expensive, but Luna had sold a few rare stamps and she felt she could treat herself to something nice.

It was largely Olivia and Luna who did the talking; they soon found themselves on the same wavelength and chatted about the past and present. Stilton mainly just sat filling in, when asked, but he felt good in their company. Luna's tattoo flashed through his head a couple of times, but he let it pass without getting hung up about it.

When Olivia poured herself yet another glass of wine the dinner was more or less over. The three of them had settled down into a pleasant state, it had taken the edge off, and she suddenly felt that she wanted to ask that question now, to Tom, the one she'd once asked without ever getting a proper answer.

So she went ahead and asked it.

'What was it that made you go off the rails?'

Luna looked at Olivia. She didn't know? Not her either? He hadn't even told her? She turned towards Stilton. Was he going to ignore Olivia's question too? After all that had happened?

Stilton cupped his wine glass in his hands. He saw the way Olivia was looking at him and presumed that Luna was doing the same. A few seconds passed, a minute perhaps, before he made up his mind.

'It was when I was dealing with Jill's murder,' he said to Olivia. 'I've mentioned that, haven't I?'

Olivia nodded. He'd told her about the murder of Jill Engberg, one of Jackie Berglund's escort girls.

'I slogged away at that case, day and night, constantly being hindered by Rune Forss. He didn't want me to go sniffing around Jackie Berglund. I slept badly, was unpleasant to Marianne, and on top of that, Astrid, my mother, was dying. So I really busted my arse during the day and then sat by her bedside during the night.'

Stilton was breathing deeply and looking down at his hands. They were trembling a little, his body still recalling how he felt.

'I guess you could say that I wasn't in great shape,' he said.

'You must have been burned out?'

'Probably. All the warning signs were there, but I just ignored them. Tough detective chief inspectors don't get burned out.'

Stilton looked at Olivia with a wry look on his face. He was telling the story to her, even though he was very aware of Luna sitting on the other side of the table.

'Late one night, when I was on my way up to see my mum, I stopped at a red light. I was exhausted and that red light suddenly became unbearable. It was as though it was triggering some kind of volcanic eruption in my body, my head started spinning, my heart was pumping and my throat tightened. I could hardly breathe. I was forced to pull over and stop the car.'

'A panic attack?'

'Yes, but I thought I was having a heart attack. Then my body calmed down and I thought I should book an appointment to see someone at the hospital, after I'd been to see my mum. Then I just drove on.'

'And were you all right?'

'Sort of.'

Stilton sipped his wine. There was a little left in his glass.

'When I saw my mother she was asleep, so I sat down by her bed and held her hand. There was a horrid black mark on it

443

from a cannula. I sat and stared at the mark and suddenly felt it starting to grow, slowly, like a snake slithering up her arm and towards her neck, as though it was going to strangle her.'

The women sitting at the table looked at him in horror.

'Of course it was all in my head,' he said.

And he drifted off into the memory…

…into the past.

'Tom?'

Stilton blinked. Astrid had woken up. The snake had gone. Those fucking images, he needed to sleep more, take care of himself, otherwise it really would be a heart attack next time.

'Do you remember having nightmares as a child?'

Her voice was weak. Stilton looked down at this pile of skin and bones that was his mother. Age is unfair, he thought, terribly unfair. He suddenly felt incredibly tired.

'Yes,' he said, 'you used to say that dreams are dreams, they're only in your head and have nothing to do with real life.'

Which is a bloody lie, he thought.

'But it wasn't true,' she said. 'It did have something to do with real life.'

Astrid looked at him with a steady gaze as she whispered these words. He steeled himself. Her expression foreshadowed something he wasn't sure he wanted to know. At least not now, he wasn't really in the right state.

'You don't need to, Mum.'

'I have to.'

She had to? What? If there was a secret she'd been bearing her whole life, then she may as well take it to her grave. She'd never been religious. She couldn't have been thinking that some God would pass judgment on her when she died? He gently stroked the black mark on her hand, it was not growing again.

'You remember the nightmares?'

Astrid kept her gaze fixed on him.

'Yes.'

'They were always about the same thing, a fire. Do you remember? That we were running from a burning house?'

'Yes, something like that.'

Why did she have to tell him this?

In his profession, he was manically focused on finding the truth, and he got incredibly frustrated if he was unable to solve a case. He wanted to know the truth at any cost.

But not now.

Not this truth.

He'd managed to run away from it, hiding himself so well that he had no idea what it was about. All that remained were fragmented pieces that still appeared in his dreams sometimes. His nightmares.

Couldn't they just stay there in that oblivion?

'It was us,' he said. 'We ran from a burning house, you and I.'

Astrid took a deep breath.

'And I was the one who started the blaze.'

'You?'

'I set our house on fire, yours and mine.'

Stilton breathed a sigh of relief. A fire. It wasn't any worse than that, the secret. He could cope with that.

'But there's more to it than that,' Astrid said.

'Mum, you don't need to…'

'I must. Don't you understand? You were only six then. Do you remember?'

Suddenly a floodgate opened in Stilton's head. The memories came pouring out, intertwining with his mother's voice:

A dark wardrobe. His mum pushes him inside. He doesn't want to go. He's afraid of the dark. She says: 'Stay in there, Tom, and don't come out, no matter what you hear, do you understand?' He nods. He knows he has to do as his mother says. She closes the door on him. The darkness envelops him and he shuts his eyes. Tightly. The smell of mothballs finds its way up into his nose. He doesn't like the smell. It makes him feel sick. Then he hears the voices. Mum's and that man's. That man who Mum doesn't want coming to their house. The man's voice is throaty; he can't hear what he's saying. But it sounds like they're arguing about something. Then Mum screams. He presses his hands over his ears, tightly, so tightly, but it doesn't help, her screech cuts through his body. Then there is silence. He carefully takes his hands from his ears. Is it over now? Then he hears the roar. A guttural roar. He presses himself as far back into the wardrobe as he can. Warm urine trickles down one leg and he starts crying. Uncontrollably. And he doesn't know whether he's crying because of that terrible scream or because his mother will be angry at him for wetting himself. Now it is quiet out there. There are no voices to be heard. Suddenly the door opens and light comes streaming in. A hand takes hold of him. 'Come, Tom, quickly!' He falls out of the wardrobe. He hurts himself. He senses a pungent smell of kerosene. Of smoke. Then he sees the flames. They have started engulfing the curtains in the kitchen. Mum's beloved curtains are on fire! His mother takes his hand, tightly, and pulls him along. It hurts. Why does she always need to be so rough?

'Ow! You're squeezing my hand Tom, it hurts!'
'Sorry!'
Stilton loosened his grip on Astrid's hand. He felt sick now. From the images and the smells. Everything. His heart was pounding and there were white spots dancing in front of his eyes. Here comes that heart attack, he thought.
Then Astrid whispered: 'I killed him.'
Stilton looked at his mother and tried to take in what she had said.
'Who did you kill?'
He didn't know whether he wanted to know the answer, but there was no escape, Astrid's eyes were staring into his. Her voice was barely audible, she was almost hissing.

'Your father.'

'My father?'

New images flashed through Stilton's head.

Mum tells him to close his eyes when they make their way out of the house, but he's peeking so as not to trip. And he sees the man on the floor, blood pumping from a large wound in his chest. He's still moving. Next to him is Grandpa's big sealing harpoon. The smoke means it's hard to breathe.

'Yes, the man who burned in there was your father.' Astrid's voice suddenly became noticeably sharper. 'A brute.'

Stilton began having trouble breathing. He sat up to get some air.

'You killed my father?' he said.

'Yes, and I don't regret it,' Astrid say. 'Not even now.'

'Why did you kill him?'

'Because he raped me. Several times. That's how you came about.'

The room started to sway, the white spots flickering in front of his eyes. It was an effort for him to ask the question: 'Why are you telling me this? Why now?'

'So that you can understand.'

'Understand what?'

Astrid looked at him, he felt her hand gripping his more tightly, she was breathing more heavily now.

'Understand why I haven't always been like a mother should be. Why I've always had such trouble… such trouble loving you.'

He let go of her hand. He saw it fall down on the covers in slow motion. That black mark was turning into a snake again, and like a flash it was slithering up towards his mother's neck. He staggered up. Panic gripped him. He had to get away! Out! He needed air! Quickly!

447

'Tom!'

It was Olivia's voice. She'd put a hand on his arm. He felt the sweat running over his eyes; his heart was pumping inside his chest. He emptied his wine glass and looked at her.

'It ended with me running out of the room, screaming. The last thing I remember is throwing up in the corridor. The rest is just a haze. I was taken care of immediately. You could say that I chose the right environment in which to develop psychosis.' Stilton's lips curled into a crooked smile. 'Detective Chief Inspector Tom Stilton, the fruit of a rapist and a murderer. Psychotic and totally burned out, in every respect.'

Stilton's eyes sank down towards his hands again.

'And then you went off the rails.'

'No, not at first. I was put on sick leave. That's when I cut contact with everyone around me. I didn't want anyone to see me in this state, least of all those who cared about me. I pushed them all away. Marianne, Mette, Mårten, Abbas – I was bloody awful towards them. Marianne in particular had to put up with a lot. Then after my sick leave I was planning to carry on working at the Squad.'

'But it didn't work out?'

'I tried, but it went tits up.'

'Because of Rune Forss?'

'Yes. He spread a load of rumours, talking shit behind my back, spouting lies here and there, until I was shut out. Friends changed tables when I sat down in the canteen, shit like that. In the end I'd just had enough and handed in my notice and lost it. Totally. I cut all ties that I still had and decided to let myself fall. And I managed that.'

Luna looked at Stilton.

'And your mum?'

'She died the same night she told me. I'd just been admitted as an emergency in the psych ward.'

Stilton fell silent. Luna poured some more red wine into his glass and thought about his nightmares. There was still a great deal plaguing him, it seemed. Stilton gulped down the wine and stood up.

'Thanks for buying the meat. And the wine. I'm off to bed now.'

Olivia got up and gave Stilton a warm hug. He peered over at Luna during the hug. She looked at him with calm eyes and moved her hand along the side of her neck, near her tattoo.

Stilton nodded and went towards his cabin. He lay stretched out on the bunk and closed his eyes. Just as he was drifting off into the sleepy fog he suddenly saw it in front of his eyes. The tattoo on Luna's shoulder. Suddenly he remembered where he'd seen it before.

Chapter 28

Alex Popovic was standing by the news desk, watching a BBC broadcast. It was an interview with a very stylish female representative of Albion International. She was standing on the steps of the company's head office in London. Next to her was Magnus Thorhed. He was still wearing a black armband over his tweed jacket and his plait was blowing in the wind. They had just come from a board meeting and the woman was assuring the reporter that it was business as usual, despite the tragic loss of the former head of the company, Jean Borell. The international expansion would be proceeding as planned. Moreover, a new CEO had been appointed to take charge of the Nordic division.

The woman presented Magnus Thorhed.

He explained, in perfect English, how Albion would continue its successful welfare venture in Scandinavia. A multi-million contract was due to be signed in Stockholm during the next few days.

'Alex!'

Alex turned around. A long-haired guy was on his way over with an envelope in his hand.

'This arrived by courier.'

Alex opened the envelope. A USB stick, nothing more. He went over to his desk and inserted it into his computer. It contained just one document. The title was clear: 'MATERIAL ABOUT THE CARE SCANDALS AT SILVERGÅRDEN'.

Alex looked up at the large television screen. Magnus Thorhed was just being asked the final question on the steps.

'You don't believe that the tough media criticism in Sweden has harmed Albion?'

'Not in the slightest. There's been smoke without fire. There are no problems whatsoever in our organisation. It is being impeccably managed.'

Alex clicked to open the document.

* * *

Stilton walked through the large glass passageway to the Stockholm police headquarters. He went up one flight of stairs and over to a specific door. He'd been here a year ago and presumed that Rune Forss still had the same office. He opened the door without knocking.

Forss was sitting behind his desk.

'Normal people knock,' he said.

Stilton closed the door behind him. Forss didn't move: he guessed what this visit was about. It was nothing that worried him. He'd calmed down after seeing that whore and decided that she didn't present a threat to him. He'd said it then and it was just as applicable now: it was his word against hers. It was like shooting fish in a barrel.

Stilton pulled out a chair on the other side of the desk and sat down.

'What's this about?' said Forss.

He afforded himself a little smile. The man sitting opposite him had once been a respected policeman. Even Forss had been impressed by his investigative ability. Then the man had made a wrong move and ended up down in the gutter. Now he was trying to claw his way up again.

Pathetic.

'It's about your relations with prostitutes,' Stilton said.

'Is that so?'

'One of them was Ovette Andersson.'

'Who's that?'

'She's the only one still alive out of those girls you bought sex from.'

'Is that what you spend your time doing these days? Gossiping with old hookers?'

'She's willing to talk.'

'Are you done?'

'No,' said Stilton.

'There's the door.'

Forss raised his hand towards the door. He was still very calm. Stilton didn't move. He glanced over at the family photo next to the phone, Forss with his wife and two grown-up sons. He knew that one of his sons was on his way into the police profession.

'This is how it is,' he said. 'A high-ranking chief inspector buying sex from a prostitute is going to sell newspapers. You know that. You also know what verbal assault is. Or threats, to put it simply. That's a prosecutable offence.'

'It is,' Forss smiled. 'And who is said to have been threatening whom?'

'You threatened Ovette Andersson, to prevent her from revealing your sexual relations with her.'

Forss leant forward a little. His patience was beginning to wear thin. He wanted to put an end to this.

'You can tell that whore that she can say whatever the fuck she likes to whomever the fuck she likes because it's all a bloody lie. If you want to believe what she's saying, that's your business. No one else will.'

Now Stilton's patience was wearing thin also. He pulled out a mobile phone from his pocket and put it down on the table in front of him. When he played a sound file it was totally silent in the room.

What the hell are you doing here?

The hissing voice belonged to Rune Forss. Stilton watched him on the other side of the desk. Forss didn't move a muscle. His brain was buffering feverishly, it took him quite a few seconds to get what was going on. Finally, the realisation sank into his brain like a spike: that whore had recorded their conversation on the street!

Stilton played that whole conversation. It wasn't very long, but there were a few key statements.

Do you know that you are the only girl from whom I bought sex who's still alive? Forss said on the tape.

He also said: *I should probably give you a good beating, but you have a son. Maybe it's better if something happens to him. What do you think?*

You're going to harm your own son?

Just after Stilton turned the recording off, he put his mobile back in his pocket. Forss hadn't uttered a word. He didn't need to. The beads of sweat trickling down towards his eyebrows did a good job of describing what was going on inside him. Stilton got up. Forss followed him with his eyes.

'What are you going to do with that?' he said.

His voice was wavering. He couldn't find the right pitch. He was in shock.

'Keep it,' Stilton said.

'Keep it?'

'Yes, until you've resigned. You have two days. If you're not out of this place before then I'll send this file to a journalist at *Dagens Nyheter*, and a copy to the county police commissioner. That also applies if you go anywhere near Ovette Andersson ever again.'

Stilton headed for the door.

He'd delivered his ultimatum. He had done what Forss did to him. Pushed him out of the police.

He turned around in the doorway.

'Scum like you have no place here.'

* * *

Olivia had left the barge and gone home in the middle of the night. Luna had tried to stop her: it wasn't a great idea crossing half of Söder as a woman on your own at that time of night. Olivia knew that, so she walked down streets she knew. At Mariatorget she was joined by a middle-aged man who tried to convert her. He was a Mormon and obviously drunk, and one of the few things that Olivia knew about Mormons was that they were teetotal, so his efforts seemed a little hollow. She told him to go to hell somewhere near Götgatan.

But she clearly felt the effects of the night before as she stood in the shower. She had a headache and an annoying burning pain in her stomach, which was not soothed when she thought about what she would have to deal with as soon as she'd had some breakfast.

Sandra.

She knew she had to meet up with her: she didn't want to do it over the phone, and she was dreading it. At the same time, she knew that time was running out. It could reach the media any time that a priest called Tomas Welander had confessed to the murder of Customs Officer Bengt Sahlmann.

And maybe even the background to it all.

She wanted to get there first.

She took a glass of juice with her into the bedroom and started getting dressed. Afterwards she looked at the bed, at the place where Sandra had been lying not so long ago. So small and alone. She leant against the wall and looked around the room. 'You don't have any photos.' She heard Sandra's thin voice inside her. But I do, she thought, and put her glass of juice down. She bent down and pulled out a cardboard box from under the bed. It was full of photographs. She lifted up a handful and went over to the wall above the bed. The small white pins were still there. She put the photographs up where they'd been before. She grabbed more and put them up. Finally, all of them were back in place, as they'd hung before they were taken down. Before the big shock. Pictures of her and Maria, with Arne and Maria, of the whole family at their summer house out on Tynningö. She looked at the wall and the pictures and thought about Sandra again.

Then her mobile started vibrating.

It was a short text message from Alex. He thanked her for the material about Silvergården. He assumed that she'd been the one who sent it. She didn't reply. When the time came she'd get in touch with him in person: he was a good contact whom she'd mishandled, or misinterpreted – she'd realised that when the whole Welander story unravelled. Alex had always been straightforward and she'd mistrusted him at times. But he was a journalist, it wasn't always easy to navigate their waters.

She went out into the kitchen and sat with her mobile in her hand. She couldn't put it off any longer. She was just about to key in Charlotte's number when she herself called. Charlotte. A very shaken Charlotte, who told her that Sandra was beside herself and had locked herself in and was crying uncontrollably.

'I can't reach her! She's just screaming! Could you come here and help me to talk to her?!'

Olivia drove as quickly as she dared. In the car on the way out to Huvudsta she went through what she had to do. What Tom hadn't dared to do last year. Tell the truth. She didn't want to be like him.

But she understood him now.

She understood what he hadn't been able to do. Recount something that would seriously damage a young woman. Now she was the one who'd be hurting Sandra. Not through any fault of her own, but still. She'd be the one who'd sit in front of Sandra and look her in the eye when she found out the truth. See her face, and know the long path that Sandra had ahead of her.

As she had had.

She drove into Johan Enbergs Väg and parked the car. Charlotte's flat was in the block furthest away.

She'd gone through it a thousand times, how she'd present this, how she'd soften the blow, how she'd formulate it as gently as possible.

The only thing she'd decided was to say it straight out.

'Your father and Tomas witnessed a murder during a live porn session. Tomas murdered your father to cover it up.'

She approached the building and looked up at Charlotte's flat.

'SANDRA!!!'

It was Olivia who screamed. Her scream made Sandra look down. She was standing on the edge of the balcony, nine floors up, barefoot, her body swaying gently. Then she lifted her head and looked up at the sky, for a few seconds, before she leant over and fell, with her hands outstretched, as though she wanted to fly.

She screamed all the way down.

Chapter 29

Olivia stood by the Chapel of Serenity and observed a little squirrel with her gaze. It was halfway up one of the mighty pine trees. Then it stopped and turned its head towards the church, as the muted tolling of the bells rang out over the cemetery. Olivia followed the squirrel's gaze and saw people dressed in black on their way through the large church entrance, among them Maria. When she looked back, the squirrel had gone.

Olivia sat down on the third pew from the front, at the very end. The rest of the pew was full. The church could accommodate a couple of hundred people and it was a third full. Olivia kept her eyes fastened on her hands clasped in front of her on her knees. When the female priest described Sandra's short life, she heard muted sniffs from young people, whom she assumed were school friends. She kept looking down at her knees, she didn't want to look at the altar, to the place where the priest, Tomas Welander, had been standing not so long ago. She would not allow him to disturb this moment.

When the female priest invited the mourners to bid their farewells by the coffin, she remained seated. She had a single, red rose in her hand, she would place it on the coffin, but she wanted to wait, she didn't want to queue up, she wanted to walk up to it alone.

As she saw the last mourners walking away from the coffin, she got up and went forward. There was a bed of flowers lying on the lid of the coffin. She stopped at one end and looked down at the narrow, light wooden coffin. Carefully, she let the rose drop down on the lid, along with her tears. She carried on standing there for a long time, until she finally felt she could say it: 'I'm thinking of you, Sandra, like you asked me, I promise,' she whispered.

Maria had stopped a little way from the coffin. She saw her daughter lift her head and dry her cheeks, she saw her tremendous sorrow as she straightened her body.

Olivia moved away from the coffin, looking down at the floor. When she reached Maria she stopped, took a step forward and gave Maria a long and heartfelt hug. As they hugged, she whispered into her mother's ear: *'Te amo.'*

Olivia released herself from the embrace and walked towards the door. Maria stood still and surrendered to the lump in her throat.

The solemn organ music reached out through the church entrance. Olivia stood on the steps and saw the pale sun shining down over the cemetery, a very old cemetery, dating back to the twelfth century. Now it was covered in a blanket of sparkling white crystals: it had been snowing all night. Olivia went down the steps and walked out through the cemetery. She didn't want to meet other mourners, she wanted to mourn alone. She walked over to the tombstones, large and small, back to the Chapel of Serenity. This had been the most agonising thing she'd ever done.

Bidding farewell to Sandra.

She stopped by the beautiful chapel and leant up against a large, dark pine tree. She could see people streaming out of the church, on their way towards cars and buses. Their lives would carry on, everything would carry on, the sun would shine until it rained, everything would keep going. She pulled out a little yellow Post-it note from her pocket and looked at it. Why couldn't things carry on for you? Why weren't you strong enough? She felt tears streaming down her cheeks again and put the note back in her pocket. Or was I the one who should have been stronger? Could I have acted differently? Was it my fault?

She moved her foot around in the snow in front of her.

It wasn't my fault. It wasn't me who destroyed your life. Olivia felt the rage rising inside her. It was some repugnant men who destroyed it. Destroyed the life of a completely innocent young girl.

She stood up straight and looked over at the church. There was still a small group of people dressed in black standing on the steps. She went the other way clasping her hands, with sadness and rage pressing against her chest. As she approached the last white grave, she'd made a decision.

For Sandra's sake.

She passed by the grave and never saw a lonely jackdaw landing on the grey marble stone behind her.

Acknowledgements

We would like to thank Criminal Inspector Ulrika Engström and the French author and journalist Cédric Fabre for the valuable information they provided.

We thank Estrid Bengtsdotter for her painstaking efforts in reading the text.

We also thank Lena Stjernström at Grand Agency and Susanna Romanus and Peter Karlsson at Norstedts for the inspirational support on all levels.

Biographical note

Cilla and Rolf Börjlind have written twenty-six Martin Beck films for cinema and television, as well as most recently working on the manuscripts for the Arne Dahl's A-group series. In 2004 and 2009, their crime series 'The Grave' and 'The Murders' were screened on Swedish television. In addition to this Rolf Börjlind has written eighteen films and received a Guldbagge Award for the manuscript for the film *Yrrol*.

As well as being among Sweden's most praised scriptwriters, Cilla and Rolf Börjlind have now embarked on a new career as bestselling authors. Their books are characterized by charismatic protagonists and depictions of Sweden, full of social conflicts.

Before its release, *Spring Tide*, the first book in the series about Olivia Rönning and Tom Stilton, had sold rights to twenty countries. And when published, it received rapturous reviews from Swedish critics.

Under our three imprints, Hesperus Press publishes over 300 books by many of the greatest figures in worldwide literary history, as well as contemporary and debut authors well worth discovering.

Hesperus Classics handpicks the best of worldwide and translated literature, introducing forgotten and neglected books to new generations.

Hesperus Nova showcases quality contemporary fiction and non-fiction designed to entertain and inspire.

Hesperus Minor rediscovers well-loved children's books from the past – these are books which will bring back fond memories for adults, which they will want to share with their children and loved ones.

To find out more visit www.hesperuspress.com
@HesperusPress